SHADOW STITCHER

AN EVERLAND MYSTERY

MISHA HANDMAN

EDGE SCIENCE FICTION AND FANTASY PUBLISHING
An Imprint of HADES PUBLICATIONS, INC.
CALGARY

Shadow Stitcher
An Everland Mystery

EDGE SCIENCE FICTION AND FANTASY PUBLISHING
An Imprint of HADES PUBLICATIONS, INC.
P.O. Box 1714, Calgary, Alberta, T2P 2L7, Canada

The EDGE Team:
Producer: Brian Hades
Acquisitions Editor: Michelle Heumann
Edited by: Kathryn Shalley
Cover Design: Brian Hades
Cover Art: Risa Hulett
Book Design: Mark Steele

ISBN: 978-1-77053-199-4

EDGE Science Fiction and Fantasy Publishing and Hades Publications, Inc. acknowledges the ongoing support of the Alberta Foundation for the Arts and the Canada Council for the Arts for our publishing programme.

Library and Archives Canada Cataloguing in Publication
CIP Data on file with the National Library of Canada
ISBN: 978-1-77053-199-4
(e-Book ISBN: 978-1-77053-198-7)

FIRST EDITION
(20190730)
Printed in USA
www.edgewebsite.com

Publisher's Note:

Thank you for purchasing this book. It began as an idea, was shaped by the creativity of its talented author, and was subsequently molded into the book you have before you by a team of editors and designers.

Like all EDGE books, this book is the result of the creative talents of a dedicated team of individuals who all believe that books (whether in print or pixels) have the magical ability to take you on an adventure to new and wondrous places powered by the author's imagination.

As EDGE's publisher, I hope that you enjoy this book. It is a part of our ongoing quest to discover talented authors and to make their creative writing available to you.

We also hope that you will share your discovery and enjoyment of this novel on social media through Facebook, Twitter, Goodreads, Pinterest, etc., and by posting your opinions and/or reviews on Amazon and other review sites and blogs. By doing so, others will be able to share your discovery and passion for this book.

Brian Hades, publisher

Prologue

Then

The worst thing, I think as I gasp for breath, is the sound. Above the waves breaking over my head, my own labored breathing, and the occasional screams as my crewmates are slaughtered by a pack of half-starved children, I can faintly hear that little bastard, Slightly, counting in a flat monotone.

"Thirteen," he says.

It shouldn't have ended like this. I can feel blood leeching out of my side. It's in the water now, and it'll be a miracle if I can reach the shore before the mermaids catch the scent.

"Fourteen." His voice rings out over the waves.

Seventeen men in our crew. Fifteen men that were my responsibility, plus my captain and myself. I shouldn't have run away. I should have stood by the crew when everything started to go sour, declared mutiny against the captain, drawn my sword and rallied the men. We all hated him. Maybe, if he'd been dead, the children would have let some of us live.

"Fifteen."

We hated him, but we feared him more. When he advanced on me, with that light in his eyes and that terrible hook, I took the coward's way out. My arms are heavy and stiff. Why am I still trying? If I make it to shore, what will I find but more savage children, armed with makeshift weapons? Pan has been thorough. The pirates are dead.

"Sixteen."

Sixteen dead. Only me now. I should just surrender. I've looked out for the crew through dozens of battles, and I haven't saved a single one. It doesn't seem right that, at the end, I should find a way to save myself.

"Seventeen."

Well, there it is. Seventeen pirates, seventeen corpses. I must have died as well. I wonder vaguely if I will ever stop swimming. Maybe this is the curse for my cowardice, at the moment when it matters most. Maybe my ghost will swim forever through the seas of Neverland. "Gentleman Starkey, the first mate of the Jolly Roger," they will say, "the pirate who fled his mates and drowned". What a pathetic excuse for a vagabond.

There is warmth beneath me, and my arms, moving of their own volition, are pulling me up. The water is receding. I feel the sun beating on my back and the ache of the wound in my side. Not dead. Not cursed to swim forever.

I manage a guttural laugh. Slightly has miscounted. I wonder absently if he'll ever find out.

Groaning, I flop over on my back and try to put my thoughts together. The sun is warm overhead. For the moment I can forget the faces of the men I left behind and simply revel in the fact that I'm alive.

There is a sound, like footsteps, on the beach.

I open my eyes. There is a tomahawk blade directly above my neck.

"Well," I mutter, as the Piccadilly Indians gather around me, "survival was nice while it lasted…"

Chapter One

Now: Thursday, February 5th, 1953

There is a game I like to play whenever a client walks into my office. I sit him down — or her, occasionally, but usually a 'him' — and ask the simple question, "How can I help you today?" Then I start to count. I've found that you can tell quite a bit about someone from how long it takes for them to respond.

My latest client does not disappoint. As I silently count, I consider the man sitting across from me. Jack Harding looks to be in his fifties, although looks could be deceiving — especially for those who have lived in the city for some time. I myself don't look a day over thirty in a good light, despite the fact that I am … well … I don't know exactly how much older. Old enough to remember a time before the city existed.

Regardless, my client appears to be in his fifties. He is slightly portly, with thinning gray hair and a pair of thick glasses. His suit is well-made and carefully pressed, so I gather that he has some money, but I don't recognize him, so he can't be too important. There is a small amount of sweat beading on his brow, despite the fact that it is quite cold outside and my office is not well heated. That, combined with the five seconds he spends composing a reply, suggests to me that he is about to give me a problem that seems important and embarrassing to him, but which is actually quite mundane. The fact that he's playing with his pocketwatch without opening or looking at it is even more evidence.

"Well, Mr. Stark..." he begins, stammering slightly, "I hope that you can help me."

He's stalling. I glance at Harding's hands, crossed in his lap, and am not surprised to see a ring on his finger. It will be about a woman. A younger woman, most likely. I give him a polite smile. "Mr. Harding, helping people is what I do."

That is not technically correct. What I do, more often, is help one person in a manner which upsets several others. Occasionally I help no one at all, and upset a great many people. But I've found that, despite what my mother taught me, it's more important to be polite than to be accurate.

"Um. Yes." Harding's return smile is forced. "I need you to find someone."

"Well, Mr. Harding, finding people is one of my specialties. I am particularly good at doing so discreetly." I lean forward slightly, fixing my best smile on my face. I've been told that it can use all the help it can get.

"Ah. Good. Good." Harding smiles again, and with some effort I manage to restrain a sigh. This is, bar none, my least favorite part of a case.

Fortunately for my increasingly-frayed patience, my assistant chooses this moment to enter the room with a tray, a pot of tea, and a pair of china cups. "Would you care for some tea, Mr. Harding?" she asks politely.

"Ah, yes, thank you. No coffee, I suppose?"

Holly and I share a quick look, and then she smiles brightly. "Of course, Mr. Harding. Just let me warm up the pot."

"Seems a nice young lady," Harding says once Holly has left the room. "Piccadilly?"

I nod once, refraining from comment. Mostly, I'm curious to see where Harding intends to go from here. Many of my clients try to show how open-minded they are by making a comment about how kind I was to hire a Piccadilly Indian as a secretary, and prove themselves to be anything but in the process. Others make crass comments regarding her beauty, suggesting that I keep her for more than her dictation skills. A few simply show their disdain for my life choices, which I am sadly used to. One particularly foolish gentleman suggested that she was my half-breed daughter, which was absurd. Aside from the both of us having black hair, I look nothing like Holly. She takes after her mother — short, bright-eyed, a bit round, and rather gorgeous. I am taller, bony, and I have never been described as handsome. A few people have charitably called me rakish. Usually I get 'weathered,' and once I was termed 'horse face.'

I am pleasantly surprised when Harding does none of the above. Staring down at the teacups between us, he simply returns my nod and finally starts to speak. "My marriage has not been a happy one, Mr. Stark. It was clear quite early on that my wife and I were not suited for one another."

Oh dear. "It's not my place to judge, Mr. Harding, only to help. I take it this missing person is someone ... close to you?"

Harding smiles faintly. He pauses when Holly returns with a steaming mug of coffee. Taking it from her with a smile and a nod of thanks, he applies a liberal dose of cream and sugar before stirring. Once she has left, he continues. "Yes, quite close. Angela Vickers is her name. I have a photograph." Reaching into his jacket, he comes out with a well-worn and folded photo. I take it, then carefully unfold and study it. Definitely a young woman, even younger than I would have guessed — not much older than Holly, unless I miss my guess. She's smiling, eyes twinkling and hair pale, wearing a glittering evening gown and a fashionable hat.

"Your camera, I suppose?" I ask.

Harding nods. "I'm something of a photography enthusiast." He takes a sip of coffee, makes a bit of a face, but then takes another. "I first met Angela at a formal dinner I was attending. I must admit that she was not there as a guest, but as a hostess."

"You became smitten, and asked her to attend some other event with you, I suppose?"

Harding colors and a wistful smile crosses his face. "That's right. Not one of my usual haunts, mind you. It was a spur-of-the-moment thing, but I was delighted when she accepted. Over the past few months, she has been ... well, lovely."

Typical. "You bought the dress and the jewelry she is wearing in this picture."

Harding's smile fades as my tone gets through to him. "I bought her some gifts, yes. The smile on her face was worth every penny." He takes a deep breath. "And for the first several months, it was wonderful, only ... in the last few weeks, I've felt that something was worrying her. Nothing that she would admit to, of course. She claimed to be perfectly happy. But Saturday night, she wasn't at her flat when I arrived to pick her up, and now I can't find her anywhere. The landlord has informed me that she moved without paying her last week's rent, and I can't locate her. Frankly, I'm at my wits' end."

"Have you spoken with her friends?"

"Well..." Harding bites his lip, taking a long sip of coffee to cover his distress. "I don't really know many of them, you see. We mostly attended events that were more ... upscale."

Oh dear.

I pick up the photograph again. "Mr. Harding, I hesitate to suggest this, but you do realize the most likely explanation?"

Harding nods, staring down at his coffee. "You think she's grown tired of the old fart. Now that she has the gifts I bought her, she's moved on to greener pastures." He looks up. "But I didn't imagine her distress, Mr. Stark. I can't go to the police; I really have nothing but my intuition to rely on, and besides, if it got out that I'd been seeing a girl on the side, the scandal would be very bad for my career. But you're known for your discretion. I would just—" He breaks off and swallows heavily. "If you do find her and she doesn't wish to see me again, that will be the end of it. I just want to know that she's not in any trouble."

I consider this and the photograph for several moments before responding. "May I hold on to this for a few days?"

Harding looks up hopefully. "You'll take the case?"

I nod. "I'm sure Holly explained my rates to you. I'll need her address and any other information you have on her, as well. I can't guarantee anything, Mr. Harding, but I'll look into it. And rest assured, I will be discreet."

Harding stands with a broad smile, taking my hand as I follow him to the door and shaking it enthusiastically. "Thank you, Mr. Stark. Thank you so much."

I warn him, "Don't thank me yet, I might wind up taking your money and finding nothing. A missing person who intends to stay missing isn't easy to find. She might have taken a ship back to America by now."

"Nonetheless," Harding says. "If anyone can find her, you can."

"Thank you for the vote of confidence, Mr. Harding," I say. "Now, tell me everything you know."

Once I have the lady's address and supposed work address, along with what Harding can remember about her friends and a list of the presents he gave her, I escort him to the office's front room, and wait while Holly hands him his coat. "I'll be in touch as soon as I have any information," I say. As the door closes behind him, I breathe out slowly, turning to look at Holly. "Really?"

She smiles a bit bashfully. "Oh I know, Uncle Basil. But it's just so romantic!"

Holly is not actually my niece. But I am a friend of her family's, I have known her for her entire life, and she's never gotten out of the habit of calling me that. It's not worth the energy fighting her on the subject.

"Romantic. Right." I shake my head, pacing back and forth. "You know that I've already solved this case."

She sits on the edge of her desk, giving me a dubious look. "I'm listening."

"An older man meets a young lady who successfully charms him. He spends several months courting her. After winning enough expensive gifts from him, she vanishes into the night. You know exactly what happened."

"You don't know that for sure," Holly protests.

I raise an eyebrow. "Angela Vickers," I said. "That dreadful movie you dragged me to last year? Angela Vickers was the name of Elizabeth Taylor's character. So not only do we have a fraud, but a fraud with a dreadfully poor imagination."

"That movie won six Academy Awards, Uncle Basil."

"Dreadful," I repeat.

"And yet you remember the name of one of the main characters," Holly points out. "Over a year later."

This was not an argument worth having. "As I was saying, we have someone who has clearly constructed a character, and the character that she has constructed is telling: a high-society debutante, someone flashy and friendly who lures men to their destruction. She accepts a great many gifts from her rich, much older benefactor who works in—" I break off, a thought occurring. "What does Mr. Harding work in?"

"Port authority," Holly says, trying to hide a smirk. When I change the subject, she tends to assume that it's because she's won. "He's their Human Resources director."

"God save us from government," I mutter. "Where was I? Yes. A rich benefactor, a government-type with money to spend and an unhappy marriage. Rich, but not extravagantly so. She grows uncomfortable — or so he believes — and eventually departs without so much as a note." I shake my head. "In deference to your romantic ideals, Holly, I'll give you three possible solutions to this situation, all of which have the same ending."

"Go on," Holly says, sitting back behind her desk and artfully posing her chin in her hands.

Ignoring her, I continue. "The first solution is also the most likely. Harding's gifts were getting less impressive as his funds ran down, or else our 'Angela' felt that they were about to. She has left in search of greener pastures. The second solution, slightly less likely, is that our mysterious vixen only wished for a certain amount of money, and has departed to live her own life. The third, and I should note by far the least likely option, is that ... well ... let's be honest. Harding is a bit of a sad sack." As I talk, I start pacing around the room. Our space isn't large. technically, it has three rooms — my personal office, the reception, and a small kitchen. I don't mind, but it does mean that when I start to walk and talk, I find myself turning around frequently.

Holly is used to me. "I can't argue with that," she says. "I felt sorry for him just getting his coffee."

"It's entirely possible, if not plausible, that his paramour started to feel guilty about bilking him so thoroughly and has decided to move on to someone she feels is more deserving of her tricks." I shrug, pulling on my coat. "Unfortunately for our Mr. Harding, all three of those stories have the same ending and that ending involves me wasting quite a bit of time tracking down a woman who does not want to be found, learning that she does not want to be found, and returning to explain to Mr. Harding that, as mentioned—"

"She does not want to be found." Holly mimics my expression and intonation, and then smiles. "So why did you take the case?"

I pause by the kitchen door and turn to face her. "I enjoy being able to pay the rent," I say dryly. "Harding seemed to be aware of how unlikely this little mission is. If he wants to spend his dollars confirming what he already knows, my conscience is clear. Besides, I could use the fresh air."

"I know the feeling," Holly says, sitting back in her chair. She frowns as I grab my coat. "Are you heading out now?"

I consider the current tram lines and the area of town I intend to canvass. "I don't see why not. You can lock up behind me and head home for the night."

This is clearly not the response that Holly wants to hear. "It's almost six, Uncle Basil," she points out. "Dinner is at seven."

"According to Harding, our mystery lady lives in Marooners. Fifteen minutes on the tram, twenty minutes to talk to a few people and have a glance at our mystery lady's apartment, twenty minutes to get back to Piccadilly Cross. Which leaves me with five minutes to freshen up before dinner."

"Mom is going to flip her top if you're late."

"Plum won't even notice. Besides, I've been late plenty of times before. Also, I am not going to be late because I have a schedule."

"Totally. Flip." Holly lets the syllables roll across her tongue.

"Holly, we don't get enough clients that I can afford to leave a case be. I'm just checking out the apartment."

Holly shakes her head. "I'm just saying, it's not good manners to ditch a dinner invite. Repeatedly."

"I'm not ditching anything," I say, putting on my hat, picking up my cane for protection, and opening the office door. "I'll be at your house by seven."

Leaving Holly grumbling behind me, I walk out into the waning light of winter in Everland.

——— «» ———

Everland was founded from a collaboration between the American scientist George Ellery Hale and the British businessman John Darling. The two of them had spent years corresponding about certain shared dreams and realized that there might be a wealth of worlds hovering two places to the right of reality as we knew it. The land they arrived at was astonishing — a magical island, home to nothing but a few ragged tribes of half-savage children and orphaned American Indians, along with a host of magical creatures and one particularly problematic and powerful boy. Once he was removed, things moved very quickly, and the island of Neverland was rechristened 'Everland' in a spirit of misplaced optimism.

For several years, drunk on the promise of pixie dust refineries, weaponized mermaids, and the possibility of eternal youth, investment in the form of both money and immigrants rushed into the newly-founded colony. But with each passing year, it became increasingly clear that there had been a flaw in the original plan. Magic can't be reproduced, which is why it is magic, and Neverland's magic in particular was based on innocence and childish games; spotty at the best of times, it was largely useless when put up against cold, hard reality. The vaunted timelessness that once held the island collapsed.

Then came the Great Depression, and thousands of poor farmers flocked to Everland, filling the buildings that had been meant for the rich and claiming jobs farming the arable land around the main city. Finally, during the Second World War, Second Star Industries managed to develop a few simple weapons technologies that brought in new money and cemented Hale and Darling's control over the city.

Today, Everland City holds about eighty thousand people, with another fifty thousand scattered around the island in a dozen villages and treaties ceding territory to local non-human populations. Government is a nightmare conglomeration of American, British, and random elements arranged into the rough approximation of a country, which is semi-independent but also still tied to both England and the United States. The island's cruelty, sadly, has stayed more or less the same as it was in the days when the island crawled with monsters and pirates. Childish or not, some things never change.

———— «» ————

My information says that Angela used to live down in the Marooners, the section of town that surrounds the port itself. It can be a rough neighborhood, but there are worse. In the Marooners you are likely to run into drunken sailors and drug dealers, but the gangs are kept mostly in check and violence is low enough that I don't bother taking my pistol. There are gun laws of sorts in this town and I've run afoul of them often enough that I don't go armed if I can avoid it.

The western line goes right through the Marooners and down Jane Street to the harbor proper, so I save myself the walk and hop a ride. I don't have a car; not many people in Everland do. Between import fees and the price of gasoline it's just not worthwhile, and the city's small enough that you can reach most places walking. When you can't walk, there's always a tram nearby — although that does mean having to read whatever absurd propaganda posters have been plastered all over the car.

Back in the early days, the posters were about safety issues in the city; newcomers didn't always read the manuals they were given, and hardly a day went by without some idiot turning up dead. During the War, it was all about conscription and crushing Germany. Today, there's an even mix. On the one side, an incongruous poster left over from Christmas extorts citizens to join the Air Force to fight in Korea, with the Air Force banner covered in a holiday wreath. On the other, a looming black shade terrorizes a pair of small children, while red text underneath implores us to keep watch for unstitched shadows.

Hopping off the tram at Bulwark Street, I make my way down to the apartment where our mystery lady pretended to live. Not much chance of getting reasonable information there, but the landlord might remember something if I nudge him the right way. The building itself, like most of the Marooners, is a first-generation brick tenement from the 20s, already looking the worse for wear. They built dozens of them in the glory days, and then overfilled them during the Depression when thousands flocked to Everland looking for a good life that didn't exist. You can read all the city's problems in one of these buildings: built more with hope than common sense, with crumbling mortar that couldn't survive Everland's extreme and sudden weather shifts, and a smattering of boarded-up windows from years of neglect. It's in better shape than some of the buildings on this street though, which gives me hope that someone around here might give a damn about what happened to a missing neighbor. The light under the front porch is even working, although no one's gotten around to putting buzzers in.

After a half-minute of knocking, the door is answered by an older lady who regards me suspiciously. "What do you want?" She glares up at me, and I wonder what she sees. Whatever it is, it makes her no less unfriendly. "If you're looking for rooms, we're full up."

That seems unlikely. "I'm actually just stopping by for Ms. Vickers," I say. The reaction is impressive; I didn't think her eyes could get any narrower and still be open. I keep my cane at the ready in case I need to shove it into the door before she can slam it in my face. "She wanted me to pay her last week's rent and pick up a few things."

The landlady looks me up and down and becomes fractionally less hostile. "She owes me twenty dollars."

I raise an eyebrow. "Ten."

A moment of grumbling and then she nods, holding out a hand. I slip a bill into it and the door opens like magic. The inside of the building is slightly more worn than the outside, but as we trudge up the stairs to the second floor I note that the carpets are swept and the lights, again, are on. "Well-lit building," I observe.

The woman looks at me over her shoulder. "I run a good place here. Don't need the kind of trouble that your 'Miss Vickers' brings with her." She pauses by a door, reaches into her long coat, and pulls out a ring of keys. "People coming by all hours of the night, gentlemen callers. This is a nice house."

Ah-hah. "I'm sorry that Angela was so much trouble for you."

"She agreed to keep things quiet. It's not right," the landlady complains as the door swings open. She gestures inside. "I'll be down the hall."

The landlady waves vaguely as she walks away and I shake my head. Angela certainly didn't endear herself to the management. Bad trait in a would-be con artist, but I won't complain. I walk inside, automatically locking the door behind me, and lean my cane against one wall. I won't need it while I'm looking around.

The apartment's inside is more or less what I expected: three rooms, clean but sparse; some light furniture and a bookshelf with a handful of books; walls essentially bare. There are a handful of photographs on the shelves in inexpensive wood frames. A quick look convinces me that they aren't actually family members or friends — no individual is in two pictures, and Angela herself isn't in any. They're props, just in case one of her gentlemen comes upstairs for a few minutes. Though I suspect that she discouraged that.

A refrigerator is humming in one corner of the kitchen. Opening it, I find a few wilted vegetables and some juice, but nothing else. The kitchen's shelves are stocked with a handful of glasses and plates but nothing particularly fancy. There are crackers still in the pantry; I absently take the box as I continue looking.

A few minutes later, my search finished, I stand in her bedroom and thoughtfully pull a cracker out of the box. I haven't found much of any use. It looks as though the girl packed everything that she could into her bags and left the rest. This validates my theory that she left under cover of darkness, but it's also a bit odd. After all, if she was planning this, surely she had time to finish gathering her things. The detritus left behind isn't worth much, but it will cost her more than the twenty dollars rent to replace all of it.

What I did find was a half-torn ticket to a play wedged under a chair leg, which could just be something that Harding took her to, but might be a clue to another admirer. What I didn't find was anything concrete — a diary, journal, or even a phone number tucked on a piece of paper in a wastebasket. There are papers on the desk, but there's nothing of interest on them. And the crackers are terrible. As near as I can tell, the girl covered them with powdered sugar. They certainly weren't meant to be eaten that way.

I return the box of crackers to the pantry and start for the door. I've just wasted ten dollars on a dead end. I can follow up on the ticket and hope someone at the theater recognizes her, but it's slim. At the door, I pause to give the apartment one last look-over on the off chance I've missed something. And I come to a stop.

There's a breeze ruffling the papers on the desk, but the window is closed.

Crossing back to the wall, I find a loose flap in the wallpaper. Underneath, something has scratched away at the mortar of the window, leaving a gap no more than an inch wide, just large enough for a mouse to push its way through. But a mouse would gnaw through the wallpaper too. This gap was designed to be hidden. I retrieve my cane and prod at the hole for form's sake, in case there's anything hidden inside, but I'm fairly sure I know what's going on even before I come up empty.

I get the crackers back from the kitchen and open the window. Leaning out, I take a cracker out carefully and leave it on the sill. Pitching my voice high and leaning back, I call out softly. "For you, sister."

There is a short pause, then a faint chime sounds and a tiny light blossoms in the shadows of the fire escape. It drops down, landing next to the cracker, and I wonder if the landlady knows that she has a fairy nest in her rafters. I suspect that if she did, the city would be by to fumigate it within hours.

The fairy looks up at me, eyes narrowed, and I set my cane down and climb out onto the fire escape, staying a foot away from her as she looks me over. After a moment, she takes a nibble from the cracker and then favors me with a burst of musical speech. My fairy is a little rusty, so it takes me a moment to decipher. "Mercy?" I repeat, raising an eyebrow. "I'm not here to hurt anyone … Oh! Is Mercy the name of the lady who lives here?"

The fairy indicates that it is, and goes off on a rapid-fire tangent about not having had any crackers lately and something about the weather. I wait for her to spin down, and then say, "I'm Basil. I don't think I caught your name, lovely lady."

Fairies are embarrassingly susceptible to flattery, although it never lasts. This one grins, flits into the air for a moment, does a curtsy, and introduces herself as either Glimmer Moss or Glimmer Moth. Or possibly Glimmer Mop. I decide to stick with calling her Glimmer. "A pleasure to meet you, milady Glimmer," I say with a bow of my head. "As it happens, I'm a friend of Mercy's, but I don't know where she's gotten to. Have you seen her?"

Glimmer, bless her tiny heart, doesn't wonder why I didn't know Mercy's name. It's a fairy trait: their own memories are poor and they often don't realize that others don't behave the same as them. It's one of the reasons that there are so few fairies left. She complains softly that Mercy has been gone for ages, settling across from me and pausing to tear into the cracker.

I consider this, letting her eat; I'm not going to get anything useful out of a hungry fairy. "Ages" most likely means more than a day and less than a week, and is about as good an answer as I'm likely to get. "Did she often have men over?" I ask when it looks like she's done.

Glimmer replies with a shrug.

I pass her another cracker from the box, phrasing my next question carefully. "Did she seem scared when she left?"

This takes a moment of thought, but eventually Glimmer admits that Mercy seemed sad, but that she seemed sad a lot.

If Holly's romantic musings turn out to be true, I am going to be slightly embarrassed. But I have one last question. "Glimmer, does Mercy have anywhere that she likes to hide things?"

Glimmer narrows her eyes and launches into a new rant accusing me of treating her as a thief just because she's small. She looks like she's about to drop the cracker, fly across the fire escape, and pummel me. I get ready to duck when I hear the distinctive sound of a deadbolt turning from inside the apartment. Glimmer and I instantly drop silent. I press myself against the wall as the door slowly opens. There's the sound of heavy boots — just one pair though, so at least Mercy's newest guest is alone.

My consideration of my options gets interrupted when I hear them approaching the still-open window. I could punch whoever leans out, but if Mercy has taken to wearing combat boots I'm going to feel fairly stupid doing so. I curse myself for leaving the cane in the room — it's exactly for situations like this that I carry it. Instead, I tuck the cracker box in my coat pocket and stand, gesturing for Glimmer to vanish. She does so, grabbing the remains of her cracker as she flits away. I prop myself against the fire escape, arms crossed.

The man who leans out is definitely not Mercy. I suppose he could be two people of her size in a coat, but no one would willingly wear that face, even as a mask. He has my cane in one hand, though it looks more like a stick in his beefy grasp. His bushy brow furrows angrily as he takes me in and growls, "I don't know you."

"That is true," I admit. The window is fairly narrow and I'm about as far back as I can get from it. If the bruiser decides to climb out, I should be able to get a few good hits in first. On the other hand, this is a narrow area and he outweighs me by at least half again. This feels like a good time for diplomacy. "My name is Basil," I offer, trying to restore a bit of balance to the conversation. "And yours?"

And here I make my first mistake. For just a moment, instinct overrides common sense, and I hold out my hand to shake his.

Sadly, the bruiser's instincts are rather different than mine. Instead of politely shaking my hand, he chooses to grab it by the wrist, yanking me towards him as he raises my own cane and prepares to flatten me. "Where is she?" he roars.

I'm quite close to him now, and I can smell a good deal of alcohol on his breath, so I decide that the time for diplomacy has passed and respond to his question by way of an elbow delivered directly to the sternum. As he doubles over with a gasp, I break free, retrieve my cane, and vault the railing of the fire escape, grabbing the ladder with my free hand and shimmying down at top speed. I'm not a moment too soon; the goon is right behind me, less climbing and more leaping down the ladder in hot pursuit.

Once on the ground, I'm feeling a bit more confident in my ability to dodge, which leads to my second mistake — pausing to try and talk some sense into the man still roaring his way after me. "I think we're getting off on the wrong foot," I duck under his first wild punch, knock the second aside with a smack of my cane, and back-step quickly away from the next three. "I still haven't gotten your name."

The stranger isn't interested in conversation. "Where's Victoria?" This roar is even louder than the one before, and he follows it up with a glancing blow that sends me sprawling, cane clattering into the gutter. I've barely scrambled to my feet before he's on me again, and it takes all of my focus to avoid the next few blows that come my way. The man is drunk, but not enough to seriously impede him, and he knows how to fight.

I glance up to the apartment. "Victoria? The girl who lives there?" I shake my head. "Don't have the slightest clue, I'm afraid."

"I'll make you tell me!" The man isn't convinced, but all of the yelling seems to be wearing him down a bit so I decide to press my luck.

"It's the truth," I tell him, dodging out of the way and retreating toward the street. My opponent pursues me doggedly, even when I knock a trash can into his path. "Haven't seen hide or hair of her. How do you know her?"

"So Schaefer hired you to spy on her?" The man's mind has switched gears, which is good. The gear that he's switched to still seems to involve hitting me though, which is not as good, and I can't respond for a few moments because I need all of my breath to get out of the way. Another light clip knocks me back, and I take advantage of the pause to shake my head.

"Not sure who you mean," I start and then hesitate. "Wait. Douglas Schaefer?"

"You're not fooling me!" In my moment of confusion, the gorilla decks me in the face, and I go sprawling again. Before I can get up, the man has me in a headlock, his face inches from mine as he roars in my ear. "You tell him to leave her alone!"

I'm having some trouble responding, on account of the pressure on my windpipe. I settle for stomping on his insole and then driving one hand into his jaw to disorient him. His grip loosens, and I take a deep breath of fresh air, but he doesn't quite let go.

"Awright, break it up!" A familiar voice echoes across the street, and I can't quite suppress a groan. My assailant doesn't respond immediately, which is all of the excuse that my old friend Constable Daggett needs to cross the street and give him a sharp rap with his nightstick. The bruiser lets go of me and rounds on his new attacker, but breaks off as he realizes it's the police.

Daggett looks between the two of us. His partner, Constable Stevens, is already arriving with two pairs of handcuffs. "If it isn't two of my favorite people," Daggett drawls sardonically. "Maybe I should let the two of you sort this out, come back in a few minutes."

My head is pounding from the fight, and I'm feeling tired and strained. With that in mind, I make my third mistake. "Well, we do all know that lazing about is more your style," I snap. "But then, you do enjoy hitting people. Difficult choice."

———— «·» ————

The Everland First Precinct building is essentially the same as the last time I was arrested. I nod to the desk sergeant as Daggett marches me up to him. "Evening, Freddie," I say. "I'd tip my hat, but … you know." I raise my cuffed hands apologetically.

Freddie nods back, "Evening, Basil." Glancing over my shoulder to where Stevens is hauling in my dance partner, he raises an eyebrow and chuckles. "Rough date?"

"This gentleman took some exception to it," I admit with a shrug. "We were discussing the situation when Constable Daggett chose to get involved. He's quite the heartbreaker."

"Doesn't look like that was all he broke," Freddie says, trying not to laugh, while gesturing for his clerk to come over.

It's Susan Dunham tonight, which is good — she thinks I'm funny. Daggett glares at the both of them. He's trying to manhandle my walking stick and a small iron cage, wincing whenever he uses his left arm and glaring at me through a swollen eye. From within the cage comes a constant stream of high-pitched, musical swear words that likely aren't comprehensible to anyone but me.

I suppose this was largely my fault. When Daggett took a swing at me, Glimmer chose that of all moments to get involved; when Daggett took a swing at her I got a bit more violent than intended; finally, when my former opponent came in on my side everything got a bit out of hand.

Daggett, at the moment, can't decide whether to glower at myself, Glimmer, or Freddie. He settles for dropping the cage on the desk and taking a step backwards, nudging me. "Drop your stuff."

It takes me a moment, with my hands cuffed, but I empty my pockets in short order. Freddie looks them over. "No pistol," he observes.

Thank God. "Don't need one."

Freddie makes a suspicious noise and picks up my cane. He taps it against the counter, looks back at me, and says, "Where's the release?"

Damn.

"Just under the handle. You need to press it and twist the head."

"Mm-hm." Freddie does so, and for a moment the room gets quieter as everyone looks at the steel blade in his hand. "One sword-cane."

"You never know what sort you'll run into. No law against concealed blades in Everland."

Freddie slides the blade back into my cane and returns it to the pile. He resumes looking through the array of goods and reading them out to the clerk, who dutifully types them up. "Notepad, fountain pen, penknife, cigarette case and lighter—" He breaks off, glancing up. "You don't smoke."

"Other people do," I point out. "I would offer you one, but Constable Daggett here would probably cite me for attempted bribery."

Daggett decides that I'm the one to glare at for the moment, and prods me in the back with his nightstick. "Shut it," he advises. Freddie shushes him and continues to look through my belongings.

"One box crackers, one photograph of a young lady." He looks up again. "Have you found yourself a sweetheart, Basil?"

"Strictly business-related."

"Well, that's a relief. Wasn't sure how I was going to break it to the ladies at the precinct," Freddie laughs. "Susan'll be happy, eh, Susan?"

Susan rolls her eyes, glancing over to me with a long-suffering smile, which I return. Freddie continues. "One fairy in a cage. Your cage?"

"The constable's cage, unless he's donating it."

"You have the papers on you?"

I hesitate. "Not as such..."

I catch Dagget smirking out of the corner of my eye as Freddie gives me a flat look. "Right," he says, as I finish digging through my pockets. "Well, can't be helped for the moment. One wallet, containing twenty-three dollars and twelve cents, along with your identification. One—" He breaks off, giving me a sour look. "One small flask which, by the smell, seems to be full of whiskey."

Daggett's smirk drops off his face, and he starts rummaging frantically in his pockets.

I shrug. "Found it lying in the street. It's downright criminal what people throw out these days."

Freddie rubs the bridge of his nose, looking over to where Daggett is slowly turning crimson. "Basil..."

"Unless you have another theory about where it came from?"

Daggett twitches, clearly debating the relative value of arresting me for picking his pocket during our fight against the consequences of Darling finding out he was drinking on duty. As usual, self-preservation wins out over spite. "Figures you'd be a drunk," he mutters under his breath.

Freddie looks between the two of us, giving Daggett a moment to calm down, then logs the flask as my property.

"That's everything, I believe. John, take him over to Room One. The commish'll want to see him."

Over Freddie's shoulder, Daggett perks up. I ignore him. "He's still in, then?"

"He never leaves before eight," Freddie reminds me. "And he has standing orders when it comes to you."

"Got it. Watch over Glimmer for me," I say, as Daggett moves to push me towards the interview room, rougher than is strictly necessary. "No need to lead the way, Constable, I know where I'm going."

They leave me sitting in the interview room for at least an hour, time that I spend considering various ways that I could have avoided this particular outcome. By the time the door cracks open, I've drawn up a list of seven options, starting with not having taken this case in the first place and ending with developing a more respectful attitude towards my opponents within Everland's finest.

"Starkey. What a delightful surprise." Commissioner Steven Darling's low drawl echoes through the interview room as he walks in, eyebrows slightly raised, and looks me up and down. He taps the clipboard at his side with one finger, clearly unimpressed.

I don't bother to correct him with regard to my name, although I can't keep my brow from furrowing in response. The Commissioner and I have something of a tumultuous relationship. I tried to kill him a few times, before he was an officer. He tried to kill me back. I didn't take it personally; he did. He left the island with the Darling children, spent half a lifetime growing up and forgetting this place, and then returned with his adopted brother to take over law enforcement duties. Then he tried to have me arrested for a half-dozen counts of murder, but my counsel successfully argued that I had already been convicted and punished by the local authorities, and I was let go. Darling never quite forgave me for that.

Generally, I try not to let it get to me. On a certain level, he's right to distrust me — I am a former outlaw, and I'm not proud of my past. Besides, a man has a right to be upset with people who've tried to kill him. But I have a contrarian streak, and I can't entirely resist talking back. "Commissioner," I say politely. "I've been here an hour and no one has even offered me any tea. Your standards are slipping."

"How rude of me," he replies evenly, taking the seat across from me and setting the clipboard down on the table. "I'll have to talk to the butler. How is it that you keep showing up here?"

"Well, if I had to hazard a guess, I would say that I seem to have offended the good Constable Daggett at some time, since he's usually the one bringing me in. Perhaps it was when his mother invited me to the opera. I probably shouldn't have accepted, but she seemed very lonely."

Darling doesn't respond, although I hear a faint sound through the one-way glass and allow myself a tiny smile. "Cut the crap, Starkey," he says. "We have you on breaking and entering, assault, and—" He breaks off, and looks more closely at Daggett's report. "Illicit possession of a fairy?"

"Not illicit," I suggest. "I just haven't finished processing the paperwork. You know how fairies get when you leave them alone."

This could actually get a bit sticky, more so for Glimmer than for me. There are good reasons not to allow illegal fairy ownership. But as I hoped, the Commissioner only looks at me for a long moment before setting the clipboard down. He may have forgotten a lot about this island, but he still respects the fairies. "I do," he says. "What were you doing in that apartment?"

"I was thinking of moving in," I say. "The landlady let me take a look at the place."

"While it was occupied?"

I shrug. "It seems the young lady in question owed some back rent."

"I see." Commissioner Darling looks as if he sees entirely more than I'm comfortable with. "And the man you were brawling with in the street?"

"A case of mistaken identity. I'm sure that he will tell you the same." I lean forward. "Although, I should note that he started it."

"Always a bad idea when dealing with a pirate," Darling says wryly.

I feel my teeth clench. "We've all worked for murderous psychotics at some point, though. Haven't we, *Slightly*."

Alright, it was possibly not the best idea to deliberately antagonize him with his old name while under arrest, but I can only stand having my past thrown at me so often. Sometimes, I think it is best to remind him that I'm not the only one who feels that way.

Commissioner Darling takes a deep breath, and for a moment I think I've pushed too far. But he lets it out, and raps the table a few times instead of punching me in the mouth. "Stark," he says, putting hard emphasis on the last consonant, "I am going to ask you one more time. What were you doing in that apartment?"

I glance over at the one-way mirror on the wall, wondering just how much of the precinct has lined up to listen to this chat. "I'm trying to find someone," I admit. "It's business-related. I have every reason to believe that she isn't around the city anymore, but I'm giving it an honest effort. I really don't know what the other man was doing there, but if I had to hazard a guess I would say the same thing as I was, but for less legal reasons."

"And who wants you to look?"

"You know I can't tell you that," I say. "Client confidentiality, Commissioner. We've been down this road before." At least a dozen times.

"You just don't want me warning your clients off."

"There would be precedent," I point out. "But in this case, it's simply that privacy is the reason that people hire a detective, rather than going to the police in the first place. I assume that if my client had wanted to involve you, you would know." I give him a humorless smile. "And you know that unless it involves a crime scene, which the apartment is not, you can't demand that information."

"If we hold you for the fight, I could declare it a crime scene."

"We were fighting in the street. Totally unrelated matter." I lock eyes with him. "You are, of course, welcome to get a warrant and prove me wrong."

Darling takes another deep breath. "I've got my eye on you, Stark." He stands abruptly, glaring daggers at me. "You're free to go. Frankly, I could hold you overnight, but I'm somehow certain that it would be more trouble than you're worth. Should I assume that you're not going to be pressing charges against your companion?"

"I don't see the need," I confirm. "As I said, it was just a case of mistaken identity. No sense getting him in trouble for something that was no one's fault."

Darling nods glumly. "Get out of here, Stark, before I change my mind. And take your damned fairy with you."

I nod, standing as the door opens. I consider a parting shot, but manage to refrain. Perhaps I'm learning.

On my way out, I pause at the front desk to gather my possessions. Freddie chuckles as he returns them, marking each one off against his list. "I hear that the chief gave you a free pass this time," he teases. "One of these days, you're not going to be leaving by the front door."

"Darling loves me," I say with a slight smirk.

"He's suggested as much," he says innocently, and then adds, "Or at least he's suggested that you should love yourself more."

I raise an eyebrow, and then chuckle as I get the joke. "Somewhere uncomfortable, I take it?"

Freddie nods. "Going to be glad to give you that fairy back. It's been cussing up a blue streak — or at least I think it has. I've never had the knack for fairy-speak." He gives me a serious look. "Get that paperwork signed, Basil. Chief's giving you a pass this once, because he's a softy at heart, but he will nail you to the wall if you keep an unlicensed fairy around."

"Understood," I say, signing the paper he passes me. "Oh, and I won't be pressing charges against my friend whose name I didn't catch."

"Gentlemanly of you," Freddie says with a smile. "Now get out of here and stop making trouble for us. We're busy enough as is."

"Yes, sir."

I hear the sound of discordant music from down the hall, and Susan Dunham returns with Glimmer. The policewoman is trying to carry the heavy cage and cover her ears at the same time, with limited success. I move to help her, taking the cage off of her hands. "Calm down, Glimmer, everything is under control."

Glimmer gives me a long, complex description of what I can do with that control, which I interrupt by opening the cage door and passing her a cracker. She takes it, still glaring at me, and flies out of the cage, looping around the room three times before hovering by the door. I turn to Susan, putting the cage on the counter. "Sorry about that."

"I don't know why you want to keep a fairy," she admits, handing me a set of forms to sign. "Aren't they dangerous?"

"Everything interesting is dangerous if you give it a chance." I pull out my pen and sign with a flourish, then glance at the next page. "And what's this?"

"An affidavit, if you're planning to charge the man who attacked you," Susan says.

I wave it away. "I really don't see the need. No harm done." Aside from a few hours in the local lockup.

Susan sighs softly, nodding, and pulls the offending paperwork away. "If you're sure. Try to stay out of trouble, Mr. Stark."

"I always *try*, Constable Dunham," I say with a wry smile, giving her a tip of my hat as I join Glimmer at the door.

Fifteen minutes later, my former assailant steps out of the station. I've spent the time lounging on the steps across the road, mollifying Glimmer and considering my options. The fairy is not happy with me, but a few crackers and a promise of a nicer nest than her previous one has calmed her down a bit. When I see the big man walking out the door, his coat pulled high and his expression glum, I push myself to my feet and step over to him. "Good evening," I say, falling into step beside him.

He gives me a grim look. "What do you want?"

"An apology would not go amiss."

For a moment he just stares at me, and then he chuckles and holds out a beefy hand. "Sorry, I thought you were one of Schaefer's goons." Up close, and now that he isn't trying to kill me, it's obvious that he's younger than I'd first assumed, probably in his mid-twenties. An Everland native, I would guess, from the smoothness of his skin.

"You mentioned as much while you were trying to pummel me," I say, shaking his hand. His grip is surprisingly soft. "If you're referencing Douglas Schaefer ... well, I'd be lying if I said we weren't acquainted, but we aren't close."

"That's the guy," he says darkly. "I'm Todd, by the way. Todd Malcolm." His suspicious look returns. "If you're not with Schaefer, what were you doing in Vicky's pad?"

"Basil Stark. I'm a private investigator." After a moment of consideration I add, "A lovesick admirer hired me to see if she was safe." It's a gamble, but if I'm lucky Todd might know something. "She seems to have fallen off the grid."

Todd runs his tongue over his teeth thoughtfully. "Another one, huh?" He checks his watch. "Listen, I gotta run — I'm really late for work and the boss is going to kill me. How about you stop by tomorrow afternoon, and we have a talk about this? I'd like to lend a hand, if it means making sure Vicky's safe."

"That seems—" I break off, looking at his watch. 8:46.

Oh dear. "That seems like a good idea," I finish weakly. "I have somewhere to be as well. Where should I meet you?"

"The Drowned Mermaid, down on Wharf Street. You know it?"

Less than a block from the apartment where we'd met. "I know of it. I'll see you tomorrow, Mr. Todd. Take care."

And with that, I start down the street, moving somewhat more quickly than I had intended. I've learned some interesting things tonight, but the case isn't foremost on my mind right now. I'm late for dinner, and Plum Blossom is going to be furious.

———— «» ————

Piccadilly Cross is the last refuge of the Piccadilly Tribe of Neverland.

The Piccadilly tribe is a funny thing; they were here before the island was colonized, but they're not native to Neverland. They don't all spring from the same source, properly speaking — some very curious anthropologists have suggested that they're mostly drawn from Cherokee, Seminole, and Muscogee peoples, but their name was given to them by Lost Boys, who wouldn't have known native linguistic conventions from a hole in the ground.

The Piccadilly arrived here the same way everyone did, once upon a time — abandoned or lost by their parents, with nothing left on Earth to claim, they simply faded away from Earth and crossed the Sea of Dreams. A motley collection of children, they somehow grew up, adapted to the strangeness of the island, and were forced into its stories, fighting pirates and beasts —occasionally Pan — until John Darling and George Ellery Hale arrived with their machines and soldiers.

During the Children's War, the Piccadilly reluctantly joined the mermaids and the beasts fighting on the side of the invaders. When it was over, they signed treaties giving them full rights to the old peninsula west of Everland's new city center, which had been tribal land until it was stolen by pirates years before. Someone wisely decided to put all of their buildings on the eastern edge of the thirty or so square miles that made up Piccadilly territory, even though the city was a good two miles away. Enough homes for a hundred-odd members, a few stores and community buildings, and a friendly but very specific fence to make sure the rest of the city knows whose land they're on. These days, Everland runs right up to that fence, and Border Road divides Everland property from tribal lands.

I'm not one of the Piccadilly — in fact, in my past I killed a fair number of them — but I'm a fellow native of the island, and I served my sentence for my crimes. Now most of those in the generation I fought with have passed on, leaving only their children and grandchildren, who know me as the man who helped take care of them when they were young. They've more or less adopted me as a result, and I am allowed to live on their lands.

That said, tonight may be the night that one of the Piccadilly finally kills me.

"Two hours!" Plum Blossom, arms crossed and eyes narrowed, has cornered me in the front hall before I've had a chance to get my coat off. She's developed a fondness for gingham dresses recently, and no one has the temerity to suggest that they don't quite suit her — or, in my personal opinion, anyone. This one is a pale green, and the vague thought crosses my mind that my blood is going to absolutely ruin it. "Two hours we wait, with the pots bubbling over and the potatoes going cold, while you wander around the streets consorting with God-knows who! Where have you been?"

Plum is beyond furious. Holly didn't get much past opening the door and giving me a warning look before she barged over, jaw clenched and eyes set as she glared up at me. I try to look apologetic. "I got arrested, Plum. It wasn't my plan for the evening, trust me."

"Arrested!" Plum's voice goes up several decibels, and I think I might hear plates rattling in the kitchen. Panther, Plum's husband, appears from the direction of the Blossom family's kitchen; He looks grim, and I give him a weak smile. He steps past Plum, gently putting a hand on her shoulder, and then turns to me.

"Arrested?" he roars. "What did you think you were—" Plum taps Panther on the shoulder as Glimmer, who slipped through the door behind me, peers over my shoulder in terror, and Panther groans. "Oh Basil. Not again."

"Plum, Panther, this is Glimmer. Glimmer, these are my good friends, Plum Blossom and Stalking Panther." Glimmer peeks over my shoulder and offers the couple an uncertain wave. "Glimmer is helping me with an ongoing investigation."

"And getting you arrested?" Plum throws her arms in the air, turning away towards the kitchen. "I don't ask for much, I'm sure. Just for one of my oldest friends to come to a lovely dinner…"

"Plum—" I try to interject. But I've missed my one chance, and Panther has stepped in.

"Instead, what happens?" he rumbles. "I spend extra for a beautiful chicken, I put it in the oven. No Basil. Plum prepares our secret family beet recipe. No Basil. We get the table ready, set out appetizers. No Basil. Adelaide arrives, we settle down to talk, and where is Basil?"

I jump in before he can give a suitably withering reply to his own question. "Who arrives?"

Panther's mouth snaps shut, and he gives Plum a sudden, panicked look. "Um."

It's my turn to give them a sour look. "Adelaide?" I ask warningly.

"Well…" Plum says, not meeting my eyes.

"That is…" Panther adds, biting his lip.

"I suppose I should introduce myself," comes a low drawl from the den. There is a woman there, wearing a dark blue blouse and a long skirt. Her hair is platinum blonde, and she offers me a cool smile. "Adelaide Evans. It's a pleasure to meet you, Mr. Stark." She looks over at the conspirators meaningfully. "Plum has been telling me so much about you." Panther has slipped into the kitchen without a word, and Plum is doing her best to keep looking like a put-upon aunt, only momentarily slipping into 'chastised schoolgirl'. I spare a glance toward Holly, who is entirely innocence and spun sugar — so she was clearly in on this.

"I met Adelaide a few days ago, she's new in town, writing a piece on the history of Everland, you know, and I thought it would be nice to treat her to a proper Piccadilly dinner." Plum coughs, looking toward the kitchen.

"So Panther bought a chicken?" I ask.

"Hush!" Plum recovers some of her fire. "Speaking of which, Panther, how is it?"

"It's fine," Panther says levelly, carrying a covered tray toward the dining room. As he brushes past me, he tries to combine a look of wounded innocence and judgment , but mostly he just looks guilty. "Let's eat."

We filter into the dining room. I pause to pull out a few crackers and give them to Glimmer, telling her that we're probably going to be much too boring for her. She grabs them and vanishes into the kitchen to perch on the window. Panther gives her a suspicious look as he takes in the vegetables, but refrains from commenting. As we head to the dining room, I tap Holly on the shoulder and raise one eyebrow.

She shrugs helplessly. "I told her you'd be late," is her only defense as she slips past me to her chair. Once there, she quickly starts helping herself to bean bread, glancing up frequently at me, Plum, and Ms. Evans, who is watching me frankly as I take my seat. To no one's surprise, I'm sitting next to her, with Plum on her other side.

"So, Mr. Stark," Ms. Evans says, taking some green beans. "Arrested, you say? It can't have been particularly bad, since you're here now."

"It probably wasn't anything," Plum says, shooting me an annoyed look. "That Commissioner Darling has always had it in for poor Basil. And please, do call him Basil. We're all friends here."

"Yes, Ms. Evans," I manage after a moment. "Please, call me Basil."

"Only if you call me Adelaide," she says with another broad smile. I watch her for a moment, and then look down at my chicken; I can't read past her pleasant demeanor. "But please, go on. You have a history with the Commissioner, then?"

"Just a minor personal matter," I reply as smoothly as possible. I pause to take a bite of chicken, and then add, "And you're a reporter?"

"A magazine reporter, yes," she says, her smile not slipping for a moment. "National Geographic, to be precise. We're going to be doing a spread on Everland, and I was lucky enough to be sent to do some field research." She glances past me. "Was that a pixie? I've never seen one."

"A fairy, yes," I correct her politely. "They aren't so common as they used to be around here, although they say that a new one is born whenever a child laughs."

"Yes," Adelaide says with a musical laugh. "I heard that myth."

I pour myself some wine and offer some to Adelaide, which she accepts. "What makes you think that it's a myth?"

Her smile slips just for a moment. "You're having a bit of fun with me, Basil," she chides.

"No one has ever seen two fairies mate," I point out, "or lay eggs, or anything of the kind. They just appear."

"But there are billions of people in the world," Adelaide says, considering me thoughtfully. The polite mask is fading, but she's still trying to gauge our reactions to each sentence. "If each one had given birth to a fairy, we'd be overrun."

"They also say that when a child first says that they don't believe in fairies, one dies," I answer around a bite of chicken. "Maybe children are losing their innocence earlier these days. Or, more likely, this isn't the only island in the Sea of Dreams. Did you ever hear about the *Mary Rose*?"

"The cargo ship that got lost on the way to Everland and claimed to have found another shore? The endless desert, stretching as far as their eyes could see?" Adelaide raises one eyebrow at me. "I know the story. I'd always assumed they were delirious. It would explain why everyone who stepped off the boat was supposed to have fallen down dead as soon as they touched the sand — they just sank into the sea."

"Maybe," I admit. "Or maybe there are more things on Heaven and Earth—" I break off, seeing the edge of an honest smile. "I can only say that I've never seen a fairy born. A child's laugh seems as reasonable an explanation as any."

Adelaide still looks a bit dubious, and I'm not surprised. Most people who weren't here in the early days think that Everland's unique flora and fauna can still be explained scientifically, and that the rest is a delusion of some kind. I was once told, with some sincerity, that the waters of the island had contained naturally-occurring hallucinogens until Darling Industries arrived, and the timelessness that I'd felt living here was just a result of a lifetime spent high. "So, Basil," she says smoothly, "Plum was telling me stories about you."

"Not flattering ones, given that I was late," I say with a smile in my host's direction. Plum doesn't smile back, but Adelaide chuckles.

"Nice enough," she says. "I'm told that you're a detective."

"Guilty as charged," I say after a moment, swallowing my food. "It pays the bills. Well, it usually pays the bills."

"That must be exciting."

"Not as often as you would think. Mostly, people want me to spy on their wives or husbands. It's enough to turn a man off of marriage entirely."

"So, you aren't married?" Adelaide asks.

I laugh. "Not likely."

"Adelaide was just telling us about New York," Plum cuts in, before I can say anything else and ruin her matchmaking plans. "It sounds like such a wonderful city. I'd like to visit some time."

"It really is," Adelaide agrees, launching into a conversation about the city's nightlife, and some of the plays that she's seen there. From there we wander into a conversation about Ibsen, and somewhere along the line Adelaide and I get into a rather spirited argument about the underlying messages of *A Doll's House*, which we only break off when I belatedly realize that we're the only two people at the table who saw the play in question.

We drift to safer topics. I discuss some of my less controversial cases, or at least the ones where I don't think anyone involved would mind a retelling, Adelaide shares a few more stories of some celebrities she's talked to — Holly is enthralled to learn that Adelaide once met Ingrid Bergman — and Plum and Panther are happy to talk about some of the strange things they've seen in the woods. Panther, like many of the Piccadilly men, works as a lumberjack, and has a knack for finding excellent trees and avoiding dangerous predators. I think that Adelaide might be caught off guard by Panther's offhanded mention of avoiding bear and lion treaty territories, but it's hard to tell; if so, she covers it well.

By the time dinner is over, I'm more than a little surprised to discover that I had quite a good time.

"Are you in town for long, Ms. Evans?" I ask as we're getting our coats to leave. Plum has insisted on calling for a cab for her, regardless of the cost, and is in the kitchen trying to convince someone over the phone to come down at this time of night.

"Probably a week or two," she answers. "I'd like to really get the feel for this town, and I'm budgeting some vacation days to do it." She smiles broadly. "This seems like a very exciting place."

"It's actually quite sleepy most of the time, but it certainly has its moments. You definitely want to take a boat out to Mermaid Point. It's absolutely breath-taking."

"Thank you, Basil, I'll keep that in mind." Adelaide looks back at the kitchen, and then to me. "I don't suppose you'd be available for an interview? Plum suggested that you'd been on the island even longer than her, and I'd love to have your insight into what it was like before people came."

I stop, take a deep breath, and shake my head. "I ... don't spend a lot of time thinking about those days, Adelaide. Not anymore. It wasn't nice, and it's gone. That's all that I really need to know." I smile ruefully. "You should go down to the First Precinct and speak with Commissioner Darling. He's been here as long as me, and he's more than happy to speak at very, very great length on the subject."

"Should I tell him you sent me?"

"Only if you want to be kicked out the door," I laugh. "Darling and I are not the best of friends."

"There's an understatement if I ever heard one," Holly says, coming into the hall. "Take anything the Commissioner says about Uncle Basil with a grain of salt, because he has a grudge like you would not believe. Adelaide, the cab will be here in about ten minutes. Basil, are you staying, or heading home?"

"Home, I'm afraid. Lots to do tomorrow."

Adelaide's ears perk up. "On a case?"

"Nothing major, but yes," I say, shooting a warning glance at Holly, who shoots it right back. "Like I said. Lots of husbands who want me looking into their wives, and vice versa."

"Of course," Adelaide says. "Well, I will try the Commissioner, and then I'll come back and make you give me your side of the story. Saturday?"

I shouldn't have mentioned it. "I'll see what I can do. Have a good night, Adelaide."

"And you, Basil. It was very interesting meeting you."

As I walk home, I turn the night over in my head. Interesting is the right word for it.

Chapter Two

Friday, February 6th

Friday morning, I would have liked to be up with the sun, but the truth is that I rise slowly and painfully. I didn't sleep well; either the case was weighing me down, or it was the bruises. It isn't until I've had a shower, two cups of tea, and a light breakfast that I'm ready to face the day. Glimmer, who spent the night industrially building herself a house out of cardboard boxes in the corner of my living room, is now curled up inside it, dozing heavily, so I leave a jam biscuit on her doorstep and head out on my own.

Holly is sitting on her porch, just across the road, looking only slightly better than I feel. "Morning, Uncle Basil," she says, standing up and crossing to meet me. "Heading into the office today?"

"Just for a few minutes, to check the mail and open the window. I have some footwork to cover."

"So I'll be spending the day reading old books and doing crossword puzzles," Holly says.

I raise one eyebrow. "There's always cleaning, if you get bored." I glance over my shoulder. "And you'll want to check on Glimmer at some point. She tired herself out, so I expect she'll be sleeping for another five or six hours, but I'd prefer not to leave her alone for too long." I pull Daggett's old flask out of my pocket and pass it to her. "Sugar water, in case she gets jumpy."

"I didn't know you had a flask like that."

"Present from a dear friend."

Holly snorts. "Of course it is. I'll come in a couple of hours then, and open up formally. Should I handle the paperwork?"

"The paperwork?" I ask. Holly coughs meaningfully, and I clue in. "For Glimmer. Of course. Yes, that might be best."

"If only because left to yourself, it'll slip your mind, and you really will end up in jail. Again." She shakes her head. "You know, it'll be the Regulators after you if they think you're a fairy smuggler, not Darling. You have enough marks against you already."

"Yes, yes," I groan. The Unnatural Resource Regulation Department, commonly known as the Regulators, is in charge of watching over all of Everland's dwindling magical threats, and while they're less corrupt than the police, that just means they're more troublesome. "I'll stop by the office at some point this afternoon to sign whatever they need. In my day, they didn't worry about it."

"In your day, the mayor hadn't made fairy vandalism an election issue," Holly points out, "and no one was using fairy dust as an ingredient in a major street drug. Don't worry about it, I'll handle the paperwork. You find our missing paramour."

My intentions upon arriving at the office are to set up a second nest for Glimmer, to keep her from tearing apart our files when I bring her in, and to see if there are any outstanding bills that need leaving on Holly's desk. Instead, I find a client standing outside the door.

"Mr. Stark?" he asks, as I approach. I give him a quick onceover. Well-cut coat, but it's a little shabby. Same can be said about the hat. The man himself looks fit, maybe a little on the underfed side, but his mustache is ridiculous and he's not half as respectable as he's trying to seem. He's also been standing in the hall for a while; his coat is wet, and while there's a dusting of snow on the ground outside, it had stopped by the time I left home fifteen minutes ago.

"One and the same," I say easily, walking over and holding out my hand. "You seem to have the better of me, Mr.?"

"Yancy. Frank Yancy." Yancy shakes my hand eagerly, then steps back to let me unlock the door. "I'm sorry to be bothering you so early. I wanted to be your first case of the day."

"I'm afraid you missed the boat there, Mr. Yancy," I tell him, letting him into the office. "I'm actually on a case at the moment, and it's only just started. I can take down some notes, if you like, and give you a short opinion, but I'm not likely to have time for an immediate investigation."

"Oh, I think you'll change your mind when you hear this," he says, grinning. "Whatever you're working on, this is bigger."

I turn to look at him, slowly. "Is it?" I gesture to the chair. "What is this amazing case, then?"

"I," Yancy says, leaning in, "have discovered the lost treasure map of Captain James Hook."

I give him a long look. "Thank you, Mr. Yancy, but I don't think I will be able to help you. Have a good day."

He blinks. "What?"

"Have a good day," I repeat. "You'll find the door behind you. As you just came through it, it should be easy for you."

Yancy looks lost. "Now, hang on …"

"I'd rather not." I shake my head, moving to the corner and clearing a space near the table by our window. It should be just about the right width for a good fairy nest.

"This is the genuine article!" Yancy says. He reaches into his jacket pocket, pulling out four yellowed scraps of parchment. "I've spent two weeks putting together the pieces. I found the first map piece from divinations by a Piccadilly wise woman—"

"No such thing."

"What?"

"The Piccadilly don't have 'wise women'. Not part of their culture," I say. "But let me guess. You cunningly followed a trail of mystical clues, using only your wits and your intellect, and now you have … what, a map that you can't decode?" I take a quick look at the pieces as I speak.

Yancy looks hurt. "Captain Hook, of course, used a cipher on his map. You see, the symbols are all coded. But I've heard of you — you're his first mate. And you would know."

I shake my head. "I've heard it all before, Mr. Yancy. Believe me, you're not the first person to think that I had a line on a secret treasure. You're not even the first to be conned by a fake mystic. It's a con. Not a bad con. I'll admit the maps are quite real-looking. A century out of date, mind you; we used paper for our charts. But I suppose paper doesn't have the same mystical gravitas."

Yancy stands up slowly. "You're wrong, Mr. Stark. This is the real deal. I found the first map section in an old journal in the town library, right where the wise woman said. The second was concealed in Marooner's Bay. And with your help, I can—"

"Get eaten by any number of creatures," I say. "If the Captain had a secret treasure, which I suppose he might have, its location died with him. And if you go wandering into the woods in search of it, you'll join him. Go away, Mr. Yancy. I'm busy."

He grabs the map pieces off the table. "Fine, then! I'll solve this problem, with or without you! And when I find Hook's treasure, I'm not giving you a share!"

"There, at least, we will be equal."

Yancy slams the door hard on his way out. I don't even look over. Between supposed ancient maps and Glimmer's nest, I'd rather focus on the thing that actually might affect my well-being and happiness.

———— ‹› ————

The whole regrettable business with Yancy hasn't taken up very much time; I still have several hours before I'm supposed to meet with Mr. Malcolm, which means that my next stop is to follow up on the play ticket that I found. It's a long shot, but I've had luck with those before. The ticket in question is for a production of Show Boat that just wrapped up down at the Olympus Theater, which gives me some hope that they may have tracked who purchased it. Furthermore, the tickets are box seats, which makes my chances even better. The Olympus isn't very busy in the morning, but their office staff are already in, and I'm able to reach the front desk without anyone wondering exactly what I'm about. A polite inquiry and a few dollars work their usual magic, and the receptionist agrees to take a look at his records, politely pretending to believe my story about wanting to return a lady's purse for which this ticket is my only lead.

"You're in luck," he tells me, flipping through the book of reservations from that night. "We had those tickets listed for a Miss Victoria Lane."

Hence Mr. Malcolm calling her 'Vicky'. I mentally note down the particulars of her newest alias, and nod my thanks. "I don't suppose that it lists a contact number, in case she isn't listed?"

"Mm … let me see…" The receptionist checks a few more pages. "No direct contact number, but I do have a reference on the purchase. The purchaser paid by check, so you could possibly go to his bank?" He shakes his head. "Seems like a lot of work to return a purse."

"I'm old-fashioned that way. Who was the purchaser?"

"A Mr. Douglas Schaefer," the receptionist says blandly. He is clearly not enmeshed in the city's underbelly, or he would have spoken the words with the same hollow echo that reverberates down my spine. I had really been hoping that Mr. Malcolm's accusations the night before were just so much invention.

I let him give me the bank branch where I might enquire further, and avoid telling him that I won't need to. I know exactly where Schaefer can be found.

⸻ «» ⸻

Douglas Schaefer is one of Everland's self-made men, although the materials he used for construction are sadly familiar. He arrived in Everland twenty years ago, a young man among the hordes that swarmed the island during the Depression, and found himself a place within the budding criminal organizations that were still in the process of setting out stakes. He set his own out more quickly, and more enthusiastically, and soon he was on the top of the heap. While it would be wrong to say that he owns the city, it is only a slight exaggeration to claim that he has a governing share in its stocks. Between gambling parlors for the wealthy and smuggled goods for the poor, he has his fingers in more pies than I care to consider.

There have been times in the past when my investigations have carried me into his orbit, and he's now familiar with me. We've put together a rough truce; I try to turn a blind eye to how his activities might have a bearing on my cases, and he tries to avoid doing the sorts of things that will unduly strain my moral compass in the process. So far, we've managed. I hope that we continue to do so, because if I ever have to face off against him, I don't think I'll survive the experience. The mayor and half the city's councilors are in his pocket, along with at least a fifth of the police force — and it's only due to Commissioner Darling's diligence that he hasn't suborned more. The Darlings are not supporters of Schaefer, and my relatively friendly relationship with him is, in the Commissioner's books, a sign that I'm not as far from my roots as I like to claim. He may be right.

Today, Schaefer is holding court at the Blue Moon, a luxurious gentlemen's club in the downtown core. I, of course, am not a member; membership is restricted roughly to the hundred richest men in the city, and I do not qualify. But if I put on a nice enough suit, comb my hair back, and make sure to bring my cane, I can at least make it to the front hall. There, a polite word — along with a dollar — can get a message to one of those in residence. I do so, and sit back in a red-backed leather seat to wait for a reply, which comes gratifyingly quickly. Within five minutes, I am being shown to Schaefer's table. He is alone with a glass of red wine, and if you didn't know him, he would just be another rich old man. His suit, his hair, even his clean-shaven face, all of it is carefully calculated not to stand out. His eyes, though — there's no way to disguise those. I don't know many people willing to lock gazes with Douglas Schaefer.

"Basil," he says politely, motioning for me to sit across from him. Aside from one young waitress, hovering just out of earshot but close enough to respond instantly, and a pair of muscular men who are quite a bit closer, it's just the two of us. One of the men takes my walking stick, although he does it politely. "Can I get you something to drink?"

"A cup of tea would be lovely."

"Nothing stronger?" He looks faintly disappointed.

"I'm afraid that this isn't quite a social call," I explain. "I don't like to drink on the clock."

"A wonderful policy," he says with a smile. "You don't mind if I indulge."

"Of course not, Mr. Schaefer."

"Please, Basil, call me Douglas." He raises one hand lazily, and the waitress hurries over and refills his glass. "What can I do for you?"

I take a deep breath. "This is about Victoria Lane."

Schaefer's smile melts away like dew on stone. Behind me, I hear his guards shifting to readiness. "What about her?"

"Someone wants me to find her," I say neutrally. "Should I?"

There is a long, dangerous pause, and then he nods. "I take it my name came up."

"Tangentially," I lie. "But I was wondering if I was about to wander into your territory by mistake."

"That is not a simple question," Schaefer admits after a moment, taking a long sip of his wine. I relax an inch, and I think the guards do too, but I don't dare to look back to see for sure. "Yes, I know the girl, quite well in fact. No, I'm not responsible for her disappearance — at least, not deliberately. I can't deny that my ... reputation ... might have been a factor." He takes another sip, then meets my eyes. "We had a relationship."

For once, I'm not happy to be right.

I keep my face composed with some effort, but I think something might have slipped through, and he catches it. He nods, with a grim smile. "I assume that another paramour is the one asking for your help. You don't have to waste your breath denying it — I suspected as much several days ago."

I breathe out slowly. "I certainly wouldn't know anything about that." And if I did, I wouldn't say it. Schaefer's life is built on his reputation. The knowledge that he was being two-timed would not be good for business.

From his smile, I think he caught my subtext. "No, I suppose you wouldn't." He leans back and downs his drink. The waitress starts to step forward again, but he waves her off. "I'm afraid that I can't help you, Basil. I don't know where Victoria is, and I haven't seen her since Sunday. I should have seen her on Tuesday, but she failed to appear at an engagement. I sent a man around to her apartment, and she wasn't there."

That's a lot more recently than when Harding said he last saw her. "That actually might be very helpful," I say slowly. "Could I ask you a few questions about her?"

"I suppose so," Schaefer says easily. "I have a few minutes."

"Where did you first meet?"

"A year ago, at a private function. She was with some industrialist, looking bored out of her mind, and I couldn't help but introduce myself. I assume that you haven't met her, Basil, but she ... well, she has a way of drawing the eye, and she has fire." He shakes his head. "I let myself get a little bit carried away, I confess. Seems a bit silly looking back on it."

"She seems like a very impressive woman," I say carefully.

He laughs. "That she is. You'll know if you find her. Even an old cynic like you won't be immune." The laugh fades, and he sips his wine thoughtfully. "I spoiled her, had her brought around to my clubs. She was enthusiastic, seemed excited to be here. I knew it couldn't last, of course, but I figured we could get some good months in before the attraction faded. It was a private affair."

Explaining why I hadn't heard anything — Schaefer hadn't wanted to advertise the girl. "And then she vanished?"

"The last couple weeks, she'd been distracted. On Sunday, she met me at the club for a private event, and admitted to having 'lost' a very valuable silver necklace. I assumed that she was having money troubles, gave her a replacement for the evening, and didn't think about it again. It seemed a small price to pay for her attention. Then she vanished. No word, no trace." Schaefer shakes his head. "And I started looking into it."

"And then you stopped looking into it."

"And then I stopped," Schaefer agrees. "All I can help you with. Now, I'm sorry to kick you out, but I have a business meeting shortly, of a private nature."

"Not a problem. Thank you for your time, Mr. Schaefer, I appreciate it."

"My pleasure, Basil. It's always good to talk to you. You should stop by some time for a social call — I'll let the doorman know to let you in."

I nod politely. "I'll see what I can do."

"Good man." He pauses, lets me stand and retrieve my hat and walking stick from his guards. "And Basil?"

"Yes, Mr. Schaefer?"

He leans forwards, and for a moment there's nothing pleasant about his attitude. "If you do find her, let her know that it would be safer if she stayed lost. I'd rather let bygones be bygones, but I can't have her appear around me again. Understood?"

I nod. "Yes, Mr. Schaefer."

I beat a hasty retreat. I want nothing more than to go home and consider what I'd learned, but I still had to meet with my erstwhile attacker, Todd Malcolm.

———— «» ————

There's nothing quite as depressing as a bar like the Drowned Mermaid at four in the afternoon.

Later, when the sun sets and the crowd comes in, it'll be a little more welcoming — a smoky room, patrons talking and flirting, a few card games scattered around, and probably a half-trained band with more enthusiasm than common sense playing in the corner. It would take more than anyone here is capable of to turn the sagging posters and stained walls into a decent place, but there'll be life to it.

Right now, though, the only people here are the career drunks and the waiters who couldn't turn down some extra hours. Sunlight drifting in from the windows catches the dust and the grime in a way that the soft lights themselves don't, and the few guys scattered around some tables, mostly close to the bar so they can get their fix faster, are disheveled and glum enough to fit right in. If I were here for a drink, I'd turn right around and head back out.

Todd is sitting by the door, looking a little bored. When I come in, he starts to size me up before abruptly recognizing me. "Mr. Stark," he says with a grin, standing. He gestures to the bartender, a hulking guy almost big enough to be his twin. "Ernie, take over for a minute, willya?"

"Mr. Malcom," I hold out my hand. "How are you?"

"Better than last night, I can tell you," Todd says. "Lemme buy you a drink to apologize?"

"I don't drink before sundown," I say, which is not technically true. "But I'll take tea if you have it."

Todd considers for a moment. "Yeah, I think we got some of that, right, Ernie?"

Ernie nods as he takes up his spot by the door. "Under the cash," he says.

Todd leads me to the bar, and pours himself a glass of orange juice with a healthy dollop of vodka while the water for the tea is boiling. "Look, I just wanted to say sorry again for last night. I was a little drunk, and a lot worried." I don't say anything, and he flushes. "Okay, I was a lot drunk too."

I smile at that. "Don't worry." I wave it off. "A lot of people take shots at me. I've gotten rather used to it."

Todd smiles. "So, you're looking for Vicky too, huh?" He shakes his head. "How much trouble is she in?"

"I don't know," I admit. "Hopefully not very much." I pause, trying to figure out how to ask this diplomatically. "Were you and she ... involved?"

Todd laughs. "A girl like her with a guy like me?" He looks down at his worn shirt and rough hands. "Naw, Vicky and me were friends, that's all. Good friends, but friends. Besides, she had enough guys in her life as it was."

"I suspected that might be the case."

Todd looks up sharply. "She wasn't like that," he says, absently pouring water into a mug and dropping a tea bag into it before passing it across to me. "She just liked to live, you know? She always said life was too short to spend it pretending to be someone you're not."

I raise my hands soothingly. "A good philosophy, although maybe not as good when you're dealing with Douglas Schaefer."

Todd winces. "Yeah," he says more quietly. "Maybe not."

"So," I prod, "what chain of events led you to be searching her apartment?"

Todd takes a long sip of juice, watching me carefully. "I've known Vicky for almost a year now. She used to come here a lot, you know? Was seeing one of the guys that sings here, helping him with his band, that sort of thing. After they broke up, somehow she ended up staying around here and he ended up leaving town." He smiles sadly. "That sort of thing happens a lot with Vicky. She gets what she wants."

I nod slowly. "And then she met Douglas Schaefer?"

"Pretty much. I mean, she spent a lot of time hanging around the bands here. Always liked jazz guys, you know? One day, she followed one of them to a classier joint, and she caught Schaefer's eye. He made a pass, she figured it might be a fun time, and one thing led to another."

"Dangerous people to play games with," I say, noting that Todd's story doesn't quite match the one Schaefer told me. Todd shrugs.

"It's not that rare around here," he says. "Schaefer likes his girls, but he's got a bit of a roving eye and he doesn't get mean. You stick with him for a while, he gets bored, you go your own way with a lot of nice presents and a good story to tell. That's all it shoulda been this time. But then Vicky met some guy down at the Port, and totally fell for him."

I straighten. Harding enters the picture. "And she didn't tell Schaefer?"

"Like hell she did," Todd says with a snort. "You wanna try breaking up with the biggest name in crime?"

"Might be a better plan than two-timing him," I point out. Todd winces and nods, so I move on. "You ever meet this port guy?" I ask.

"Never even got his name," Todd says. "She didn't like to talk about it. I get the feeling she didn't want him to know about all of this — and hell, she didn't want anyone around here to hear anything that might get back to Schaefer."

That doesn't sound much to me like living your life without pretending, but this is an interesting story, so I don't interrupt. Instead, I just drink my tea and wave him on. It's dried, instant stuff, but it's marginally better than nothing. Todd continues. "I think, at first, she figured that Schaefer would get bored of her pretty quick, and she could slip off when that happened. But he didn't, and by the time she realized she was stuck, well ... she was stuck."

"And Schaefer never figured it out?" I ask. "He's a pretty sharp guy." I already know the answer, but getting it from this perspective might help with a few things.

"Well ... that's what worries me, see," Todd admits. "About a week ago, she showed up looking spooked, and drank herself near into a stupor. Wouldn't talk about it at all, just kept changing the subject whenever I tried to ask. At the end of the night, she told me she was thinking of getting out of town for a while. I made sure she got home safe, but ... I haven't seen her since."

"You think Schaefer caught on."

"That was my thinking, yeah," Todd says. "I think he knew she was two-timing him, and I think she found out. I hope she went into hiding the next day, but I dunno." He smiles self-consciously. "I was getting pretty worried, you know? I slipped the landlady a twenty to call me if someone tried to get into her apartment. Figured it would be one of Schaefer's people, and I could talk to them."

That cunning old lady, taking money from both sides. I chuckle, shaking my head. "So that's how you showed up right on my heels yesterday."

"Pretty much, yeah," Todd nods. "Only I'd been worrying, and I'd had a few drinks to calm my nerve, and one thing led to another..." He trails off, and rubs the back of his head. "Again, I'm real sorry about that."

"Like I said, I'm no stranger to violence," I assure him, finishing my tea and moving to stand. "Thank you for your time, Mr. Malcolm. I can't be sure, yet, but I don't believe that Miss Lane is in any danger. Most likely, she's following through on her plan to take a vacation to less ... problematic ... climates, and I think that everyone involved in this mess is going to be willing to let her go."

"I'm not so sure," Todd says, scratching the back of his head, "There's one more thing." He takes a deep breath. "See, in the last couple of days? Someone's been tailing me."

I sit back down on the stool. "Really?"

Todd nods glumly. "Yeah, really. Not all the time — at least, I don't think so. The guy is good, real professional, you know? Sticks tight to the shadows, or in crowds."

"Are you certain it's one person? No offense, but this neighborhood doesn't lack for shady sorts."

"Yeah, I know," Todd says. "This is different. Trust me, I've lived around here long enough to get a feel for when I'm being followed. Thought I'd caught him night before last — was heading home, and I saw movement. Just in the corner of my eye, a tall guy with a low hat. Couldn't see his face. I turned around, and he ducked into an alley. By the time I got to it, he was gone."

I sit back in my chair, which squeals in protest at being forced to handle human movement. "And were you ... ah..."

"Drunk at the time?" Todd asks sourly. "That's what Eddie thought. I'm telling you though, the guy was following me. I haven't seen him since Wednesday, but I don't know that means he's not still around. Tell you the truth, I thought you might've been him when I ran into you."

"I see..." I say slowly. "That does put a different spin on things, doesn't it? Well, I suppose I'll just have to find Vicky before this other mystery man does." I reach into my coat, handing him a business card. "My office number. If you spot him again, or if anything else comes up, I'd appreciate it if you give me a call."

"You're going to look after her, right?" Todd asks.

"I'm going to do my best. Good day, Mr. Malcolm."

Todd nods, still looking worried, as I head for the door. I can't blame him. Assuming that he wasn't just jumping at shadows, which I'm not entirely willing to discount, it looks like I might not be the only guy trying to track Mercy down. The only question is, who's hired the other guy, and what does he want with her?

I'm starting to get the feeling that this case might not be as easy as I'd hoped.

——— «◇» ———

Halfway down the street, I become aware that I'm being followed.

With Todd's story still on my mind, I decide to play this a bit more bluntly than I usually would. I can't get a clear look at my tail without letting on that I know they're behind me, but I turn a couple of corners to be on the safe side, and a half-block behind me someone in a blue coat does the same thing. I disguise my route, pick up a newspaper from a stand and then stop at a small fruit market, grab a bag of slightly overripe apples, and then calmly walk around a corner, cross my arms, and wait.

I don't have to wait long. As the person in the blue coat comes around the corner, I raise my eyebrows and meet her gaze. As it turns out, it isn't Todd's mystery man at all. "Miss Evans," I cross my arms and look her up and down.

"Why, Basil," Adelaide says with well-feigned surprise and a broad smile. "What brings you down to the market today?"

I don't smile back. "You're a better reporter than a spy, Ms. Evans. And there are easier ways to get an interview than by 'bumping into me' on the street."

Adelaide laughs ruefully. "Alright, then. All cards on the table it is. You're right, Basil, I was following you."

"Who were you hoping I would lead you to, precisely?"

"Maybe I was just trying to get a feel for your job."

"That's the sort of thing that tends to end badly. But as long as we're having this chat, we might as well have it over a slice of pie. Have you visited Jessie's? It's just down the street." I take a step away, and then glance back at her. "Your treat."

Adelaide shakes her head. "Not very chivalrous of you."

"My chivalry takes a hit when people start stalking me," I say dryly. "Count yourself lucky I'm in a curious mood, or this conversation would already be over."

"Somehow," Adelaide says with a faint smile, "I think you're always in a curious mood."

I don't have an easy answer for that, so I start to lead the way to Jessie's. As we walk, I take a sidelong glance at Adelaide, only to find her doing the same thing to me. "Enjoying the city so far?" I ask, vaguely.

"It's certainly living up to its reputation," Adelaide starts, and the pauses. "Basil," she says very quietly and carefully, "that man over there is flying."

I glance over. "He's dusted. Just ignore him."

"He's *flying*," Adelaide repeats.

"Floating, more like," I say, giving the man in question another look. He's pretty far gone, to be taking dust outside in broad daylight, but he can't be more than a foot off the ground, wobbling along with a goofy smile on his face and narrowly missing pedestrians.

"This is normal?"

"It's a drug," I say. "Dust. You must have heard of it. Fairy dust, mixed with opium and Delysid to suppress unhappy thoughts. Totally illegal, of course, but no one cares enough to do anything about it."

"I always thought fairy dust making people fly was an urban myth."

"It practically is. Children can do it, a little. Adults pretty much have to be as high as a kite to fly for more than a second or two, ironically enough. Too many buried worries otherwise. But I'm told it's quite the experience."

"You've never tried it, then?"

"I don't like drugs," I say, "and dust is a nasty and addictive one. Not worth the trouble, trust me." Adelaide has a pensive look in her eyes, and I hope I haven't given her any ideas, but she doesn't say anything.

It's not long after that that we arrive at our goal. Jessie's Fine Dining and Family-Friendly Restaurant is a fixture of the market district, a pleasant little diner that attracts a small tourist crowd and a lot of locals. I'm not sure why it's called Jessie's, since there has never, to my knowledge, been a man or woman by that name working there, but it's really none of my business. Maude's behind the counter as we walk in, a middle-aged lady who I've known for the last twenty years, since she came here as a bright-eyed young woman seeking her fortunes. These days she's a little overweight, with a few streaks of gray in her hair, but still has a broad smile for an old warhorse like me. "Well hello, Basil," she says, stepping out from behind the bar. "Who's your friend?"

"Maude, this is Adelaide Evans, with the *National Geographic*. They're doing a piece on Everland, and I thought it wouldn't be complete without a look at Jessie's," I say. Adelaide catches the subtle emphasis on her supposed occupation, but Maude just lets out a little squeal of delight.

"Oh, you old dear," Maude says, patting me on the shoulder. "Let me get you a slice of our famous Peach Cobbler, Miss Evans! On the house!"

"That's not really necessary—" Adelaide starts weakly.

Maude rolls right over her. "Oh, it's no trouble. Any friend of Basil's is a friend of mine!" She bustles her way into the kitchen, and I slide into a booth near the bar. Adelaide sits down across from me, looking slightly uncertain.

"Don't want to trade on your fake credentials?" I ask.

Adelaide frowns at me. "You know, you're really smug when you think you know things that you shouldn't."

I raise my eyebrows and smile.

Adelaide mutters something deeply uncomplimentary about me under her breath. "Why," she says quietly, "do you think I'm not with National Geographic?"

"Because there's no reason to be tailing me if you were." I try not to sound as smug as she claimed I was. "Also, because I've had a subscription for the last several years, and I've never seen your name."

"I'm new. This is my first solo assignment."

"And where's your photographer?"

"I'm hiring one here," Adelaide almost snaps.

Maude interrupts us, bringing a slice of cobbler for Adelaide and apple pie for me. "There you are, you two. And Basil, your tea will be ready in just a minute or two. Would you like something, Ms. Evans? We have a lovely soda machine."

"Just water will be fine," Adelaide says sweetly. Maude laughs.

"Is that Basil getting under your skin?" she asks. "He has that effect on women."

I turn to give Maude a wounded look. "Really, Maude?"

She chuckles and pats me on the shoulder again. "He's really just an old softie," Maude says. "Trust me, I've known him for half my life."

Adelaide nods noncommittally as Maude pours her some water and slips back into the kitchen. "This may have been a mistake," I mutter.

"Old flame?"

"No, no. I helped her out a few times when she was younger. We stayed in touch." I shrug. "It's not a very interesting story."

"Oh, I think quite a lot of your stories are interesting. Take the Piccadilly, for example. However did you go from their enemy to being an adopted member of the nation?"

I go still. "You have been talking to a lot of people, haven't you?"

"It's not often that you find yourself in the presence of history," Adelaide says. "How old are you, Basil? Eighty? A hundred?"

"I'm forty. More or less."

Adelaide snorts. "You were here when the first colonists arrived, and you were an adult then. That was thirty years ago."

"Like I said. More or less."

Adelaide smiles, shaking her head. "So it's true, then. You were really here before the colonists came."

Light dawns. "You went to Commissioner Darling."

"You suggested it."

"I make a lot of mistakes," I say. "I suppose he had nothing but harsh words about me."

"Actually, the Commissioner was surprisingly reticent on the subject of your past. He gave me some leads, but nothing that a day in the library's newspaper archives couldn't have dredged up," Adelaide admits. "He did mention you killing children."

"I never killed children," I say grimly.

Adelaide raises an eyebrow. "At the risk of seeming rude," she says, "what would you say you did?"

"I killed very young adults," I say. "Neverland robbed them of their childhoods. Darling doesn't remember as clearly as he thinks he does. He grew up away from the island, and came back. I never left." I shake my head slowly. "He always hated me, though. I suppose it makes a certain amount of sense. When he lived on the island, he considered himself to be the second-in-command of the Lost Boys. That left him in charge of their survival, since their leader certainly didn't care if they lived or died." I paused, taking a sip of tea to cover my expression. Old memories, and bad ones. "I was, as you probably know, Hook's first mate. That left me in much the same position among his pirates as Slightly was in Pan's, and for much the same reason." I give her a bitter smile. "We each lost friends to the other's men, Adelaide, too many to ever be anything but enemies. But I was already an adult when it began, whereas he grew up in the middle of it. I don't blame him for holding a fiercer grudge than I did."

"Which brings us back to the original question, Mr. Stark," Adelaide says, with a hint of a smile. "Just how old are you, really? And don't say forty."

I chuckle. "The truth is, it depends."

Adelaide furrows her brow. "How can it depend?" she asks. "When were you born?"

"Oh, well, if you go by that clock ... I don't remember," I admit. "Some time in the 1860s, I think. I spent too long in Neverland; my life before that is a bit of a blur. But it hardly matters. I'm somewhere in the order of ninety years old by that reckoning."

"You look good for your age," Adelaide says with a smile, taking a bit of cobbler.

I grin. "Well, by any metric that counts, I'm not. If you count a man by the time that he lived ... well, in that case I'm probably about fifty. Years in Neverland flow into each other, and my time as a pirate is one long event in which I didn't grow, change, or develop as a person. My time with the Piccadilly involved some growth and change, mind you, but not as much as it should have for the time that passed. And then the Darlings came back, and everything changed." I pause thoughtfully, and add, "Physically, though, my doctor tells me I'm about right for forty, and that's the age on my citizenship papers. As though all the time in Neverland before it changed was just a bad dream."

"Was it?" Adelaide asks softly.

"Bad enough," I admit. "But that's in the past. How's the cobbler?"

"Good."

"Good enough for me to find out who you're really working for?"

"Not that good. Why don't you impress me with some old-fashioned deductive reasoning?"

I chuckle. "Alright. You've got a talent for interviews, and an eye for details, but you're a terrible shadow and if you have any combat training, it's not enough to be instinctual. So you're not a cop. You talked a good talk at dinner, and you seem to know a bit about the press, so I'm guessing that you're a reporter, and you've got a story that you think is pretty juicy. You don't trust me enough to tell me what it is, so it involves the local criminal scene — you aren't sure who I'll discuss it with. And you're not new to the game, but you're new enough to be making rookie mistakes, so this isn't your usual beat. Which means the story has to involve something that you came across back home and followed here, and I don't recall any sensational disappearances recently, so it's probably either a smuggling story or something involving the local Mob. And you were following me, so you think I'm involved somehow." I sit back, and take a bite of my cobbler. "How'd I do?"

Adelaide's smile has fled. "That obvious, am I?"

"I do have keen deductive reasoning."

She bites her lip, pushing her food around her plate with her fork. "Remind me never to play poker with you. If you figured that much out that quickly, other people are going to clue in sooner than I'd like."

"Seems likely. So, which is it? Smuggling, or the Mob?"

"Maybe both." Adelaide leans in, lowering her voice. "You're right. I'm a reporter, with the New York Times. We were given information about a smuggling ring operating out of Everland, and I'm here investigating."

"Just the one?"

"What?"

"Adelaide, there are more smuggling rings operating out of the port authority than there are legitimate traders. I'd venture half the ships have some kind of illicit cargo on them. Fairy dust, starmetal, iron oak trunks, gemstones, even the occasional beast or live fairy, although those get cracked down on pretty hard." I shrug. "No one's going to be too worried about a newspaper 'exposing' that. It's the worst-kept secret in the city. I swear half the port authority are on some criminal's payroll."

"This one's different. It's on a whole other level."

"I don't suppose you'd be willing to share your evidence with me."

Adelaide smiles and stands, patting me on the shoulder. "Sorry, Basil. Maybe next time. Sorry for following you — I don't think you're a part of this." She reaches into her purse, dropping some cash on the table. "But I have this funny feeling that I'll see you around."

Maude stops by the table as Adelaide walks out. "She's a feisty one, Basil," she says. "Be good for you, I think."

"There's nothing going on there, Maude," I say politely, grabbing my hat.

"Oh, I wouldn't be so sure," Maude says with a twinkle in her eye.

Everywhere I go, someone is trying to set me up.

———— «» ————

When I step into my office, I'm immediately attacked.

I drop my cane, duck under the sparkle-trailing assault, spin around, and raise my right hand in time for Glimmer to slam into it instead of my face. "Good to see you too," I say with a chuckle, as she reels backwards, spouting profanities. "Mint?" I pull it out of my coat as I speak, waving it in front of me.

For a moment, Glimmer tries to remain annoyed, and then she gives up and takes the treat. She retreats to one corner of the office, alternately smiling and scowling at me, and I glance over at Holly, working at her desk.

"This is a funny definition of checking in on her."

Holly shrugs, not even looking up from the paperwork she's finishing. "She seemed lonely," she says. "Was chattering a lot. I'm not actually ... good ... at speaking fairy, but I gather she's a little nervous right now."

"Too much change," I agree, walking over to Holly's desk and sitting down across from her. "She'll calm down in a day or two."

"Well, until she does, I'm happy to have her keep me company while you're out all day," Holly says. "Also, I think she's building a nest in the coat closet."

"She's what?" I rub my forehead. "There was a perfectly good nest by the window."

"Perfectly good is a matter of opinion. You're crap at construction. Oh, and before you take your coat off, you got two calls."

I pause with my coat half-buttoned. "Who wants to see me now?"

Holly blinks. "Long day, huh?"

"Rather, yes," I say. "In order?"

"Frank Yancy stopped by the office a few minutes after I arrived."

"For what possible reason?"

"Something about a breakthrough that he said would prove a point? He didn't want to give me details, and then he spotted Glimmer and went over to bother her, and then she attacked him. She's still pretty angry about it."

I walk over to Glimmer and pat her lightly on the head. "I'm sorry, Glimmer. People can be rude."

Glimmer blows a raspberry.

"He did leave a hotel address," Holly says.

"Toss it in the trash."

"I just thought I should mention it, given that he seemed to be waiting for something."

"With any luck, he'll wait until the sun goes out. Who else called? The Publisher's Clearinghouse Sweepstakes?"

"Our client, about twenty minutes ago. He wants you to stop in and give him a progress report." Holly gives me a sympathetic smile. "Would you like a cup of tea before you go?"

"If I drink any more tea," I say sourly, "I'm going to be sloshing as I walk. What the devil does he want me to tell him? I've been on the case for one day."

"You always tell me that if you haven't learned anything useful in a day, you're not going to learn anything useful at all," Holly points out.

"Useful and 'worth reporting' are two very different things. And going into his office? People are going to talk."

"So, you're not going?"

"Of course I'm going. He is the client, after all. But I will have to talk to him about boundaries. You might as well go home. I certainly plan to after this little tête-à-tête."

"Alright, then. Try not to get arrested. Once I lock up for the night, I'm not coming back to fish bail money out of the safe. What's the verdict on the case? True love, or a cruel con?"

"I'm not certain yet. It's beginning to look like she did something rather foolish, and had to leave in a hurry." I decide to throw Holly a bone. "It's possible, that she wasn't specifically duping Harding. She may even have had feelings for him." When Holly's eyes light up, I raise a finger warningly. "I don't know that yet."

"I told you so!" she laughs, ignoring me. "Just wait and see!"

I sigh, turning around, and open the door. "Before you get too excited, you should know that she was seeing another man when she started seeing Harding."

"Oh?" Holly pauses as she is turning away. "Who?"

"Client confidentiality, Holly," I say lightly, closing the door behind me before she can throw anything. We have too few mugs as it is.

——— «» ———

The Everland Port Authority is a big place, because Everland lies in the Sea of Dreams. Any ship can set sail from any port, fix the settings on a starlight rangefinder, and sail nonstop for three days and three nights, and they'll see us on the horizon. Turn around, go in any direction, and you wind up back where you started. Try to match your sailing to another ship that arrived from somewhere else, and they'll fade away before your eyes. Make a mistake with your rangefinder, and you'll never be seen again. Some sailors claim to have found other islands out there, stranger dreamlands than Neverland ever was. They're probably right, but no one's figured out exactly how to reach them yet, and probably no one ever will. It was only a fluke that opened this one up.

The really interesting thing, though, is that the effect is ship-by-ship. Come to Everland, unload a lot of cargo, load it onto a different ship, and you have the fastest sea trade route in the world. It's not without its drawbacks — tankers are too large to make the journey, ships vanish somewhat more often along the route than anywhere else on Earth, and there's the occasional threat of sea monster or pirates — but the rewards are generally considered well worth the risks. As a result, Everland's storage warehouses are filled, not with the magical geegaws that its founders dreamed of, but with whatever goods need the most rapid transit across the sea.

The result of this is that port fees are one of our city's major sources of income, and the Port Authority is one of our largest employers. A result of *that* is that the Human Resources department of the Port Authority is itself quite large, and the result of that is me spending ten minutes wandering the halls before I actually find Mr. Harding's office.

"Thank you for coming in, Mr. Stark," he tells me, shutting his office door.

I can't quite suppress a grimace as I remove my hat and sit across from him, waving off an offer of coffee. "It's very hard for me to be discreet, Mr. Harding, if you invite me directly to your office."

Harding has the good grace to blush. "I'm sorry. I couldn't find time to slip away, and I wanted to know what you'd uncovered. Besides, I'll be home all weekend, and I'd rather have workers wondering than my wife. If anyone asks, I've got a story about hiring you to look into some discrepancies that have cropped up in our cargo reports. Nothing to worry about, honestly, but it will act as an excuse, and keep the workers on their toes."

I'm not sure I like being used as a boogeyman, but I've heard worse plans. "Alright, Mr. Harding. It's your dime." I pull out my notes and run him briefly through my progress, glossing over the details of my meeting with Schaefer. "My suspicion," I conclude, "is that she is planning to leave town within the next few days. I think she's safe, but she's laying low. I may be able to find her before she leaves — I have a few possible leads — but I can't guarantee it."

Harding licks his lips uncertainly, staring down at his paperwork. After a few moments, he says, "I need to know, for certain, whether she's safe. If she leaves town, there's nothing I can do. Keep investigating over the weekend; you can come by Monday morning and tell me what you've found out."

"Exactly what I was going to suggest. At the very least, I'll be able to tell you whether she's gone."

"Thank you, Mr. Stark. You've been very patient with me."

I nod, standing up, and grab my hat from the coat rack. "It's no trouble, Mr. Harding. Have a good night."

A few minutes later, as I'm strolling down the hall, a man falls into step beside me. I give him a quick glance up and down. Fit, blonde hair, handsome. Walks like he's used to getting what he wants. "Mr. Stark," he says with a smile, holding out his hand. "Tim Sanderson, head of security."

Just the person I was hoping not to meet.

I stop, giving him my most polite smile, and shake his hand. "A pleasure to meet you, Mr. Sanderson. What can I do for you?"

"I just wanted to say that I'm a big fan of your work." Mr. Sanderson's smile is just as polite as mine, and just like mine, it doesn't reach his eyes. His hand squeezes mine tightly for just a moment too long before letting go. "When I saw you in our halls, I didn't know if I would get another chance."

"Oh, you might," I say easily. "Do you need to see my visitor's pass?"

He laughs. "No need. Reception told me you'd checked in." I start walking again, to see if he will follow, and he does. "What brings you down to the port? Looking for records?"

"Just here on business," I say. "I can't discuss all of the details, of course, but Mr. Harding ... well, if he hasn't already told you, I probably shouldn't be the one to spill the beans."

It's petty, but I can't resist. I don't like the way that Sanderson is looking at me, and my barb hits home. For a moment, his smile fades entirely, and when he speaks it's only with a shadow of his former warmth. "Of course," he says politely. "I understand the need for operational security." He looks at me searchingly, and then leans in. "If you need any help with employment records, you should talk to me. Harding is a good man, but he doesn't always see what's under his nose."

I'm beginning to suspect that Sanderson is right. "Thank you," I say politely. "I'll be sure to keep that in mind. I'm due to come back Monday — maybe I can speak with you then?"

"Of course." Sanderson's smile is back to full and just as insincere as ever. "I'll be happy to."

As I walk off, I wonder if Sanderson's going to be spending a long night burning incriminating evidence. It's an open secret that the Port Authority is rife with corruption; Harding might not have chosen the best cover story for my presence. But when nothing comes of it, he'll calm down.

A stray thought occurs to me — if Sanderson works for Schaefer, my story is going to get back to him, and if he thinks there's truth in it I could have some goons trailing me soon. Maybe I shouldn't have tweaked Sanderson's nose. Too late to worry about it now, though. Shrugging, I put my hat on and step out into the cold air. It's been a long day, and there's every chance that tomorrow is going to be longer. I desperately need some sleep.

Chapter Three

Saturday, February 7th

I wake up even more sore than I was on Friday. The bruise on my face is purpling up nicely; as I examine it in the mirror, I decide it gives me a bit of a roguish complexion. Still, I don't want to look too rough, so I apply the lightest touch of makeup to it before staggering out the door, privately hoping that I'll feel better on Sunday. I stop by Silver Donner's as early as possible, hopefully before Donny has a chance to hear that I might be coming. Of course, his store doesn't open until almost noon, so early is a relative term.

"Hey, welcome to Silver … oh, it's you."

"Nice to see you too, Donny." I nod politely, glancing around the shop.

Donny, proper name Sam Donner, is the proprietor of a pawn shop right on the edge of the harbor. If you've ever visited Everland, you've probably heard his ads on the radio — he's a bit of a local celebrity. He likes to say; "Whatever you need, you can find it at Silver Donner's," and he's not far off from the truth. Need to sell something to tide you over until payday? Donny won't gouge you, and he's always looking for repeat business. Want a diamond necklace at the last minute for an anniversary present? He'll help you out, and he's got a good eye for fashion. Need to hire a bodyguard in a hurry because you pissed off the wrong folks, or fence some art that got a little too hot? He'll help you out there too.

Most importantly, he's the only guy in town I know of who smuggles folks off the island without going through

Schaefer directly. He's tangentially a part of Schaefer's criminal empire, pays his percentage and makes sure that it's lucrative enough for Schaefer to have a vested interest in keeping him in business, but it's mostly a formality. Most of the time, Donny's on his own, and that's the way he seems to like it.

He doesn't look thrilled to see me, but he never is. "What do you want, Basil?" he mutters as I glance around. "Looking for a new coat? Maybe one from this decade?"

That was uncalled for. "What's wrong with my coat?"

"Nothing, if you was a hundred. That style went out with the War. You want something more sleek, less … square."

I take a moment to look over a rack of guitars, wondering if Holly still plays. "Nothing wrong with a big coat in the winter, Donny."

"Yeah, sure. So, if you're not finally fixing your wardrobe, why are you here?"

"It's about the girl you're smuggling out of town."

Donny hesitates, reaching down to the counter for his book. "Don't know what you mean."

I cross to the front, tapping the display case. "Let me refresh your memory. She sold you that necklace, there, to help with her passage. The silver one, with the ruby."

Donny makes a face and sits down heavily. "I knew I shoulda left it in the back," he mutters. "Yeah, okay, maybe I saw a girl. Doesn't mean I'm doing nothing illegal."

I give him a slow look. "Donny, this is me you're talking to. Since when do I care if you're doing something illegal?"

"Since you started hanging out with a broad who's been asking around about criminal operations around here. Some of us are starting to wonder, you know?"

Adelaide's certainly been making waves. "It's not related. Look, I'm trying to track down one girl. Just the one. I don't care if you've got a hundred guys lined up to head back to the Real."

"I wish," Donny snorts. He looks me over. "You always play straight with me, Basil. Okay. If you say you're not working with the reporter, I believe you."

"Thank you," I say, pulling up a stool. "Mind if I sit?"

"Go ahead."

I take a seat, and Donny offers me a cigarette, which I wave off. "So, what's up with this girl?" he asks me. "Crosses my mind you might be the guy she's trying to hide from."

"She's hiding from someone?" I ask, sliding a bill out of my pocket and placing on the counter. It vanishes so quick you'd think it was magic.

"Hell yeah. Seriously freaked out. Nice-looking kid, and she can play it cool as they come, but she was jumpy underneath. She wanted a trip out, soon as possible, no questions. Didn't specifically pay me not to talk, but kinda suggested that I shouldn't tell anyone." He pauses, looking a bit embarrassed. "It weren't you, I wouldn't have. But I figure you're not like to be meaning trouble for her, unless she really deserves it."

"Not planning trouble," I allow. "But I'm not surprised she's hiding." I decide not to mention that she's hiding from Schaefer. That's a story that doesn't have to get around, and I'd rather not test Donny's virtue. "So, she paid in cash and jewelry?"

"Yeah, even mix. I got her a berth heading out Monday morning, dummied up some ID for her saying she's a tourist heading home. Pretty simple stuff, really." He leans in. "So, what's the deal?"

"Someone's worried about her. Any idea where she's staying? I'd like a word with her if I can."

He shakes his head. "Nah, she didn't say ... actually, wait. Maybe. I told her she'd have to make her own way to the berth, and that cabs don't go out there that early, and she said she could manage it. But she didn't come by car. So she's probably in one of the flats down in the Green. Either that, or she's planning on a hell of a long walk Monday morning." He shrugs. "Could go either way, I guess."

"It's a place to start." I stand up. "Thanks for the help, Donny." I smile slightly. "If I run into Adelaide, I won't mention your name."

Donny scowls at me, muttering, "Great, you're on a first-name basis with her already. This is gonna end in a disaster, just wait and see."

"It usually does," I say, walking out of the door.

———— «◇» ————

I swing by the office to make some calls. There are only a few places in the Greens that rent out rooms by the week, so I call them up, portraying myself as a prospective tenant, and make some appointments for the afternoon. I rule out the hotels; too much traffic for a woman trying to lay low. That leaves the flats, and there are only four places that seem to be within her budget while being discreet enough for her goals. I make appointments with all four, and then ask Glimmer if she wants to visit them with me. If anyone is going to be able to spot Mercy, it'll be her. She's happy to help find her friend, so I tell her we'll head out soon and leave her to get herself ready, asking Holly if she'd like to join me for lunch before Glimmer and I head out.

"Sounds good to me," she says. "I was just going to eat some leftovers from Thursday night anyway. Where are you thinking?"

"Just the cafe down by the corner. Nothing fancy, and we can bring something back for Glimmer."

"The price is right," Holly agrees, grabbing her coat. "I'll put a sign on the door."

The cafe is a nice little place; I prefer it in the summer, when the patio is open and you can watch the passersby, but in winter there's an old-fashioned fireplace and steaming mugs of cocoa, and Holly and I pass half an hour trading stories. As we're finishing our sandwiches, though, Holly glances over my shoulder and grimaces. "Trouble," she murmurs.

I raise an eyebrow, quietly shift my hands so that they're flat on the table, and half-turn.

Trouble, indeed, in the form of three well-cut suits and a nice dress, and I know the face attached the largest and burliest of the set.

Schaefer's set up his organization less like a family business and more like a revolutionary cell. He has four lieutenants at the moment, each of which has their own gang. Officially, none of them work for Schaefer, and the few times that the police have managed to take one of them down, there's been nothing to connect them further up the chain. Schaefer basically just keeps things organized, solves disputes, and takes a small cut these days.

And of all the lieutenants to visit me personally, Quentin Lark is probably the most dangerous. He's big, he's brash, and he's brutish, but he's too powerful to ignore.

"Basil, buddy," Quentin says, grabbing a chair and dragging it over to sit on the side of the table, between Holly and me. His two thugs are flanking him like a mismatched couple of statues, and there's a quiet black woman in the back, her dress topped by a fur coat and her eyes glinting gray. Idling outside is a long black car — I wonder if it pulls double duty as a sedan and a hearse. "How are things?" He adjusts his suit as he sits down. It's not a flattering fit, but they rarely are. Quentin wouldn't know fashion if it bit him on the nose.

"Doing well, Quentin. Who're your friends?" I ask.

"Jason and Max." Quentin points at one man, then the other. "New blood, you know? Always looking for talent." He gestures vaguely behind him. "And my colleague is Stephanie Tate. She was interested in meeting you, so when I saw you in the window I thought that we would stop in and introduce her."

Ms. Tate nods. "It's a pleasure to finally meet the elusive Basil Stark."

"Charmed, Ms. Tate. Please, have a seat." I glance sidelong at Quentin, who is already seated, and is leaning back, toying with his pocketwatch as he studies me. He doesn't notice that I've called out his breech of etiquette. Ms. Tate does, and the ghost of a smile touches her lips.

"Thank you, Mr. Stark," she says politely, "but I don't think we'll be staying long."

"Oh?" I look back to Quentin. "Not merely a social call, then?"

"Not entirely." Quentin slips the watch back into his pocket. "We're on a schedule, so I won't take up much of your time. What's the business with you asking questions around the docks?"

"The business, Mr. Lark, is none of yours," I say calmly, pausing to take a last bite of my sandwich. Across the table,

Holly tries not to laugh. The big guys look confused, and Quentin looks annoyed, so I continue. "It's a private matter."

"That reporter chick hire you to look for someone?"

I have a smooth rejoinder lined up, but Quentin's non sequitur catches me off guard. Instead of a smooth denial, I end up with, "What? Adelaide? What does she have to do with my case?"

"You tell me," Quentin says, leaning forwards. "A reporter shows up in town, doing an 'interest piece' on the city that involves a little too much snooping around in places she should keep out of, she has dinner with you, and suddenly you're crawling around the docklands, claiming to be on the lookout for some girl. Even stop in and bother the boss himself. Seems a little suspicious, wouldn't you say? Maybe a little like someone's getting involved where they shouldn't?"

"Someone certainly is," I say. "You."

Quentin's jaw clenches, but I'm not done. "Quentin, I do not work for Douglas Schaefer. Neither do I work against him. I realize that the existence of that option confuses and infuriates you, but here it is, and here we are. Now, if you aren't going to order, please leave. The owner is giving us looks."

Quentin shoves the table back an inch as he stands. "Word of advice, Basil," he says, trying to sound unfazed and almost succeeding, "stay away from the dame."

"Which one? You've presented me with a dizzying array of options."

"Take your pick," Quentin snarls, turning away from the table. "Come on, boys, we're outta here."

As Quentin storms out the door, Jason and Max hot on his heels, Ms. Tate hangs back, turning back to face me. "You certainly got under his skin."

"I have a talent," I say, leaning back in my chair. "So, Ms. Tate. Is this the part of the plan where Quentin threatens me, leaves, and then you linger to butter me up?"

"No, Mr. Stark," Stephanie says with a smile. "This is the part of the plan where Quentin threatens you, leaves, and then I linger to threaten you."

"Ah. Refreshingly direct. Alright, Ms. Tate, I'm listening."

Stephanie leans forwards, her smile vanishing as she meets my eyes. "We are both in the business of secrets, Mr. Stark. The only difference is that I bury them, and you dig them up afterwards, like a dog searching for a bone." Over by the car, one of Quentin's goons — Jason, I think — is giving us a steely look, and Stephanie waves vaguely at him to wait without taking her eyes off of me. "The problem with that is that if you dig the wrong thing up, I have to put it back in the ground. And when I have to do that, I'm not very particular about what else gets put in the ground along with it. You understand, I'm sure."

"We all want to avoid unnecessary ... work," I say, glancing out of the corner of my eye. The goon is gesturing insistently at us. Stephanie ignores him.

"Exactly. If I were you, I would give up this little investigation. But I've only known you for two minutes and I already know you aren't going to do that, so at least walk very, very carefully around it."

"Ms. Tate, I always walk carefully around anything that involves Douglas Schaefer, however tangentially."

"Of course you do," she says with the hint of a smile. "You're a smart man. It was a pleasure meeting you, Mr. Stark. You're everything Douglas said you would be. Have a lovely day."

"And you, Ms. Tate. Until next time."

I stand and nod to Stephanie, who turns and leaves the cafe. The thug standing by the car looks like he's about to have a coronary, but he just opens the back door for her, closes it behind her, and circles around to the front. I watch the car drive off, frowning thoughtfully.

"Wow," Holly says from across the table. "I feel totally unappreciated."

I laugh. "You would have preferred them to be threatening you too?"

"Acknowledgement that I was here would have been kind of nice," she says, shaking her head. "I realize that you get people looming over you all the time, but they were just rude."

"That's Quentin for you," I say absently, tapping my fork against the table. "He only talks to people who he thinks are important, and his judgment is atrocious."

"So what's bothering you?" Holly asks, glancing at my tapping fork.

"Mostly, that entire exchange. It didn't make any sense." I lower my voice a little, just in case. "There's no way that Schaefer sent them. So what are they up to?" I drain my cocoa. "I need to look into whatever Adelaide is digging up."

"Oh, she's Adelaide now?" Holly says with a grin.

"What?"

"Not Ms. Evans."

I groan. "Holly…"

"No, no, not saying anything else. Just thought it was an interesting observation." Holly's grin is wide as she stands up. "I'll let you pay. I'm heading back to the office in case another case falls into our laps. Have fun pissing off mobsters."

"I always do." I wait for Holly to leave, settle up, and head out myself, my mind still on the case. Obviously, Adelaide's story wasn't as absurd as I'd originally thought, but I can't imagine why a bit of smuggling would worry Quentin Lark. He has more than enough pull to make a minor crime like that vanish. Either the story is bigger than I thought, or else Adelaide has accidentally started investigating something else. Or possibly Quentin is just being a paranoid idiot, which wouldn't surprise me. Either way, I should probably find a way to give Adelaide a subtle warning about the wasps' nest she's poking at.

I'm distracted by my thoughts, and it's not until three blocks from the coffee shop that I become aware that I have a tail. He's good — just a hint of a shape walking around the corner, a glimpse of his shadow as he ducks into an alley when I look back. The streets are sparse, and no one else seems to notice as I put on a bit of speed. Inside, though, I'm fuming. It's one thing for those two to stop me at lunch with my niece and threaten me; I get threats on a weekly basis, it's just part of the job. But if they actually think that they can stick me with a tail and I'll lead them to whatever it is that they're worried about, well … that's just insulting.

I spend a couple of hours bumming around town, dropping into a few clubs and theaters that I know Mercy never visited, just in case Quentin gets smarter and starts actually following up on my business. Then, once I'm sure I'm not being followed, I collect Glimmer from the office and head down to my interviews. Our process is simple; I go in, make like I'm planning to rent, and find out whatever I can about the flats that are available. When possible, I nudge the conversation towards other tenants, but I have to be careful — most of these folks make their living on discretion, and they're not going to just admit who might have rented recently. Still, I'm able to put together a list of likely buildings, and start checking everywhere that seems like a good bet, sending Glimmer in to act as my bloodhound while I stay inconspicuously nearby, keeping an eye peeled.

It's almost sundown by the time I narrow my search to a small row of flats eight blocks from the harbor. The novelty of this game is starting to wear thin with Glimmer, and she gives me a sour look, promising that this is the absolute last time she'll do something like this. It's the third time that she's said it, so she's probably getting pretty serious. I sit back on a nearby park bench, pull out my newspaper, and start working on a plan in case she's serious this time.

Fortunately, I don't have to worry. It's only a few minutes until Glimmer returns, and this time there's someone with her; a woman, heavily bundled up against the cold, her hat pulled down low and her hands in her pockets. She sits down next to me without fanfare, and I nod absently.

"Miss Lane. A pleasure to finally meet you. Or should I call you Mercy?"

She gives a little start, and then gives Glimmer an accusing look. The fairy blushes fiercely and moves to hide behind my hat. "You can call me whatever you like. Mercy will do as well as anything. So, you're the great Basil Stark, then."

"My reputation precedes me."

"If you hang out in the right circles, it does." Mercy looks me over and gives me a hopeful smile. "Another two days and I would have been right out of it. Is there any chance I could persuade you not to tell Douglas where I am?"

I smile back and gesture to her coat. "You can take your finger off your pistol, Mercy. I'm not here to drag you back to anyone, and I'd appreciate it if this conversation didn't turn violent."

There is a very long pause, and then Mercy carefully pulls her hands out of her pockets. One is holding a small, very wicked-looking gray derringer, which she is now not quite pointing at me. "A girl can't be too careful," she says calmly.

I weigh the pros and cons of trying to grab it from her before she panics and shoots me. "Todd Malcolm is worried about you."

Mercy hesitates, and then chuckles bitterly. "Todd's a peach, but he doesn't know when to leave it alone. You're not telling me that he sent you after me?"

I decide against answering directly for the moment. Mercy's clearly spooked, and I'm not sure how she'll react if she finds out it was one of her ex-lovers who sent me. "He gets worried easily, I suppose. Seems to think that Mr. Schaefer is upset with you."

"If that were true, would you tell him where to find me?" she asks, turning slightly to give me a speculative look.

"Schaefer, or Todd?"

"Either of them."

I smile faintly. "I don't break my commissions, but I don't see the need to create a fuss. I'm supposed to go in Monday morning and tell my client whether you're alright. I don't see that I have to do more than that."

Mercy studies me, and then nods slowly. "You promise?"

"My word is my bond. Besides," I add wryly, "I get shot at enough as it is."

"That, I believe," Mercy says. "Glimmer likes you," she adds, tucking the gun back into her pocket, "so you can't be all bad. Tell Todd I'm sorry I didn't tell him more, but he's better off this way. He'll understand, I hope." She stands up, and holds out her hand, Glimmer drops down on it and hugs her index finger. "Take care of yourself, Bug. I think I'm going to miss you the most."

Glimmer sniffs, and gives her a second hug, then flits back to my hat. I nod, standing up. "If you don't mind my asking, why leave Todd out in the cold?"

"Like I said, he's a little slow on the uptake. I figured it was safer for both of us if he didn't know too much." She looks out across the park, watching the shadows cast by the trees. "I should have known he'd do something stupid, though. At least he stopped at this. Hope you aren't bleeding him for too much."

I chuckle. "I wouldn't dream of it. Take care of yourself, Miss Lane."

Mercy considers me for a moment. "It's Nelson, actually."

"Hm. I think I prefer Lane."

This surprises the first honest giggle out of her. "Took my whole time here for someone to see it my way," she says, standing up. "Goodbye, Mr. Stark. I don't think we're going to meet again."

"It seems unlikely."

I keep an ear peeled for the sound of a gun sliding out of a pocket, as I walk away, but I don't really think that she'll shoot, and she lives up to my beliefs. Once we're about a block away, I turn back to look, in time to see her slipping through the front door of one of the flats, and then I keep walking. There's a lightness in my steps that I haven't felt since this case began. In the end, despite everything odd that happened, it really was that simple. I can go in Monday morning and tell Harding that he just missed her but she's fine, collect my pay and call it a week.

It belatedly occurs to me that I forgot to ask her whether she was in love with Harding. Probably for the best; if the answer wasn't 'yes,' she'd have been liable to go for her gun again. Holly will just have to live with not knowing.

Chapter Four

Sunday, February 8th

Since Harding doesn't want a report until Monday I have the day off, but the entire business with Quentin is still bothering me. Calling Adelaide to tell her that some criminals don't like her investigation seems pointless without more information — I can't imagine that she expects local criminals will be lining up to give her a parade, after all. So I figure that if I'm going to bring her bad news, I might as well bring her some good to go along with it. Besides, it's a lovely morning. Crisp, clear air, not a hint of frost, just cold enough that I can justify bundling up in my coat and hat as I stroll down towards the docks, cane in hand. Glimmer comes along, darting through the air above me with glee and occasionally dipping down to make snide comments about this or that passerby.

My first stop is an old friend who owes me a favor. In fact, now that I think about it, I figure she owes me two, and I have a pretty good idea about where she'll be. I slip over to the docks, where today's passengers from Europe should be coming in. The *Everland Dream* is one of only a few passenger ships serving the city; we have a lot of transport, but not many tourists. I slip into the crowd, sending Glimmer up into the air to avoid blowing my cover, and pace the richest, dumbest looking single men stepping off the boat, all starry-eyed, with carefully pressed suits and the latest fashions in hat and tie. They don't even notice me strolling among them, they're so focused in their own worlds.

As we leave the harbor and the men start flagging down taxis, a gnarled old Piccadilly woman comes tottering in our direction. She has a knitted wool shawl hanging just above her eyes, and leans heavily on a staff that is studded with beads and small brass bells. One hand reaches out, and her staff taps on the ground. "Young man, wait," she warbles to a man who has paused to look at her curiously. "I sense a kindred spirit, yes? You are a newcomer to the Isle of Spring, but you remember it in your dreams, yes?"

"Isle of Spring?" the man asks, as I edge closer through the crowd.

"An ancient Piccadilly name for this blessed place," she says. "Some precious few have visited it once before, yes? They are always called back to the land of their dreams." The man is listening, rapt, and the woman tilts her head slightly to look at him better, which is the moment that she spots me approaching.

"Damn it!" The last two words are neither high nor warbled, and the old, tottering woman is abruptly neither bent over nor unsteady as she moves from standing still to a dead sprint, leaving her stick to clatter on the ground in front of her bewildered mark. I curse under my breath and race after her. Glimmer comes swooping down towards me. "Keep an eye on her!" I shout, pointing to the fleeing 'wise woman'. Glimmer gives me a very imprecise salute, and lifts back into the air.

Having Glimmer in the game is a huge boon. When I reach a gap between two alleys, she points me to the loose board in the fence that the woman shimmied through, and I'm able to loop around Sutter Street to cut her off as she tries to dart out of the alley. When she doubles back and takes a left into the warren of alleyways behind the Marooners' bar district, Glimmer flies above and occasionally lets her light flicker brighter, and I track it from a distance. Because of that, I'm leaning against the wall next to the alley she attempts to stroll casually out of, her wise woman getup replaced by a low cap and a man's jacket, and I reach out with my cane and block her path as she tries to slip past. "Hello, Amaryllis."

"Oh!" Amaryllis Bloom gives me a very wide, very insincere smile. "Basil! I didn't see you there."

"Or at the docks fifteen minutes ago, I assume?"

"That was you? I just saw someone moving kind of ... uh ... forcefully? Yeah. Forcefully towards me. Thought it was a dock worker. You know how they get about people trying to make a living in their turf."

"Con artists trying to make a living, you mean."

Amaryllis wobbles her hand. "I'm in the business of dreams, Basil."

"You're in the business of being a disappointment to your parents." Amaryllis is another member of my adopted extended family, but to her parents' chagrin, she's even wilder than Holly. I let her go, and she takes a half-step away from me, rubbing her shoulder, but doesn't run. "Are you the one selling fake treasure maps this time?"

"What? Basil, I'm shocked. How could you even — alright, yes, but it's a great system." Amaryllis reaches into her robes and pulls out another fake map scrap, identical to the one Mr. Yancy tried to show me a few days earlier. "I've got a whole game set up this time. I'm in business with Rurrra — did you ever meet her?"

"We're acquainted," I say dryly.

"Oh, right, she tried to eat you that one time. I'm sure she's sorry. Anyway, I scatter a few of these scraps around, set things up so that the mark thinks they're real, and then we get him coming and going!" Amaryllis, in her excitement, seems to have forgotten that I disapprove. "First he pays me for the first map piece, and then he bribes a guard I know for access to the second one — I get free drinks out of that — and then he buys supplies, hopefully from a shop the guard recommends, and we get a small payout from that, and he goes into the woods, and Rurrra pretends to want to eat him—"

"And what happens when he reaches the end of this little trail?"

"Oh, it's a dank, deserted cave, and there's signs of old digging, and a couple of old doubloons I bought from an antique shop. Someone else already found the treasure! Or at least, that's what it looks like. All that's assuming they get past Rurrra, of course. They usually panic and throw all their supplies down and run away around then. The last guy did, just today."

"And what happens when your tiger friend gets shot?"

"She'll be fine. She knows the risks, anyway. And we're splitting the funds fifty-fifty."

"This seems like an amazing amount of work for relatively little gain."

"It's not about the money, Basil," Amaryllis says primly. "You know that. It's about these idiots who come to Spring and think they own the place just because they have fancy suits and ties. It's not their home."

"One of your marks showed up at my office."

"...Oh."

"Find a new con, or I'm telling your parents about this one."

Amaryllis glowers at me. "You don't play fair, Basil." I just waggle my eyebrows at her, while she weighs the relative cost of changing cons and dealing with a two-hour lecture about Piccadilly responsibilities from the Blooms. "Fine. I'll let Rurrra know we're moving on. Did you track me down just for that?"

"Actually, no. I'm following up on a case, and I thought you might be interested in making some real money. Almost legal, even."

"Boring. What's the pay?"

"It pays in 'you still owe me from the business three months ago,' plus reasonable expenses."

Amaryllis extravagantly yawns.

"It involves spying on the port authority."

"I'm in. What do you need?"

I can't help but laugh. "I rather thought that would prick your interest."

"Yeah, yeah, you've known me literally my whole life, don't get all smug about having an idea of how I tick. I repeat, what do you need?"

"I'm hearing rumors about a new smuggling operation. Something involving the authority, and possibly using Quentin Lark's men."

"Is this about that reporter lady?"

"You've seen her?"

"Not personally, but I heard some things around the bar. She's quieted down a bit lately, but a couple days ago she was all over the place. Even stopped by Plum and Panther's for dinner. Lark put the word out not to chat with her."

"What a breach of hospitality."

"I know. I almost went to introduce myself right off when I heard, but then I thought, who cares what a couple of yonega are up to. So, is this about her?"

"Might be. She's looking into something that could get dangerous." The wind picks up, ruffling our coats as we face each other. "Quentin's putting a lot of energy into this."

"Alright, could be fun. I'll look into shady operations around the docks, see if anything's gotten shaken up by Miss Reporter sticking her nose in everywhere. What do you have so far on this thing?"

"I've shared it with you."

Amaryllis stares at me for a moment. "Basil, you realize I'm not *actually* magical, right? That's just an act for the tourists."

"But you do have a lot of friends among the dockworkers, not to mention street dealers. I'm going to work on this from the mob angle, be a big, annoying presence for Quentin to threaten and bluster at. I figure it'll give you a chance to stand on the sidelines and watch for the fallout. See what ships change their plans at the last minute, what products are suddenly scarce on the street."

"Well, it's a plan, I guess. And I do like the part where I'm not the one getting shot at. But you do realize this means I'll have to be careful about how to approach you."

"I know. You'd better give it a few days. If you need me, you can always have your brother slip a message to Holly. They're still friends, aren't they?"

"Inexplicably. Holly's too cool for Fox, and he knows it." Amaryllis nods. "Okay. I'll ask around, see if I can't find something out. But for something this tricky, I'm still charging half my usual rates, plus that marker you called in."

"That seems fair." It's the best I'm going to get.

"How dangerous is this smuggling ring, anyway?"

"Dangerous enough for Quentin to risk threatening me over it, but not so dangerous that he's willing to shoot a foreign reporter dead for looking into it."

"That sounds pretty dangerous." Amaryllis grins. "Why didn't you open with this, instead of all of that stuff about the con?"

"Because I didn't want you doing the con anymore, and I knew if I opened with this you wouldn't have listened to a word of that. I'll talk to you later, Amaryllis."

"You'd better have your checkbook ready. I'm planning to show up with all kinds of juicy intel."

I leave Amaryllis to start planning her campaign, and catch a bus heading uptown. Church should be letting out soon, and the best way to make Quentin nervous is to seem to be tailing him.

Like any good Anglican — or least any good Anglican with money to spare — Quentin Lark is a member of the congregation of St. Alban's, over in Glen River. I'm a little out of place here, not quite fashionable enough to blend in with the locals, but not quite out of place enough to be bothered by the police. Normally, if I wanted to slip around unnoticed, I would go back to the office and change into a smart suit and jacket, trade my hat for something a bit more of this decade. But blending in isn't the goal today.

I buy a danish from the local bakery, settle on a bench down the street from St. Alban's with a good view of Quentin, pull out a newspaper that I have no intention of reading, and watch as the churchgoers stream out in small knots and clusters. I expect that Quentin, never a man who understood shame, will have attached himself to a group to go to lunch for 'business' discussions, and I'm not disappointed. He leaves the church with a trio of businessmen, in the middle of an animated conversation, one of his goons keeping pace ten feet behind him. I glance down at my paper again, looking over the top as they head up the street towards a local deli, and then stand, fold it carefully, and pocket my pastry for later.

Quentin has picked a good table by the street, and is settling down with his friends. As I'm strolling towards him, he glances up at me, raising an eyebrow, and makes a tiny gesture with his head. His goon casually stands up and walks toward me.

"Mister Stark," he says, stopping me a few feet away from the café's gate. "Fancy meeting you here."

"Jason." I keep my hands in my pockets.

"It's Max, actually. Jason's the other guy."

"Pardon me."

"Apology accepted." To my surprise, Max gives me a smile. "You here to talk to the boss?"

"Would you believe I didn't even expect to see him here?"

"No."

"Not even if I said I was looking for Miss Tate?"

"You're at the wrong church. She's Methodist."

"Must be fun at the office." I look Max up and down. He's talking casually, but his eyes keep drifting to my hands, and he's tense. Does Quentin actually think that I'd start something in the middle of the street? "I'm guessing that's where your partner is."

"Don't need two of us on Mister Lark all the time."

"You never know. Trouble can come out of nowhere." He tenses at that.

Definitely on edge. I pull my danish out, just to see what will happen, and I'm rewarded by seeing Max half-draw his gun before he realizes what I've done. I take a bite, smiling. "I'm just passing by, Max. You don't need to be so nervous. You can go and tell Quentin that I was just stopping by to see about burying the hatchet."

"He's got a meeting now, but I'll tell him that," Max says. "And I gotta say, I'm glad to hear it. Wasn't too sure about tusslin' with you. You're giving up the case, then?"

"I got what I needed." Let Quentin stew on that. "Be sure to thank him for his help."

"Help?"

"He'll know what I mean." I nod to Max and turn to leave. I'm more than a little surprised to see another familiar face right behind me. "Mr. Sanderson."

"Mr. Stark." The head of port security is dressed in his Sunday best, and looks as surprised to see me as I am to see him.

"You two know each other?" Max asks, blinking.

"We've met," I tell him. "In a purely professional capacity."

Sanderson nods. "I didn't know you lived in the area."

"Only here on business, I'm afraid. You know how it is."

"I do. I have to admit, I was surprised not to see more of you around the port authority. Is this related?"

"Oh, my business at the port authority is basically wrapped up." I glance over my shoulder at Quentin's table. "I hope I'm not delaying your meeting."

"I'm early, actually." Sanderson is watching me, eyes narrowed. He looks almost as nervous as Max, which is saying something. "I hope I haven't interrupted yours."

"I was just leaving."

"Sorry to hear it."

"Another time, maybe. I'm sure I'll find other reasons to be down at the port." I tip my hat to both Sanderson and Max. "You gentlemen have a good day."

As I walk away, I consider everything. Quentin is more high-strung than I thought, if he's sending his bodyguards to keep me away, and it's clearly related to the port if he's meeting with Sanderson. Maybe Adelaide was on to something after all. On the other hand, that could mean that this is more dangerous than I'd imagined. If Quentin and Sanderson think that my case for Harding was related to whatever operation they're cooking up together — or worse, if each of them thinks I'm involved in something the other is doing — this could get messy.

On the bright side, I have definitely succeeded at distracting Quentin from Amaryllis. After this little disaster, I'm going to have his people following me day in and day out. It's time to really start making him nervous — which means spending the afternoon doing chores and shopping, but doing it just outside of my usual neighborhood. I spot people watching me while I'm having a long conversation with the owner of a local hardware store, and they follow me to the barbershop where a lot of Quentin's men get their hair cut. I deliberately lose them on the way to the market to pick up fresh vegetables, but they catch up with me while I'm talking with some buskers by the boardwalk.

By the end of the day I've fixed up my squeaking front fence gate, gotten a new haircut, picked up food for the week, made a couple of friends, bought some cocoa for the evening, and picked up a new supply of firewood, mostly while just inside various storefronts, letting Quentin's boys literally cool their heels in the freezing rain. As I head back to my house to settle in front of a warm fire, I see the car that has been following me give up and pull away instead of getting too close to Piccadilly lands. I imagine the two heavily-bundled men inside are rehearsing what to tell Quentin. It's been a good day.

Chapter Five

Monday, February 9th

The dulcet song of my phone ringing off the hook shakes me awake to a dark room. I manage to stumble out of bed and into my kitchen, grabbing it and mumbling some variation on hello.

"Where the hell is my fare, Basil?"

The harsh tone helps to clear the fog from my brain. "Donny?" I ask, looking from my kitchen clock to the moon hanging outside window. "It's not even six o'clock."

"Yeah, cry me a river. Where's the girl?"

It takes me a moment to realize who he means. "On a boat out of town by now, I would have thought."

"Like hell she is. Dame never showed. Now I've got a pissed-off captain, I'm out of pocket about fifty dollars on account of I had to give him the cash she gave me and then some to calm him down, and the only guy I talked to about the whole shebang is acting like he doesn't know a thing. Well, I'm not buying it, pal. You found her, didn't you?"

"Since when do you not take full pay up front?"

"Don't change the subject," Donny says. "Where the hell is she?"

"I don't know, Donny, try her flat."

"Like I know where that is."

I can see that I'm not getting back to sleep any time soon. "I'll look into it," I say curtly, hanging up before Donny can say anything else. To be totally honest, I'm starting to get a bad feeling, now that I've woken up enough to seriously consider the situation. I can think of several reasons that Mercy might have missed her boat, and very few of them bode well. I suppose, early or not, it's time for me to find my way across town as best I can.

The two guys from last night have been replaced by two more, but it's laughably easy to slip past them out my back gate. Sometimes, I don't even know why Quentin bothers. I keep an eye out for more tails on my way downtown, but it looks like he's putting minimal effort in right now. Maybe I burned him out yesterday. It still slows me down a little, and by the time I make my way to Mercy's flat, the sun has crept over the horizon. There are a few early risers out and about as I walk through the crumbling tenements of the Green, and a few people give me the eye as I walk past, but most just keep on with what they're doing.

I knock on the door at Mercy's, but it's only a formality. One way or the other, I don't expect an answer. Instead, I pull on my gloves and slip around the house to the alley in the back. The back-door's lock doesn't hold out long against my picks, but there's a chain on the door that takes a few tries to slip loose. In a couple of minutes I'm stepping through the door, hoping that no one spotted me and called the cops. Given the neighborhood, it seems unlikely.

A moment later, I'm worried about the cops for an entirely different reason.

Mercy is sprawled on the ground, across the living room doorway, still wearing the clothes she had on when I spoke to her. I cross over and kneel next to her, but it's obvious that she's been dead for a while — a day at least. It looks as though she had reason to be worried.

Moving mechanically, I pat Mercy down for evidence. I find three small, brown paper packages tucked into the pocket of her housecoat, but nothing else. I crack one open, frowning at the shimmering golden powder inside, and then carefully close it and return all three to her coat. Fairy dust. I'm not sure I buy it. Dust addicts are pretty easy to spot, and Mercy wasn't either floating giddily or twitching from withdrawal when we met. On the other hand, if she was only an occasional user, I suppose she might have taken a packet to calm herself before the big day and gotten a strain that was poison.

I check the living room for any signs of forced entry. It's a drab, worn room with peeling wallpaper and decades-old furniture, almost exactly what I expected from the outside, and it doesn't look like Mercy had time to put much of a stamp on it. The front door is locked and bolted, and I notice that the chain is drawn there, too. I check the bedroom, and note that her bags are lying open on her bed and that the window's open a crack — but there's a bar there too, to keep it from opening all the way. No way for a person to have gotten in.

My bad feeling is an alarm klaxon by now, but I've seen what I can. The only question is how I'm going to spin this when the cops come calling. I'm tempted to just slip out the back, but I need time to think, and I don't want Darling bringing me in two days down the road because he found a footprint or some other piece of evidence I've forgotten, so I return to the kitchen, pick up the phone, and place a call to the police.

———— «◊» ————

Commissioner Darling is a ray of sunshine in my otherwise dreary day. "Have you disturbed anything?" he growls at me, as the coroner moves into the room to take a look at Mercy's body.

"I turned her on her side when I was checking for a pulse," I say smoothly, "and my footprints are probably on the scene. Otherwise, I kept it clean." I do not, of course, mention my short investigation.

Even Darling can't fault me for that, although I can see that he'd like to. "Fine," he grumbles, waving me back. "Go give McClennan your deposition."

I step to one side as the police take a look over the room, joining the young officer sitting by the door with a notepad. "Surprised that the boss is here," I say casually. "I wouldn't think he had the time for every suspicious death."

"When you're involved," McClennan says dryly, "he makes time."

It's lovely to be wanted. I give McClennan my statement, which is generous with the truth. I go with the first story that jumps to my mind, and tell him I was investigating on my own time, trying to rustle up some leads on a story that Adelaide Evans was working on, about what life's really like for the poor of Everland. Some people I talked to suggested that Mercy might be up for an interview, but I found her dead when I arrived. It's a terrible excuse, and McClennan is rightfully less than impressed, but this is getting messier than Harding would want and the last thing I need is the police beating down his door. While I give him my story, the officers are poking around, and once I've finished explaining I listen in.

"Time of death was more than a day ago but less than two; I'll know more if we do an autopsy. Cause of death seems to be choking," the coroner is saying. I bite my lip, because that matches my big worry — Mercy died the night after I saw her the first time, which I can't tell the police now that my deposition says I've never been here before. "Dust overdose, I would guess; there are signs of it under the fingernails, and packets in her housecoat."

"There's another three hidden under the windowsill," one officer reports from the bathroom. The coroner nods in a self-satisfied way.

Darling shakes his head, walking for the door. "Bad luck for you, Stark," he says. "Worse luck for her."

When I don't answer, he stops and looks at me. For a moment, our eyes meet, and then he wheels on one foot and looks back to his officers. "Search the apartment."

"Sir?" The coroner is clearly new.

Darling jerks his thumb towards me. "Stark has that damned look on his face. He's spotted something, which means you had better spot it too."

In another situation I would chuckle, but with a girl lying dead on the floor it doesn't seem appropriate. I decide to give them a minute, while Darling crosses back to look at the girl. "Any signs of violence?"

"No," the coroner says. "She's perfectly normal. I suppose she was cooking when she fell."

Darling's brow furrows. "Cooking," he repeats.

The coroner gestures to the floor. "There's some salt scattered on the floor. She must have fallen backwards, crawled towards the phone for a moment, and then died."

Darling takes a deep breath. "Salt," he says slowly. McClennan looks up sharply, as the Commissioner glances over at me. "Check the kitchen."

"You already know what you're going to find," I say softly. Darling nods, but waits for the patrolman to come back out.

"No sign of any cooking," he says. "Everything is clean."

Darling grits his teeth. "We've got a rogue shadow."

The coroner goes pale. "What?"

I take some pity on him. "Asphyxiation is the method by which shadows kill their targets, and a circle of salt keeps them from reaching you. If you're not strong enough to pin one to the wall, it's the best course of action. Mercy must have seen it coming, started to sprinkle a circle, and been attacked before she could finish." I shake my head. "It's been a while since the last rogue shadow," I said to Darling. "What, three years?"

"Four, I think," Darling agrees. "I remember when they got loose every other month." He grits his teeth. "This is a police problem now, Stark. Your job is over — go tell this reporter that she'll need to look elsewhere for an interview. And don't spread this around. Last thing we need is a public panic."

"Yes, sir." I turn and walk away. A rogue shadow is everybody's problem, but Darling isn't going to let me take part. In any event, shadows only move around at night — during daylight hours, they prefer to hide. But I have one last arrow in my quiver. I turn back at the doorway. "Oh, Commissioner?"

Darling turns towards me with a scowl. "Yes?"

"One last thing for you to think about. There's salt scattered around the girl, but the box is back in the cupboard. So who put it there?"

By the time he's recovered from his shock, I'm out the door and walking quickly down the hall. I think I hear him shout something as I hit the stairs, but the door shuts between us and gives me a reasonable shot at claiming I didn't.

The truth is, I wouldn't have any answers for him even if I had turned around. Someone had been in that apartment after Mercy died. Probably the same someone that planted the dust on her. Which meant this wasn't only a rogue shadow. Someone was covering for it.

I don't like the way this is shaping up.

———— «◊» ————

Having shaken the police, I make my way down to the port to report in to Harding, cursing my luck. If Harding hadn't made it clear I shouldn't report before today, I'd have spoken to him on Sunday. I could have told him the girl was fine and he didn't need to worry. Now I have to tell him the truth, because he's going to see it in the paper soon enough, and I can't help but feel like this is going to impact my fee.

I pretend to spend a bit of time poking around the shipping offices, just to keep up appearances. I have the feeling that Harding is going to be twice as interested in keeping his connection to Mercy quiet. Then I let his secretary know that I've arrived, wait a few more minutes while he finishes up with some meeting that he's in, and head in to talk to him.

"Mr. Stark," Harding says, waving me to the seat across from me. "You have a report."

"I'm afraid so," I say soberly. "You may want to pour yourself a drink."

Harding looks at me for a moment. "Something's happened to her."

"I tracked her down, but … I'm sorry. Seems she passed away Saturday night."

Harding swallows, and stands abruptly. He goes over to a small cabinet by the wall, pulls out a bottle of scotch, and pours himself a stiff drink, downing it in one motion. "What happened?" he asks slowly.

I've thought about this part carefully. "Hard to say. It looks like a dust overdose, but the police are treating it as suspicious."

"The police?" Harding asks, turning to stare at me.

"I'm afraid that Miss Vickers was mixed up with some shady fellows. Gangster types. I think that's what she was worried about. She cut off ties because she didn't want you involved, and I'd recommend it stays that way." Harding is looking at me, pole-axed, and I feel a twinge of sympathy. "I've kept your name out of it, so far, but it might be that they'll run into her connection to you eventually. Might be a good idea to brush up on your alibis."

"For the weekend?" Harding asks, sinking back into his chair.

"Saturday in particular."

"Well, that won't be a problem. The wife and I spent the day at a garden party." Harding pulls out his watch, starts to check the time, and then stuffs it back in his pocket without actually looking at it.

"I'm sorry for your loss, Mr. Harding," I say, picking up my hat and standing. "I wish that I could have done more for you and Angela."

"No ... no." Harding stands to shake my hand. "I knew the poor girl was in trouble. You did everything that you could. I'll have my secretary drop off a check at your office. And Mr. Stark ... thank you for your discretion. I think that you're right. It's best if I ... don't become involved in this any further." He blinks. "If you'll excuse me, I would like to be alone."

"Of course, Mr. Harding." I nod to him, and show myself out.

To my annoyance, Tim Sanderson is standing in the front office as I step out. "Mr. Sanderson," I say politely.

"Mr. Stark," he replies with the same inflection. "Here to see Mr. Harding again. I must say, I'm surprised. I thought you said your work here was done."

"We were just concluding some formalities. I'm finished here."

"Are you?"

The secretary is looking worried. Neither Mr. Sanderson nor I is pretending to be pleasant anymore. "Yes," I say. "I am. I think it's not likely that we'll be speaking again anytime soon, Mr. Sanderson. Terribly sorry, I know that you are, as you said, a fan."

"You never know, Mr. Stark," Sanderson says coolly. "Like I said, I follow your work quite closely. I trust you can show yourself out?"

"Quite." I put on my hat before my mouth gets me in any more trouble. Obviously, our earlier encounters have left a mark. One more place that I'm not going to be welcome going forwards.

———— «⟩⟩ ————

"You're late," Holly points out when I finally stagger into the office just after noon, a cardboard takeout box in each hand. "What kept you? New case?"

"You could say that. Mercy Nelson was murdered Saturday night." I collapse into my seat, drop down the food, and rub my forehead. "I've just been by Harding's office to break the news to him."

Holly swallows. "Oh, hell, I'm sorry, Uncle Basil. Was it...?"

"Harding?" I finish. "I don't know. He seemed honestly upset, but he could have been struck by the magnitude of his crime. But then, it could have been practically anyone." I feel a strong urge for a drink, but I need my senses sharp. There's a pot of tea steeping, and I pour myself a cup. It's over-brewed and a little cold, but it's better than nothing.

Holly sighs, shaking her head. "Well, that's it, then."

I take a slow drink of the tea.

Holly looks up sharply. "Uncle Basil ... You did call the police, right?"

"Yes, I called the police."

"Well, then. That's it," Holly says. "You can't get involved in an active police investigation; Darling would nail you to a wall."

"If he finds out."

"Of course he'll find out!" Holly stares at me. "You need to let this one go."

"I don't know yet. I need to think about it."

"It wasn't your fault, Uncle Basil. You said she was trying to hide. Obviously, someone found her."

"And if that someone was Schaefer, the case will be buried."

"If that someone was Schaefer," Holly points out, "so will anyone who looks into it." She grabs her takeout container and stabs a fork into her food. "You don't think it was, do you? I mean, you said that he said..."

"People say a lot of things, Holly."

"Alright, then. You're not ready to let this go, at least walk me through it."

"Mercy was killed by a shadow the night after I met with her," I say. "That means it's either a terrible coincidence, in which case we'll know in the next day or two when a rogue shadow kills a few more people, or it was the strangest crime of opportunity I've ever seen, or someone hired a stitcher."

Holly stands abruptly. "I'll buy some salt."

"They haven't hired a stitcher to kill us," I say mildly.

"They will."

I chuckle sourly. "You are a cynical girl. Clearly, I did something right teaching you."

While Holly shrugs, I sit back to consider what I know about shadows, and it isn't pretty. Think about every dark thought you've ever had that you didn't follow through on. Moments when you wanted to hit someone. Moments when you wanted to take something. All those times, daily, when just for a fraction of a second you were just about ready to strangle some jerk. You didn't follow through. You just put the thought aside, and calmed down.

Those thoughts don't just vanish. They all pass into your shadow.

As a rule, that doesn't actually matter. Our shadows are firmly attached to our bodies, with no will of their own. But sometimes, here in Everland, they get snagged in a door that closed a little too fast, or caught on a tree branch as we rush past. And once in a blue moon, they get torn right off, and take on lives of their own.

In the bad old days, this happened fairly often, but it wasn't much of an issue. The irony of shadows is that the worse a person you are, the less dangerous your shadow becomes. If you've never held back from a cruel deed or hurtful comment, your shadow will be a playful and innocent thing. The shadows of children and psychopaths are safe. It wasn't until normal people came to Everland that the really bad ones started to appear. The first decade after the colonization was the worst, but things have tapered off over the last ten years.

The darkest rumors, though, are the stitchers. Supposedly, there are hitmen in the city who can detach their shadows at will, and who can, for a price, deliver an almost untraceable, nearly unstoppable assassination. Most people think it's just an urban legend. As for me, I've never found any proof that the stitchers are real, but I've also never investigated those stories too closely. On the one hand, they might just be lies — enforcers who've found a particularly gruesome legend to attach to themselves. On the other hand, they might be true, and if they are I don't want to mess with that sort of person. Either way, they wouldn't get a lot of work in town — this city isn't big enough to have a robust economy in hired murders. Some of the stories say they get hired out — take their shadows to Paris or New York, kill someone, and come back before they can grow weak from lack of magic. It's possible, I suppose.

The important thing is, there are only two ways to stop a shadow. They become more solid the more light you shine on them; in total darkness they're impossible to catch, but can't touch you, and in bright light they're solid enough to kill, but also solid enough to trap with iron or steel. They're most deadly in twilight and dim light, when they can suffocate you, but you can't grab them back — although even here, iron will slow them down. So light is one defense. The other one is salt. A salt circle blocks no matter what the light level. Don't know why, but it doesn't much matter.

"Maybe," I admit slowly, "a few boxes of salt around the office wouldn't hurt."

"What makes you sure it is a stitcher?" Holly asks. "I thought that you didn't believe in them."

"Someone snuck into Mercy's house and planted drugs on her after she died. Tried to make it look like an overdose. You don't do that for a rogue shadow attack unless you're covering it up, and no one covers up rogue shadows. There's no angle in it."

"I think I understand why you think it was Schaefer."

I nod. "The kind of money those guys are supposed to command, he can pay. And he didn't want people to know he'd been two-timed, so I could imagine him wanting to conceal his part in killing her too."

"But…"

"But it seems more than a little circuitous. Schaefer has plenty of ways to make a person disappear if he needs them to, and he's not usually the type to kill someone for personal vengeance. It's one of his few better features." I shake my head. "The man is brutal. If word got out, he would have something done. But he kills people to send messages, and by definition you can't send a message if you cover up the killing."

"Other options?"

"Well, Harding, obviously," I say. "Jilted lover, demonstrably wanted me to find the girl, was pretty averse to getting the police involved. But he's an HR man. As far as I know he doesn't have criminal connections, and a stitcher is above his pay grade."

"Also, why hire you to find someone he'd already found?"

"He might have hired more than one person, if he was serious." My cane is still leaning against my desk. I grab it and toy with it thoughtfully. "It doesn't quite match up, though."

"Anyone else?"

"Yes. Quentin Lark."

"The sleazebag from the cafe the other day?"

"The very same. He didn't want me looking into Mercy. I thought he was just worrying about whatever that thing with Adelaide was, but it might actually have been connected. If I'm looking into this, I have to start with him."

"*Are* you looking into this?" Holly asks.

I look over to the corner of the room. Glimmer has slipped out of her nest, and she's sitting on the edge of my side-table, watching me. "Probably," I admit. "But not without doing the research. I'm going to call Niall, see what he knows, and put this aside for today. I have another stop to make first, anyway." Niall Williams is an old friend, despite the fact that he works at Second Star Industries. As one of the few scientists on the island who actually likes me, he's a good source of information when I come across the weird cases.

Holly raises an eyebrow. "Where?"

"Miss Evans. I may have gotten her involved with all of this, and if the police haven't followed up yet, I should let her know what she's getting in for."

"And if they have?"

"Then," I say, picking up my hat as I stand, "I definitely need to apologize."

I go to open the door, and surprise Frank Yancy just as he's trying to yank it open from the other side. The edge of it catches him in the shoulder, and knocks him off-balance, and for a moment it looks like he's going to fall. "Oh, no," I mutter. "I don't have time for this, Mr. Yancy. Go away."

"You're not getting rid of me that fast, Stark!" Yancy looks faintly unwell. It takes me a moment to realize that he's trying to be threatening. "What did you do with it?"

"With what?"

"Where's my map?"

Holly has risen from the desk behind me, looking quizzically over my shoulder. I grit my teeth. "Your map."

Yancy looks over my shoulder, and points accusingly at Holly. "You had your Piccadilly steal it from me! It's the only place it could have gone! You almost had me believing it wasn't real, but I figured it out!"

"Right. That is enough." Something in my voice catches Yancy's attention, and he takes a step back as I push past him. "I do not have your fake map. I do not care about your fake map. I most certainly am not wasting my time trying to decode your — and I cannot emphasize this enough — your *fake* map. And I am definitely not using my secretary to steal anything, maps or otherwise! Now get out of my hallway, Mr. Yancy."

"Or what?"

"I haven't entirely decided yet. But I might remind you that I was a pirate once, and old habits die hard."

Yancy tries to match my glare, but he doesn't have the fire for it. He backs down the hallway. "I'll call the police, Stark! We'll see how proud you are when I come back here with the law!"

"Be. My. Guest."

I slam the door in his face, and turn to face Holly. "The nerve of some people."

"Not going out?"

"I'm giving him five minutes to stew on the front steps first."

"You think he'll actually go to the police?"

"If he does, they'll laugh him out of the station. Captain Hook's lost treasure map indeed." I frown, glancing around. "Where did Glimmer go?"

"She went and hid in her nest when you and that Yancy guy started yelling at each other."

"Poor thing. Well, after the last time, I don't blame her." I return to my desk. "Mr. Yancy is enough to put anyone off."

———— «◇» ————

Since I'm waiting anyway, I use the office phone to call up Niall. He isn't free today, which I expected, but I make an arrangement to meet with him for lunch tomorrow. With that taken care of, I slip out of the office by the side entrance, checking the street for trouble. No sign of any of the people that Quentin had following me, which is a bit of a surprise. I wouldn't have thought that he'd give up that quickly. Still, it makes my life easier, so I don't begrudge it.

I stop by the hotel Adelaide is staying at. She is unsurprisingly not in, which leaves me with a few hours to burn and no leads to burn them on. I spend the time dropping in on some of my general contacts, just to keep in practice and to muddy the waters in case someone is paying attention to who I'm talking to. I consider stopping by the Blue Moon and seeing if Schaefer is holding court, but it seems a little too much like tipping my hand if he is responsible, so I ultimately decide to hold off for the moment. I also think of looking into where Quentin was on Saturday, but I figure that should wait too. Around five, I return to the hotel, and this time I'm in luck; Adelaide is in, and when I tell the front desk I'm here I'm told to wait a few minutes and she'll be right with me.

———— «◇» ————

"Well, Basil, this is quite the unexpected pleasure," Adelaide says the promised few minutes later, stepping out of the elevator. "What brings you around here so early in the evening?"

"I may have inadvertently caused you a little trouble," I admit. "I thought that the least I could do would be to apologize in person."

Adelaide raises an eyebrow, which means she wasn't busy being questioned by the police. "Trouble?" she echoes. "Well, then, why don't you buy me a drink and tell me what you did."

"Are you sure?"

"Either I'll be amused, in which case you can join me, or I'll be angry, in which case I'll need it," she shoots over her shoulder as she walks into the hotel bar.

I can't fault her logic, so I join her. Two minutes later, she's holding a glass of white wine, and I'm swishing a whiskey sour around in one hand. It's been a while since my last drink, but I figure this week deserves just one. "So," Adelaide says, "what is this terrible transgression against my honor that you've committed?"

I don't smile back. "I claimed to be on an investigation to impress you, and in doing so inadvertently connected you to a murder."

Adelaide's smile fades, and she takes a long sip of wine. "A murder?"

"A murder."

"And why did you use my name?"

"It was the first thing that popped into my head," I admit. "I told the officers about your official expose, about the life and times of the city, and that I was looking for someone that I thought would be interested in talking to you, only to find her dead."

"And she was...?"

"A young woman by the name of Mercy Nelson." Adelaide is still giving me a flat stare, so I take a swig of my own drink to cover my embarrassment.

"Damn it, Basil."

"I know, it was crass of me," I say. "But I didn't want to implicate my client in a murder, and it wasn't as though she was involved in..." I trail off as Adelaide downs the entire glass of wine in a single gulp, and motions to the bartender for another.

"You're paying for this one too," she warns me.

"What did I do?" I ask slowly.

"I think you might have just connected me to a murdered source," Adelaide says.

It's my turn to finish off my drink and signal for a second one. "Do tell."

"This smuggling ring, the one I'm really working on," Adelaide says. "I assume you realized it wasn't coming out of nowhere. Last week, our office got a letter purporting to be from here, with some very suggestive hints about a major smuggling operation working out of the area. It was light on details, apparently because the source was worried about her mail being intercepted. After some discussion, the editor decided it was a viable source. We sent a letter back to the listed box, advising our source to be ready for an undercover reporter, and I came along a couple days behind it."

The timeline works for Mercy to have been the source. I take another sip of my drink. "And no one showed up?"

"Oh, someone showed up, alright," Adelaide says, eyes narrowed. "There was an anonymous letter dropped at the lobby Saturday afternoon, arranging a location to meet Sunday evening. When I arrived, I met a young woman, reeking of gin, who proceeded to spin me an utterly fanciful tale about dust smuggling and illegal poaching. She took me around to some warehouses she claimed were full of contraband."

"Which were empty?" I ask.

"Got it in one," Adelaide says.

"Well, then, I understand your frustration. I don't see how your paper getting scammed connects to my case. The woman I found was killed early Saturday morning."

Adelaide makes a very unhappy grunt. "The problem is, that girl was not my source. She didn't know any of the things my source had hinted at in the first letter, only the much more generic information we'd written in our reply." She runs a hand through her hair. "The first letter and the one dropped at the hotel when I first arrived, were written by a completely different person. I'd bet my life on it. And now you're telling me there is a completely different person, who was killed the day before my source was supposed to meet with me."

"That is unpleasantly suggestive."

"And you're also telling me that you told the police I was involved."

"Now, hold on, I didn't tell them that you were involved," I protest. "I only told them that I thought the girl might have interesting information, but didn't find her in time." Adelaide is still giving me a flat-eyed glare.

"Possibly ruining my cover story, and drawing me to the attention of people who are willing to commit murder."

"With shadows," I say unhappily.

Adelaide chokes on a sip of wine. "With what?"

"Keep your voice down!" I glance around, but no one seems that interested in our argument. "The girl was killed by a rogue shadow, and then someone tried to make it look like a drug overdose. That's the official story, by the way."

"Lovely," Adelaide says frostily. "So you brought me to the attention of a gang of *magical* murderers. Is there anything else I should know? Maybe you told the local crime lord that I was trying to overthrow him, or left the police chief a mocking note in my name?"

"Er..."

"What?" If Adelaide's tone was cool before, now it could freeze molten lava.

I breathe out slowly. "You did not hear this from me."

"My lips are sealed."

"The dead girl was connected to Douglas Schaefer."

Adelaide takes a deep breath, and finishes her second glass of wine.

"I didn't expect it to be a problem," I say miserably.

"I don't even know what to say," Adelaide says. "That is ... I thought you were supposed to be good at this."

I wince. "I would say that was uncalled-for, but given our situation — fair enough. But look — all this about blowing your cover? If you're right, your cover is already blown. They knew exactly who you were, or they wouldn't have sent another woman to lead you on a wild goose chase."

"But they did not know I hadn't bought it," Adelaide points out, a little archly.

"And they still don't," I say. "They just know that I was looking for something else." I frown, thoughtfully. "Things are starting to add up, though. A jilted lover wouldn't have access to something like a trained shadow. An international smuggling ring, though? I suppose, if they were smuggling something valuable enough, and if it is actually possible, they would have the cash, the connections, and a desire to avoid being noticed." I rub my forehead. "And the girl was spending time in a crime lord's home, and at the port. Either place, she could have stumbled onto something big and recognized it for what it was."

Adelaide nods slowly. "Any smuggling operation would have to have someone at least paid to look the other way, and — damn it, Basil, I'm not theorizing with you, I'm still angry!"

"But it still doesn't work," I mutter. "Not to belittle the situation, but there can't be that large of a human smuggling situation. It just wouldn't be worth the cost to get them here." I look up, to find Adelaide giving me a look. "I'm sorry, I was thinking out loud. Angry. Yes. You have every right to be, I cocked this one up. How can I apologize?"

Adelaide stands up. "The drinks weren't a bad start," she says. "Are you going to be investigating?"

"It's a police investigation," I say. "My hands are tied." Adelaide raises an eyebrow, and I smile. "Alright, I'm considering it. But it's going to be more than a little tricky."

"Well, you had better keep me in the loop. You've walked into my scoop, Basil, and I'm not letting you take it away from me. Get it?"

"Got it."

"Good." Adelaide smiles. "The girl gave her name as Molly, but I expect she was lying. A little shorter than me, brown hair, gray eyes, wore an old gray coat over her dress." She scribbles down the address the two met at, and hands it to me. "I figure you can start looking into it tomorrow."

"I can start looking into it tonight, but I probably won't find anything until tomorrow."

"Right. I'll be following my own leads, and I'll let you know what I turn up. And if the police talk to me, I'll back up your little story. I'm a little surprised that they haven't yet."

"They obviously don't think you have much to contribute," I say, smiling. "Darling probably assumes my story was a complete fabrication, which, in his defense, it was. You may be in the clear as far as anyone else hearing about it."

"I hope so," Adelaide says. "I can only imagine what he'll say if he finds out I lied about my job." She drops a few bills on the table for the waiter. "Good night, Basil. Not quite as nice as the last one, but no less interesting, I suppose."

"I do my best." I stand up and grab my hat, wait a few minutes for her to leave, pay the bartender, and go to check out this 'Molly'.

On my way out, I pause at the hotel lobby when I notice the doorman on duty is Jimmy Liu. He's someone I've met before, this being one of the few decent hotels in the city, and his memory for faces is exceptional. If Mercy was Adelaide's contact, she would have been here to try and catch her before leaving town, and Jimmy might remember it. "Evening, Mr. Stark," he says with a smile. "Saw you with that dame. Business or pleasure?"

"Business, I'm afraid." I reach into my pocket and pull out my cigarettes. "Smoke?"

"Don't mind if I do." Jimmy deftly slips one out of the pack and pulls out his own lighter. "You need a light?" I wave it away, and he chuckles. "What can I do for you?"

"Wondering about a couple of girls who stopped by earlier this week," I say. "First one would probably have been here Thursday or Friday." I show him my photo of Mercy, and Jimmy whistles.

"That's a nice-looking girl," he says. "Don't think anyone that fancy stopped by who wasn't staying."

"She wouldn't have been done up quite so fancy. I'd expect she was in a brown coat, maybe a hat pulled down."

"Now, that does ring a bell," Jimmy says after a moment. "I remember a girl in a brown coat Friday afternoon. Wouldn't have paid her any mind, but she was being so cagey I figured she might be a thief."

"It fits," I agree. "Was anyone with her?"

"No, she was alone."

"Did she leave anything with the front desk?"

"Not that I saw, but Mike was on duty at the desk, and you know how he is."

I do indeed. Mike has never seen a bribe he didn't like, and his only saving grace is when you buy him off, he stays bought. "I don't have a picture for the other one. She would be a bit older, brown-haired, with signs of being a habitual drunk. Probably wearing fairly ragged clothes."

"Doesn't ring any bells," Jimmy says, shaking his head. "Sorry."

"Not a problem, it was a long shot." Jimmy offers me the pack of cigarettes back, and I wave them away. "Hold onto them. Some bigshot might need one." I start to turn away, and pause. "Oh, Jimmy — has anyone else stopped by asking after Miss Evans?"

Jimmy grins. "Yeah, there was a guy. Tall, blond, real handsome-like. Asked after her at the desk on Friday, but she wasn't in. Worried about the competition?"

"In a manner of speaking. He leave a name?"

"Don't know."

"It possible that the guy wanted to take a look at a note he claimed to have left, maybe fix a few things?"

Jimmy shrugs. "It's possible, Mr. Stark. You'd have to ask Mike."

"Thanks, Jimmy. You have a good night."

"You too, Mr. Stark." Jimmy gives me a small wave and stubs out his cigarette as I head out. Tall, blonde and handsome, huh? It could be a coincidence, but I already know one man involved in this case who fits the description, and the security chief for the port authority has plenty of reasons to be messed up in this business. One more person for me to follow up on.

I don't bother heading down to either the location of the warehouses that Molly showed Adelaide; a criminal would have to be ludicrously incompetent to use one of their usual operations as part of this kind of scam. The café where they met, on the other hand, seems like a better bet. Unfortunately, it's also closed this time of night. Instead, I stop in at a few bars in the area, chat with the customers. It takes me a few before I hit paydirt.

"A payday, huh?" Jack Mulligan runs the Crooked House, one of the grimier bars that I frequent. Still, it's hard to beat the prices, and Jack doesn't water down his drinks, so it has a dedicated clientele. I'm nursing a beer that I have no intention of actually drinking, and he's making a show of wiping down a glass he has no intention of actually cleaning, so we make a good pair. "Sure. Sally Montague was in just last night, flush with cash. Drank herself to sleep, woke up this morning, staggered off. Probably still sleeping off the hangover. She in trouble?"

"I just want to ask her a couple of questions," I say. "She might have got herself mixed up in something."

"Wouldn't be the first time," Jack grunts. "She's not a bad kid, really, but she's not half as bright as she thinks she is. Want me to tell her to look for you?"

"I'd rather you didn't. I want to talk to her quietly, and for some reason when people know I'm looking for them they have a tendency to spook."

Jack snorts. "Sure thing. Tell you what, stop by again tomorrow night. If she didn't spend the whole score last night, she'll be here."

"I may just do that," I say, grabbing my hat. "And, Jack? She's probably not in any danger ... but the possibility exists."

"Got it," Jack says. "I'll keep an eye on her."

"Thank you," I drop a bill on the bar. "Keep the change." As Jack takes the bill, I head out. I'm just about at the end of what I can do tonight, and my bed is calling to me. High time I answered.

Chapter Six

Tuesday, February 10th

I'm sitting in my office, working on the morning crossword while I eat breakfast, when Holly taps twice on the door and then walks in. "There's somebody here to see you, Uncle Basil."

"It had better not be Mr. Yancy again."

"No, no. This is a big guy. Said his name was Todd Malcolm, and you knew him."

"Built like a truck, with looks to match?"

"Uncle Basil!" Holly gives me a reproachful look, which I take as a yes.

"Right," I say, taking my tea and plate. "I suppose I'll have to see what he wants." I stand, and then pause as a sudden thought occurs to me. "Did he seem angry?"

Holly considers, and then shakes her head. "Definitely upset, but not angry. Why, did you do something to him?"

"Water under the bridge," I say, heading over to the door. "I hope." I step out into our main room, before Holly can call me on my statement, and take a look for myself. Todd has squeezed himself into one of the chairs by Holly's desk, and he's cradling a cup of tea as if he's not quite sure what to do with it. He looks hungover, but that's a step up from drunk. There's a paper tucked under his arm, and his hat is sitting on her desk.

When he sees me, he quickly sets his cup down next to the hat and tries to scramble to his feet. "Mr. Stark," he says, grabbing his chair before it can fall over. "I, uh, I dunno if you remember me, but, uh…"

"Of course I remember you, Mr. Malcolm. It's only been a few days, after all."

"Aw, call me Todd," he says with a surprisingly shy smile. "Sorry to bust in on you so early in the morning."

"Don't worry about it, Todd." I pull up our other chair and sit across from him. It seems simpler than inviting him back into my own office. Holly crosses past us, sits at her desk, quietly pulls out a notepad and pretends to write things on it while obviously eavesdropping. "How can I help you this morning?"

"It's about Vicky," he says, grabbing his newspaper and spreading it out. I take a glance at the page, and then do a double-take and look more closely.

It's today's edition, and it isn't the front page. Buried on the fourth page is the unprepossessing title, "Woman Dies of Drug Overdose". There's a short blurb about a poor anonymous soul found down by the ports, and a picture of Mercy. Anyone with information about the girl is asked to call the Everland coroner's office.

"I just came from the coroner's," Todd says as I study the paper in growing confusion. "It was her. Just lying there..."

"Are you alright, Todd?" Holly asks, looking like she's about to stand.

"Yeah," Todd says after a moment. "Yeah. Not the first friend I've known who's died." He swallows, and looks up at me. "They told me it happened on Saturday."

"And you want to know if I know anything else?" I ask slowly.

Todd reaches into his coat, and I tense. It isn't until he's pulling out a large envelope that I'm sure he isn't about to jump me. "Vicky didn't do dust," he says grimly. "I know she didn't." He drops the envelope on the table. "I want to hire you, Mr. Stark. I wanna know who killed her."

I look down at the envelope. "You're sure?"

"Yeah," Todd says. He meets my eyes. "But I gotta be honest. I think it was Schaefer. I dunno if that's enough money to go up against him, but ... if anyone would do it..."

I open the envelope, take a look inside, and whistle. "That's a decent stash of dough, Todd. You haven't done anything foolish, have you?"

"Nah," Todd says. "I work a lot, and I get drinks on the house. Don't have much else to spend it on, you know?" He shakes his head. "But I don't like the idea of Angela getting a hatchet job like this. She wasn't that kind of lady, Mr. Stark."

"I believe you. But you realize that if I do learn something that leads back to Schaefer, there's not much either of us could do about it. And I'm not as sure as you are that he's responsible."

"You find the evidence, I'll figure something out," Todd says.

I'm not sure that I like his tone, but I let it pass. Reaching into the packet, I pull out a few bills and pass the rest back to him. "That should cover my expenses for a week."

Todd looks down at my bills, and at the larger wad in his hands. "It's not much money."

"You're not the only one unhappy with this situation. This stinks to high heaven, and I don't charge much for cases like that. This is just the price to keep you in the loop. Besides, I have reason to believe there might already be a police investigation going on — if there is, I'm going to have to leave it to them, and I don't want to take your money before I know for sure."

"Well, alright, then. You need anything — any kind of help — you let me know. I don't let people do my friends over like this."

"If you can keep your ears open for the name Mercy Nelson, it might be a help."

"Another name she was going by?"

"Her real one, I think."

Todd looks a bit hurt that he didn't have her real name to begin with, but nods and agrees to keep an ear open. Holly waits until he's out the door before giving me a flat look. "Uncle Basil, you're already investigating this. Why did you take his money for a job you're already on?"

"It pays the bills," I say mildly, tucking the money into my own coat. "Besides, I've seen looks like that before. Todd needs to feel as though he's doing something or he's liable to go off on his own and start poking around. The last thing I need is him charging into the middle of Schaefer's operations and bringing a world of trouble down on his own head."

Holly considers that. "Fine. You have any leads?"

I look down at the paper. "I have a few. Yesterday, Commissioner Darling was convinced this was a rogue shadow. I thought otherwise, of course, but I don't think he believed me. Notice anything missing from this story?"

"So they didn't want to worry people."

"They should want to. Rogue shadows are front page news, and rightly so. No, someone's covering up the circumstances of Mercy's death, and that may give me the in that I need." I grin, reaching for the phone. "I just need to make a quick call." Holly gives me a suspicious look as I dial. "Hello, put me through to Commissioner Darling at Everland Precinct 1, please."

"What?"

"Shh, Holly, I'm on the phone. Ah, hello, Commissioner. How are you today?"

"What the hell do you want, Stark?" Darling growls.

"I'm doing well, thank you."

"Stark..."

"Fine, I'll get to the point," I say before he can hang up on me. "I couldn't help but notice an article in the paper this morning. What happened?"

There's a pause on the other end of the line. "The death was declared not suspicious," Darling finally says. "The coroner's office put the call for more information to the papers last night, and they published an article. It's not exactly complicated."

"What about that was not suspicious?"

"The coroner couldn't prove that a shadow was responsible. Between that and the dust, he had a chat with the DA, and agreed to file the death as an accidental drug overdose."

"Which is absurd, of course."

"Pay attention, Stark. The investigation is closed. Don't bother me about it again, understand?" Before I can say anything else, Darling slams down the phone. I hang up as well, smiling broadly.

"You look like the cat that swallowed the canary," Holly observes. "Why?"

"Did you catch much of that?"

"I caught just about all of it. Commissioner Darling isn't exactly a quiet guy."

"Well, there you go." I lean back in my chair, grinning. "I'm back on the case, in an official capacity."

Holly blinks for a moment, and then nods slowly. "The investigation is closed."

"Darling practically shoved it into my lap," I agree. "Told me exactly what was up. He must really think there's something going on, if he's willing to set me on it like that." I shake my head. "It would be nice if he was less antagonistic about it, though. My life would be much easier without him dancing around the point all the time."

"You'd be bored."

"I could use the rest. This also explains why the police didn't want to speak with Adelaide." I lean back in my chair. Glimmer has slipped out of her nest, attracted by my conversation, and she watches us curiously. "I wish I'd known about this yesterday. I wasted a lot of time worrying about how to sidestep Darling's investigation, when I could have been going ahead with mine."

"It's good practice for you. So. Someone put pressure on the mayor to put pressure on Darling, and it must have been a lot because he doesn't back down easy. Who'd you think did it?"

"The obvious answer is Schaefer," I say, drumming my fingers. Across the room, Glimmer grins and copies me. "Almost no one knows there's a connection between him and the girl, and that would be how he prefers things."

"But?"

"But the point in that theory's favor is also the point against it. Almost no one knows there's a connection between Schaefer and the girl. His best bet is to leave it that way — this kind of influence has a way of backing up on you."

"So, other options?" Holly's pulled out a notepad, and I smile as she writes down something about Schaefer in shorthand.

"Other option — the mayor is trying to keep this story under wraps in the hopes that it will vanish on its own. A shadow-murder is usually bad news, and it's an election year."

"No, it isn't."

I look up. "Hm?"

"We've got more than a year until the next election, Uncle Basil."

"Oh." I pointedly ignore Glimmer's giggles. "Well, close enough. The point is, our mayor is conflict-averse, and rogue shadows don't always strike more than once. This could be just a run-of-the-mill obstruction designed to keep anyone from getting worked up about dangerous monsters on the loose. 'Girl dies of drug overdose' is a sadly common refrain. It didn't even make the front page."

Holly makes another note. "And the third option?"

"Someone highly-placed in the city's structure is involved with our possibly-fictional stitcher, and doesn't want anyone looking into *them*. It might, or might not, be directly related to the case. Just more muddied waters."

"This is a pretty muddy case already."

"You don't have to tell me. I've got more suspects that I care to, and I don't know which one to follow up on first. And I'm about to have lunch with Niall, which almost always leaves me with more questions than answers, so by this evening the list is only going to be longer."

"Sounds like you should be talking to Adelaide, then." Holly closes the notepad and smiles. "She's investigating this whole thing too, right?"

"She is," I admit. "And as it happens, I've already promised Adelaide that I would keep her in the loop."

"Well, there you go. You'd better call her, and tell her about all this. Might do some good."

"Not a bad idea," I stand and reach for my coat. "We need to meet up tonight and share what we've learned, anyway. Assuming she isn't still furious at me, which I won't rule out." Then I pause. There is something about that smile that makes me suspicious. "You do mean good for the *case*, don't you?"

"Sure, let's go with that," Holly's smile has turned into a grin. "I'll go get the hotel number and you can give her a call."

I sigh under my breath as she skips off. I really need to spot this sort of thing in advance.

———— «» ————

Normally, if I'm trying to pick Niall Williams out of a crowd, it isn't difficult. There just aren't that many fifty-year old, six-foot-three, black men walking around the streets of Everland in brown coats and red bow ties. Down at the Cathay Delight, he stands out slightly less, if only because the number of men in brown coats is much higher. Brown coats are, for reasons I've never quite grasped, considered quite fashionable at Second Star Industries, and Cathay Delight is the best Chinese restaurant in the neighborhood — or, arguably, in the city.

I don't actually have to pick Niall out of this crowd, though. He spots me coming in the door and waves me over to his table. "I ordered wonton soup for the both of us," he says by way of introduction. "Is that alright with you?"

"If it wasn't, I would have said so over the phone," I say, taking off my coat and hanging it and my hat on the hook provided next to the table, where it sits alone.

Niall chuckles. "I am a man of habits, aren't I? How's it going? Panther mentioned at poker that you'd adopted another fairy?"

"She's back at the office. I don't need another incident with someone thinking she's a stray around here."

Niall winces theatrically. "We don't do fairy experiments anymore, you know that."

"Officially."

"Officially," Niall agrees. "But I think actually, too. Too much effort, too much trouble, no results. The big thing this year is mermaids. They're much friendlier."

I raise an eyebrow. "Take care you don't get drowned."

"That's mainly an urban myth." Niall digs into his soup. "There's no documented case of someone getting attacked by mermaids who didn't attack them first."

"Stumpy Johnston," I say. "And Charlie Three-Swords."

Niall chews a wonton quietly for a moment. "I'm not sure that pirates count," he says. "Your basic relationship with the island was hostile from the start, so it wouldn't really surprise me to learn that the mermaids considered you, at heart, to be enemies."

"It's possible. But still, I would watch them if I were you. They don't show their emotions easily."

"Oh, you don't have to tell me about that," Niall says. "We've been working on the healing properties of mermaid tears, and let me tell you, our current plan involves showing them tragic movies. It's been absolute hell finding ones that will cause a proper reaction, but at least we don't have any shortage of volunteers."

I stare at him for a moment. "Showing them movies."

"I realize that it sounds a little—"

"Silly?"

"Unorthodox," Niall says a bit tersely, "but it's a matter of scientific ethics. Mermaids are sentient beings, and unlike fairies, they're as complex as humans. If we're ever going to synthesize proper palliatives out of their tears, we need ethical ways of generating samples, and working to find the right movies is a lot better than going around to funerals with a sample kit and a smile."

I chuckle. "Alright, alright." We pause to order, and he tells me a bit more about his research. As absurd as the idea of treating mermaids to *Gone With The Wind* in order to cure smallpox seems, Niall takes his studies very seriously, and he manages to make the idea seem a lot more reasonable as he goes into the particulars — or at least, the particulars that are neither confidential information nor much too scientific for me, which are luckily usually the same thing. After our food has arrived, and he's spent another ten or fifteen minutes on the subject, he finally starts to run down. "But then," he finishes up, "I doubt that you called me up to talk about my research."

"Well, that's not completely true. Although I did want to see you — it's been too long."

Niall's been with Second Star Industries for almost twenty-five years; he was one of the first scientists who signed up when they came to Everland, and he's been involved in several major breakthroughs over the years. His primary field of interest is in life-extension formulas, and he managed to convince me to submit to being poked and prodded for several years back in the early days, before he gave up on restoring youth through simply being here and moved on to more chemical approaches. He's quite close to George Ellery Hale, the Old Man himself, and would probably be a vice-president by now if it didn't take him out of the lab too much. As it is, he muddles along, studies the interesting chemicals of Everland, occasionally producing a useful result that helps make his company quite wealthy, with a sizeable percentage of the profits going back to him.

Now, he raises an eyebrow. "I'm not sure I like the sound of that," he says seriously. "You're generally patient when I blab on, and you're occasionally interested, but you do not, as a rule, come looking for my knowledge. Something to do with a case?"

"I hope not, but there's a chance. How much do you know about shadows?"

Niall shudders. "Nasty things. Probably I don't know much more than you."

"But Second Star studied them during the war, didn't they?"

Niall makes a face. "Not so loudly," he shushes. "Wartime research is heavily classified. Even I don't know most of the things that we were working on, and there are people here who'd love to try and bring you in as a spy."

"The Old Man still holding a grudge?"

"He's calmed down over the years. But it's well known that he's not your biggest fan, either. You know you're a bit of a local legend around the office." He sits back, using his chopsticks to toy with his noodles, and then nods. "Look, officially, we never did anything like that. But you can't work at Second Star without hearing rumors. There was research done. The hope was that we could create untraceable, unstoppable agents to be used as spies or assassins against the Axis powers."

"Shadows aren't nearly unstoppable."

"Unstoppable enough if you don't know what you're up against," Niall points out around a mouthful of chow mein. "The project was a dismal failure, of course, even by the somewhat lax standards of the time. One of the researchers was killed, and the whole department was mothballed. As far as I know, that was the end of it." He pauses to swallow his food. "Why?"

I toy with my spoon. "I think I may be about to go toe-to-toe with a stitcher."

Niall shakes his head. "That's impossible, Basil. There's no such thing."

"You're sure about that?"

"Absolutely." Niall pauses to take a mouthful of noodles, chewing carefully before he speaks. "Now, I will grant that, from time to time, a shadow becomes unstitched, and there are those who have managed to recover their shadows before they cause very much harm. I assume that's where the stories started. But even if I grant the ability to detach your shadow at will, it's simply impossible to control what it will do next. Every dark impulse you've ever had is buried in there, and the shadow doesn't prioritize. You can't even *predict* what it would do, let alone control it."

"What if the shadow's source had iron self-control?" I ask.

"That would just make it worse. I suppose, if you had some sort of fellow who acted on every impulse and desire he had, except for ones he specifically wanted his shadow to do for him, it could — just barely — work. If the only impulse the shadow has is to kill a specific person, that would be all it would do. But a person like that wouldn't be able to keep a low profile. He'd be arrested within days of setting up shop. Hours, probably." He shakes his head. "No, Basil, I don't know what evidence you have, but I think you're coming at this from the wrong angle. What evidence *do* you have, incidentally?"

I explain the broad strokes of my investigation, leaving out names but not details. Niall is polite enough not to interrupt, and soon he's sitting back and considering the case. "Have you considered the possibility that someone simply… lost control?" he asks. "If one of your suspects really wanted to hurt this girl, and happened to lose their shadow, it could explain why they covered it up afterwards."

I grimace. "It's possible. Everland is a land of coincidence, after all. But it doesn't sit right. The cover-up suggests something else is going on."

"And so you thought of Second Star."

"George Hale has more pull than anyone in the city. More than the mayor and Douglas Schaefer combined. If this whole thing was the result of a Second Star project gone bad, he wouldn't want his company dragged through the media circus that would come out of it."

"Well, if anyone else gets shadow-murdered, that should indicate it was deliberate," Niall cracks open a fortune cookie. "But if I were you, I'd keep my eye out for anyone walking with a limp. 'Now is the time to try something new'."

"What?"

He waves the fortune at me. "That's what my cookie says."

"Your cookie says to look for someone with a limp?"

"What? No." Niall gives me a baffled look. "Now is the time—"

"Niall," I interrupt. "Why a limp?"

"Stitches on the feet. Only way to get a shadow back on, and from what I've heard it smarts for a few days. I'd expect limping from anyone that spent Sunday forcing their shadow back on. May I have your fortune cookie?"

I pass him the unopened cookie, and he cracks it as well, already munching on his own. I flag down the waiter for our check. "Thanks for the information."

"What little there was of it," Niall says. "But I'll do some digging, look into where the project leads ended up. I suppose it's possible one of them continued the project on his own time."

"Appreciate it. And we need to do this again sometime soon, when there isn't a case to distract me."

"Or a project to distract me," Niall agrees. "Best of luck, and I'll be in touch."

—— «» ——

I'm not due to meet with Adelaide until nine, and I have a few more hours until the bars open and I can start looking for Miss Montague, so I stop by the municipal records office to do some research on the port authority, and my new friends Harding and Sanderson. I don't learn much of interest. Harding has been working in the authority for a good ten years, since moving here from New York, and is rich enough to show up from time to time in the society pages. His wife is, apparently, related to the previous mayor, and reading between the lines it looks like her money and connections helped him get his current job, after which he's helped to get a lot of her friends' relatives their own jobs around the port. It's always nice to see that the system works.

Sanderson, on the other hand, doesn't have those kinds of connections. He's only been head of security for about eight months, before which he wasn't important enough to have any records or notices. Under his watch, smuggling has seemingly dropped about ten percent, although the cynical part of my brain can't help but wonder if that's due to smugglers getting arrested, or due to palms being greased. Mr. Sanderson is also a strong supporter of the local theater community; his name pops up in a half-dozen lists of donors, all within the last two years. As I check the lists, I come across an interesting little fact. Also present, not far from Sanderson's name, is another familiar one — Quentin Lark. It could just be a coincidence; there are, after all, a lot of supporters of the arts, and Lark is the sort of guy who likes to throw his money around. Somehow, though, I'm not so sure.

I take a look over the theater company in question, the Jane Arlett. It's not one that I'm very familiar with, although they seem to be moderately well-established — enough so that they have their own playhouse, which they rent out to other companies and for private events. More than a few important people are on their donor lists, and I recognize a number of names. What makes the theater interesting, however, is their board of directors. There are five names there, and I recognize three of them — Quentin Lark, Douglas McKay, and Stephanie Tate. McKay is one of Lark's paid accountants, and I'd just met Tate with him earlier.

So, what does that make this theater? A vanity project, funded largely by Lark's friends and allies? Or some kind of a scam? Either way, Sanderson's involvement suggests a connection between himself and Schaefer, which is exactly what I'd been worried about. I note that he only appears on the two most recent donor lists, going back about four months, so it's a recent connection. Something else to look into.

I'm interrupted from further investigations by the clerk, who stops by to remind me that the office will be closing shortly. I return my files, and head on my way. I figure I can stop by the office, check in with Holly, pick up Glimmer, and head out again for my evening of investigation.

———— «» ————

"Any interesting calls?" I ask, as I step inside. For some reason, Glimmer is sitting on my desk, arms crossed and in a huff. She studiously ignores me as I enter, although she does give me a sidelong look to make sure that I know she's doing it.

"Mr. Yancy..."

"I said interesting calls."

"Well, he said something about this being your last chance."

"I'm trembling." I look between Holly and Glimmer for a moment. Holly has one of her detective novels open, and there's a stack of papers on the desk next to her. "Did I miss something?"

"Nothing major. Glimmer just tried to add a few archival files to her nest. We sorted it out." Holly beams over at Glimmer, who doesn't beam back. "Oh, that reminds me. Has Amaryllis stopped by recently?"

"That would be a pleasant surprise, but if she did, I wasn't here. Why?"

"Well, for a start, Fox called. Wanted you to stop by his house, and wouldn't say why. I assume that it's Amaryllis-related." Holly holds up a few torn scraps. "For a follow-up, the nest was lined with these little scraps of paper. It looked like Amaryllis' handwriting on them. I thought maybe you gave a note from her to Glimmer to make sure it got destroyed."

"No, not unless she slid it under the door. But you were here all day today, so I wouldn't think..." A horrible thought strikes me. "Could I see those for a moment?"

On my desk, Glimmer has moved from studiously ignoring me to feigning invisibility. Holly, looking quizzical, passes me the scraps, and I stare at them for several seconds. "Oh, damn it."

"What?"

"These aren't scraps from a note. They're scraps from a map."

"Why would you have..." The other shoe drops. "Mr. Yancy's map?"

"Likely." I look over at Glimmer, who is actually whistling innocently. "Glimmer?"

Glimmer explains to me that those pieces just fell out of the bad guy's pocket, and anyway I said they weren't valuable, and anyway he deserved it, and besides which she has no idea where they came from, and anyone could have torn them up and filled her nest with them.

I blame myself for not keeping a better eye on her. "Well, at least it's just a minor case of vandalism. No chance of convincing Mr. Yancy of that, though"

"So what are you going to do?"

"The same thing I was going to do before I knew that my fairy friend here is a little bit vindictive. Ignore him, and hope he goes away. It's not as though he lost anything of value." I narrow my eyes at Glimmer. "I'm not taking you with me tonight, though."

Glimmer makes a rude noise.

"I don't care why you did it! You can't just take things from people because they're mean to me." I walk over to the desk. "Glimmer, I need to be able to trust you in the field. No more stealing."

She makes the noise again, but more softly. It's the best I'm going to get. "I'll bring you back a pastry," I tell her. That wins a reluctant smile, although she doesn't quite turn to look at me. I've hurt her feelings by not appreciating the help, but there's nothing for it. I make too many enemies on a regular basis for a vengeful fairy to be an asset.

"Are you still meeting with Adelaide?"

"After I finish my increasingly lengthy day. I just needed to wait long enough for the bars to open. I'll swing past Fox's house on the way down. Lock up the office for me?"

"Of course. And I'll have Glimmer here to watch my back." Glimmer beams at that, forgetting to be angry with Holly, and I grin and tip my hat to them both, before heading back out.

———— «» ————

Fox lives on his own, in a small cottage on the northern edge of Piccadilly Cross. It's only a short walk over, and I arrive with the sun still hanging low on the horizon. I can see light through the closed shutters, so someone's home, at least. I knock briskly on the door, wait about twenty seconds, and knock again.

I'm about to go for another pass when the door opens, a hand grabs me by the collar, and Amaryllis yanks me through the threshold and slams the door shut behind us. "Damn you, Basil, what have you gotten me into?"

I stumble a few steps, recover my footing, and take a look around. Every window is shut tight, every lamp in the place is on, and there are salt lines across every possible entryway. I see a few seashell charms hanging from the window frames. "Do those work?"

"Mermaids claim yes. Never had a chance to test them before this. Also, don't you dare change the subject."

"I take it that you found something."

"Something found me," Amaryllis says darkly. "Tea? Bourbon? I'd join you, but I've already had a drink to take the edge off, and I want to stay focused."

"Where's Fox?"

"I called him and told him to stay at our parents' tonight. I didn't want the shadow following me back here and getting him."

"You saw it?"

"Aha! You did know that there was a shadow!" Amaryllis points at me accusingly. "And you didn't tell me! I repeat, what the hell have you gotten me into?"

"I didn't know about the shadow when I spoke to you. And I wasn't sure that it was connected until … well, to be honest I'm still not entirely sure." I take a seat on one of the three chairs in the room. "Walk me through it, Amaryllis."

"Fine, but you are going to pay handsomely for this blunder." Amaryllis sits across from me, where she has a good view of the shutters. "Sunday and Monday were pretty low-key. I asked around, got some information. It wasn't until yesterday that word filtered out, and I had to get creative."

"You were followed?"

"Yep. It was the usual suspects, at first — a couple of obvious goons trying to fake the dockworker look, an undercover cop, probably a mugger." Amaryllis shrugs. "I lost them pretty easy, kept digging. But this morning the goons were gone, and I started seeing someone who was ... I don't know how to describe it, Basil. Stealthy as hell and obvious as the sun at the same time. A shadow ducking around corners, into alleyways. Never close enough to corner, but always there."

A chill runs down my spine. "A man with a hat?" I ask.

"Oh, so you know about him too?"

"Not exactly," I say. "I saw him, a few days ago. Thought it was just a particularly stealthy tail Quentin had left on me. I shook him in a park, haven't seen him since."

"That would probably have been a good idea."

I rub my forehead. "You doubled-back, didn't you?"

"Don't lecture me on danger, shadow-boy," Amaryllis snaps. "Anyway, yes. I lured him to one of those cul-de-sacs with a loose board, slipped through it, and then vaulted back over the fence to grab him, which was about when I found out that the shadow didn't have a person casting it." She breathes out slowly. "If it had been brighter out, I might not have made it, but the alley way really shaded. The thing didn't have a good grip, and I got a few knives into it when it went for my throat. Just enough for me to take off while it pulled them free. It didn't follow me into the street."

"At which point you called the Regulators, I hope?"

"Like hell I did. I bolted right back here and locked the doors and windows, pulled out every half-baked charm I own, and told Fox to call you." Amaryllis snorts. "What were the Regulators going to do? Disbelieve it to death?"

"Catching shadows is literally one of their jobs."

"Basil, you aren't listening. This thing followed me for at least two hours! It knew not to attack me while anyone else could see!" Amaryllis waves her hands in the air. "That is not what shadows do! They decide on something, they attack, or they grab a thing, or whatever. They don't make plans, or stalk people, or consider what's going on before they strike." She shakes her head. "I think something was commanding it. I think there's a stitcher involved."

"Damn it," I mutter. "Niall was so sure that was impossible."

"You knew about that too?" Amaryllis gives me a flat stare that I'm growing increasingly used to on the faces of my acquaintances. "You really know how to mess up a lady's evening, Basil."

"I didn't know about that until today, either. Do you even believe in stitchers?"

"Maybe. Lots of old stories about people who could use medicine to control their shadows. Could be something to it, could just be fireside tales. And I'd heard the stories that there were stitchers in Everland, but I didn't buy them." Amaryllis looks over to the salt by the door. "I'm buying them now."

"Whatever you learned at the docks must have really upset someone, if they sent a shadow to kill you."

"I can't imagine what. I asked around — quietly, I thought, but obviously not quietly enough. A lot of smugglers are pretty pissed at the moment, but it's not anything that isn't basic knowledge."

"Oh?"

"Yeah. Quentin's locked down the docks. The last six months or so, there've been a lot of early retirements, a few firings for 'taking bribes,' and a handful of suspicious injuries. The guys who've replaced them don't deal directly with any of the usual crowd. But Quentin's put out the word that people who need to get stuff in or out can go through him."

"For a cut, of course."

"Got it in one. It's a nasty little power grab, and it sounds like some of the other bosses are getting pretty pissed about it. If Quentin can't hold it down, things are going to go south for him in a hurry, and no one will shed a tear."

"Unless he has stitchers on his payroll."

"Yeah, that would make things a bloodbath. But the only reason that we think that is because a shadow tried to kill me. It's not like I'd learned anything about them." Amaryllis shakes a finger at me. "And now, buddy, we're even. More than even. You owe me big time. Setting a damned shadow on me. What the hell."

"I am sorry about that." I pause. "Wait, no I'm not. I have a damned tourist threatening to sic the police on me because he thinks I stole a map that you gave him. I think that evens us up quite nicely."

"Tell you what, if he tries to kill you, let me know and I'll accept that argument. After I finish laughing. Otherwise, I am absolutely calling this favor in. You need anything else? Because too bad. I'm planning to stay out of town for a few days, go visit Rurra until things calm down. She can sniff out shadows from a mile off."

"You've done more than I expected you would need to already."

"Great. Give 'em hell. Help out whoever you're helping. And leave me out of it."

"You have my word on every count," I say. "Now if you'll excuse me, I need a drink."

"You and me both, Basil."

——— «<» ———

The Crooked House largely appeals to the dockworker and factory crowds, most of whom stop by to grab food and a few pints before going home for the night. By the time I arrive, the first of them are already on the scene, and by the time Sally Montague slips in an hour later, the place is filled to the rafters, with a few card games being played and a lot of beer being consumed. I've got another beer in front of me, and am sitting in a booth not far from the bar, where I can keep an eye on the door and the clientele at the same time.

Miss Montague is almost exactly what I expected; she has a faraway look that suggests she's dusted up, and she makes for the bar with a hop over someone's foot and a slide out of the path of a waiter that confirms it, her feet hanging in the air for just a moment too long each time. Only slightly dusted, though; if she was really high, she'd be trying to drift right through people. She slides up to the bar, and a minute later there's a gin and tonic sitting in front of her as she turns to chat up the worker drinking next to her. I give them a few minutes, long enough for her to decide he's not as exciting as she thought and, incidentally, to finish her drink, then I stand up and walk over, flagging down the bartender. "Gin for me, Charlie. Straight." While he's pouring, I look over and give Miss Montague a smile. "Ma'am."

She smiles back, a little bit incredulously. "This isn't a ma'aming sort of place."

"Their loss," I say, taking my gin from Charlie. "Sally Montague, isn't it?"

"Have we met?"

I shake my head. "Jack Mulligan at the bar mentioned you." I hold out my hand. "Basil Stark."

Sally's brow is furrowed, but she takes my hand. I make an elaborate show of kissing the air over it, and she blushes. "Nice to meet you, Basil. Funny name. Sounds familiar…"

"I have a bit of a reputation," I say politely. "You might have heard of the time I caught the Hook Street Filcher."

"No!" Sally's eyes are wide. "I read about him! He stole a hundred watches in a week and nabbed the Commissioner's wallet in the middle of his speech, and then he turned himself in one day out of the blue!"

"The one and the same." I gesture to Charlie. "Another drink for the lady, Charlie?"

Sally beams at this, leaning in with wide eyes. "I heard the Filcher was actually a hypnotist, and he could make a whole crowd zone out for a few seconds. That was why he went after watches."

I chuckle. "I've heard that story as well, but no, he was merely a very skilled thief with a talent for blending in. Although, and this is not common knowledge, he was descended from a Lost Boy, long ago, and had a knack for the ways and paths of the island that let him evade capture. When he ran down an alleyway, it didn't always end where it should…" I launch into a rambling tale, heavy on description and light on details; there are facts about that particular case that I would rather not share, but Sally is just dusted enough to be caught up in the excitement of the story, and I doubt she would notice any flaws in the structure. Or perhaps I'm not giving her enough credit, and she's the sort to get caught up in a good story with or without drugs. Either way, she barely touches her drink while I talk, and by the time I've reached my confrontation with the Filcher, the two of us alone on a sailboat ready to launch, she is totally enthralled.

"...and so, having lost our duel, the Filtcher felt obliged to follow its terms. I escorted him to the police station, where, in order to protect my identity, Commissioner Darling helpfully did not give me any of the credit."

"Wow!" she claps excitedly, drawing raised eyebrows from a few of the nearer patrons. "That's a really, really amazing story."

"Well, I'm sure you have good stories of your own."

Sally's brow wrinkles. "I dunno ... I don't usually do really exciting things. I mean, I just work as a waitress."

"Really? A talented, cunning young lady like you?" I feel a little bad, drawing her out this way. It's simply too easy. "I bet you've tricked some folks yourself from time to time."

"Well, yeah..." Sally looks a little dubious. "I mean, just for fun. Not really."

"Jack mentioned you'd met with a reporter. You must have had a good story for her."

Sally makes a face. "That was nothing. Just messing around." She takes a drink. "I don't even know what it was about. Not really a good story."

"Oh, you must have known something."

"Just some reporter, trying to make Everland look bad," Sally says vaguely. "Like everything's trouble and bad things around here." She blinks a couple of times. "Got a hundred bucks to lead her around for a day, and tell her some things. Like, drugs and things." She gives me a smile. "I don't do drugs, but I know some things. I mean, I don't usually do drugs. Just once in a while, to take the edge off."

I nod reassuringly. "Of course. Who doesn't?" Charlie the bartender, passing by, gives me a raised eyebrow, but Sally doesn't notice. "So, someone wanted to take this reporter lady down a peg?"

"Yeah. Nervy dame. I don't ... I don't know if she really bought it, but she seemed pretty annoyed. Thought she was gonna slug me when we went to that empty warehouse." She giggles. "That was pretty funny. Might have been worth getting slugged. But I'm glad I wasn't."

"Me too," I agree. "Your partner would have been pretty upset, too, I expect."

"What?" Sally blinks slowly. Two drinks on top of the dust is not doing wonders for her thoughts.

"Your partner. The guy you worked with to trick the newsie."

"Oh, that guy," Sally snorts. "He wasn't a partner. Never met him before. He just knew a guy that I'd done some work with before, on ... uh ... some things. Acting. Was looking for someone who could do a job for him, and I was around."

"Some kind of bigwig, then? Sounds like you could get more good jobs going forwards."

Sally giggles again. "Yeah, maybe I will. Sure hope so."

"Hey," I press, "what's this guy's name? Maybe I can get some work from him too. I can be pretty cunning."

"Oh, yeah," Sally says, wide-eyed. "I can see that, wow. Maybe you could. You should ask him!"

"I should," I say, surreptitiously gauging her. There's being high, and there's giving me the runaround, and Sally seems to have slipped from the former into the latter a little too smoothly to be as drunk as I thought she was. Before I can press the point, though, someone walking past catches my stool with their leg, and falls into me. Gin and beer spills everywhere.

"Watch it, bud," the guy barks.

"Hey!" Sally says, looking down at the gin now soaking her dress. "You watch it!"

"Shut your gal up, bud, or I'll do it for you," the man growls.

Sally gives me another stare, eyes even wider than before, and clutches at my arm. "You can't talk to us like that!" she shouts at the man.

I look at Sally, and back to our new friend. Quickly, I push off of my stool, leaving Sally on my arm, and smile mildly to the man. Of all the times not to bring my cane. "Now, why don't we all calm down? I'm sure Charlie doesn't want any trouble here."

In fact, Charlie has already backed away, and is talking urgently with another large man, sitting at the end of the bar. The bouncer — presumably — is looking a little slow to stand. I see the shape of things developing.

"You don't want trouble, you shouldn't push your chair back like that," the grunt opposite me says, giving me a shove. I sigh, grabbing my hat with one hand and the bar with the other, and slip it on my head as I step lightly around him.

"I didn't say that I didn't want trouble," I say, giving him a light tap on the back. At the bar, Sally is watching with an excited smile. "I said Charlie didn't, and I don't like to disappoint friends. So, why don't I buy you another beer, and we'll forget this little incident."

"Why don't I pop you one?" the guy growls.

I keep my smile. "You can try," I start.

Before I can say anything else, the bouncer makes his way over, having run out of excuses not to. "There a problem here?" he rumbles.

"Not at all, I was just leaving." Tipping my hat to Sally, I add, "It was lovely to meet you, Miss Montague, and your friend."

Sally blinks innocently. "My friend?"

I nod to the goon. "A lovely evening. Until next time, enjoy your drinks." Quickly, I step through the door, glancing around me as I step onto the street to confirm that there aren't any people around. I start down the sidewalk at a brisk pace, trying to get as much space between us and the bar as possible before the inevitable confrontation.

"Hey!" The voice comes from behind me, and I smile, turning around. The goon from the bar, beer still staining his shirt, is right behind me, his coat half-off as he charges forwards. "We aren't done talking!"

I take a few steps back, gauging his approach as he comes in for a swing. Sloppy, slow, but not as drunk as he's faking. I lean back from his first punch and step into his reach, delivering a quick jab to his chest. "Fair enough," I say, while he staggers back, coughing. "Did you have something to say?"

"You have something to … I … go to hell!" The goon tries for a bear hug, and I dance to one side, shaking my head. "I'm gonna flatten you!" He manages to grab the edge of my coat, but when I spin and drive my heel into the top of his shoe, he yelps and lets go. I take advantage and kick him in the shin, knocking him over. "You're a dead man!" he roars.

I lean over him. "Whatever you think I'm worth," I say softly, "it is not nearly enough."

The guy's jaw drops. "How — I mean, what do you…?"

"Please," I say. "This whole setup? Basically the oldest trick in the book." I put my hands in my pockets, looking him up and down. "Sally pretends to be higher than she really is, and looks for someone well-off enough to be worth mugging, and who'll try to take advantage of her. You move in once they're in a secluded spot, threaten him, take his money, and rely on his humiliation to avoid getting the cops involved. The really interesting part, though, is that you moved in as soon as Sally started getting nervous about the questions I was asking her."

The goon coughs, staring up at me. "I dunno what you're talking about," he says, one hand dipping into his pocket. A moment later, his expression turns panicked, and he starts rummaging frantically around.

"Looking for this?" I pull his switchblade out of my pocket and flick it open.

"I … uh … huh?" He looks up at me, eyes focused on the blade now less than a foot above him. "Look, buddy, maybe we got off on the wrong foot, huh?"

"Maybe we did," I agree, turning the knife over in my hands. "I assume you and Sally took some extra cash to keep quiet about who hired you. I was wondering if you might want to change your mind?"

"You threatening me?"

"Me?" I smile. "I'm just a simple investigator. Why would I need to threaten you?" I flick the knife open and closed a couple of times. "Good blade. Must have cost a pretty penny."

"Uh, yeah." The guy tries to scramble backwards, and I casually shift my stance, my foot coming down on his jacket.

"Suppose you want it back," I say.

"Uh…" The guy looks up at me, and over at the knife, and swallows. "If you don't mind, mister."

"No, no. I was planning to return it once our chat was finished, anyway. The only question was how." I pause. "I'm sorry, that came out sounding a lot like a threat. Funny how that happens." I let my foot slip off his coat, so that he can get some distance.

"Yeah. Funny." He pulls himself to his feet, wincing when he puts pressure on his bruised leg, and takes a step backwards, out of easy stabbing range. "I, uh, look, that little scrap just now, I was out of line, you know? Just let the moment get away from me, didn't mean nothing by it. No hard feelings?"

I give him a flat look. "Of course not." I tuck the knife back into my pocket, and toss him a business card, which flutters to the ground at his feet. "Tell you what. You have a change of heart, you let me know. Maybe you can get this back and some cash besides. Until then, I think I'll hang on to it. Might come in handy at some point." There's not a chance that he's actually going to call me, but I have an idea that I'd like to test out.

The goon tries to grab the card without taking his eyes off me, which results in him nearly falling over. I almost reach out to steady him, but I've still got the knife and he'll just collapse again, so I settle for watching dispassionately as he hastily snatches up the card and limps back inside the bar, keeping one eye on me the whole time.

As soon as the door closes, I pocket the knife again and hurry to the alley next to the bar, taking up a position near the far end and crouching low behind some overfilled trash cans. It takes a few minutes for my hunch to pay off, but it does — eventually, my friend steps out of the Crooked House's kitchen entrance, takes a perfunctory look around, and then starts off down the street. I let him get some distance before I follow along.

As far as tails go, I think it's one of my better ones. Things get complicated for a few minutes when he hops a streetcar heading uptown, but I manage to wave down a cab and catch up before he hops off again. I have the cabbie pull over on the corner a block away, overpay him, and continue my pursuit. We're in a quieter area of town, but it's not so late at night that I can't stay out of sight by blending in with the locals, and my goon is still treating his leg gingerly, so I can keep up without any trouble.

He takes a turn down a smaller street, made up of small bakeries, shops, and the occasional bar, and steps into a small, well-lit restaurant, past a fairly imposing doorman. The sign over the door proclaims it as "Murray's", and the décor is pretty high-class — not the sort of place I would expect a guy like this to hang out, which suggests that my hunch played out. I look the place up and down and consider my options. I can't walk in the front door without getting spotted, and this isn't the sort of place that'll just let anyone waltz in the back way, but the small brownstone next door looks like a promising approach. I pause, lifting my foot up onto the sill as I mime tying my shoe, and keep an eye on the inside of the place as my goon strolls through. He passes by the patrons and through the 'Employees Only' door, heading upstairs to the second floor, which confirms one hunch; whoever hired him is working out of the back, either officially or not. The doorman is starting to give me nasty looks by this point, so I quickly finish tying the shoe, give him a smile and a nod — neither of which are returned — and continue on my way. If I'm lucky, he won't think twice about it.

As soon as I round the corner, I make for the alley between the restaurant and its neighbor. I'm in luck; there's a fire escape on the brownstone, and a dumpster I can use to reach it. I climb up as quietly as possible, until I'm high enough to peer through the second-story window. There's a flimsy curtain in the way, of course, but I can just make out the two people arguing. One is my goon, without a doubt. The other one is a figure I'd recognize just about anywhere. Seems I've found a connection to Quentin Lark.

《》

"And just who is Quentin Lark?"

I sit back in my chair and consider how to arrange my answer. Across from me, Adelaide is toying with her linguine. The two of us have met up near her hotel to share our findings from the day over a late dinner — a bottle of wine sits untouched between us, along with my promised pastry wrapped up for Glimmer, and we've barely had time to eat. "Quentin Lark," I say thoughtfully, "is an idiot."

"Well, then," Adelaide says. "Problem solved, I suppose."

"Unfortunately, he's a very dangerous idiot."

"Of course he is," she mutters. "He couldn't just be a run-of-the-mill one."

"Essentially, Quentin Lark is one of the five most powerful criminals in the city. You've only been here a week; how much do you know about Douglas Schaefer and his operation?"

"I know the rough framework, but I could use details," Adelaide admits, pulling out a notepad. "Do you mind?"

"Go ahead, with the understanding that you probably don't want to publish most of this." Adelaide gives me a look, and I shrug. "None of this is heavily hidden, but it's also not discussed too openly. An expose on Everland's criminal underworld is going to result in Schaefer suing the hell out of your paper, and I don't have any evidence for anything I am about to tell you beyond my personal experiences."

"Alright. Consider me warned."

"It'll have to do. I'm sure you're aware by now that Douglas Schaefer controls most of the organized criminal activity in the city. Mostly, he makes his money through illegal gambling, smuggling, and drugs, with a light touch of protection rackets and graft to round things out."

"That pretty much covers what I've learned," Adelaide agrees. "He stays out of it, lets his lieutenants do the dirty work. Lark is one of them?"

"Exactly." I pause to take a few bites of chicken, and then continue. "Quentin has been with Schaefer for a while, and he's been a lieutenant for a good three years. He's not half as clever as he thinks he is, but he has an eye for talent and he's a lot like Schaefer in one way — he's more interested in the power of his position than in the money. That means he's willing to give a great percentage to his people as long as he can share in the credit, so he's got a lot of folks working for him who are more interested in cash than prestige, and who don't want to make waves. He's carved out a strong niche in town, even gotten into a few minor clashes with Schaefer's other people. I figure he's got another year or three before he over-reaches and ends up either in jail, or in the morgue.

"I'd have preferred it if we were dealing with almost anyone else, to be honest. Quentin is just smart enough to figure out we're on to him, and just dumb enough to burn his operation to ashes trying to protect it from us — and the downside of his priorities is that he's more concerned with winning than with profit margins." I shake my head.

"But you don't think we're in trouble with Schaefer himself?" Adelaide asks.

"It's possible, but I doubt it. Schaefer is in a league of his own, and this is strictly amateur hour. If he wanted you distracted, he would have put a better plan together, or just pulled some strings and kept your visa from being approved. I can, frankly, think of a half-dozen better ways to make you less suspicious than hiring an actor, and I am not a criminal mastermind."

"Well, that should make things easier." Adelaide catches my expression. "But it doesn't?"

"It does not," I say. "Because amateur-hour theatrics fit Quentin to a T, but the hit on Mercy was smooth. Someone put that together with enough layers that I'm still not sure exactly what went down, and that someone had access to an untraceable, magical murderer to do their dirty work for them." I lean back. "And a magical murderer who I've been told, by someone who should know, can't possibly exist. No, if Quentin could call down shadow hits by himself, he'd make sure everyone knew that crossing him meant being killed in your sleep, and he wouldn't care about the heat it would attract."

"I heard that shadows used to slip free by accident. Could Quentin, or one of his men, have lost control and only gotten their shadow back after the girl was killed?"

"Maybe, but someone was on the scene soon after the killing, with exactly the right props for a frame-up; if it wasn't right away, it was at least within a few hours. Whoever it was, they knew a shadow killing had taken place, and they framed the scene to draw attention away from it. If they hadn't missed the salt, we never would have figured it out. It could be it was one of Quentin's people, I guess." I shake my head. "I hope you learned more than I did."

"I learned a few things," Adelaide admits around a mouthful of pasta. "Did you hear about what happened to the last head of port security, Perry Lodge?"

"Retired, didn't he? I vaguely remember hearing about it. He was a little young, but the pensions for the port authority have always been generous."

"Basil, please. That was just the cover story. He was embezzling, and he got caught. The city didn't want a scandal on their hands, so they gave him the choice of returning the bulk of the money and then quitting immediately, or going to jail for a very long time."

"Where did you hear all of this?"

"It's amazing what you can get with a smile, a press pass, and a disgruntled employee." Adelaide smiles at me. "One of the security staff thinks that the new head of security is the one who turned his boss in, and gave me all of the information, along with a few written letters that really should have been shredded. It's not enough for a conviction, but it would be enough for a story in the paper. I even managed to finagle a look at the tax summaries for last year. Officially, there were some accounting irregularities due to changes in the way the port was recording its finances. They were sorted out, coincidentally, a few weeks after Lodge retired."

"So, an ambitious underling sold out his boss to gain power, and shortly afterward a mysterious smuggling ring starts up," I say thoughtfully. "That does seem suggestive. Did you know the port authority's chief of security stopped by your hotel and asked after you last Friday?"

Adelaide's eyes narrow. "Last Friday?" she repeats. "Isn't that interesting."

"I thought so. Had you started looking into the authority yet back then?"

"I had not," Adelaide says. "I was still poking around the port district itself." She frowns. "I've had a couple of run-ins with Mr. Sanderson since then. Kind of pompous, doesn't seem to take me very seriously. He did take an interest, though." She shakes her head. "You think he's connected to all of this?"

"I think that, if you wanted to run a major smuggling operation through the port instead of running small boats up the island, a crooked port security guard is worth five cops. A crooked head of security means you have all the guards you need. I also think that if you're a major crime lieutenant, you might just know when someone is trying to launder money they've been stealing. Quentin could have given Sanderson what he needed to overthrow Lodge."

Adelaide nods. "And it seems fairly coincidental that our dead victim is connected to both Lark and Sanderson."

"I agree," I say. "I think it's high time I looked into the circumstances behind Miss Nelson meeting and falling for Mr. Harding. It could be that either Lark or Sanderson encouraged her to do so, either as a distraction or as a spy."

"Then why would she leave?"

"She recognized the danger of the situation, or she started to feel guilty and wanted out, but knew full well that she couldn't just back out."

"Hmm, well, it's as good a theory as any, I suppose," Adelaide says dubiously. "If you're doing that tomorrow, I'll spend some time looking into our Mr. Sanderson."

"While you're at it, why don't you see if you can learn anything from the police? Darling seems to like you, and God knows he doesn't feel the same way about me."

"Give a girl all the hard work, why don't you," Adelaide says, but she's smiling so I think I'm fine. "In that case, I'd better turn in. Sounds like we've got a few long days ahead of us."

"Best kind," I say. "Meet up Thursday morning?"

"No, I'll call you when I've got something. No sense us being too predictable. You can do the same if something comes up."

"Fair enough," I say. "Until then, whenever then may be."

Chapter Seven

Wednesday, February 11th

I get in to my office later than I would like to admit, having gotten to bed well after midnight. Holly is already present, of course, and a pot of tea is steeping in the kitchen for me. She's good enough to wait until I have some of it in me before she gives me the messages.

"Donny called for you. I'm surprised he didn't try you at home."

"He might have," I say, glancing around for food. There are some biscuits, but Glimmer has gotten to them and looks like she might actually fight me for them, so I let them be. "The phone rang while I was in the shower. What did he want?"

"Didn't say. But he didn't sound very happy."

"Right. I should probably call him back."

"Oh, and a Mr. Jay Pearson stopped in. Divorce case."

"I assume you told him to come back in a week?"

"No, I said we'd take the case."

I pause with my tea halfway to my lips. "I'm sorry, what?"

Holly gives me an absolutely unrepentant look. "I told him that we'd take the case," she repeats.

I set the teacup down. "Holly, I don't have time…"

"I know. You're on this murder investigation, and it's busy, and frankly, I approve. But we aren't making much money off of it. Todd's a sweetheart, but he's not exactly loaded, and you're throwing a lot of cash around."

I spend a moment trying to parse the idea of Todd Malcolm and 'sweetheart' in the same breath, and another moment parsing the idea that Holly has somehow gotten on a first-name basis with my client in the last twenty-four hours, which distracts me from the more pressing issue at hand. "I thought you didn't like me taking his money at all."

"That's my point. We need money, and we're not taking it from him. So I'll go snoop around and find out a few things for Mr. Pearson."

I wince. "Holly, you're my secretary, not a partner-in-training."

"And you," Holly replies without a blink, "are poor. You can't afford a partner. A secretary will have to do."

"Your parents..." I try weakly.

"Won't ever know," Holly says. "Anyway, I already said yes, so the point is moot. What was I going to do, send him somewhere else?"

"The thought had occurred. Send him over to Carson. He needs the work."

"Carson's a pillock," Holly points out.

"That is why he needs the work. But he's the only other detective in town."

"Which is why," Holly finishes triumphantly, "I told Mr. Pearson we were taking his case. You don't really want me to call him and say that you changed your mind?"

"Just tell him that my secretary had an attack of indiscretion," I say, glowering.

"And ruin your reputation by suggesting that you don't control your own employees? Uncle Basil, I would never do that to you!" Holly shrugs dramatically. "There's nothing for it. I'm just going to have to do it."

I groan. "You're not going to let this go, are you?" On the other hand, if things heat up it might be better if Holly isn't in the office full-time. "Fine. But be careful. And take someone with you. I don't want you out there alone."

"I can take care of myself."

"If something did happen to you, and Plum found out, you'd be short one boss," I shoot back. "Take someone with you."

"Fine," Holly grumbles, trying not to grin. I decide to take the win, and go to dial up Donny.

"Silver Donner's, how many I direct your call?"

"Knock it off, Donny, I know you don't let the other employees answer the phone."

"Oh, Mr. Stark. Nice to hear from you."

I'm instantly suspicious. "Well, you told Holly you needed to speak with me right away," I say carefully.

"Yeah, yeah. You remember that girl, the one you were looking for? The one what sold me that necklace?"

"Absolutely." I consider my next words before speaking. "Did you learn something else about her?"

"Yeah. We got a locket from her too. Turns out one of the stock boys had it stored in the wrong place. Thought maybe the picture here would be useful. Low price, just for you. Whaddaya say?"

"I'd say that seems like a possible clue. How soon do you want me over?"

"Sooner would be better, Mr. Stark. Stuff like this, you don't want to have it hanging around."

"Then I'll come right over."

Holly catches my look as I'm hanging up. "Something wrong?"

"Donny's in trouble."

"How do you figure?"

"He called me Mr. Stark. And conveniently had a clue lying around, and didn't so much as mention how pissed he still is at me."

Holly stands, and reaches to pass me my cane. "Yeah, that doesn't sound like Donny. You're going?"

I nod. "Donny's a friend. Well … he's an acquaintance, at least. I don't like the idea of leaving him twisting in the wind. But do me a favor. If I haven't called in an hour, call the police."

"Will do, Uncle Basil."

I arrive at Silver Donner's just before noon, but instead of taking the front door I slip around back to the service entrance. Picking the lock is just a matter of moments, and I crack the door open slowly, thankful that the day is dreary and overcast. The back of the shop is dark and jumbled, full of old crates with things that Donny hasn't figured out how to sell yet, a bit of furniture that he's holding, a few shelves of records and books that he keeps for himself, and the miscellaneous bric-a-brac that hides his safes from any would-be burglars. There's also a large, shadowy shape sitting at the table Donny uses to count his take at the end of the day, at just the right angle to ambush someone pushing through the curtain that leads to the front of the shop. In this light, I can't get a good look at him, but it sure looks like a pistol sitting on the table.

Keeping my cane at the ready, I creep up behind the thug, low to the ground. I'm very nearly quiet enough; he hears me as I come up behind him, and his hand shoots out and grabs the end of the cane. I kick his chair leg, he grabs at me as he goes down, and a moment later the two of us are on the ground, the can clattering into a pile of boxes. He reaches out to grab me by the neck, and I take a moment to introduce his side to my fist. It doesn't do much, but it distracts him enough for me to slam my head forwards into his face, and he lets go of me with a muffled curse. As he rears backwards, pushing himself to his feet, I snatch his pistol from the ground and raise it.

"Easy, hotshot," I say. "No sense ruining Donny's things."

He freezes, looks me up and down, and decides that I'm serious. He settles back from 'about to attack' to 'looking for a good moment,' which I guess will have to do for now.

"What the hell are you doing back there — oh, it's you, Basil." Donny is back to his usual self. He pushes through the curtain and flicks the lights on, giving me a good look at my would-be ambusher. Imagine my surprise to see a familiar face.

"Good afternoon, Jason," I say to Quentin's goon. "Fancy meeting you here." I glance over to Donny. "Could you do me a favor and close up for a few minutes? Gunshots frighten the tourists."

"Aw, come on, Basil," Donny whines. "Not on my stuff."

"You hear that, Jason?" I ask. "What'd I tell you, Donny just hates a mess. Come on, Donny."

"Yeah, yeah," Donny mutters, pushing the curtain aside. Outside, I hear him arguing with a customer, who presumably heard the ruckus and isn't sure he should be leaving. I turn my attention back to my prisoner.

"Fancy meeting you here, just as I'm supposed to arrive to investigate something your boss doesn't want me investigating. I don't like those kinds of coincidences. Makes me think someone is trying to get me." My eyes narrow. "I get twitchy when people try that."

"You and me both, pal," Jason says. "You ice me, there'll be hell to pay."

I hear the door locking out front. Fifty-fifty whether Donny's coming back with support, or without it. "You went to a lot of trouble to get me, Jason. Well, here I am. What do you want?"

"Boss wants to talk to you."

"My office is always open. He can talk to me there."

"Maybe he wants to talk to you quiet-like. Maybe he don't want everyone in the damn city to know something's up."

"Maybe I don't respond well to men with guns."

"When a boss like Mr. Lark wants to talk to someone, they tend to get a little nervous. Sometimes they rabbit. The gun saves time."

"Well, you've certainly dodged a bullet there. I'm not nervous at all." Donny snickers as he steps back through the door. "So," I add, "Quentin wants to have a word. What about?"

"None of my business."

"You don't ask a lot of questions, do you?"

"People that ask a lot of questions get whacked," Jason says pointedly.

"Threat noted. You're pretty sure I'm not going to shoot you, aren't you?"

"Pretty sure."

"I hope so," Donny interjects, looking between us. "Hey, Basil, you're not mad at me, right? I mean, this guy made me call you. Threatened to smash up the place."

"And you, one of Schaefer's best customers."

Donny misses the sarcasm. "I know! I tell you; I've got half a mind to go straight to Mr. Schaefer himself about this."

Like hell he does. Donny wouldn't risk getting caught in that kind of a crossfire. But it's a nice sentiment. "I'm pretty tempted to give you a corpse-disposal problem to solve, Donny." Donny doesn't even blink. He knows me too well to believe I'd follow through on a threat like that. "But it's your lucky day. I don't really want to get into that kind of a fight with Quentin. Yet."

Jason, who does not know me so well, relaxes just a hairsbreadth. "So, whaddaya going to do?" he asks.

"Where did Quentin want to meet me?"

He looks at me, considers lying, visibly decides against it. "Old warehouse he owns. Pretty quiet this time of day."

"How thoughtful of him, but I wouldn't want to impose." I consider for a moment. "Why don't we meet somewhere slightly more ... friendly. There's a lovely little restaurant nearby, name of Murray's. I believe Quentin stops by there frequently?" Jason doesn't look happy that I know that. "Why don't I go over there and order lunch, and Quentin can join me whenever he feels like it."

Jason swallows. "Uh, yeah, okay."

"Wonderful. Donny, may I use your phone? I need to call someone and let them know I'll be a few minutes late."

Keeping the gun in hand, I head over to the phone, one eye on Jason in case he decides to go back to the original arrangement. I dial up Holly and let her know how things are going.

"Are you sure this is a good idea?" she asks. "I mean, doesn't Lark own that place?"

"That's what makes it perfect. There'll be too many people there for him to do anything obvious, and he's too openly tied to it to wreck it coming after me. I hope." I can hear Holly gathering breath to speak, and I add, "If he's that upset, he'll attack me anywhere. Better to know now."

"Right," Holly says dubiously. "I'll tell you what. I'm going to be out doing research on the divorce case, and I'll call the office in an hour to find out how badly you got beaten up. If you aren't there, I'll start panicking and call the police."

"Make it an hour and a half. Lunch could run long."

《 》

I beat feet to Murray's, figuring Jason will be on the phone the moment I'm out the door, so if I'm going to get there before Quentin's men I want to be quick about it. As it turns out, I'm just quick enough. A couple of toughs are approaching down the street as I stroll up. No bouncer today. Suppose they don't need one until after sunset.

Quentin's not in, but another familiar face is. "Mr. Stark," Stephanie Tate says as I step inside, gesturing me towards one of the window booths. I glance around, spot a half-dozen patrons, and decide that it'll do. I slide in opposite Ms. Tate and nod to her.

"Ms. Tate. A pleasure."

"The pleasure's all mine, Mr. Stark. And please, call me Stephanie."

"Whatever you say, Ms. Tate."

She laughs. "You don't take orders well, do you?"

"If I took orders well, I'd be a cop."

"Well, aren't we all lucky that didn't happen. When I heard you were on the way over, I just had to get here first. You must know who owns this joint."

"I have a suspicion. Not exactly neutral ground, I admit, but close enough for our purposes. I assume that Quentin is on the way?"

"He'll be a few minutes. I understand that it took Jason a while to get a hold of him."

"What a terrible shame. Fortunately, I brought a newspaper." I pull it out of my coat, opening it on the table.

"We're all heartbroken," she agrees. "Pass me the business section?"

"Of course, Ms. Tate."

The waiter arrives. I order a sandwich, and we spend a couple of minutes in silence, both pretending to read, before she says anything else. "I have to admit, I was a little disappointed to learn that you'd kept on this case," she says, not looking up from the paper. "I can't help taking it a little personally."

"A woman is dead, Ms. Tate," I say, also not looking up. "A woman I was supposed to find, at that. I take that very personally."

Stephanie nods after a moment, closing her paper and looking out the window. Quentin's boys are outside, having a hushed conversation. "May I ask a possibly indelicate question?"

I consider a moment, and then nod. "You might as well. I do, of course, reserve the right not to answer."

"Of course. What happened to you?"

I turn, lowering my newspaper and raising my eyebrows. "Excuse me?"

"You were Gentleman Starkey, once. I've read the stories, studied the histories. You were the first mate on one of the most fearsome pirate crews in history. They say that you knew the politest ways to murder a man, and that you were utterly cruel and ruthless."

I smile faintly. "Not utterly cruel. Only one man could hold that position, and he was my Captain."

"Nonetheless," she says, tapping her pen against the table. "The man you were, he would have been ruling this town. At the very least, he'd be in Quentin's shoes by now, as first mate for a new captain. How did you go from Gentleman Starkey to...?" She gestures vaguely.

"To Basil?" I suggest.

"To Basil," she agrees.

I sit back in my chair. "Do you know much about the Piccadilly Indians, Miss Tate?"

"Not much. They've been here as long as anyone. Children of Indians, brought up by the island, right? I know you have an attachment to them."

"After the fateful battle in which my crew died, the Piccadilly captured me. They delivered to me a humiliating punishment — to live among them, learn their ways, and care for their children as a nursemaid."

She blinks. "I always assumed that story was just so much hot air."

"Oh, no, it's one of the few about me that's true."

"I can't imagine it," she says, shaking her head. "You could have killed the children at any time."

"I may have fallen far, but not that far. I gave my word, and besides, they weren't my enemies. Actually, I grew rather fond of the little blighters." I chuckle. "They honed the rough edges right off me, I'm afraid, and do you want to know the most terrible secret of all?" I lean in, lowering my voice, and Stephanie leans in to match me despite herself.

"What?"

"I'm much happier this way," I say conspiratorially. I can see from the look on her face that she's disappointed, so I press on. "The Piccadilly grew fond of me too. They even gave me a Piccadilly name."

"Oh? What was it?"

"Basil."

Stephanie blinks. "But ... that's just your name."

"Piccadilly names, traditionally, are those of the plants or animals that they most embody," I explain. "I wasn't born with the name Basil. It's a covenant, made with many people who aged a little bit faster than me and are now gone. Double the reason to hold to it."

"What does it mean?"

"Basil is a complicated plant. It either represents the best of wishes, or undying hatred. There is no middle ground."

"Very fitting. Which way do you think the plant points today?"

"I haven't decided yet. When Quentin arrives, I'll let you know."

"Hm," Stephanie grunts, looking down at her paper. "Maybe you haven't changed as much as I'd thought."

"One of my constant fears," I assure her. "I'll try not to burden you with any bodies." I see the waiter returning, with Quentin in tow, and I turn to give them a smile. "Ah, Quentin, we were just talking about you."

"Alright, Steph, I'll take it from here," Quentin says, as the waiter drops my sandwich down as quickly as humanly possible and backs away. I don't blame him; Quentin looks like he's just about ready to break the table across one knee.

Stephanie looks up mildly. "Of course, boss," she says, layering a whole lot of emotion into that last word as she stands up. "I'm rather getting used to running into you, Basil. You may be habit-forming."

"Really? I usually hear quite the opposite. Take care, Ms. Tate."

Quentin clears his throat noisily, and Stephanie nods once to him, casually snatches up my half of the newspaper, and walks away. I chuckle ruefully. "Wasn't quite done with that," I say.

"I don't think reading material is your primary concern right now, Stark." Quentin doesn't sit. Instead, he takes a step closer to tower over me.

"Stark? What happened to 'Basil, buddy'? It had a nice ring to it."

"I told you to leave the dame alone."

"I told you no. And I don't like being strong-armed." I take my sandwich, meeting Quentin's eyes. "Anyway, the 'dame' is dead. Murdered. You wouldn't happen to know anything about that, would you, Quentin?"

"I heard it was drugs," Quentin sneers. "Dust isn't my racket."

"No, you're more in the smuggling business these days, aren't you?"

I watch his eyes narrow. "Meaning what?"

"Not everything has to have a grand meaning, Quentin. Sometimes, I'm just making conversation. Why'd you send your pal Jason to bother poor old Donny?"

"Donny's in his own mess of trouble. You should worry about yours. I don't like it when folks ignore my friendly warnings, Stark. Makes me a little grumpy."

"And then you start doing stupid, stupid things, so we can't have that." I watch Quentin's face get red, and shake my head. "Come on, Quentin, what are you even trying to pull here? The only thing you've managed to do so far is convince me you're involved in all this mess. And using Donny? Did you honestly think he'd call me up out of the blue with a hot tip on a missing girl? Not his style."

"Stark, you are playing with fire."

"Oh, dear me. What are you going to do, send a goon around to vanish me?" I meet his eyes. "Here's some advice, Quentin. I don't know how you were involved in all this. Not yet. But I don't care about your little power games. I care about the girl. How did she get caught up in all this?"

"None of your business."

"So you do know."

"What I know is also none of your business." Quentin slams his hands down on the table, ignoring the looks from the nearest patrons. "I wanted to do this quiet, Stark, but you sure like blasting other folks' plans to rubble. So we'll do it straight. Give up this case, or I will bury you so deep they'll never find the body." He gestures to the table. "Enjoy your sandwich."

"I plan to," I say. "Oh, and Quentin? Since you were so nice as to give a warning, I'll give you one right back. If you actually work yourself up to taking a shot, you'd better make sure it lands. I've outlived better men than you." I smile politely. "Have a lovely day."

"Go to hell, Stark," Quentin snarls over his shoulder as he storms off. It takes a few minutes for normal conversation to resume, while I finish my sandwich and consider my next move. Chances are, I could convince one of the local diners to report that little threat of his to the cops, but that won't do much more than annoy him. It isn't as though Darling doesn't know who he is, after all. All I've managed to do is frustrate him, which, to be fair, was my main goal, and with enough witnesses to the event that if I do end up having to shoot him, I'll have someone around who can tell Schaefer he had it coming, which was the second. I don't think Quentin's got the balls to come after me in force, but if he's as deep in this as I think he is, he might not have a choice.

———— «»————

When I get back to the office, it's locked up tight. I let myself in carefully, glad for the first time that Holly's busy with that other job. I don't think I want her caught in the middle of all this. I spend a moment seriously considering pouring myself a stiff drink, resist the temptation, and go for a glass of milk instead. Then I prop my feet on my desk, grab one of Holly's trashy detective novels to pass the time, and wait for her to call.

"Basil Stark Investigations," I say, when the phone rings right on schedule. "How may I direct your call?"

"Oh, good," Holly says over the line, "you're alive and well."

"Alive, at least," I agree. "How can you read this stuff?"

"That is a classic work by a classic author."

"How can he be a classic? This was published last year." I shake my head. "You would think there would be enough detecting in your life. On which subject…"

"The stakeout is going fine, Uncle Basil."

"Stakeout?" I straighten abruptly. "You said you were doing *research.*"

"A stakeout is research. Anyway, I can't talk long, I've left my friend upstairs with the camera while I came down to the lobby to call you. Oh, and I took a couple of calls before I went out Niall wants you to call him, but he's going to be in meetings all afternoon, so he suggested you try him at home this evening. Which probably actually means—"

"I know what it means." It means that he has something to tell me that he doesn't want Second Star's switchboard operators listening in on, but not something so pressing that it needs to be delivered in person.

"Well, you could let me say it anyway," Holly grumps. "Also, Adelaide called for you." I swear I can hear her eyebrows waggling over the phone. "Oh, and Glimmer's been pouting in her corner, so wherever you're going tonight, take her with you, please? We both know which of us is going to be cleaning all day tomorrow if she decides to break everything in the kitchen out of spite."

"Understood, boss. Any other orders?"

Holly snorts. "Don't get arrested."

"No promises. This is one of those cases." I take a breath. "When you finish up, I'd suggest heading home instead of back to the office. Quentin just made a move against me, and I'd be a lot more comfortable if you were home with Panther and Plum. This friend of yours, can he fight?"

"You assume it's a 'he'."

"Holly, please tell me that you did not go out alone on a *stakeout* with another young woman."

"You know, some people would be more worried for my safety if it was a young man I was spending time alone with."

"I trust your judgment where men are concerned. I'm only worried about your youthful sense of immortality."

"Calm down, Uncle Basil. Yes, it's a man, yes, I trust him, and yes, he can take care of himself. The whole point was to have some muscle, right? We'll be fine."

"Right. I'm sorry," I say after a moment. "I do trust you, Holly. It's just this case. I already know someone was willing to kill over it, and Mercy wasn't much older than you. Just ... be careful. Please."

There's a long pause on the other end of the line before Holly answers, more subdued. "Right. I will, Uncle Basil. You be careful too."

After she hangs up, I sit and stare at the phone for a minute before I pick it up again, trying to decide if I'm handling this right. Should I be storming down to ... to wherever Holly called from, to pick her up and drive her home? But then, she is an adult, and she knows the risks. And, of course, she's still probably safer there than she would be here, with Quentin on the warpath.

I shake my head, and dial Adelaide's number. I knew that there were risks when I agreed to take Holly on. So did she, and so did Plum. Too late now for what-ifs.

"Good afternoon, Adelaide," I say, when the hotel connects me. "Holly tells me you wanted to speak with me?"

"Hello to you too," Adelaide says. "I thought we might work together for a bit. You remember the Jane Arlett?"

"That theater that Quentin and Mr. Sanderson were both members at, yes. What about it?"

"I think I have a lead, but I need to get at their records. The problem is, there are definitely people in the office, and I don't think I can slip in unnoticed. I've been mulling it over all morning, and then I realized — I don't have to slip in unnoticed. Sanderson already knows I'm poking around his life. I just need to get really ostentatiously caught *trying* to get in, and have someone else slip in while I'm creating a big ruckus and yelling about freedom of the press."

"Why, Adelaide, are you suggesting that we engage in burglary?"

"I'm a reporter, not a cop. Are you interested?"

"You're a woman after my own heart. Shall we meet a block away in, say, an hour? I need to get a bite to eat in case

I get arrested." I pause, and grin. "And I think I know how to really dial up your distraction."

"Oh, really?"

"Oh, really. You've met Glimmer, yes?"

———— «» ————

Just over an hour later, I'm lurking on a fire escape one level above the second-floor offices of the Jane Arlett Theater, waiting for the commotion that is bound to happen momentarily. I've cracked open the window of the mostly-empty office above, and am listening intently for the telltale sound of Adelaide's entrance.

I'm not disappointed. Within a few minutes, I can hear raised voices from the stairwell — Adelaide, loudly declaring that the theater is a hotbed of bad taste, misspent donations, and decrepit actors, just generally a blemish on Everland's bohemian community, and clearly not worthy of the time she intended to spend writing about it.

"The jewel of the community, they said! Ridiculous!" Her voice carries up to where I am, well over the alternately brusque and pleading tones of a beleaguered theater manager who had no idea that a journalist from the National Geographic was coming by for a two o'clock interview, certainly didn't tell any actors or the artistic director to be present, and was frankly more than a little annoyed that some mainland critic thought that she could just barge in and cause trouble. As the row intensifies, I hear the sounds of the remaining office staff going down the stairs to see what's happening, which is the moment that Glimmer makes her move.

I'm proud of the little scamp. She explodes out of Adelaide's purse like a firecracker, and I hear various small objects hitting the ground. Within seconds, someone frantically shouts, "Get the door!" and someone else slams it shut before Glimmer can swoop into the office proper. I smile, slip down the ladder, and use a bit of wire through a loose crack to get the outside window open; it only takes a few seconds, and then I'm in the office. Outside, I can see Glimmer's shadow as she dashes back and forth through the lobby, frazzled actors and managers in her wake as they try valiantly to corner her. Adelaide, in the guise of helping, is getting in everyone's way, pleading with the staff not to hurt her darling little fairy and making wild pleas for Glimmer to come back to the nice purse.

I figure I've only got a few minutes before either someone decides to come into the office to get a net, or Glimmer forgets that she's playing a game and actually runs off, so I move quickly to the records room. The door is locked, of course, but it's a crummy padlock and it barely slows me down. I flip through the theater's financial records as quickly as I dare, looking for damning evidence, and check their personnel files while I'm at it. Soon enough, I have a solid idea of what's going on, and it's time to slip out again, a few pieces of paper tucked into the folds of my coat.

It's thus something of a disappointment to open the records room door and find Tim Sanderson lurking outside it, a scowl on his face and a pistol in his hand.

"Mr. Sanderson," I say gamely. "What a remarkable surprise." I glance to the front door — Glimmer is still doing her routine outside, and no one seems to have noticed us. "Shouldn't you be at work?"

"I took a sick day," he says, eyes narrowing. "Thought some fresh air would do me good."

"And you just happened to end up here," I say, and then break off and sigh heavily. "You followed Adelaide."

"And found you, in the process of burglarizing our offices. The police are going to have a field day with this."

"They would, if you told them. But you aren't going to do that," I say, straightening. If he wants to play rough, I will too. "Because if they come in here, they're going to want to know what I was doing, and that's going to lead to them poking around your financial records. And won't that be a black mark on your resume."

Sanderson swallows, but he holds firm. "I don't know what you mean."

"Well, you're on the board. Did you know that half of your stagehands — of which you have far too many, by the way — are known enforcers for Douglas Schaefer? And your anonymous donations, such good fundraising. And your ticket sales are frankly amazing given the middling reviews."

Sanderson holds the gun on me for a moment more, trying to stare me down. "You're talking your way into a bullet, Stark."

"I doubt it. Too many witnesses outside, too many people knew I was coming here, and the window is open. No, I think we can both agree that the best thing to do here is go our separate ways, and no one has to explain mysterious gunshots or bloodstains to the police, or discuss the specifics of the theater's operations."

Sanderson glares at me a moment longer, and then grunts and takes a step backwards. "Get out of my office. And if I ever see you again..."

"Yes, yes, I know, horrible pain, suffering, never find my body." I wave him off as I move to the window. "I've been threatened by the best, and you're not going to come up with anything that I haven't heard before."

"I don't have to be creative. I just have to be accurate."

I pause. "I take it back, Mr. Sanderson. That is a new one. I like it." I take one last look around, and the cast pictures spread across one wall catch my eye. I suck in my breath. "So this is where you met Mercy," I say without thinking.

Sanderson's hand tightens on the gun. "Maybe I'll shoot you after all."

"Right. Have a lovely afternoon, Mr. Sanderson."

Sometimes, discretion is the better part of valor.

——— «◊» ———

"You're lucky he didn't kill you," Adelaide says, taking a sip of her coffee. It's half an hour later, and we're sitting in a small café discussing what I learned while she was raising hell. Glimmer is sitting by the window, munching on a small sugared tea biscuit and watching a few snowflakes drift out of the cloudy sky.

"He didn't seem the type, although there was a moment there when I wasn't sure. And I admit it was a shock running into him just then. Rather ruined my investigation, and I'm afraid that he'll have reported back to Quentin by now."

"So, aside from tipping off the bad guys, did we learn anything?"

"Absolutely. We learned two, very important things. First, the Jane Arlett is a money-laundering operation, and a slick one." I smile, leaning back in my chair, and take a bite out of my muffin. "There are crooks on the payroll, they're giving stolen or smuggled cash to the theater as donations, and everyone on the board is drawing a tidy salary. They run real shows, hire real actors, but the staff is all Quentin's, and I'd bet half the hall rentals are fakes."

Adelaide whistles. "Can we prove it?"

"No, but we can prove enough to make Quentin shut the theater down if the police come sniffing. I grabbed a few papers. There's a chance he'll do it anyway when Sanderson tells him what happened, but it could be leverage."

"Alright," Adelaide says, nodding. "What's the second thing that we learned?"

"How Mercy fits into this damned mess. Finally."

"Aside from dating two of the principals?"

"Aside from that. I know how she met them, now. She was one of the Jane Arlett's actors. For at least a year — I saw her in two different production photos. That's probably how she met Schaefer; Quentin used some actors as hostesses for some upscale event, and Schaefer was smitten. It's also how she met Harding — Sanderson's on the Arlett's board, and I'd bet a dollar that he's borrowed the staff for events too."

"Well, that ... doesn't actually help us, does it? It's interesting to know how she got mixed up in all this, but we already knew she was involved with Quentin Lark's operations. I suppose it's more evidence that he's responsible for her death."

"And that Tim Sanderson was in on it. How's this for a theory — Mercy is working as an actress, under an assumed name. She meets Harding through Sanderson, either by chance or because he's trying to undermine Harding by throwing beautiful women in his path, and she actually gets fond of him. Then ... she finds something out, which I'm going to assume is connected with the shadow that killed her. Possibly she learns that Quentin or his mystery partner has an actual stitcher on staff. She calls you, planning to meet with you and spill the beans on her way out of town. I don't know why she didn't do that in New York, but I'm guessing that whatever proof she had was local."

"Then why did she tell me the story was about smuggling?"

"If she told you it was about lethal shadows, would your editor have paid your fare? Besides, there really was smuggling, it would hold up to casual scrutiny, and if Quentin's people caught on, they'd cover the wrong bases."

"Good point." Adelaide taps her spoon against her cup, nodding slowly. "Alright. Quentin finds out that Mercy learned something, and panics. He creates that fake to distract me, and his partner — and I cannot believe that I'm saying this — sends a shadow to kill her. Then he manipulates the crime scene to discredit her.

"If it had worked as planned, you would have been on your way back to New York, and no one would have investigated Mercy's death. Too bad for Quentin that Harding had already hired me to look for her. Threw the whole plan into chaos."

Adelaide laughs. "You have that effect on people."

"Part of my charm."

Her smile fades as she looks back down at her coffee. "It holds together, but why keep the shadow a secret?"

"At the moment, my guess is that was the stitcher's requirement — he wants to be a shadow partner, if you'll pardon the pun." Adelaide groans, and I smile. "When you get down to it, there are a lot of ways to fight a shadow if you know it's coming for you. The longer Quentin can keep this secret, the stronger his position when it comes out. More evidence that Quentin isn't fully in control of this operation."

"Right. You realize that there isn't a scrap of proof, and given that we're suggesting someone has mastered shadows, which as I understand it is literally impossible, you're probably going to want some of that before I try to write any of this up."

I take another bite of muffin before speaking again. "Yeah. With the added wrinkle that Quentin and Sanderson both know that we're onto them, and have both made some rather nasty threats, and of course the other wrinkle that there is, in fact, a murderous shadow out there. While my body turning up in the harbor could probably be used as proof of wrongdoing, I'd rather it didn't come to that."

"Me neither. Do you have a plan?"

"I always have a plan." I grin. "This one is particularly patchy, though. I'm hoping a contact will be able to give me a lead. If he does, I could get back to you tomorrow."

"Lovely. What am I supposed to do for the rest of the day?"

"I don't know. Have you talked to the police yet? They won't talk to me, but for a beautiful and talented foreign reporter, I bet you could get them to tell you just about anything."

"Basil, you flatterer." Adelaide pats me on the arm, and I find myself blushing.

"Someone shut down the case," I say, quickly changing the subject back. "It might just be the mayor trying to avoid a panic, but it might be another avenue of investigation. Something to do, at any rate."

"Right. Tomorrow, then?"

"Until then, Ms. Evans." I stand, and offer her a bow.

She chuckles. "Until tomorrow, Mr. Stark."

———— «» ————

I get home shortly after five, and spend some time playing cards with Glimmer and watching the sunset while I wait to give Niall a call. Glimmer's strutting across the table, thrilled at how well she evaded everyone back at the theater, and I have to admit that I agree with her. "Glad you decided to stick around," I say, when she winds down a bit and starts studying her cards.

She makes it pretty clear that she doesn't have anywhere better to be, and anyway she liked ol' what's-her-name and is pretty pissed that she died, and besides, there's free crackers.

"Point taken." I let her win the next couple of hands, then excuse myself to give Niall a call on his home number. He answers almost immediately.

"Basil, glad to hear from you. How's your investigation treating you?"

"Lousy. I'm hoping you're about to tell me that things are turning around, though."

"Things are turning around."

"You have something for me?"

"I do, actually. A name, and an address. Conrad Higgs. Works out of a small lab on the corner of Seventh and George, in Mud Point."

I consider that. "Not a very prestigious neighborhood."

"No, it isn't. Higgs was a Second Star researcher, but he was given his walking papers a few years back. Not much detail, but I gather he was continuing research in his off hours that the Old Man didn't approve of."

"That's a wide net. The Old Man disapproves of anything he doesn't control."

"Now, Basil…"

"Alright, alright, I'll be nice." I glance away from the phone. Glimmer is amusing herself by quietly stacking the deck we were using, so I figure I've got some time before she gets really bored. "Let me guess — Higgs was one of the shadow researchers."

"Lead developer on the project, and it was cancelled over his very strenuous protests. He went so far as to put them on record."

"So, if we were looking for someone who would know about controlling shadows…"

"It would be him, yes."

"What are the chances that he'll be happy to see me?"

"At a lab like that? I'd imagine he'd be happy to see anyone."

"Now who's being judgey?" I chuckle.

"In all seriousness, Basil, if you just treat him seriously, I expect that he'll tell you everything he knows. God knows it's usually harder to get a researcher to stop talking than it is to get us to start."

"Thanks, Niall, I'll check it out first thing tomorrow morning. I owe you one."

"I'll add it to my tab. Have a good night."

After hanging up, I spend a few moments staring thoughtfully off into space, and then reach for my cane. Niall's a good egg, but he has a bad habit — assuming other people are too. A disgruntled scientist devoted to potentially illicit research seems like a good lead to me, but it also seems like there's a good chance that he's in this up to his neck, and as much fun as alerting Quentin and Sanderson to my investigation has been, I don't really see the need to go three for three. I will be interviewing him tomorrow morning, but first, I want to poke around.

——— «» ———

I wait until after sundown before returning to town, and arrive at Higgs' lab a little after ten. Mud Point is a bit rundown, but as neighborhoods go it's fairly quiet. Located on the cliffs near the western edge of town, it was the site of some factories and plants in the old days, when the town was being planned. When the island's economy shifted to trade and away from production, most of the factories closed, leaving a lot of old, rusting buildings, and a lot of small houses surrounding them in a town rapidly spreading west towards Piccadilly territory.

Higgs' lab is in one of those old factories, along with a dozen other low-rent businesses. The building's front door is open, which strikes me as terrible security, but I take advantage. The door to Higgs' office, on the other hand, is quite well-locked, and I spend a good two minutes working on it before I manage to make my way into the front office. Looking around in the dim light of the streetlamps outside, it's about what I expect. A few faded pictures on the walls, a small desk with a typewriter and phone for the secretary, a side office for files, and a door leading into what was the adjacent suite, but which Higgs has presumably converted into lab space.

What catches my eye is the furniture. The wallpaper is on the verge of peeling, but there's wall-to-wall carpeting on the ground, which is unheard of in this sort of building, and the chairs and table for waiting guests look trendy, if not expensive. The typewriter's a new model too. It looks suspiciously like Doctor Higgs has come into some money recently. I cross over to the secretary's desk, and find a small filing cabinet, securely locked. This one looks like it might be more trouble than I can manage, but whoever does the filing isn't too careful — there are keys in the less securely locked desk.

There are, I muse, as I open the filing cabinet, an awful lot of locks in this place.

Nothing particularly interesting in the files here, though. Phone records for all of Doctor Higgs' old contacts at Second Star, most of them crossed out in faded red ink. In a few, the pen tore through the paper, it was pressed down so hard. There are also numbers of a few captains of industry over at Hawthorne Logging and the docks, some of them also crossed out, but most of the files are about supply purchases and import notices, which could be a smoking gun or totally innocent. I take note of a few of the more memorable names, to run past Niall later, and move on, keys in hand.

The next logical stop is Higgs' office. I move to open the door, and am caught off guard when I find that someone has beaten me to it. The office door wasn't quite closed properly, and opens easily. I step inside quickly, looking around, and close it the same degree behind me, leaving the lights out just in case.

Higgs doesn't believe in a Spartan design. A bookshelf dominates one side of the room, packed floor to ceiling with a mixture of old tomes, science journals, and volumes of poetry and mythological fiction. Another wall sports a half-dozen portraits of fanciful Everland historical moments: the Jolly Roger pulling into Marooner's Bay; a flight of faeries; and the signing of the Beast Pact, complete with two tigers and a lion opposite John Darling and George Ellery Hale, and a wince-inducing racist caricature of a Piccadilly standing between them, grinning. More carpet on the floor, a proper brandy cabinet on the third wall between two more filing cabinets, and another phone on Higgs' desk — a new one, unlike the one in the front office.

It seems nice enough, but the filing cabinets aren't locked, and neither is his drawer. Inside, I find a few notepads, mostly covered in indecipherable scribbles, a few keychains, and a photograph of Mercy Nelson. She is posed in a fine dress, looking at the camera with a hint of a smile. I consider it thoughtfully, and check the back. No signature or personal message, sadly. On a hunch, I rifle through the professor's account-book. It is, as I suspected, a mess, but there are payment lines for two assistants — one Sadie Metcalf, listed as a lab assistant, and a Victoria Lane as a publicist. The fake name that Mercy used with Douglas Schaefer and Todd Malcolm, popping up again.

I go to check the main filing cabinets; in case they have something else useful. The first is filled to bulging with old notes, and I flip through a few of them idly. They look like experiment records, and while they're coded there are suggestions that Higgs might have decided to keep going on his shadow experiments in secret. The second filing cabinet has much of the same, but it's only about half-full. I grab the most recent one. It's over three weeks old, and doesn't have much of interest.

I'm about to start looking more closely when I hear the office door open. Quickly, I grab my cane and hat and duck behind the doorframe. "Doctor Higgs?" a woman's voice calls. "Are you here yet? Hello?"

I hear the door close, and the sound of someone fumbling for a light. It must be the assistant. She goes on, calling over to the lab. "I don't know why you needed me out here at this time of night, Doctor, but I must say that I don't appreciate being dragged out of my—"

The light comes on in the other room, and her voice cuts out. For a half-second I freeze, thinking that she's spotted something, but then there's the sound of something hitting the floor and I decide I'll just have to risk it. I throw the door open and spring into the main room, to find myself facing a terrible sight.

Miss Metcalf — at least, I assume that it is Miss Metcalf, not having any picture to identify her by — is lying on the floor, still wearing a long brown overcoat, her hat on the ground next to her and her hands clutching her throat. The room is bathed in light from the overhead bulb that she had just got to, but there is a shadow in the room not cast by me or by her, falling across her body. Its hands are lined with hers, and her face is shrouded in darkness as the creature attempts to pour itself down her throat. I can see faint ripples of motion on her side and on the ground leading towards the desk, the shadow continuing to flow out in an impossible, sinuous attack.

I stand frozen for a moment, and then grab my cane and twist the head, pulling out my sword. I lunge towards the creature, slamming my blade into the floor in the shadow's center with all of my might. My shoulder groans in protest, but the blade bites home, stabbing through the shadow and carpet and lodging in the hardwood beneath. Thanking all the stars that there was wood, and not concrete, down there, I grab the secretary by her free arm and start to pull her away from the shadow.

The creature tries to resist, but it isn't very strong — better at flowing around obstacles than resisting them, it can't keep its hold on Miss Metcalf, and I yank her, still gasping, free of its reach. The creature is stretching as best it can, but too much of it is behind the desk, and my sword is keeping it pinned. Its grasping fingers reach for her chest, but her throat is safely away, and it doesn't have the mass to do real damage. A moment later, the two of us are crouched against the far wall, watching the floor as the monster thrashes and spasms. The worst of it is the silence. Aside from Miss Metcalf's ragged gasps, and my heart pounding in my ears, there is nothing.

After holding that pose for a moment, I look over to her. "Where's the nearest phone?"

Still wordless, she points to the desk.

"Other than that."

"Doctor Higgs' office," she manages, in a raspy voice. And then she gasps, and points back to the middle of the room. The shadow's body is starting to tear slowly, splitting around the sword pinning it to the ground, and it is pushing itself towards us, its lower half slowly turning into two ragged tails that trail behind it as it oozes across the floor, arms outstretched and fingers like claws.

"Well, that's new," I mutter. I gauge the distance to the front door, and decide that the lab is a better choice. I pull Miss Metcalf to her feet, and push her ahead of me. "Come on!"

Fortunately, the lab door isn't locked, which gives us a chance to race through it and slam it behind us. I glance at the bottom, and find it sealed tight against the ground. No chance of light – or a shadow – slipping under there. Ahead of me, Miss Metcalf screams, and I spin, drawing my pistol.

It won't do much against a shadow, but it's all that I've got, and if it's a human we have to deal with, it could be enough.

As it turns out, I don't have to worry. Doctor Higgs is already dead.

By the look of it, he hasn't been dead for very long. He's still wearing a lab coat, with a few buttons torn off, and there's a pair of smashed glasses on the ground beside him. His eyes are open, staring up at the ceiling, and his hands are at his throat. Miss Metcalf's hands go to her own throat in response, and I step up beside her. "Miss Metcalf. Sadie. Look at me. Here."

Sadie looks at me, with shock-filled eyes. "He was ... he ... I just spoke to him an hour ago on the phone. He's not ... he can't be..."

"I'm sorry. That shadow outside must have gotten him."

"No! He was careful! He always took precautions—" Some element of self-preservation pushes through the shock, and Sadie shuts down that line of thought. "We're safe in here," she says instead. "It can't get under the door."

"You know what that was out there?"

"Everyone knows what a shadow is. Oh, God, Doctor Higgs..."

"Is there a phone in the lab? We need to call the Regulators."

"The Regulators! No!" Sadie moves to block my way to the phone. "Who are you, anyway? What are you doing here?"

"I came to see Doctor Higgs about shadows," I say, which has the benefit of being half-true. "I arrived just before you. It looks like I wasn't quite quick enough. Miss Metcalf, that shadow outside is not behaving how it should. It was willing to tear itself in half just to reach you, and it is not going to go away, and I left my only good steel out there in your office. So unless you have a fancy tool in here that can banish the thing, we are calling the Regulators."

I half-hope that she will reveal that she does, in fact, have a fancy tool. But instead she swallows, and fights back a sob, and gestures to the phone. I cross past her, tucking my gun back into my pocket, and dial the emergency line.

After I've given my address and a brief summary of the issue, Sadie and I settle down to wait, as far from the body as she can manage. "Shouldn't be more than a few minutes," I say. "Regulators take shadows very seriously."

"Too seriously. They don't hire people who care about this island. They just hire people who want to stamp it out, turn it into another productive little factory town."

"True. I'm not their biggest fan myself. But they have one advantage over most of the city — they aren't in anyone's pocket."

Sadie rubs at her throat. "I suppose not." She almost looks at Higgs' body, but quickly turns back to me. "You never told me your name."

"Basil Stark."

"The pirate?"

"Ex-pirate, please. Although I'm touched that you've heard of me."

"Some of us read our histories. I never thought I'd meet you, though." She pauses, and looks down at her coat. "I'm Sadie Metcalf."

"I guessed as much. Doctor Higgs' secretary, yes?"

"Assistant. I have a masters' in cryptozoology. Doctor Higgs says I should study for a doctorate, but—" She breaks off. "That is, he said that. Before ... you saved my life out there, didn't you? Thank you."

"Don't mention it. Your first experience with someone trying to kill you?"

"I should think so! And poor Doctor Higgs is right there. Shouldn't we do something for him?"

"Nothing we can do. He must have been killed right after he called you."

"I mean... lay him out properly, or close his eyes, at least."

"The police would have harsh words for you if you did. This is a crime scene."

"Oh. Of course." Sadie sinks against the wall, trembling, and staring at him.

"What was he like?"

She smiles faintly. "Difficult, but supportive. I must have threatened to quit once a week, but where else could I learn the things he knew? The man was a genius. Hale never knew what he lost when he fired Doctor Higgs." She looks over to me. "Do you have anything to drink?"

"I try not to carry the stuff, I'm afraid. Although right now I could use a drink myself." I pat her on the shoulder.

"Damn. I could use it. It's not every day … that is, I've seen my share of corpses, but not quite so fresh. Or so personal. I expect I'm in shock."

"I expect so. Why did he call you?"

"Something to do with the latest project. He was nervous, more than I've ever heard him. I wonder if he knew that it was loose? But no, he wouldn't have called if he suspected I'd be in danger."

"The project working on shadow control?"

"Well, yes, but—" Sadie breaks off, and her eyes narrow. "How did you get into the lab, anyway?"

"Door wasn't locked."

"Really."

"That's my story."

"How do I know you didn't bring that thing into the office with you?"

I raise an eyebrow. "Are you saying that shadow control *is* possible?"

There's a short pause. "I think it might have been," Sadie admits. "I helped with a lot of the research, but Doctor Higgs didn't trust even me completely. He was certainly attempting to control his shadow. Imagine — a scout that could examine the most desolate, secret places, and send back information. Someone who could find trapped workers in a mine collapse."

"Or who could kill anyone."

"That wasn't the point!" Sadie snaps. "It was about knowledge."

"And it was just the two of you?"

"Doctor Higgs couldn't afford any other assistants. Are you worried about someone else arriving?"

I show her my picture of Mercy. "Do you know this girl?"

She frowns. "No, I don't think so. What does she have to do with all of this?"

I spend a moment considering her. The shock is wearing off, and people can go a lot of ways when grief takes over. Anger might be better than breaking down right at the moment. "Someone is going out of their way to frame Higgs for murdering her," I say bluntly.

"What? That's absurd! Why would Doctor Higgs want to kill someone?"

"Why would someone want to kill Doctor Higgs? The world is a complicated place, and this woman is in your books as an employee."

"She certainly is not! I manage those books myself." Sadie looks over to Higgs' body, and the light dawns. "Oh. I see. Whoever killed him altered the records."

"And you were meant to be too deceased to contradict the findings," I agree. "It's slick, if nasty."

"Those bastards!"

"Who?"

"He's had private backers, the last year or so. Someone with real money, someone who's interested in how the island really works. I don't know much about them; I've just been depositing the cash. Higgs said they offered him whatever he needed."

Unfortunately, anything else Sadie has to say on the subject is interrupted by the sound of a door being smashed in, and floodlights shining through the windows. A voice shouts. "Regulators! Everyone be calm!"

Someone else yells, "There it is!"

The next minute is pretty loud, but when it ends, and the door is opened, the shadow is in custody, the lab is swarming with leather-suited figures in heavy helmets bearing silvered blades and guns loaded with holly-tipped bullets, and we're being looked over by a pair of very studious medics while a group of investigators study Higgs' body. One medic is shining a light over my clothes while the other is carefully dabbing Sadie's throat with some gel or another. "Was there more than one of the creatures?" he asks.

"Not that I saw."

"And it didn't attack you?"

"I know, it's unusual. But no. It left me alone until Miss Metcalf entered the room. I hadn't bothered with the lights — I thought that Doctor Higgs was in his lab, and didn't want to disturb him until he was done. That might have been it."

"Maybe." The medic sounds as dubious as I am. He finishes flashing his light, and gestures to one of his friends. "You tussled with it?"

"Barely. I stabbed it, pulled Miss Metcalf free, and we retreated into the lab. I didn't have any more steel on me."

"Right." The man behind the medic makes a sudden movement, and the medic yanks me forward. Caught off guard, I stumble as a pair of floodlights are shone directly behind me. There is a nasty-sounding clang, and a metal half-dish is slammed on the ground on top of my shadow.

"What the hell?"

"Fragment." The medic pats me on the shoulder. "Happens from time to time. Your shadow probably crossed the attacker while you were fighting, and a bit of it got loose. They aren't generally dangerous, but we prefer to round them up."

"I didn't know that about shadows."

"Really? An old hand on the island like you?" The medic laughs and pats me on the shoulder. "Don't worry about it. You're clear now."

Sadie has also been given a clean bill of health, but by now a familiar figure is stomping through the door. "I might have known you'd be here," Commissioner Darling growls as he looks over the scene. With the Regulators wrapping up, it seems the police have been allowed access to the crime scene. "I hope you realize that you are absolutely under arrest."

"On what charge?"

"We'll start with suspicion of murder, breaking and entering, trafficking in illegal research, and theft, and move on from there." Darling scowls at Sadie. "And you are?"

"Sadie Metcalf," she says, eyes flashing. "I'm the lab assistant here. And if you're arresting the man who saved my life, you're going to have to arrest me too."

"Oh, I am absolutely arresting you too."

There is a short pause. "Oh," Sadie finally says.

I give her a pat on the shoulder. "It won't be so bad. I've been arrested plenty of times. We'll be out of there in two hours. Three, tops."

Chapter Eight

Thursday, February 12th

We are not out of there in three hours. In fact, Darling keeps us cooling our heels in separate cells for a good four hours before the interrogations start, and they go on for some time. My paper-thin story that I was stopping by to arrange an interview with Higgs is rightly viewed with suspicion, given that I picked a lock, snuck into the office, and rifled through his files, all of which are technically felonies. By the time Darling steps into the interview room for a personal talk, I'm getting fed up with the whole process.

"Alright, Stark, let's take it from the top."

"Let's. It's not as though I have actual work to do today. I saved someone's life, from a threat which, if I need to remind you, you officially stated did not exist, and in return I've experienced another fine night as a guest of Everland's finest."

Darling coughs, and sits down across from me. "Alright, fine. You're right, Stark. And you'll probably be thrilled to know that Miss Metcalf refuses to charge you for trespassing, so you're basically in the clear."

I blink. "This is a new tactic. Usually you don't open an interrogation by explaining why someone is not in trouble."

"We just got our preliminary crime scene report. Did you know Higgs was researching shadow control?"

"If I knew, I would have reported it. It's illegal research." Darling gives me a flat look, and I can't help but smile. "I don't trust shadows, Darling. Especially not right now. I promise, I would have warned you if I'd had a shred of evidence. But I did have a few suspicions."

"And you, I assume, have suspicions on who is funding this little operation."

"Quentin Lark, possibly with backing from someone in civil government. He's paid off some port authority people for reasons that may or may not be connected." I shrug. "Again, no evidence."

"So this is why I've been getting reports of Quentin's boys following you around town?"

"In a nutshell."

"Is Quentin involved beyond the funding? There were documents in the lab suggesting Higgs was having an affair with the Lane woman."

"Nelson. Her name was Mercy Nelson."

"Regardless. It all holds together. He was on the verge of a breakthrough, but he couldn't quite control his shadow. Miss Nelson must have broken it off with him, his shadow went after her for revenge, he planted the drugs on her in an attempt to cover his tracks, and then when he found out you were on the way to his office, he tried to unleash it again, and it killed him."

"It's a nice thought, but there's a problem with that."

"You mean Miss Metcalf's claim that Nelson wasn't on the payroll."

"Along with why he called her in to begin with, and why his shadow went after her, but not after me." I shake my head. "Doctor Higgs didn't lose control of anything. Quentin had him killed to keep him from talking to me."

"How could he possibly have known you were on the way?"

"I think he planted a shadow-spy on me."

"Stark, making up words is not going to convince me that you don't need to be locked up for a few days."

"The regulators found a fragment of a shadow on me. They thought it was from the one in the lab, but I know I didn't cross it. Our shadows were facing opposite directions. It must have already been there."

"And it ... what, reported to him? How, exactly?"

"Ask Miss Metcalf. She mentioned using a shadow to explore and report back on things. My guess is it somehow communicates with the main body of the shadow, which is somewhere near Quentin. He's been using my own investigation to find out what he needed to cover up, and I, like an idiot, never saw it coming." I rub my forehead. "I think Higgs and Mercy are both dead because I tracked them down."

"You must be angry."

"Incandescent. How did you guess?"

"I don't think you've ever admitted to making a mistake before. Not to me, at any rate." Darling leans back in his chair. "You do realize that your theory requires Higgs to have actually finished his work."

"Let me guess — none of his files say that's the case."

"Got it in one. Of course, if someone planted some files, they could have removed others. But you're handing me a theory with, once again, not a shred of evidence beyond your gut. And your gut is not a reliable witness."

"So where does that leave us?"

"With you walking out the door. We're holding Miss Metcalf for a while. Officially, it's on suspicion of involvement in forbidden research, but I'm putting her in a reinforced, well-lit cell in case another shadow comes wandering by."

"So you agree with me."

"Like hell I do. I just don't trust tidy cases like these." Darling leans in close. "Listen up, Stark. This case, once again, is about to be closed. I am on my way to the DA's office to argue strenuously against this course of action. I expect to be overruled."

"Quentin does have friends in high places."

"Not high enough to withstand your bull-in-a-china-shop methods." Darling takes a deep breath. "I can't believe that I'm saying this, but you'll find that Miss Metcalf slipped a few files into your possessions. Don't make a fuss about it, but they might help you stay one step ahead of him."

I blink, and then slowly smile. "I'm your stalking-goat, then?"

"I want him brought in, Stark, and you're just the force of chaos to make him mess up enough to lose his protection.

And who knows, maybe I'll get really lucky and you'll get shot in the process."

"Your faith in me is heartwarming. Any chance I could see the rest of your investigation notes, or get the names of the Regulators assigned to the shadow hunt?"

"Stark, I am unhappy enough not dragging you into a cell, let alone giving you confidential information. You started this mess. Finish it."

Well, for Darling, that's practically an apology. I take it gracefully, and let him leave without further comment.

———— «» ————

After being released, I make my way towards the records room. Unfortunately, Constable Dunham spots me coming as she starts out of the room. "No."

"I haven't asked for anything yet."

She waves a finger at me. "Basil, do you know how much trouble I can get in just for talking to you? I'm not giving you the case files."

"Which case?" I ask innocently. "I was just going to ask about those nice Regulators who helped me out earlier tonight."

"Regulator identities are sealed. I don't even know the names myself. The Commissioner probably doesn't know them. Shoo. Get your things, go outside, and talk to your girlfriend."

"Susan, I just … what?"

"Tall lady, blonde, wearing a coat that's way too heavy for around here, sounds American from the accent. She's been waiting outside for half an hour." Susan grins and taps me on the shoulder. "And you told Freddie that you weren't seeing anyone."

"I'm not… why is everyone so interested in my love life?"

"You pry into everything. Stands to reason we'll pry into the one thing we know about you."

"Again, we are not dating."

"Just go outside. We don't have anything useful for you, and I'm not putting my job on the line in order to not help you. I'm this close to finally making detective, and the boys would pounce on a breach like that."

"Fine. See you later, then. And good luck."

Susan gives me a wave, and I give up. If Darling catches me in the record room, leeway or no, I'll be back in a cell so fast my head will spin. Instead, I go to get my personal effects.

"Basil. Hear you've found yourself a girl after all."

"Don't even start, Freddie. Do you have my cane?"

"Freshly cleaned and given the Regulator stamp of approval." Freddie passes me his itemized list of my latest goods. "And your pistol, which you really shouldn't be carrying around, your lighter, wallet, file folder..." He pauses and winks. "Miss Metcalf asked if she could leave it for you. Nice girl." He passes it over. "We made copies in case there was anything incriminating, but it's just a bunch of old notes."

Old notes indeed. "Thank you. Is there any extra salt around?"

Freddie checks under the desk. "I think we have some in the emergency kit, just in case. Worried about getting attacked again?"

"Very."

"Fair." Freddie passes me four small packets of salt. "Here you go. How many days do you think until you stop by again?"

"Hopefully quite a few." I quickly collect my things, stuffing them into various pockets. "But with my luck, I'll be back in here by the weekend."

"I'll have some tea ordered in for you. Say hi to your new girl from me."

"She is not ... you know what, never mind. Have a good night, Freddie."

Adelaide is, indeed, standing outside, wearing a coat that's probably appropriate for a winter in New York, which leaves it a little warm for February in Everland. She raises an eyebrow as she sees me walking up. "You look terrible."

"Lovely to see you too. How did you know I was here?"

"I stopped by your office, and Holly said to try the First Precinct. And so here I am, and here you are. What happened to you?"

"It's a long story. Let's head outside, and I'll tell you the whole thing."

We step outside, and as we stroll down the street I explain the events of the evening, leaving out only one detail. "If I hadn't decided to leave early, it all would have been over by the next morning. Miss Metcalf would have died with Doctor Higgs, and all the evidence would have labeled him the guilty party. Quite neat and tidy. Hold this."

Adelaide takes my walking stick, and leans on it while she waits to see what I'm up to. "You think someone's covering their tracks?"

"It's the only possible situation. Darling disagrees, he thinks that — hah!"

My hands come out of my pockets with two of the salt packets, which I tear open and throw over Adelaide's shadow. She yelps in surprise, taking a step back as her shadow suddenly distends, a spot near its shoulders pinned under the salt as her step rapidly transforms into a leap. It only lasts for a moment, but it's enough for us to be free, and the tiny fragment of shadow can't last on its own. It lets off an almost-silent hiss as it dissolves into the normal pattern of morning light on the pavement.

"What the hell!"

"Quentin's found a new trick," I say grimly. "Who knows how many of these he's spread around. As many as he can produce, I would guess, which could be dozens, or just yours and mine."

"My and your what? Was that some kind of … tiny shadow-monster?"

"A piece of one. I'm hoping that Miss Metcalf's notes will shine some light on it." Adelaide scowls, and I belatedly say, "No pun intended."

"Well, you'd better look at them quickly. Do you have a suit?"

"What? I mean, yes, of course, but why?"

"You're my plus one this evening."

"…to where?"

Adelaide grins. "While you were being dashing and saving lives, I was securing an invitation to the mayor's gala fundraiser tonight. I'm told that everyone who is anyone will be there."

I fight back the urge for a stiff drink. "And you want to see if anyone panics when they see me?"

"That, and who sidles up to try for some conversation. Everyone who matters already knows that I'm working with you. That ship has sailed. But I don't actually know all the social structures around here."

"That high up, neither do I."

"I'd still feel more comfortable having you there, especially if there are murderous magical shadows on the loose. And I do think that you'll be a great distraction."

"What is it with people using me as a distraction today?" I wave my hand in defeat. "You win, Adelaide, I'll go. But only because I enjoy hors d'oeuvres. And because I think Quentin might be there, and I want to see if us being shadow-free scares him half as much as it should."

"Do you think he knows?"

"I have no idea. It really depends on how the system works. If the things have to report in, it could be hours before he figures it out. If they're basically magic radios, he might have known before you did." I shrug. "One more thing to find out tonight. We're making progress."

"Are we? Two people dead, and mobsters out to kill us both."

"All we need now," I say seriously, "is proof. Shall I pick you up at six?"

"Better make it five. It's an early dinner."

"Then, madam, I will see you tonight."

———— «❍» ————

"Holly, you would not believe the day that I've been having," I say as I step into the office.

"It's eleven a.m., and you didn't pick up Glimmer this morning, so I think I probably would."

I take a moment to glower at her. Holly is over by the filing cabinet, filling out what looks like an expense report. There's a check sitting next to it, and a small bundle of case notes. "Divorce case?"

"Closed. Another tragic tale, but I think they'll work it out."

"Your faith in mankind, as ever, fills me with awe. Did you bring Glimmer in, then?"

"Oh, yeah. I stopped by your house first thing. There's tea steeping, by the way."

I cross over to the kitchen and pour a cup, and then check the cupboards. "Where's the brandy gone?"

"You gave it to Mom to cook with."

"What? That can't be right. When was that?"

"November, I think."

"Damn, that's right." I consider. "Gin?"

"Used the last of it after the Hawthorne case. When you sobered up, you told me not to buy any more because, and I quote, 'it's a bad idea to keep it within arm's reach on cases like that'."

"Well, I've changed my mind." I add some milk to my tea instead. "I've had a rough night."

"I know the feeling."

There is a very short pause as we both realize what she just said. I lean back out to look into the office. Holly, with a guilty expression, is suddenly hard at work on the accounts.

"Holly," I say slowly, "were you on a stakeout last night?"

"Most of it."

"Didn't I tell you to lay low?"

"Who's going to find me in an old motel room under an assumed name? If I'd been any lower I'd have been anonymous. Speaking of which, have you seen Amaryllis around? Apparently she left some kind of cryptic note to her family and vanished into the woods."

"She'll be fine. Don't change the subject. Did you tell your mother?"

"Basil, I don't even live with my mother. I don't tell her everything."

"What about your father?"

"Not a chance."

"So you knew they wouldn't approve."

"Big words, given that you were busy … what, breaking into Quentin's offices?"

I cough. "No."

"Someone else's offices?"

"Alright, we have both made mistakes. Congratulations on closing your first case." I notice the lack of a high-energy fairy bombarding me. "If you brought Glimmer in, where is she?"

"Um. Could be anywhere, really."

"Holly, you are a terrible liar." I walk over to the kitchen window, which is slightly open. If Glimmer is around, and Holly isn't worried, it means that someone else is here. And that someone is … "Todd?"

Todd Malcolm, hulking on the fire escape, gives me an embarrassed look. He's wearing the same jacket I saw him in last time, and he looks like he hasn't slept recently. Glimmer is sitting on his shoulder, looking incredibly amused, and sucking on a caramel as big as her head. "Uh, hi, Mr. Stark. She can eat sugar, right?"

"Why are you hiding out the window? You're a client, you can stop by at any—" I break off. I look over to Holly, who looks guiltier than ever, and back to Todd, who looks about the same. "Holly, could I speak with you in the office for a moment?"

"Uh, sure."

"Mr. Malcolm, wait in the kitchen. You look very uncomfortable out there."

"Uh ... yessir." As Holly and I leave, Todd sheepishly starts the task of getting back through the window.

In the front room, I lean against a desk and give Holly a long look.

"I can explain," she says.

"You went out on a stakeout with *Todd Malcolm*?"

"You said you trust my judgment!"

"I'm revising that opinion!" I throw my arms up. "The man is a drunk. And we know almost nothing about him!"

"He's a big puppy. And he's not the only one who's been having a few too many the last few days." Holly glares at me. "Look, he stopped by to ask about the case, he was worried, I mentioned the divorce thing, and he got kind of protective. I said I'd bring him along to stop him worrying."

"What does he know about stakeouts?"

"Well, for a start he's got about two hundred pounds of muscle and a great glower. Have you seen him glower? It's amazing."

"Yes, I've seen him glower, when he was introducing my face to the pavement."

"Oh. Right. I think he really is sorry about that."

"Holly, you decided to spend a day alone, in a small, isolated space, with a total stranger, whose only qualification was that he once tried to beat your boss half to death in a violent rage. I cannot even begin to describe what a monumentally bad idea that was. What were you thinking?"

Holly takes a deep breath, and her fist clenches. "I was thinking that he was a guy who was so loyal that he was willing to go up against Douglas Schaefer to protect a friend. A guy who pulled together his entire life savings just to find out how she died."

"His … what?"

"See? You didn't even check. He's a good guy, Uncle Basil. You need more good guys in your life, and I think he'd like to hang around. Besides, it kept him from going after Quentin, and I figured you'd be glad I had some backup if any of Quentin's goons came after me."

Before I can say anything else on that front, there is a sharp rap on the front door. I groan softly. "This conversation is not over."

"You'd better believe it isn't," Holly snaps. She takes a deep breath, puts on a smile, and walks over to the door. "It's open — oh, now what?"

"Out of the way, little girl." Constable Daggett pushes his way past Holly, looking around the room. Glimmer lets out a low snarl, and I motion to Holly, who nods and moves to stand next to her before she does something ill-advised. "Stealing folks' stuff, Stark? Pretty low, even for you."

"What—" I break off, and rub my forehead. "Yancy filed a police report, didn't he?"

"He very much did. And as I was lucky enough to be on the case, I thought I would come down and have a look around."

"Did you? You realize that the map he is accusing me of stealing isn't even real."

"A-ha!" Daggett wags a finger at me. "Admission of guilt. I didn't tell you what you stole."

"You didn't have to. He came by in person to accuse me a few days back. Threatened to call the police. I didn't think he was stupid enough to actually do it." If it had been any officer who didn't have a grudge against me, it would have been nothing, so of course I got the one who still wanted revenge.

"Well, he did, unluckily for you. So I think I'd better have a look around."

"I think you'd better not." I step into his path as he walks forward, and glare down at him. "This is a private office,

Constable, and it is filled with confidential information. Unless you have a warrant, and I know that you don't because you haven't snidely waved it at me, you don't have the authority to look around my private files. And besides which, and I really don't know why this question isn't being answered, what possible motive do I have for this alleged theft? As previously noted, the map is fake. Unless you believe in Captain Hook's buried treasure?"

"Of course not. But there's plenty of reasons to steal a fake map."

"Name one."

"Fraud. Maybe you were supposed to be part of this con, and the next step involved 'selling' this guy's map back to him, only he got wise, so you started playing dumb."

"Constable, if you can convince Mr. Yancy that his map is fake, you will have my eternal gratitude. I might even give you a present."

"Or maybe you know the con artist, and stole the map to cover for them."

"Or maybe Mr. Yancy dropped the damn thing in a cab. Get out of my office before I get annoyed."

"And do what?"

"Ironically, Constable, I will call the police. You don't have a leg to stand on and you know it."

"Unless you get violent," Daggett sneers. "And who's going to know better?"

"Well, Holly, for one. If you want to explain to Darling how you barged into my office and then I took a thoroughly unprovoked swing at you, which I presume ends with you heroically wrestling me to the ground and calling for backup, you should be ready for the firestorm that will result. It would not be my first brush with the law."

For a moment, the two of us stand there, eyes locked, and then a ruckus from the kitchen draws our attention. Daggett is only a few steps behind me as I rush over to the kitchen to find Todd Malcolm, leaning by the fire escape window, and Frank Yancy, caught halfway through it. Todd has Yancy in a headlock, and Yancy is clearly trying to avoid swearing up a streak.

"Caught a burglar, Mr. Stark," Todd says blandly.

"Mr. Yancy. What a thrilling surprise. Mr. Malcolm, if you would pull him in?"

Todd does so, easily. Soon, Yancy is standing next to him, clothes rumpled from his impromptu wrestling match, rubbing his neck while his eyes dart between Todd, Daggett, and me.

"Well, well," Daggett grins. "Looks like this just turned into a crime scene."

"What?" Yancy sputters. "But you said—"

"Shuddup!" Daggett moves to smack Yancy, takes a look at Todd's glower, and decides against it. "I said I'd look into it. Said it was a real shame. Didn't say you should take the law into your own hands."

"Mr. Yancy, did Constable Daggett, perchance, indicate to you the exact time that he would be paying my office a visit, along with a possible location from which you could enter it unnoticed?"

"Well, uh…" Frank bites his lip, looking between the two of us.

"And let me guess. He assured you that there really was a lost treasure. I'm afraid you've been used, Mr. Yancy."

Yancy looks baffled. "But he's a cop," he protests.

"A cop who hates me." I turn to Daggett. "Should make for good headlines — 'Police Officer Commits Burglary'. I can't wait to see what Darling has to say about it."

"Your word against mine."

"My word, and Todd's, and Holly's, and I suspect Mr. Yancy's if you try to arrest him. But I really don't have time for the rigmarole. I have somewhere to be tonight. So tell you what — if you get the hell out of my office, and don't come back, I will forget this whole idiotic escapade happened."

"But—" Yancy starts.

"Out!" I yell.

The kitchen empties rapidly. Daggett is the first out the door, without even looking back. Yancy hesitates by the coat rack, turning back. "This just proves you're crooked, Stark. I'm going to figure out where you put my map, and I…"

Todd cracks his knuckles ominously. Yancy gets the hint, and bolts.

I tap Todd on the shoulder as he moves to follow them. "Where do you think you're going?"

"Uh, out?"

"Not you." I pull him back into the main office, which would be laughable if he weren't confused enough to go along with it. "We haven't finished discussing the whole stakeout situation."

"Uh, gee, Mr. Stark, I'm really sorry. I mean, I didn't think you'd be too happy, but Holly said it would be okay..."

"Holly is very convinced of her ability to sway me. Although, I notice, not so convinced that she didn't try to have you hide on my fire escape."

Holly grins. "I was kind of hoping to have the talk with you first. It seemed easier. Maybe write you a letter."

I rub my forehead. "Young people. The lot of you will be the death of me. Right, Todd, you might as well have some tea."

"You mean ... you're not kicking me out?" Todd's face lights up.

"No, you can stay. You did good with Daggett, and Lord knows I want to belt him more often than not. I'll fill you in on where we're at, and we can discuss strategies. Oh, wait, first things first. Both of you, stand over there."

They do, giving each other confused looks, as I pull out the salt from the kitchen and toss it on the floor. Neither Todd nor Holly's shadow reacts to the sprinkling of salt, and I gesture them back to their seats.

"Everything okay, Mr. Stark?"

"Just give him a minute," Holly says. "Whenever he does something totally bizarre, he has some reason for it."

"The reason, in this case, is dark magic — Holly, stop laughing. I'm serious."

"Sorry. Sorry." Holly is still giggling. "It just sounds so melodramatic."

"A man named Conrad Higgs invented a way of controlling shadows. He was killed by a shadow last night. It also nearly killed his assistant, and me."

"Oh."

"Hang on, a shadow?" Todd is frowning. "So he's a stitcher?"

"No, he is a corpse. His killer is a stitcher."

"I kinda thought stitchers weren't real."

"They weren't," I say grimly. "Someone got ideas." Briefly, I lay out the situation as it stands, while preparing tea. Todd's face clouds over as I explain my findings, and he looks like he's getting ready to explode. For her part, Holly is listening silently. "I don't have any evidence I can present to the police — yet. But it seems clear that Quentin is responsible. Once I figure out who's backing him on this, we might be able to bring him down."

"It's got to be someone more important than Sanderson," Holly points out. "He's involved, but he's just a security chief, and a recent one. He hasn't had time to have influence."

"Why don't we corner Sanderson somewhere and find out?" Todd suggests. "He's not Lark. He doesn't have bodyguards."

"He doesn't need them. He's an experienced security officer with political protection, an official reason to carry a gun, and a demonstrated desire to use it on me. If by chance we survived that, what do we do next?"

"Uh … find the guys he tells us about?

"Hard to do from jail. Do you think Sanderson wouldn't go directly to the police?"

"Uh." Todd mulls over that one for a bit. "Damn. So what do we do?"

"We review these files." I pull out the thick pile of files that Miss Metcalf left for me. "I have a few hours until I need to run home to prepare for my dinner tonight, and there might be something in here that we can use."

"I dunno, Mister Stark. I'm not really a research sort of guy."

"That's fair, and honestly, I would rather pass all of this by Niall, but he's at work, and I'm not taking this lot to Second Star. God knows what they would do with it. Besides, we don't need the exact mechanics; we need somewhere to go with this stuff. You know people, especially people that Mercy was spending time with. You might recognize a name that Holly or I wouldn't, or something Mercy once said could trigger a memory. We'll each take a pass over everything, but every eye on the page is a help."

Todd looks dubious, but he takes his share of the papers. I grab the tea while Holly gets cups, and we spend the next hour reading over Higgs' notes. It's a hell of a chore. Most of the notes weren't meant for public consumption — they're full of shorthand, self-reminders, and impossibly convoluted scientific jargon, alongside various administrative notes and cost estimates, and they aren't in any kind of chronology. I'm pouring over a confusing series of sketches for an 'ectoumbric modulation generator' and trying to make heads or tails of it when Todd abruptly speaks up. "Say, uh, if there's something about dead guys, is that important?"

"Dead guys?" I look up.

"Yeah. There's a whole thing here about, uh, harvesting 'cadavers'. That's dead guys, right?"

"Yes it is. Pass me that?" Todd hands the pages over, and I give them a quick scan. "Oh dear."

Holly puts down her papers. "What is it?"

"A lead, I think. Higgs was theorizing here that there could be a grace period between a person's death and their shadow losing all of its strength. If you could detach it during that period, it would be a blank slate. No living body means no dark desires. You just need to imprint a desire on the thing, and you can get it to do what you want."

"Okay, that's creepy, but how does it help us?"

"Everland doesn't have a surfeit of corpses, and a corpse without a shadow gets noticed. Higgs would have had to rob a morgue to get those bodies, or at least bribe an attendant. That could give us some proof about who he was working with."

"That does sound like a lead." Holly walks over to crane over my shoulder at the papers. "Does it say what it means by 'imprinting'?"

"Not a word. I think some pages are missing." I smile. "Which is another hint that this is the right path. Good work, Todd."

Todd blushes with pride. "You'd have seen it too, Mr. Stark."

"But you saw it first." I stand up, looking at my watch. "Alright, I think it's time to split up. Holly, take Todd down to the morgue and see if you can find anything out. Grab some of our bribe money from petty cash. Then see if you can meet up with Niall after work and have him take a look over those papers. And I hope I don't need to say this but..."

"Watch out for Quentin's people?"

"And for mysterious shadows. Take a few knives with you."

"And while we're dodging monsters and digging up clues, you'll be out on a fancy date with Adelaide?"

Todd stares at us. I glare at Holly. "It's not a date."

"I bet it's a date. Do you even have a suit?"

"Of course I have a suit. Everyone has a suit."

"I don't have a suit," Todd volunteers.

"Thank you, Mr. Malcolm."

"Sorry."

"Look, the point is, this is not a date. It is an investigation. I will be wearing a suit, because we are going to be mingling with the upper crust."

"Who will run away when they see you," Holly mutters.

"Who will probably not even recognize me."

"With that haircut? They'll recognize you."

"There is nothing wrong with my hair!" Since I seem to be losing control of this conversation, I decide to beat a hasty retreat. "The point is, I will be at work tonight. Come on, Glimmer."

"You're taking Glimmer to a fancy-dress party?"

"What, she doesn't have a nice dress?"

Holly just looks at me seriously, while Glimmer points out that her dress is very nice. I glance over at her, and while it does have a certain homespun chic to it, Holly might have a point. "Fine, we will get another dress. People love fairies."

"It's your party," Holly says with a shrug. "Glimmer, don't let him do anything too stupid."

While Glimmer is giving Holly what I desperately hope is a salute, I look at the two of them. "Be careful, both of you. We're at two people killed, and at least two more attempts, and things are going to get worse before this is over."

Holly nods. "Nothing we haven't handled before."

"It might be."

"Don't worry, Mr. Stark," Todd says. "I'll take care of her."

"Great. That just leaves her to take care of you."

Todd's brow furrows, and Holly grabs him by the arm. "Come on, I'll explain on the way."

⸺ «» ⸺

I go home and get myself and Glimmer ready to go. Glimmer is delighted to be going to a party, and swears up and down that she'll be on her absolute best behavior. I don't actually know if I can trust that, but a small package of sugared crackers should keep her occupied if the party gets to be too much, and people really do think a 'tame' fairy is a sensation. The only question is whether she'll be willing to play at tame for long enough.

Luckily, I have a small stock of clothing that is appropriately fairy-shaped, a legacy of a few companions over the years. Glimmer is too enthralled by the goods to question their provenance, and while I have a careful shave and take a few minutes to trim some loose edges from my hair, she debates furiously between a sparkling red, backless dress and a leaf-green suit. She ultimately chooses to mix and match — I catch her about to take a knife to the dress, and spend a few minutes hemming it for her so that it stops above the knee and she can wear the suit pants underneath. We take a look in the mirror and agree that the result suits her, and I go to change into my own suit.

When I come out, Glimmer is sitting on the head of my walking stick, checking her hair in the mirror. She gives me a wide grin, hops into the air, and settles on my shoulder, before gesturing to the door. I laugh, and take her lead.

The driver of the taxi I call almost balks at having a fairy flying free in his cab, but a couple of dollars wins him over and we're on our way. We reach Adelaide's hotel with time to spare, and I decide that it's better to send the cabbie on his way and grab another for the next trip, rather than leave the meter running. Taxi dispatched, we're on our way to the lobby.

Jimmy Liu's on duty again tonight, and he lets out a low whistle when he sees the two of us. "Looking swell, Mr. Stark. And who's this little lady?"

Glimmer gives him an elaborate bow, and shares her good opinion of Jimmy's taste.

"This is my friend Glimmer," I say. "She's my plus one. Which, given that I am Adelaide's, should make for some good conversation when we arrive, but I think Glimmer is worth it."

"I'd agree. Heck of a unique look. You'll be asking for Miss Evans, then?"

"Indeed. I'm a little early. She probably isn't quite ready yet."

"On the contrary, Mr. Stark." I turn to find Adelaide stepping out of the phone booth. "I've been here five minutes."

"Once again, you challenge my expectations." My suit is nice enough, but Adelaide leaves me feeling distinctly underdressed. Her dress is slender and midnight blue, dotted with tiny silver threads that sparkle like starlight, and complemented by a wide-brimmed hat. A light scarf and long gloves complete the look, although I do notice that her heels are noticeably short. She catches my glance, and smiles sheepishly. "Just in case we need to run away from someone murderous tonight. Hanging around you, I'm not ruling it out."

"Probably wise."

"And you brought ... Glimmer, was it?" Glimmer nods, and Adelaide reaches out her index finger for Glimmer to shake. "I don't mind the company, but..."

"She'll be the toast of the town," I assure her. "Do we want to wait around here for a bit, or crash the party early?"

"Oh, we're already fashionably late." Adelaide takes my arm, and the two of us start walking in a stately manner towards the door, with Glimmer perched in my hat-brim. I'm gratified to see more than one person stop to stare at the three of us as we stroll out the front door. "Any luck with those files?"

"Some. I have associates working on it."

"Associates?"

"Holly and a friend of hers," I admit quietly. "But associates sounds better."

Adelaide raises a hand, and the first taxi down the street stops to pick us up. This time, the cabby doesn't even raise a fuss about Glimmer, too busy trying to figure out who we are. "Where to, folks?"

"Hillman's Row, Number three."

I choke. "What?"

The cabby gives me an odd look, but Adelaide nods to him and the car starts up. "What's wrong?"

"I'm suddenly wondering if bringing Glimmer was a good idea." Glimmer looks up sharply, and I give her an apologetic look. "You didn't tell me our host was the Old Man himself."

"The Old Man?"

"George Ellery Hale. Second Star's president."

"I know who George Hale is. Everyone in the world knows who George Hale is. He founded the National Research Council, invented the starfinder compass, worked with John Darling to find Neverland, and proved the existence of the dreaming sea. He's a legend. What's with the 'old man' business?"

"Hale is one of the only immigrants to really benefit from the island's youthful properties." I shrug. "It's a nickname. Hale was in his mid-fifties when he first came here, and that was over twenty-five years ago. But he's still running the company, going strong. Doesn't look a day over sixty. Someone started calling him that during the war, and it stuck."

"Oh. And that address is his house?"

"You didn't know that?"

She shrugs sourly. "I got the invitation from the mayor's deputy. He just said that it was a political function. I assumed it was the mayor's house."

"It probably never occurred to him that someone might not know the Old Man's address."

"What does any of that have to do with Glimmer?"

"Let's just say that Second Star's attitude towards the locals usually falls somewhere between 'cordial' and 'avaricious'. Fairies don't have the same protections that the beasts and mermaids got; they're considered a potential menace. Not by me, Glimmer, stop glaring. The point is, they don't have protection against Second Star researchers scooping them up to try and develop a better flight formula."

Glimmer shivers, and pushes herself farther into my hat. I wince. "I'm sorry, Glimmer, I didn't mean to scare you. We'll be fine. I'll be watching your back, and you'll be watching mine, right?"

Glimmer mutters agreement, but she doesn't come out of the hat.

Adelaide leans in carefully. "Is this really a concern?" she whispers.

"Probably not," I admit. "The Regulators turn over any unclaimed flora and fauna they collect to Second Star. City contract. They have more fairies than they know what to do with, and they honestly treat them better than most. It just rubs me the wrong way."

We sit in silence for a few moments after that, but fortunately we're starting up the Hill, and there's enough to distract Adelaide and Glimmer both. I look out the window at the passing houses, and let myself be distracted as well. For all that I've been here my whole life, I don't often have reason to come up Hillman's Row.

The mansions on Hillman's Row aren't just large, although they are certainly that. I think the smallest one we pass is three stories tall and as wide as a small city block, with grounds to match. No, what truly sets the rich of Everland apart from the common folk is their access to the dwindling magic that the island is known for, and nearly every house feels the need to advertise. We pass a house lit entirely by shimmering rainbow fireflies, a kaleidoscope dancing along the eaves through carefully designed glass tubes, sending a cascade of rainbows across quartz beacons set along the path. Another is made entirely from island ironwood, a log cabin exaggerated to impossible proportions, with vines and ivy holding the façade together and window shutters made of giant leaves — I suspect there's real glass hidden behind them, if only to stop winter wind, but the illusion is phenomenal. Adelaide points to a smaller —well, smaller by the standards of Hillman's Row— building, set back from the road, with a driveway that reflects the moonlight with a deep orange hue, like roiling lava in the ground. "How do they do that?"

"One of the rarer gemstones you find on the island. Changes light as it passes through."

"It's a little ominous," Adelaide says, looking at the house beyond the seemingly-flaming path. It is lit in the same way, although in shades of purple and blue, a Victorian mansion in stone and brick.

"I'll give him this much. Schaefer has a sense of the appropriate."

Adelaide turns to stare at me. "That's…"

"Douglas Schaefer's home, yes. He had it built about ten years back. Hillman's Row is reserved for the richest, most well-placed men in the city. Where else did you expect him to be?"

"Fair enough. I wonder how Mr. Hale's home will compare?"

"You might be disappointed."

After the more elaborate homes up the way, the Old Man's house is anticlimactic. It looks more appropriate to a New England home than an Everland manor, smaller than any of the houses around it and without the magical frills. The house's one concession to uniqueness is barely visible from the front—well, not at night, anyway. Specifically, there is an observatory that takes up the back half of the property, complete with a telescope that would prompt complaints from the neighbors if Hale hadn't helped write the zoning bylaws. This high up the Hill, it's mostly immune to the faint glow from the streetlights below.

"It's nice," Adelaide says, as we step out of our taxi. I pause to pay the man, looking around at the limos parked along the side of the house, their drivers already relaxing wherever the servants hide out. "I don't know what I expected, but this is actually peaceful."

"It was one of the first European houses built on the island," I say, as we walk up the steps to the front door. "Hale tried to set the tone for the Hill, but he didn't quite manage it. Probably helped, though. I shudder to think what things would have looked like around here if he'd been more flamboyant."

The doorman gives Glimmer a suspicious look as he checks for Adelaide's name, but he allows the three of us through the doors without making a fuss. I hand my coat and hat to a charming attendant, holding onto my walking stick, and Adelaide does the same with her hat and shawl. She leans in close to me as we walk into the hall. "Is there a procedure for this, or do we just wing it?"

"I don't get invited to many fancy parties anymore," I whisper back. "Let's just be charming and a little bit obtuse, and see who gets annoyed. And keep an eye out for anyone having a chat with Lark."

"Adelaide, my dear, so good of you to make it." The deputy mayor, Shaun O'Halloran, appears out of nowhere, taking her hand and kissing the air just above. "And you've brought Basil Stark with you. How nice."

"Mr. O'Halloran," I say, giving him a slight bow. "It's been some time."

"Three years." O'Halloran can't quite repress a shudder. "I'd heard you were giving Adelaide a tour of the... poorer districts... but I didn't realize the two of you had grown close."

"Well, you know, we share certain business interests."

O'Halloran looks between the two of us, brow furrowed. "Right..." he says uncertainly. "Well, I hope you're not planning on causing another scene. I've brought my cook here to work the party, and he still gets nervous around clams."

Adelaide laughs. "Well, that sounds like a wonderful story. Basil, why don't you get us drinks, while Shaun tells me all about it."

I blink at her in surprise, and she tilts her head towards the buffet table. Following her gaze, I nod slightly. "Of course, Adelaide. Mr. O'Halloran."

O'Halloran all but shoos me away, and Adelaide rolls her eyes at me over his shoulder. I manage to avoid a laugh, as I slip across the room to where Tim Sanderson in engaged in a quiet, but intense conversation with another familiar figure. Sadly, before I can quite reach them, she spots me coming. "Basil Stark, as I live and breathe. I didn't expect to see you here."

"Ms. Tate. I didn't realize that you mingled with the upper crust. Or, for that matter, that you did, Mr. Sanderson."

"Please, call me Stephanie. This is a party, after all. And you've met Tim, I take it?"

"We're acquainted. Oh, and the little lady currently trying to make off with a shrimp puff is Glimmer. Say hello, Glimmer."

Glimmer makes a rude gesture. Stephanie almost giggles.

"If you'll excuse me," Sanderson says stiffly, grabbing a glass of wine and storming off. There is a moment's pause.

"I knew that you had that effect on people, but I've never seen it happen so quickly," Stephanie says, with a hint of admiration. "What did you do to upset him so badly?"

"I feel like you already know the answer to that."

"You might be surprised, Basil. I mean, I know it has something to do with Quentin's secret games, but beyond that..." Stephanie shrugs. "He isn't even here tonight, you know. Sent me to wave the flag."

"I'm sure that you're a champion, but it seems like a waste of your talents."

"Oh, I don't mind. It's a chance to get to know people, and this is a wonderful vintage. Is it true that you threatened to kill him?"

"Absolute slander. I only warned him about what would happen if he kept after me, and he got all nervous. Poor man gets flustered so easily."

"Now, there's a story. Dramatic, to the point, but there are all sorts of depths and ellipses lurking in the words. Suits you." Stephanie takes a long sip of wine. "I don't suppose I could persuade you to give me the whole story."

"Ask Quentin. I'm sure his version is more entertaining."

"We're on the same side, Basil. At least, I assume that we are. You don't make it easy for someone to figure out where your loyalties lie."

"My loyalties lie against the people who are committing murders."

"Must be terribly lonely. It seems like everyone's committing murders these days."

"I get by." I pour two glasses of wine. "I have to admit, I'm more than a little curious. What makes you think that we're on the same side?"

"Quentin has been a little ... aggressive, lately. I'm sure that you've heard. I'm a loyal sort of person, Basil. Quentin is my immediate boss, but I'm loyal to Douglas first. I'm getting the feeling that Quentin might not be."

"Just now?"

"Don't be mean."

"If you're so loyal to Douglas, and you think Quentin has other plans, why the elaborate attempts to chase me away in the past?"

"It's my job, Basil. I keep problems from reaching Quentin, and I help keep him in check. You, however, are a problem in every sense of the word, and since you came on the scene he's been making bigger moves by the day. There are only two ways that can end — either you go away, and he calms down, or you don't, and ... well." She shrugs. "I don't think you're going away, and I don't think Quentin is going to keep his calm. That makes this an irreconcilable difference, which means that my job has just become controlling the fallout. Which, in turn, means that I'm willing to trade some information with you if it will make both of our lives … easier."

"Great. How many of Lark's secrets are you willing to spill?"

"What are you looking for?"

"A list of associates would be a strong start."

"And set you on their trails? That sounds very much like the opposite of controlling the fallout," Stephanie says mildly, tapping me lightly on the arm. "You're going to have to be a lot more specific if you want something from me. And before you get any ideas — you can follow me around all night, if you like. I talk to everyone."

"Fine, then, just to play along. What's the deal with Sanderson?"

"Ah, now he is an interesting one. I assume you know that Quentin got him his position at the port."

"I'd guessed, although I don't know what strings he pulled to do it."

"Well, Sanderson was a loyal fellow, for quite a while. The last few days, he's gone rogue. I don't know what the exact trigger was, but I happened to be at the restaurant Wednesday night when he came in, and I thought he wasn't going to be coming out again."

"Right after Higgs died," I mutter.

"What?"

"Ask Quentin."

"You say that an awful lot, Basil. The point is, there is no deal with Sanderson. Not anymore. As I understand it, Quentin spent most of today running through Sanderson's men, figuring out which ones were on his side and which were ready to flip. It's bad news all around. The last thing that we need is a war on the docks."

"So you were hoping to calm him down just now?"

"Hoping, yes. Until you showed up and scared him off, I thought I might have a chance. What did you do to him?"

"I got too close," I say grimly. "I don't suppose you'd be willing to tell me which way Sanderson's guards are going to fall."

"I would love to, Basil. It would mean that I know." Stephanie steps away. "All that I know is, I wouldn't want to be on the docks tomorrow night."

"You think there'll be a fight?"

"I guarantee it. So thank you for that."

"I'm not the one playing with fire, Stephanie. But thank you for the information."

"You're welcome. My turn. What does any of this have to do with that reporter you brought with you?"

"Smuggling," I say with a shrug.

"Funny. If you don't know, you can say so."

"I'm serious, but you should already know that. Quentin started all of this because he was worried about what Adelaide would dig up. He killed one of her contacts, planted a false one in her path, and then tried to scare me off the trail. And all because someone told her they could spill the beans about some smuggling."

"Well, that doesn't seem likely," Stephanie says. "Are you sure this dead contact was telling the truth?"

"Enough to be killed for it."

"Fair enough. Do you know the name of this mystery contact that Quentin was so afraid of, despite the fact that there is no smuggling operation in the city big enough to resort to murder over?"

I consider the situation for a moment. The truth might be worth the show. "She was going by Victoria Lane at the time."

Stephanie chokes on her wine. A few people standing nearby turn to look at us, and she swallows quickly and steps in, hissing softly. "You cannot be serious."

"Deadly serious."

"You think Quentin Lark murdered his boss' girl?"

"I do."

"Schaefer would tear him apart. They'd be fishing pieces of him out of the harbor right through Labor Day."

"Good reason for him to be worried, then, isn't it?"

"And you haven't gone to Douglas about this because...?"

"I have a number of reasons for that. Maybe you can figure them out. Have a good evening, Ms. Tate."

I turn to leave, and find myself face to face with the Old Man.

"Ah, Basil. It's been some time, hasn't it?"

I glance back to Stephanie for support, just in time to see her slipping away with her drink. Glimmer, for her part, has winged her way across the room and is now sitting cheerfully on Adelaide's shoulder. She spots me looking and gives me a little wave. Traitor.

"Mr. Hale. Over eight years, I believe. You're looking well."

It's true, too. He's almost bald, with short-trimmed, white hair around the base of his skull, he still has his large, round glasses, and he insists on wearing a mustache that's twenty years out of date, but he's as fit and healthy-looking as the last time we met. He's aging so well that it seems more than a little unfair, which I suppose is ironic coming from me.

"Fresh sea air and plenty of exercise," he says seriously. "Keeps the darkness at bay, a day at a time. But then, you look much the same, as well."

"Kind of you to say." I can't think of anything better to add. I almost glance around to see if I'm about to be violently evicted, but manage to restrain myself.

"I heard that you had some bother last night."

"News travels quickly."

"Only to me, my boy. I was wondering if you would come tonight. When I heard that an invitation had been issued to that reporter — what was her name?"

"Adelaide Evans. I'll introduce you."

"Oh, no need. I prefer to avoid interviews. But I thought you might make an appearance, as well. Always willing to tweak my nose."

"If you'd prefer, I could always go."

Hale looks at me seriously. "Still holding a grudge, Basil?"

"No, Mr. Hale. I don't blame you for anything. I just don't like your work. Are you?"

"Holding a grudge? No, I don't suppose so. It was a different time. In war, we are called upon to do what we must to protect our countries, and I am proud of what Everland accomplished for the Allied cause."

"But the defense contracts are still in place."

"True, but more refined. Take Conrad Higgs, for example. Poor man never saw the dangers of his work, and what happened?" Hale shakes his head. "I would prefer not to have government contracts at all, to be honest. I have my own projects to interest me. But one must pay the bills however one can."

"Let's take Doctor Higgs, yes. Where do you think he was getting his equipment from?"

There is a brief pause. "I see what you're insinuating, Basil, but I won't rise to the bait. Higgs was duly removed from work for breaching ethical boundaries. I realize you would feel quite vindicated if I were involved with this whole mess, but I can assure you that Second Star was not involved in any research that Higgs might have undertaken after he left our employ. You'll have to look elsewhere for your culprit."

"What was he like?"

"Higgs?" Hale takes a drink from a passing waiter as he thinks back. "We never much got along, to be honest. Too brash, much too sure of himself. Fancied himself a light of reason in a benighted world. Oh, he was friendly and encouraging – as long as you agreed with his theories. Happy to share credit, too. But disagree with him, and the gloves were off. He came in during our wartime expansions, but he was never quite going to fit in at Second Star."

"And he was working on shadow-stitching?"

"I suppose Doctor Williams told you that. We looked into it, during the war. Think about it — a shadow holds all of a man's secret desires, his thoughts and beliefs. You can learn a lot from that. That was the first thought. We started by working on ways to communicate with shadows. We thought we might be able to have a conversation, Basil. That was all."

"Didn't work out so well, I take it."

"No. Much too dangerous. Hard on the volunteers, and hard on the researchers. We had injuries. No deaths, but it seemed to only be a matter of time. I mothballed the project, moved our efforts into other paths, and by the end of the war shadow research had been ruled illegal."

"Which didn't stop Higgs."

"As I said, Higgs couldn't stand it when someone told him he was wrong. He kept working on the project. Hired dock workers who could keep their mouths shut as volunteers, moved

slowly. He thought he was being careful." Hale looks disgust-
ed. "But there was an accident. One of the workers died."

"And yet nothing made the news."

Hale has the good grace to look embarrassed. "The
man's death was reported on, but no, the exact details were
classified."

"Must be nice to have the papers in your pocket."

"What was I supposed to do, drag ourselves over the
coals? The damage was done, and we were taking steps to
ensure it didn't happen again. Besides, Higgs wasn't lying
to his volunteers. They knew that there were risks, and he
was paying them quite well to take them. There were several
ethical breeches involved, but the penalties for violating
research laws aren't particularly strict. Higgs was removed
from the company, barred from future work with our
affiliates, paid a steep fine, and was disgraced. The last time
I had heard from him, he was working on papers involving
the island's distance properties, and occasionally visiting
the mainland to give lectures on his wartime work, or at least
those elements of it that had been declassified."

"You never change up here, do you?" I shake my head. "I
could have told you that he would keep researching. Anyone
could have."

"I didn't want to badger a man whose life had already
been ruined."

"You didn't want to be reminded of how badly you
messed up, you mean."

"I didn't need to tell you any of this, Basil," Hale says
angrily.

"Then why did you?"

"Because—" Hale breaks off, and sighs. "Because it is my
responsibility. Higgs' research started in my labs."

"I don't suppose you know who his mysterious sponsors
were, then?"

"I'm afraid not. I have my suspicions, of course. There
are people in the local government that feel that Second
Star's time is passing. I hear whispers of 'monopoly' and
'unpatriotic' thrown in my direction, and I've had a few mild
suggestions that we should be spending less time on the

Dreaming Sea projects and more on the Korean war. We put in so much to fight fascism, after all. Why stop now?" Hale looks glummer than ever. "Shadow spies. Just the sort of breakthrough the foreign department would pay handsomely for. Anyone with more greed than common sense could think it was a good idea." He pats me on the shoulder. "I should move on, visit with other guests. This whole thing is tiring, but we do what we must, eh, Basil?"

"We do what we must, Mr. Hale." I give him a bow, which he returns after a moment. "Until we meet again."

Hale moves off, and I rejoin Adelaide. She's ditched O'Halloran somehow, and is in the middle of a crowd of wealthy socialites, sharing some story about New York that's much too far along for me to parse. Most of them are strangers to me, with two exceptions. One young gentleman in the back of the crowd is a former client desperately trying to pretend that we've never met before, and I indulge his embarrassment, but the other is more familiar.

"Mr. Stark," Jack Harding says quietly, stepping over and letting Adelaide continue her tale. "Ms. Evans told me that you were here, but I hardly believed it."

"Mr. Harding. You're looking well."

"You're being polite, but thank you." In truth, Harding looks tired more than anything else, but he offers me one of his vague smiles. "Things have been ... odd ... around the port lately. I wonder if you might have an idea about why?"

"Me?" I ask innocently. "Haven't been by in days."

"It's only that my chief of security keeps vanishing from work, and I'm almost certain I heard him yelling about you over the phone."

"Oh, yes. That." I wince. "Mr. Sanderson and I may have had ... an altercation. Or two. Barely worth mentioning, really. He'll be over them in a heartbeat."

Harding looks dubious. "Really? He didn't sound it. I don't know that I've ever heard him so upset."

"Hm. Well, you know how security people are."

"I don't know that I do," Harding admits. "I let security handle their affairs, and I handle mine. It's safer." He lowers his voice further, leaning in. "It's not about ... you know. Is it?"

"Hard to say, Mr. Harding. Hard to say." I take a step away, before it can seem obvious that he's trying to be subtle, and return my attention to the party as a whole. Adelaide's story is wrapping up, and I allow her to introduce me to the other guests. Given that I don't have much interaction with what passes for high society in Everland, except for those elements of it that are notably corrupt, exceptionally desperate, or historically-minded, this is a novel experience for us all.

"Is it true that you fought the Crocodile?" someone asks.

"Fought is a strong word. I prefer to say that I survived the Crocodile."

"I heard that the Old Man gave orders to his staff for you to be shot on sight."

"Of course not, that would be illegal. And besides, he rescinded the order after — oh, three or four years."

It goes on like that for much longer than I'd prefer, but I play it to the hilt. Finally, we're able to find a moment of peace, while Glimmer is showing off her aerial acrobatics. Adelaide steps close to me. "You never mentioned that you and Hale had a history. Any chance of netting me an interview?"

"Not with the history we have. It's all bad."

"Damn. He doesn't speak to any reporters these days. So what's the story?"

"We had a number of clashes over his ideals, mainly. I don't approve of all of Second Star's ideas about what improving the island means, and he's a starry-eyed cynic who thinks that his science is a perfect cure for a broken world. But our feud is old gossip these days. We mostly avoid each other, and we haven't tussled in years."

"You weren't avoiding each other half an hour ago."

"It seems this investigation has triggered the Old Man's conscience. Or at least his fear of consequences. He was quick to assure me that Second Star wasn't involved, but was notably silent on who was. I don't suppose you've had better luck?"

"Not as much as I'd like. These people are shockingly sheltered, aren't they? Mr. Harding seems nice enough. He mentioned that he knew you?"

"He started this whole thing. Did you mention Sanderson to him?"

"No. Should I have?"

"Given that he's technically Sanderson's boss, I thought he might have spilled something useful."

"I'll follow up with that, then. I noticed you were talking to another lady before Mr. Hale showed up. Is she important?"

"Stephanie Tate. She's one of Quentin Lark's top people."

"So a trail of upset-seeming people talking to her would be a good lead, then."

"Very much so. Do you have them?"

"Very much so." Adelaide grins, and offers her wine glass in a toast. "I was talking to them when you arrived. The three who made their excuses as soon as seemed polite, to be specific. All of them work in the shipping business. One deals mostly with the lumber industry, and the other two ship food and luxury goods to the island, and technology out."

"That does sound like the sort of people we want to be following." I rub my chin. "I'll vanish into the crowd, again. If you seem annoyed enough with me, maybe they'll try to drop some misdirection on you."

"It's worth a try."

We spend the next three hours playing cat and mouse with Stephanie's contacts. They are, in fact, willing to approach Adelaide to 'warn' her about me whenever I'm not around, while I'm busy creating a scene and reminding the political elite that I exist. I do my best not to drink too much, but I'm feeling decidedly tipsy by the time we decide we've gotten what we can. We find Mr. O'Halloran to give our respects, Hale's tradition being to abandon his party at least an hour early, and after Adelaide deftly avoids an attempt at a kiss, we make our way outside to wait for a cab.

Inside the car, we take stock. Glimmer, having tired herself out performing for a very appreciative audience, has gone to sleep in Adelaide's purse, and is snoring softly. Adelaide is looking out the window wistfully. "That was a lovely evening, wasn't it?"

I grunt noncommittally. "Too formal for my taste. All that posing and posturing. I prefer a quiet gathering with a handful of friends. But the food was good, and I did enjoy the company."

"I guess Jessie's is more your speed?"

"Very much so. I spent too much time with the highbrow set in my youth."

Adelaide turns around to stare at me. "I thought you were a pirate in your youth."

"A man isn't born to piracy. Well, I suppose that a man could be born to piracy, but … the point is, I wasn't." I pause. "Why are you looking at me like that?"

"I'm just trying to imagine you as a young, dashing nobleman."

"Oh, don't. Please don't. I wasn't *part* of the highbrow set. I just had to deal with them rather a lot. No, I was solidly middle class. My father wanted me to follow him into accountancy, but a stuffy office seemed like a living hell. Still, I couldn't disgrace him, so I started teaching. It was a step below what he wanted, but several steps above a life on the open road."

"You were a teacher?" Adelaide looks incredulous.

"In the end, my life always seems to revolve around children, doesn't it?" I laugh. "First teaching them, then fighting them, and then raising them. And now it's starting to feel as though I'm back to teaching them, everyone seems so young. But technically I was an usher — oh, what do they call them now … a teacher's aide, I think. It didn't suit me. I ran away, signed up on a sailing ship. Was swept overboard one night, rescued by pirates, made myself useful, and the rest, as they say, is history."

"Your history leaves rather a lot to the imagination."

"I'm not that drunk." I lean back in the seat. "You wouldn't want to hear the rest, anyway."

"Why not?"

"Violence. Cruelty. Sorrow. Poor life choices. Take your pick."

"But you just left your life behind, to go to the sea?"

"I was young and stupid."

"There wasn't anyone you wanted to stay for…?"

"I was young and stupid," I repeat, a little more forcefully than I intended. Damned wine. Even the cabbie gives me a surprised look through the rearview mirror. "Let's discuss something else."

Adelaide gives me a long look, and then nods. "You might be interested to know that one of our three targets — Emil Amsel, I think — made a little slip of the tongue."

"Did he."

"There's a ship coming into the city tomorrow afternoon. Emil mentioned it by mistake, when he was trying to convince me to go to dinner with him."

"He was what?"

"Yes, it was sweet, if a little overbearing. He started to suggest tomorrow, mentioned that it would have to be a late night because he would be coming from a four o'clock meeting and wasn't sure how long it would take, then spent a moment panicking that he'd mentioned the ship at all before laughing off the comment and said that he had his dates mixed up." Adelaide shakes her head. "He was pretty drunk. I doubt he'll even remember making the comment tomorrow morning."

"Now, that is interesting. A ship coming in just before sunset tomorrow could take off again in the middle of the night, rumors of war on the docks, and Quentin is dodging a major chance to press palms with his supporters tonight in order to have some kind of war meeting. With a criminal conspiracy in the midst of being covered up, if there's anything important that needs to be shipped off, now would be the time to do it."

"But how would he have gotten the word out? Radio can't cross the Dreaming Sea."

"The ship is probably coming in on a normal schedule, and there's been a change in plans. It's the only reason that our drunk executive would feel the need to go down in person to explain the situation to the captain."

"Then we can call the police on him!"

"We most certainly can't."

Adelaide blinks. "Why not?"

"Quentin has people on the police force. I don't know exactly which ones. If we call the police, they'll catch the ship, but I'm willing to bet that he's planning to load things onto it this time around, not off. We might round up a few criminals, but it'll be the end of the real investigation." I shake my head. "We can't afford to let that happen."

Adelaide nods reluctantly. "I suppose not."

"You must have evaded the law from time to time on your own investigations."

"In little ways, here and there. Like back at the Jane Arlett. But this is a lot bigger than that. We're talking about murderers, and if we do the wrong thing tomorrow, they might get away."

"Then I suppose we'll just have to not do the wrong thing."

"Thank you, Basil, that's quite helpful."

"Well, it's not as though we have a habit of ... hang on."

The taxi has reached the street of Adelaide's hotel, but instead of finishing the last legs of the journey, it has abruptly turned into a narrow alleyway two blocks from our destination. I raise my eyebrows, and put a hand on my cane. "Time to go."

Before Adelaide can do more than let out a startled yelp, I've grabbed her arm and pushed her door open with my free hand. The two of us tumble out of the now slow-moving cab, which immediately accelerates down the alleyway and out the opposite side. Adelaide lands in a pile of garbage bags, and come up sputtering. "What the hell, Basil!"

I pull her to her feet. "Good shoes for running, you said? Well, we had better ... oh, dear."

The closest end of the alleyway is currently filled with a trio of very large men, one of whom is holding a gun. I look to the end the taxi vanished down, to find three more men closing it off.

Adelaide looks at one end, and then the other. "God damn it. This was turning into such a nice evening."

"I know what you mean." I look the nearest boys up and down, and sigh. "Hello, Jason."

My sparring partner from a few days before gives me a rough nod. "Mr. Stark. Miss Evans." The hand not holding a gun tips his hat to her. "Sorry about this, but the boss wants a word."

"Not a problem. My office is open nine to five."

"We stopped by."

I take a closer look, and can't help smirking. "Ran into trouble?"

"Dunno what you mean."

"Your friend has quite the black eye, and one of the folks advancing on us from behind is limping. And if you'd caught Holly, you'd have opened the conversation by using her as collateral — or, realistically, you'd have just called me with the news instead of resorting to dime-store novel tactics. A fake cabbie? Really?"

"Oh, he's a real cabbie. Pays his dues and everything. The boss just put a bit of a squeeze on him to get you here. He wasn't happy when he found out you were bothering his contacts."

"Stephanie spilled the beans, then."

"None of my business who spilled what," Jason says, gesturing with the gun. He steps towards me. "Drop the cane, and the lady's purse, and then we can go have a little chat. You cause trouble, we're not all going home."

I make a gesture, and Adelaide slowly places her purse on the ground. I let my walking stick fall as well. "Feeling paranoid, are we?"

"You're a fair hand in a fight, Stark. A length of wood like that, maybe you get the wrong idea. Maybe you try something. I'd rather not shoot you down here, if I can avoid it. Jogging is rough on the suits."

"A-ha!"

There's a moment of frantic confusion. Jason's gun vanishes into his jacket, and the goons behind us hesitate in confusion as a man triumphantly strides into the alleyway. "I've got you now, Stark!" The streetlight is in my eyes, and I can't quite make out details, but that voice sounds sickeningly familiar.

I squint at the figure. "Yancy?"

Jason takes a step towards the silhouette, putting a hand on his chest. "Hang on, pal, we're having a conversation here, so maybe you should just keep on walking."

"Oh, you'd like that, wouldn't you? Don't worry, ma'am, you're safe now!" Yancy nods authoritatively to Adelaide, who is staring at him in confusion, and then turns back to me. "You and your goons won't hurt the lady, Stark!"

"Wha... *my* goons?"

"*His* goons?" Jason echoes.

"Don't play dumb! I know that you're trying to con this lady. Selling her fake stories about Everland. Maybe even trying to convince her that you've found my treasure! When I saw your boys hanging around the hotel, I knew that something was up, and surprise, surprise, here you are!"

"Wait, wait. You were ... waiting at the hotel?"

"Well, yes, obviously." Yancy looks a bit deflated.

"Why?"

"To tell her about you! National Geographic would pay well to be on site when I find the treasure."

There's a long, long pause, and then Jason looks over at me. "What treasure?"

"I don't even know where to begin," I say tiredly. "Mr. Yancy, I appreciate this, but now is not a good time for you to be here."

"No, no, he should come along," Jason says, making a motion towards Yancy. One of the goons moves over, reaching to grab Yancy by the arm. "This sounds like a lovely story. Anyway, he's seen us together now."

"Oh, I see what's going on here," Yancy says.

"I shudder to ask," I mutter.

"These guys don't work for you. You work for them! This is a whole criminal conspiracy!"

Jason gives me an incredulous look. "Who is this clown?"

"A tourist."

Jason bites his lip. "A tourist," he echoes. "With a treasure?"

I nod. "Oh, yes, a very large one."

Yancy is giving us a suspicious look. "Let go of my arm, you gorilla," he snaps to the goon holding him. "Or else I'll sue you into oblivion!"

Jason frowns. "Buddy, if you don't stop your yapping I'm gonna make you."

"Bring it on!" Yancy tries to raise his fists but is somewhat hampered by the one arm being held down. "One on one, you and me."

Before Jason can take him up on that offer, and with some regret that I'm not going to see it, I take a step towards him and put a hand on his shoulder. "Jason, I think you should let this one go. Just back away."

Jason turns around, and plants a fist in my stomach. I collapse with a grunt, and Adelaide runs over to check on me. "Shut it, Stark! I don't know what kind of clown show you've gotten us involved in, but if this little shrimp wants to play rough, he's gonna get it."

I wheeze, taking hold of my cane and letting Adelaide help me back to my feet. "No," I groan, leaning heavily on the cane, "I don't think he is."

"And why not?"

"Because I have a sword." It's off the ground and out of the sheath in one motion, pointed at Jason's throat. The men blocking off the back of the alley start towards us, then stumble to a halt as Adelaide whips out the pistol I passed her and points it at them. "And she has your gun."

Jason very carefully pats his jacket pocket, and his eyes narrow. "Smooth move, Stark. Now what? You stab me, my boys are on you. She shoots, they're on her. Six of us, two of you."

"And Mr. Yancy, of course. Although you still have him pinned, so I suppose you're right. Stalemate."

Yancy is staring at the lot of us. "What the hell is going on?" he asks. "Is this a double-cross?"

I glance over at him. The thug holding Yancy is looking between us uncertainly. "Mr. Yancy, did you by chance call the police before you decided to follow six men into an alleyway unarmed?"

There's a short pause. "Uh...."

"Of course not. Foolish of me to have asked." Without turning around, I speak to Adelaide. "What do you think?"

"About what?"

"Could you shoot all three of them before they reach us?"

"I'd really rather not commit a triple homicide tonight, Basil."

"Boring." I turn back to Jason. "Look, the way I see it, this situation has three possible endings. First possibility, your boys rush us, I stab you, Adelaide shoots one of them, the rest jump us, Yancy gets his neck broken..."

"Leave me out of this!"

"No. Anyway, when it's over, half of you are dead, and the other half are hurt and dragging our corpses to Quentin to explain why a very loud and very obvious fight broke out and why the police are looking for them.

"Second possibility, we all just stand here like this until someone comes by to find out what all the ruckus is about, they call the police, who descend on the area, we all get arrested for weapons possession and attempted murder, and no one gets a good night's sleep."

"I like the second option," Adelaide says. "I especially like the part where you and I spend a night in jail, and everyone else is there forever."

"It has its charms," I admit. "Unless someone hears sirens and decides to go for option one, of course."

"Mm. Good point."

"So what's your third choice?" Jason asks.

"Well, no one wants to get shot, stabbed, or bludgeoned to death tonight. And honestly, cleaning this blade is a pain, and I can't sheathe it if there's even a drop of blood left on it. So why don't we all just take a deep breath, back away, and go about our lives, without any unfortunate incidents. First, you let Mr. Yancy go. Your goons behind us clear out so that Adelaide can turn around, I let you take several steps back, we leave the alleyway, and you go back to Quentin and tell him we saw you coming and bailed."

"Quentin won't like that."

"You think he's going to like you showing up in the morgue with your throat cut? You are what we call a 'known associate,' Jason. He'll be dragged in for questioning first thing in the morning."

"I like how you think that's the only reason he'd be upset at me getting smoked."

"Isn't it, though?"

Jason doesn't have an easy answer, so I press my advantage. "What do you say, Jason? Do we play the odds, or do we all go home, have a drink, and contemplate our own mortality?"

Jason attempts to take a deep breath, but my sword at his throat makes it a lot more shallow. "Let the weirdo go, Fred."

"Okay, if you say so." The goon holding Yancy lets go of his arm and takes a step away, looking dubious.

Yancy instantly takes off at a dead sprint, screaming at the top of his lungs. "Help! Police! Murder! Help! Help!"

There's a moment of shell-shocked silence, and then Jason says, "Jesus, Stark, who is that guy?"

"I don't want to get into it. Shall we do the rest quickly?"

Jason nods, and the three thugs flanking Adelaide practically melt away in their eagerness to escape the attention of the police. Adelaide spins to point her gun at Jason, and I lower my sword and take two steps back.

"You know this isn't over," Jason says.

"So be it. Tell Quentin that it's war."

He nods grimly. "I will." And then he vanishes out of the alley with his friends.

I look over to Adelaide. "Are you alright?"

"Fine. Why?"

"Because if you grip that pistol any tighter, it's going to shatter."

She looks down at her hands as if they belong to a stranger, and then drops the pistol with a shudder. I flinch.

"Don't do that!" I carefully retrieve it. "The safety was off. You might have shot yourself."

"I don't … I don't really have much experience with guns. Should we…?"

"Step out of the alleyway, very casually, leaving the gun behind?" I ask, sheathing my sword into its cane. "Absolutely. Grab your purse." I check my hat. Yancy's shouting has finally woken Glimmer, who is blearily sitting up and looking around. "Come on, sleepyhead. We need to move."

We step out of the alley, Adelaide only a little shakier than me, and are halfway down the street by the time Yancy returns with a pair of officers. "There they are!" he shouts, almost incoherent.

"Ah, Mr. Yancy," I say, tipping my hat to him. On my shoulder, Glimmer hisses. "Glad to see you."

"You are?"

"Absolutely. You probably saved my life back there." I look to the baffled police officer. "Mr. Yancy here interrupted a mugging in progress. Probably saved my life."

"I did?"

"He's a hero," Adelaide confirms, leaning heavily on me and giving the officer a wide-eyed stare.

"I am?"

I give him a firm pat on the shoulder. "Wonderful man! Scared off a group of ruffians just like that!"

"Now hang on…" The officer turns to Yancy. "You said there was a pack of murderers in the alleyway attacking a young lady."

"Me," Adelaide confirms, still leaning on me. "Basil was walking me back to my hotel when they descended on us. Why, if Mr. Yancy hadn't been there, they might have killed us both!"

"What … but…" Yancy turns a disbelieving look on me.

"We'll have to take a report," the officer says dubiously. "If you could come down to my car, I'll get the details."

"But what about my map?" Yancy asks plaintively.

"Map?" The officer asks.

I sigh. "Mr. Yancy, as your friend, I'm asking you to drop this."

"I will not, and you are nobody's friend!" Yancy jabs a finger at me. "This man may not be a mugger, but he did steal a map of incalculable value from me! I will not rest until I get it back!"

The officer turns to look at me. "What map would this be, sir?"

"I already spoke with Constable Daggett of the First Precinct about this," I say reluctantly. "Mr. Yancy is a bit excited; I wouldn't want to…"

"It's a map to Captain Hook's buried treasure!" Yancy declares triumphantly.

"Captain … Hook's…"

"Yes! An Indian wise woman showed me the way! I had to crawl through a sewer, and find a rare library book, and break into the Museum of…" Yancy, suddenly realizing what he's saying, breaks off.

"The Museum of Everland History, perhaps?" the officer asks, taking Yancy by the arm. "Now, isn't that interesting. We've been looking for a vandal who broke into that museum just last week. I think I'm going to have to ask you to come down to the station to answer some questions."

"No, I ... that is ... he's the one that stole my map!"

"Your map to Captain Hook's buried treasure."

"Yes!"

The officer turns to me. "Terribly sorry for the trouble, Mr. Stark. We'll have an officer by your rooms in twenty minutes. Unless you feel you need protection?"

"I think we'll be alright. But thank you."

Two minutes later, with a despondent and confused Mr. Yancy in the back of a squad car, the officer is taking down everything that Adelaide and I can remember about our 'muggers' — which includes detailed physical descriptions, and after a moment, that two of them called each other 'Fred' and 'Jason,' but not the fact that they're associates of Quentin Lark and that this was a targeted attack.

Once the officer has driven off, Adelaide turns to me. "Why didn't we tell him the truth, exactly?"

"This is Second Precinct territory. Half the cops in this district are on the take, and a lot of them report to people who might pass the situation on to Quentin. I didn't want to be kept at the station for 'further questioning' until Quentin could get a new crew of killers together." I look up and down the block, but any would-be watchers scattered when the police arrived. "On which note, I don't think your hotel is going to be a safe place to stay. Are you packed?"

"Unless they broke into my room."

"Good. Wait one moment." I pull out several packs of salt, and scatter them onto our shadows. To nobody's surprise, a small piece of mine starts writhing in pain. "Learn a new trick, Quentin!" I shout at it, pinning it to the ground with my cane until it dissolves into wisps of shadowy substance. "I swear, the man is incorrigible."

"When did he do that?"

"Someone at the party, I assume. That's how he knew to have a taxi waiting for us. Possibly he was spying on Stephanie, and had a shadow-piece hop from her to me when he discovered I was there." I shake my head. "Anyway, now that we're clear, we're going to Piccadilly Cross. Quentin can't send goons up there without setting off a real war, and I don't think he's ready to go that far yet. We'll both stay with

Holly tonight, and make sure she and Todd are alright, and tomorrow we'll figure out our next course of action."

As it turns out, Quentin's boys did, in fact, break into Adelaide's room. When we get up there, her clothes are scattered across the ground, the bed has been pulled apart, and her suitcase is gone. She just looks over the wreckage and sighs. "And this night started off so well."

"Did you have anything important in here?"

"No, of course not. My notes were in the hotel safe, and I'm wearing all the jewelry I brought. But it's going to be a pain to gather all this stuff up." She takes a step forward, and starts grabbing things. "My best dress! Damn it, they tore it."

"Adelaide..."

"What!"

I take a step back. "Are you alright?"

"Of course I'm not alright, Basil! I'm furious! I've been threatened, attacked, and now ... now this!" Adelaide gestures to the clothes everywhere. "And we can't call the police because apparently they're not trustworthy, which means ... what's the point? We can find everything out, and write the best damned story in the world, and nothing changes!" Adelaide turns and slams her fist into the wall. "Sometimes I just want to—! I don't know what I want."

I step up and put a hand on your shoulder. "Rougher story than you're used to?"

"Is it always like this here?"

"Not always. Too often for my liking. But fighting them isn't like solving a puzzle. We won't put Quentin away, and then the city is safe. It's more like ... gardening." On the floor, Glimmer is trying to lift Adelaide's dresses one at a time, struggling with the effort of piling them on the bed.

Adelaide blinks. "Gardening."

"Weeds don't stop growing just because you've uprooted a few, but that doesn't mean that you should stop taking care of the garden, right?"

Adelaide laughs. Turning around, she leans in and prods me in the chest with one finger. "You have a very strange way with words, Basil Stark."

"I do my best."

For a long moment, she looks down at me, and I'm surprised at how close she is. The room is quiet.

And then Glimmer starts making exceptionally loud kissing noises.

We step apart quite quickly. Adelaide is blushing, and I have a nasty suspicion that I'm doing the same. I distract myself by quickly helping to gather up clothing, while Glimmer throws her hands up angrily and then flops down on the bed. She mutters something under her breath that I don't catch. Adelaide looks over and smiles.

We go downstairs and tell the concierge that Adelaide is checking out, and that there's been a break-in. He is appropriately shocked and just horrified enough that I almost believe he wasn't paid off to give her room number to Quentin's people, and offers Adelaide another room of her choice free of charge, along with the services of the house detective. She declines, and goes to the safe while I make a call to a taxi that I trust.

Fifteen minutes later, bags in hand, we're crossing the road to Piccadilly Cross, keeping an eye out for any goons that have gotten the bright idea to stake the area out. There don't seem to be any; either Quentin's confident of his plans, or he's low on trusted agents.

"Where to first?"

"Holly's house. I want to check in with her, and make sure that she's safe." I glance over to Adelaide. "Unless you'd like to drop your things off first?"

"No, Holly's is fine. Where does she live?"

"Not far – just across the street from me, actually. Not that much is far from anything else here. Thirty houses don't take up a lot of space."

There are lights on in Holly's living room when we arrive, which seems like a good sign, so I step up to the door and give it three quick raps.

"Who's there?"

"Basil. Wait, is that Todd?"

There is a moment's pause, and then Todd Malcolm cracks the door open. He's got a beauty of a shiner, but otherwise seems healthy, and he gives me a big grin. "Oh,

Mr. Stark! Am I glad to see you. We've been worried sick." He looks past me. "And you've got ... someone with you?"

"Todd Malcolm, Adelaide Evans, a reporter friend. Adelaide, this is Todd, a ... client? Contractor? Honestly, it's gotten a bit complicated. Is Holly in, Todd?"

"Yeah, she's taking a nap in the other room. I said I'd stay up and keep watch, just in case."

"So..."

"So ... oh! Right. Come in." Todd opens the door the rest of the way, and ushers us into Holly's living room. Adelaide looks around while I remove my hat and jacket, and point Glimmer to the small nest that Holly built in the corner.

"Could you pour a stiff drink for Adelaide?" I ask. "On second thought, pour one for me too."

"I ... uh ... I don't know where the booze is."

"I've got it," Holly says blearily from the doorway. She's still wearing her clothing from earlier in the day, rumpled from being slept in. "Where the hell have you been, Uncle Basil?"

"Adelaide and I had a run-in with Quentin's boys."

"Six members of a matched set?" I nod, and Holly groans. "We were afraid of that. We called the party to warn you, but they said you'd just left. Come on, everyone sit down. I'll get tea. And yes, there'll be something in it for Adelaide."

I raise an eyebrow. Holly snorts. "You, Uncle Basil, need your wits. Anyway, I think you've already had a couple."

"You aren't my mother, Holly."

"But I am your host. Sit down."

I sit down. The couch is just wide enough to fit Todd and me, which leaves Adelaide and Holly in the room's two chairs, carefully set up in the corners with Holly's radio between them. I never bother with the thing — Everland only has two stations, and they're both garbage — but she likes the local news. For some reason.

While we're setting up, Adelaide relates the story of our narrow escape. Todd and Holly listen, Holly occasionally nodding along, until we reach the sudden arrival of Mr. Yancy.

"You've got to be kidding me," she says.

"Hopefully, that particular problem is over for the moment," I say. "With Mr. Yancy safely behind bars, we can focus on the actual problems. The long and short of it is, we have a ship to spy on tomorrow, which might have the last pieces that we need. Holly, Todd, how were your days?"

"Kind of fun, until I got beat up," Todd says. He grins viciously. "But you shoulda seen the other guy."

"I did see the other guy."

"Oh. Right. Well, anyway, I'm going around it all backwards. We started at the morgue, and, uh … Holly?"

Holly passes out teacups as she takes over the telling. "We went down to the morgue. I don't like the new guy, he's kind of weird."

"He is a coroner."

"I know, but he's kind of weird. Anyway, yeah, there were some corpses that went missing. Some assistant got fired over it. The rumor was some back-alley doctor wanted to practice his medicine, but they never found one that matched the description."

"And the examiner had that description, I assume."

Holly nods. "If you squint, it could be Doctor Higgs. They never thought to go look around scientists, just actual medical doctors, and it was just a few cadavers belonging to poor people, so the police didn't try very hard."

"How many is a few?"

"Five that they know of. The examiner admitted that it could have been as many as fifteen. But here's the thing, Uncle Basil — the last one was sold more than three months ago, and it wasn't because the seller was nabbed. He didn't get caught until someone identified a victim from a photo, and went to dig up a body that turned out not to be there. Apparently, the buyer stopped wanting bodies."

"Hm. Perhaps he made a breakthrough."

"Wouldn't he step things up at that point, not dial it back?"

"Not if the breakthrough meant that he didn't need any more corpses," Adelaide says thoughtfully. "The question is, what was it?"

"And how do we deal with any shadows that come our way?" I add. "Quentin won't dare send his boys onto

Piccadilly land, but at this point he knows that his shadow's not much of a secret."

Todd raises his hand.

"You don't have to do that, Todd. Just ask."

"Why wouldn't he send his guys up here? This place is nice, but it's kind of quiet, and it's not close to the police."

"No, but it is close to a hundred lumberjacks, miners, hunters, and farmers, most of whom are armed," I say.

Holly nods. "We've had troublemakers come by in the past — poachers, vandals, sometimes just people who think it'd be funny to beat up an Indian. We keep an eye out for each other up here." Her smile is forced innocence. "And like you said, the police are a long way away."

"Got it." Todd nods, looking satisfied. Adelaide, on the other hand, seems torn between fascination and horror.

"Is that ... a frequent problem?" she asks.

"Not if they know what's good for them," Holly says firmly.

"The point is," I say, before we can get any farther off-track, "that even if Quentin was stupid enough to order his boys up here, which he might be, they aren't stupid enough to come. In the off-chance that I'm wrong, we have a lot more backup than he does. A shadow, though — that's a different sort of trouble. Did Niall have any advice for us?"

Holly shakes her head. "I got the notes to him, but he said it would take time to look through them all. He wanted you to stop by his office tomorrow afternoon, and he would share what he'd managed to find out."

"Well, that's good news, but it doesn't help us right now. Right. We're going to need to keep watch, and make sure a shadow doesn't slip in. I saw that the door was salted on the way in. Holly, have you salted the windows?"

"All along the sills, Uncle Basil."

"Good. That's probably enough, but just in case, we'll take turns on watch." I look over to Adelaide. "Sorry. This isn't going to be a restful night."

"Yeah, I've only really got the one bed." Holly is sizing us all up. "Miss Evans, you ... might ... fit on the couch. It's the same size as the one at Mom's that Uncle Basil sleeps on once in a while when he's hiding from reporters, and you're not much taller than him. Of course, there's only one couch. I have some spare blankets, but..."

"I can drag a chair into the kitchen and sleep there," Todd says. "I've slept in worse."

"And I can pile some blankets in the corner of the kitchen, leaving Glimmer and Adelaide here."

"This isn't my first job out of town, Basil, and The Times doesn't always spring for separate hotel rooms," Adelaide says. "I'll be fine with you two in the room with me. Actually, I'll be better than fine. I'd be happier to have you all around if something oozes through the window while I'm sleeping."

"Alright, then. Holly, why don't you take the first watch, since we just woke you up already. Todd, you can go second, I'll go third, and Adelaide can take the last."

"Sounds as good a system as any," Holly says. "Two hours each, and wake everyone else if anything happens. Quietly, to avoid letting them know we're up. Come on, I'll get the blankets."

It's an oddly comfortable scene, like a children's sleepover. After some consideration, we drag the couch and chairs into Holly's room so that everyone can stay together. Just in case. Holly offers the bed to Adelaide, who turns it down. Those of us sleeping put blankets over our eyes to keep the light out — the last thing that we want is a shadow slipping into the semidarkness of an unlit room — and we settle in to get as much rest as we can. As it happens, I'm used to this sort of thing, and I settle easily into a mostly restful sleep.

It feels like it's only been a few minutes when I'm being shaken roughly awake. "Mr. Stark!" Todd hisses, impossibly loudly for an attempt at a whisper. "It's outside!"

My eyes snap open, and I groan softly as I stand. "Where?" I hiss. I see over his shoulder that Holly is already awake and crouching by the door.

Todd points to the living room, and I take two soft steps towards it. There's a shape against the window frame, a pattern of darkness across it that obscures the stars outside. Shadowy fingers are trying to slip under the frame, but

Holly's salt line is doing its job, and the shadow can't seem to find enough purchase to get past. The three of us watch in tense silence as it tries for a few more seconds, and then vanishes.

"It went left," Todd suggests.

"You two check the kitchen. I'll wake the others. Yell very, very loudly if it seems to be getting in."

As Todd and Holly head for the kitchen, I move into the bedroom to find Adelaide sitting up and watching, and Glimmer still curled up on a shelf. "What's going on?"

"Trouble," I say. Before I can say more, she looks past me, and her eyes go wide. I spin, to find a silhouette passing in front of the bedroom window — a tall man's shape, wearing a wide-brimmed hat. "It's the same one," I mutter.

The shadow tries the bedroom window the same way it tried the living room. Reaching out, I very carefully pick up my walking stick and draw it. The sound is enough to wake Glimmer, who mumbles something blearily as she starts to sit up.

I move as quickly as I can, stabbing my sword into the corner of the window, where the shadow is just poking through and teasing at the salt line. It catches the edge of the shadow, but there isn't enough of it to get purchase, and it tears itself away in what looks like a hurry — silently, of course. Damn things are always silent.

Todd comes racing in. He blinks, seeing the sword sticking in the sill. "Did you get it?"

"No. But the salt lines held. At least we know it still has that weakness."

"No sign of a human buddy?" Holly asks, joining us.

"None." I glance at the clock. "Alright. Todd, I'm awake now, and I was supposed to start my watch in twelve minutes anyway. I'll take the next one, in case it comes back. But I think we're probably safe for the night. It didn't like being stabbed, and it doesn't know how to get in. It'll go back for more instructions, and that will take time."

"Well ... are you sure, Mister Stark? I could stay up a while longer."

"It's fine, Todd. I don't know that I could sleep anyway."

"Okay, then. Yell if there's trouble." Todd sits back in his chair.

Bleary-eyed, I make a second cup of tea, check on Glimmer to make sure she knows not to chase after the shadow, and settle in to wait and watch the windows in the living room and here in the bedroom carefully. Holly fell back asleep in seconds and is already snoring softly in her bed, Todd is settling in, and for a few minutes, it's just me sitting by the corner. Then I glance over and see Adelaide watching me. She raises an eyebrow, I nod, and she slips over to where I'm sitting, carefully sitting down on the floor next to me.

"You should be sleeping," I whisper to her.

"I barely managed it the first time, and now I've been scared sober." Adelaide shakes her head. "That thing at the window ... how are you all so calm?"

"We aren't. Holly's faking it for me. She knows I'm overprotective, so she's pretending that she's okay. Almost managing it too. Todd ... I think he just trusts me, which is sweet, if misplaced. So he's convinced himself that as long as I'm here, things will turn out alright."

"And you?"

"I've been through hell and back, Adelaide. I'm under control because of the years when not being under control would have meant dying. Because there were years when I did panic, and ran away, and people died. A lifetime of failure and nightmares helps you hold the line, but I wouldn't recommend it as a tactic."

"It's nice to know someone is calm."

"I didn't say that. I said I was under control. I'm furious."

"Not scared?"

"Scared is what Quentin wants. What he's going to get ... is me."

"Your delivery needs some work." Adelaide leans in to me, and I put my arm around her shoulder. "I've been in bad places before, Basil. I've interviewed hardened murderers, helped chase down leads on corporate frauds. But this is my first assignment away from my contacts, and my state. In New York, I know who to trust. There are corrupt cops and dangerous people, but I can generally rely on getting the word out. Here, though … this is insane. Never mind not knowing who to trust, I don't know what to believe."

"That's the problem with Everland." I turn to look at the window the shadow was creeping at not long ago. "Once magic is real, anything could be. It hits everyone differently. A lot of visitors end up like Mr. Yancy did. After all, if there are shadows and fairies, why not pirate treasure and secret conspiracies?"

"Then how do you figure out what's real?"

"By learning who to trust, and listening to them. There are a lot of good people in Everland."

"Like you."

I bite my lip. "I don't know about that. I've done a lot of things in my life that I'm not proud of. Hell, I'm on a first name basis with the city's premiere underworld boss."

"Oh, don't give me that. Why are you still pushing this case, then? You had a dozen chances to back off, to let it go. Why keep digging?"

"Because someone needed to." I pause. That's not quite right. "Because that girl died alone, and no one was going to find justice for her, and her killer knew it. And the hell of it is, I think she knew it too. She had a plan to take care of herself, and it almost paid off, and I'm the one that screwed it up. Even if I didn't mean to. I have a responsibility to see it through."

"So, just because you're a hero?"

"No. Because it was my fault, and there are enough sins on my conscience. I can't abandon anyone else."

She smiles, and leans farther. "Well, then, that answers the question."

"What question?"

"Whether you're good," she says sleepily. "You said you didn't know. It would be trite to say that not knowing is the sign of a good man, but I think you can make a strong case for guilt."

"How very Catholic of you. What about you?"

"What about me?" Adelaide asks, eyes closed.

"You could have taken the first boat off-island whenever you wanted, and you were only part of this because Mercy tried to make you a part of it. You don't have a responsibility to her."

"It's my job, Basil. If I gave up on a story just because a truly amazing number of people started trying to kill me, I wouldn't be much of a reporter."

"You wouldn't be holed up in a room with three other people waiting for a monster to come and try to kill you, either."

"There are upsides to being holed up."

"Such as?"

Adelaide opens her eyes, glaring. "You'd better be trying to make a joke, buddy."

I can't help it. I laugh, and a moment later she's laughing, and a few moments after that Holly is throwing a pillow at us and telling us to keep it down, she's trying to sleep. We settle to quiet giggles, our conversation cut off. But Adelaide doesn't get up, and I don't feel like asking her to. When I look down a few minutes later, she's asleep, blanket pulled up around her chin and her head resting gently on my shoulder.

Chapter Nine

Friday, February 14th

I'm the last one to wake up Friday morning, to the smell of frying bacon. I open my eyes, sit up, and feel all the aches and pains of the last few days intently. Holly, in the kitchen, glances over and waves. "Welcome back to the world, Uncle Basil. Sleep well?"

"Soundly, at least," I say, standing up stiffly. "After I woke Adelaide for her watch, I practically blacked out."

"Well, it's been a heck of a week, so that makes sense. She's in the washroom, by the way. Todd ran next door to grab some eggs from Lynx."

The man in question returns a minute later, knocking tentatively before coming in. "Your friend says no one saw anyone around last night. That shadow-thing must have come up by itself. Explains why it didn't stick around."

"Lazy of our mystery attacker," I say. "Although I suppose he hoped Holly was alone. I'd bet my last dollar the shadow slipped by my house too."

"So what's today's plan?" Holly asks, taking the eggs and adding them to her pan. "Some kind of stakeout?"

"First things first — we're going down to visit with Niall."

"All of us?"

"Four's a crowd, true, but with things as they are I wouldn't mind having the backup." Glimmer dive-bombs my ear furiously, and I amend. "Five is a crowd. Glimmer, I'm not taking you to Second Star. It isn't safe. You're going to stay here and keep an eye on the house, in case those thugs try to come back."

Glimmer hovers in front of my face, arms crossed, and tells me that there's no way that's happening.

"Glimmer," I say patiently, "we need someone to keep an eye on things here. All of our notes on the case are safely hidden in this house, and I don't want Quentin to come up here and steal them. You're my only hope."

Glimmer suggests that I leave Adelaide behind, since they're her notes, and anyway we don't need notes if we know who to attack.

"We can't just walk up to him and — what!" I turn to Holly and Todd, who are watching this exchange in bemusement.

"Uh, nothing, Mister Stark," Todd says quickly. "Just followin' the arguments."

"Glimmer," Holly says with a suspicious sweetness in her voice, "if you come with us, who will protect the cherry pie I'm baking?"

All of Glimmer's attention is suddenly on Holly.

"I'm going to set it out to cool before we go, and someone needs to make sure it doesn't get stolen by any pie thieves."

Glimmer allows that she wouldn't want that to happen. Entranced by the possibility of eating an entire pie while we're away, she settles down on the counter, but not before demanding that I come back to get her before we go to our stakeout. I solemnly promise, and turn to find that Adelaide has come out of the washroom and was watching the whole thing.

"You're adorable with her," she says quietly.

"I ... er ... I need to shave."

By the time I've stopped by my house, grabbed my razor, and finished my own morning preparations, breakfast is served and cooling on my plate. I wolf down my food, explain our plan for the morning to Adelaide, and take a breath. "Holly, we're going to need to borrow Lynx's car."

"Oh, no, Uncle Basil. He said that if I ever asked again he would shoot me."

"Well, that's not neighborly."

"After what we did to the last one? It's downright pleasant."

"What did you do to the last one?" Todd asks.

"Not pertinent," I say quickly. "Holly, we can't rely on taxis today. Too much chance that someone will radio Quentin."

"And the chance that someone will shoot out Lynx's back windshield? Again?"

"Moderate," I admit. "But we paid him back. I don't see why he's holding a grudge."

"Anyway, he's working today. I don't think he'll go for it."

"Do you have a better idea?"

"Yeah. Mom."

"No."

"Uncle Basil—"

"Do you want to tell her that you're in mortal danger?"

There is a short pause. "I'll go ask Lynx." Holly leaves, and comes back a few minutes later. "He's already gone."

"Damn it. Alright, troops. Gear up." I take a deep breath. "We're going to go talk to Plum Blossom."

———— «» ————

"I don't see why you're so nervous," Adelaide says, as we walk over to Plum and Panther's house. "They're a very nice couple."

"Until their daughter is in danger," I say.

"There was … a lot of shouting when I decided to start working for Uncle Basil," Holly says. "Words were spoken. Accusations were made. I had to promise them that I would stay behind the desk and not get involved in any cases directly."

Todd's brow furrows. "But you went on a stakeout for that divorce case. And we went to the morgue. And—"

"Yes, Todd, I know," Holly says. "I mean, obviously I wasn't totally telling the truth. But I've been breaking it to them in little bits and pieces. They know that I follow up on leads once in a while. In safe places. They don't know about the stakeouts."

"To be fair, until Wednesday I didn't know about the stakeouts," I say dryly.

"What?" Todd looks between me and Holly. "Holly, you said—"

"I said it would be fine. And it was. See? Not lying. I knew that he would be okay with it if he thought about it for a bit."

"Okay is a very strong word for—" I break off. "You know what, we're getting off-track. The point is, Panther should be at work, so we only have one person to convince. We just need to get across to Plum how important this is without getting her..."

"Worried?" Adelaide offers.

"Murderous," I say.

"Oh."

"Any ideas?" Holly asks.

Adelaide nods slowly. "I have one. Do you drive, Basil?"

"Oh, God, no. Never learned. When we need to rent a car, Holly drives."

"Well, then. We have a plan. Let me do the talking." We're reaching Plum's house as she speaks, and find her in the front garden, carefully pruning the short holly hedge that runs along the side.

Plum looks up at the four of us. "Good gracious, Basil! I didn't expect to see you here this morning ... with Holly ... and Ms. Evans ... and?"

"Todd Malcolm, ma'am." Todd takes off his hat. "Nice to meet you."

"Well. What a nice boy." Plum looks around at us. "What trouble are you in, Basil?"

Adelaide smiles brilliantly. "Oh, it's not trouble. Basil agreed to help me with my story, since his last case finished up, but there's a lot of driving involved. He thought that you might be able to let us borrow your car for the day."

Holly, Todd, and I are all ramrod-still. "That's ... nice ..." Plum says suspiciously, looking at us. "I thought that you were staying in town."

"Well, I was out at a gala with Basil last night, and we came back to Piccadilly Cross, and I ended up staying too late. So I slept the night at Holly's house."

I just barely manage to avoid an inclination to drop my jaw at how easily Adelaide skates around the vast chasms in that summary of her night.

Plum, however, is distracted by the sound of all of her dreams for me coming true. "Well, isn't that lovely! Why, of course I could lend you my car! The two of you should have a beautiful drive!"

"Actually, Holly and Todd are coming along," Adelaide admits. Before Plum can finish looking suspicious, she explains, "I'm a New York girl, Ms. Blossom. I can't drive. And Basil…"

"Oh, that's right. Basil, you really need to learn to drive."

"Not my thing."

"Cars aren't going away, Basil."

"Anyway, Holly offered to drive us, but her friend Todd had come over, so…"

There's a momentary pause, like the world holding its breath. Plum stands up, and looks at Todd more carefully. "You're a friend of Holly's?"

"Uh … a recent friend, yeah." Todd, wide-eyed, looks to Holly for support, but she's as transfixed as the rest of us.

"You don't have any untoward intentions for her, do you?"

"Mom!"

"Ma'am, I can promise that I do not," Todd says solemnly. "Your daughter is mighty nice, and I would like to get to know her, but it's not like that."

"Well, why not?"

Todd blinks. "Uh…"

"Mom!"

"I don't see what's wrong with asking, Holly! He's a very nice boy. Very polite. Is there a girl in your life, Todd?"

"Uh. No, ma'am. Not as such."

Plum smiles triumphantly, while Holly tries to bury herself behind Adelaide. "You don't say. And what do you do for a living, Todd?"

Todd is now looking frantically for support from the rest of us, and getting nothing. Holly and I know better than to interrupt Plum while she's constructing a narrative, and Adelaide just looks fascinated. "I'm, uh, a bouncer, ma'am. Downtown."

"Well, that's … nice." Plum seems to be searching for a way to fit this into the grandchildren she's already planning for. "Must be a very exciting job."

"It can be. But mostly it's pretty boring, and then you gotta toss someone out on their ear."

"Now that must be hard work."

"Well," Todd says thoughtfully, warming to the subject, "It usually isn't, on account of people who are causing trouble in bars are really drunk, and the bouncer isn't. I mean, drinking on the job, whoo boy. You can get in a lot of trouble for that, and it's pretty bad too. Happened to me once, and the manager damn near scared me sober, he was yelling so hard. Never did it again. So yeah, a big guy like me tossing one or two drunk guys out to the street, nah, that's not too hard. But once in a while someone pulls a knife, and then … uh…" He trails off, suddenly noticing the way that Plum is sizing him up. "Yeah. So. Anyway, it's not much of a job, really. Pays the rent, but not much else. Sorry."

"Well," Plum says again. There is a thoughtful look on her face that I'm not sure that I like. "I think some of Panther's workers started out that way, you know. Loggers are always looking for security folk."

I decide to step in before Plum can finish recruiting Todd into the family business. Normally that would be Holly's job, but she's as awe-struck as the rest of us. "Todd is helping us out. I thought it might be a good idea to have someone tough and trustworthy around the office, in case of bruisers."

"You're hiring an office bouncer?" Plum asks suspiciously.

"Well, not exactly, although come to think of it, that is exactly what happened with Mr. Yancy, isn't it?" I chuckle, and pat Todd on the shoulder. "So I suppose that we are. But since Holly is driving us into town, and the office is closed, Todd's tagging along."

"Basil, you didn't even hire a bodyguard when the Hook Road Slaughterer was after you. How dangerous is this story of Adelaide's?"

"Um."

Adelaide leans in. "Basil's being overprotective," she says with a wink. "I told him I was just as tough as he was, but you know how he gets."

"Oh, that I do. Alright, alright. I know you wouldn't be asking if it wasn't important. The keys are in a cup in the front hall. You know where to look, Holly."

"Yep!" Holly doesn't wait for any follow-up questions about Todd, the case, or anything else that her mother is likely to ask. She bolts for the house, leaving the rest of us standing awkwardly around. Plum looks at us in turn. "Have a nice day in the city, all of you. And be careful! I don't want a scratch on that car when I get it back."

"Neither," I say honestly, "do I."

———— «» ————

Second Star's facilities are almost exactly as I remember them from my last visit — a massive, sprawling complex of buildings large enough to be its own neighborhood, surrounded by chain-link fences and watched by a small army of security guards. The buildings closest to the road are beautiful — gleaming, glass-faced buildings ten stories tall, towering over the brownstone buildings across the street and casting their shadow over the city. Further back, concealed from sight, are the factories, labs, and warehouses that fill twenty blocks of Everland's southeast coast, complete with their own private dock to receive goods without having to deal with the port authority.

Holly drives us to the gate, where I decide to test whether the Old Man really has taken me off his list. It turns out that he has, and we're given passes and an escort to the main parking lot, and told that Niall will be informed of our arrival. The whole thing is more than a little ominous.

Of course, I'm the only one who seems to think so. Holly is as cheerful as ever, looking around the building curiously. Todd and Adelaide are more openly awed, and Todd pauses as we enter the main doors to point at a giant skeleton of a sea monster that is suspended over the front lobby's main entrance. "Is that real?"

"Very real," I assure him. "One of the first sea serpents that the Everlanders found when they landed on the island. They killed it, of course."

"That seems wrong," Adelaide says.

"Well, to be fair, it started it by swallowing one of the launch boats. Killed three people before they were able to bring it down. I suppose it set the mood for the next several years."

Our guide directs us to a set of seats off to one side, near a small potted palm tree, and a few minutes later, Niall walks out from the elevator, eyebrows raised. "Basil! Lovely to see you. And Miss Blossom, and Mr. ... Matthews?"

"Malcolm, sir."

"Right. Tom Malcolm." Niall shakes Todd's hand, while Todd wrestles with whether to go for a second correction, and then turns to me. "And I don't think I know your last friend, but I can guess. You must be the reporter I've heard a few things about."

"Adelaide Evans. Lovely to meet you." Adelaide shakes Niall's hand.

"Quite the crowd that you've brought today, Basil," Niall tells me, leading us back to the elevator. "I assumed you would be stopping by on your own."

"Things are heating up fast, Niall. We decided that there's strength in numbers. Do you have anything for me?"

"Not as much as you might hope, but it's fascinating stuff. Terrible, of course, but fascinating. Shame about all of the missing pieces." Niall punches in a floor number in the elevator, and leans back. "I would love to have a word with Doctor Higgs' assistant, but the police aren't letting her see anybody right now, so I've had to guess my way through. Come in to my office, I'll give you what I've found."

The others look around Niall's office. It's a homey place — just high enough to peek over the rooftops of the city, but not so prestigious as to offer a view of the bay, or of the island's forests. Niall has decorated with a handful of paintings, mostly abstract, and a few awards that he's won over the years, as well as a framed picture of himself standing at his graduation with his parents. Aside from the pictures, and a bookshelf filled with various arcane texts, there isn't much that is his.

There also aren't enough chairs; aside from Niall's own office chair, there are only two others for visitors. After some shifting around, Todd elects to stand by the door, Holly and Adelaide let Niall seat them, and I lean on the desk and look at what he's found. "It's interesting stuff," Niall explains, showing me where he's annotated Higgs' notes. "If it weren't hilariously illegal, it might even be worth following up on."

"Does it work?"

"Hard to say. There are key pieces missing. I can tell you this much, though. Whoever sabotaged these files knows a lot more about paperwork than science. Unless I miss my guess, they took out any page that seemed to have concrete specifics, while trying to leave a functional record behind. Didn't want anyone to know anything was missing."

"Well, that makes sense. They wanted us to think that Higgs had just died of a very dramatic experiment. If he figured the process out, they wouldn't want us to know it."

"Right, exactly. But he figured it out quite a bit before the notes cut out. My hunch is the person taking the files didn't really know what mattered. They just grabbed the pieces that looked like conclusions, on the assumption that they could get another scientist to work backwards from there. Their work on the financial records, though — that is a thing of beauty. Holds together perfectly — or at least it would, if Higgs didn't reference a few purchases in his experiment notes that got left off the ledger."

"Not Quentin personally, then. He's an ass with numbers." I rub my chin. "Either his investor did it, or they trusted someone else with the finances."

"Could it be Quentin's fixer?" Holly asks.

"Ms. Tate? It's possible. She is more clear-headed than him, and I doubt that she's as devoted to Schaefer as she pretends." Holly has pulled a notepad out from somewhere, and I pass her a pen from Niall's desk. "I feel like she's as baffled by what's going on as we are, though, and I don't think Quentin trusts her enough to give her control over a shadow. Anyone they sent in to cook the numbers would have full access to the experiment notes and the ability to make shadows of their own. It would have to be someone Quentin trusted entirely."

"There are a few side references to a backer in the experiment notes," Niall says. "Nothing explicit. Barely even circumstantial. But it always refers to one person, who is a 'he.' There's also a very short reference to 'getting materials from his criminal friend' in the middle of a section on shadow control, who is also referred to as a 'he' just afterwards."

"So, two conspirators along with Higgs, both of them men," Adelaide says.

"Or two who were willing to talk to the good doctor," I point out. "One to be respectable, and one to be threatening."

"Either way, there's no more information. But this you might be interested in. I think Higgs actually might have gotten the process working." Niall beams at us. "Imagine! There could be a shadow under someone's control out there right now!"

"Well, yeah," Todd says. "It tried to kill us last night."

Niall's face falls. "Oh. I see."

"Confirmation is good, Niall," I say, patting him on the shoulder. "How does it work?"

"Well, it's hard to say. My guess would be through a sort of supernatural stitching. You see, shadows aren't entirely contiguous. They operate in non-geometric collusion when split by sufficient force."

I spend a minute working through the words, but Adelaide beats me to it. "So if a small piece of a shadow was cut off, the rest of the shadow would be able to see and hear through it."

"Oh, much more than that, Ms. Ellens."

"Evans," I cough.

"Miss Evans," Niall says. "If you could remove a small piece of a shadow, and restrain it somehow, you could use that piece to see and hear through the shadow as a whole. If you timed it right, you could focus on something that you really, really wanted to do, and then not do it, and your desire would pass into the shadow you were connected to and it would go off and do it." He tabs some papers. "The mechanics of the thing would be incredibly complicated, of course. And the shadow servant would have to already be detached from its original host. And you would need a proper container to prevent the shadow fragment from vanishing or dissolving." He looks up at us, and sees us all staring at him. "It's mostly a theory," he says apologetically. "But it's definitely the direction that Higgs was working in."

"How large of a container are we talking about, here?" I ask.

"Well, that depends on how much machinery you actually need, which depends on how much shadow you

have to restrain. Smaller than a take-out container, I would
think. Maybe even as small as a cigarette case."

"Well," I say slowly. "That's terrifying."

"It gets worse," Niall adjusts his glasses. "Because I can't
see how it would work the way Higgs is suggesting here."

"What do you mean?"

"Look, when someone dies, three things happen. First,
all of their unmet needs get dropped into their shadows.
Usually that doesn't do anything, but a shadow off a fresh
corpse is totally berserk. But as those desires fade, so does
the shadow's power, until they just ... fade away. And the
whole process doesn't take long. So not only would Higgs
need fresh corpses, but his shadows would be dead within a
day or two, and they'd be absolute beasts while he had them.
It's a total dead end."

"He solved it," Adelaide says. "There were at least two
shadows out there, under control, at once. The one that
attacked Basil the day before yesterday, and the one that
went after us last night."

"Yes. Well. I might know what the solution is."

I look at him. Niall is sweating faintly, and looking
unhappy and faintly helpless. Whatever the answer is, I
know I'm not going to like it. "Alright, Niall. Lay it on us."

"Coma patients."

We all stare at him. "What?" Holly asks.

"Find someone in a deep coma. Their shadow would be
weak, no volition of its own, and maybe you could safely har-
vest it without them doing anything. As long as they're still
alive, the shadow's still alive. Then you tie your own shadow
to theirs, give it marching orders, and you're good to go."

"So we should be checking the hospitals, not the
morgues."

"That was my first thought. But I called around. There
are only three people in comas in the city right now, and no
one is missing a shadow."

"Of course, with Quentin's resources, he could have a
patient or two declared dead, and move them to a private
facility. If they've been in a coma long enough, no one would
even question it."

"That's awful," Holly says. "You're saying that, somewhere in this city, there are two people, just … lying there? Without shadows?"

"Maybe only one, now," I say grimly. "There's no reason to keep a man without a shadow alive."

"That is horrible," Adelaide says slowly. "But it would also be proof, wouldn't it? We just have to run the research, find out what's happened to people who died of comas in the last few months. Higgs only made his breakthrough recently. Hell, he didn't have Quentin's backing at all six months ago. That's got to narrow the field."

I nod. "Between that, and the boat coming in today, we might actually have a shot at this. Of course, it means that we're going to have to split up."

"Why?"

"Because as soon as we start digging, someone is going to call Quentin, and he'll know we're on to him. And it's a short hop from there to burying a body in a shallow ditch in the woods somewhere. Even if it gets dug up, one shadowless corpse won't make a lot of press. We need to reach both locations at once."

"Our usual partnerships, then?" Holly asks. "Todd and I can drop you two off near the docks, and then do the legwork for the hospitals. It's not like Mom's car is going to be very useful down there. Way too obvious."

"Alright then, it sounds as though we have a plan. Niall, I don't suppose there were any secret shadow weaknesses that you uncovered in those notes?"

"Light, salt and iron, the usual set," Niall says. "Basil, you need to call the Regulators in on this."

"And tell them what?"

"That someone might be controlling shadows! This is huge! I know that you're worried about the people involved, but think about what would happen if a technology like this got out? We could have an epidemic of shadow-stitchers. And anyway, the Regulators might be able to help."

"More likely they'll trample over everything, but … no, you're right. We need to solve the case, but we also need to stop the science from getting out there. Niall, how do you feel about becoming our fifth recruit?"

"In what way?" Niall asks cautiously.

"Quentin's boat is scheduled to dock at four o'clock. Call the Regulators twenty minutes before that. Tell them what you've learned and suggest that we went to the docks without that knowledge. That's enough time for them to scramble their boats, but not enough to actually stop the ship from docking. We'll learn what we can before they descend on the scene to arrest everyone. It won't take, of course, but they should be able to confiscate whatever goods Quentin was planning to smuggle in or out. That should give us the last pieces that we need to put him away, and the Regulators probably won't misuse the information." I frown. "This goes against every fiber of my being, you know."

"I know, but you've got to admit that having thirty or forty armed agents ten minutes behind you is going to make you feel better."

"It just might make me feel shot."

"It makes me feel better," Adelaide says.

"Because you don't know them. Overzealous maniacs, the lot of them. As liable to shoot us as the real villains."

"But you're still calling them?"

"Well, Niall is an old friend. And if something goes badly wrong and Quentin gets us … better to have a second string in our bow, so to speak."

"Well, on that cheerful note, why don't we have some lunch?" Holly stands up, looking around the room. "My treat. You've got almost four hours until that boat comes in, and even accounting for showing up early to hide, we're all going to want to get some food in us."

"We'd better order in," Niall says, with a gleam in his eye. "Might be dangerous to be seen together outside right now."

"You just want to have Chinese twice in one week."

"And what's wrong with that?"

"Nothing at all." I pat him on the shoulder, and then turn to look around the room. "Alright, Holly, you have a point. We should eat, and there's just enough time to do it before we need to get to work."

《》

A few hours later, full of cheap noodles, Adelaide and I are crouching on a second-floor balcony right by the berth we expect to see our mystery ship dock at. It wasn't difficult to find out where we should be going. Adelaide created a distraction while I got my hands on the list of employees at the port today, and compared it against the list of new security guards that Amaryllis provided me with. Only one section of the port was covered entirely by new guards, which narrowed our search down to a dozen berths. Some quiet questions to local dockhands picked out the areas where no one is supposed to be working, and one of them is in a sheltered spot just before a small spit of land. A ship coming in could easily turn, moving to hug the shoreline, and make it impossible for anyone at another berth to see what was being done. A couple of warehouses provide cover, and it's far enough from the main shipping crates.

We make our way up the fire escape two hours before the boat is due to come in, and settle in for a long wait. As it happens, our wait isn't as long as I would have liked. Just under an hour before the scheduled time, we hear the sound of an engine, and I take a quick peek to find a large gray van pulling up to the dock, with two familiar-looking faces inside. Jason and one of his fellow goons, the one sporting a black eye, who I mentally dub 'Shiner.' They climb out, and start looking around.

"Will you look at that?" I whisper. Adelaide nods slowly. Shiner is wearing a port security uniform. He must be one of the four guys on duty today.

Adelaide and I look at each other, and start quietly shifting position. The ladder for our fire escape has been pulled up, and we're hiding under the rim of the building, but there isn't as much cover on the roof as I would like. There is, however, an open window, or at least a window that's vulnerable to lockpicks, which is the same thing as far as I'm concerned. As we hear the sound of Shiner coming up the ladder, we duck through the window into the dark warehouse, and I gently lock it behind us.

A shadow passes across the window, and we hear Shiner test it. Apparently, he thinks it's secure enough, because I hear a faint grunt and the sound of him walking back to the ladder. I wait until we can't hear anything, and start to crack the window back open.

Which is the moment that we hear the distinctive sound of the warehouse's padlock being opened.

Adelaide and I get through the window in what I assume is record time, and I slide it shut before the light can give us away. Inside, we can hear Jason and Shiner walking up and down the rows, and a flashlight momentarily shines in the window. I faintly hear, "Looks good, boss," and then Adelaide and I are back on the roof, crouching down and breathing heavily.

"That was too close," Adelaide whispers.

"Well, get ready. If they're good, they'll do it again before the boat comes in, and we'll have to be just as fast."

As it turns out, they aren't good. Satisfied that everything is under control, Jason and Shiner park the van at the side of the building and stand outside, keeping an eye out for anyone arriving, but ignoring everything already present. I'm almost embarrassed on their behalf, but it makes our job easier.

Until I spot a familiar shape zipping through the air towards us. "Oh, no," I groan softly.

Adelaide looks over. "Is that…"

Glimmer dives down to the roof, arms crossed, and lands on my shoulder. She hisses that I'm up here playing hide and seek while she's doing all the work, and proceeds to go into a huff, leaning against the wall and occasionally shooting us dark looks.

"Glimmer," I whisper, "this is a stakeout. Shh."

"How did you even find us?" Adelaide asks.

Glimmer snorts. She wasn't following us, she explains, still quiet enough that I figure I'll do more damage shushing her than otherwise. Some guy tried to break into the house, and ran off when he heard people coming to investigate. She grabbed the fender of his car to find out where he was going, and he drove all the way to the port, and met up with another guy, and was busy arguing with him about something. And then she saw us, and found out we were 'staking out,' and here she is. She seems pretty impressed with herself.

"What guy?"

She shrugs. She didn't recognize him, which doesn't mean much because Glimmer recognizing anyone she hasn't taken an intense liking or dislike to is a crapshoot. I wonder who would be bold or stupid enough to come to Piccadilly territory. At least it can't be Yancy.

Before we can ask any more questions, I see Quentin Lark coming down the road, with another security guard flanking him, who's yet another of Jason's buddies from the other night. This one is a Chinese guy, the one who was limping — and still is, if not as badly. I point them out to Glimmer, who confirms that Quentin is the guy the other guy was yelling at. She doesn't recognize the guard.

"Do you think the stitcher was the one at the house?" Adelaide asks.

"Could be." We settle in to watch. It would be too much to hope that he'll show up, but maybe Glimmer will remember his face if we meet him again soon enough.

Below us, Quentin is having an intense, very quiet conversation with Jason. I can't make out the details, but whatever Jason is saying in reply, which sounds like variations of 'yeah, boss,' and 'sure thing,' isn't making him look any calmer. He doesn't stop talking until we hear the sound of another, louder engine approaching from the north, at about the same time that a boat comes around the edge of the harbor.

It's not a large boat — about the smallest size that can reach Everland, really, designed for a crew of ten or twelve people, and with its own crane for unloading bulk cargo. It drifts into the dock, and Quentin's boys move forward to help tie it off. While they do, the truck I've been hearing pulls up. At this angle, it looks almost as large as the boat — a big eighteen-wheeler. "Maybe we were wrong," I say. "What's Quentin off-loading?"

The ship is in the process of lowering a large metal shipping crate to the dock, and Quentin storms over to talk to the crew. Even from here, we hear him yelling for them to hold up. "We need to get closer," Adelaide whispers.

"Along the roof, here," I point to where the balcony around the edge of the warehouse almost touches another one. "We should be able to make that step. Carefully."

She nods, and we spend several heart-pounding seconds crossing from one building to the next, praying that Jason and his friends don't look up. Fortunately, they've been distracted by the truck, and are directing the driver to try and turn it around to back it up to the dock. This is taking more than a little time.

We reach the area above Quentin just in time to hear him say, "Fine! I'll pay for the damn cargo, just put it back on the ship. Can you load up last month's supply at the same time?"

"I dunno, man." The captain of the ship, a lanky, dark-skinned man with a scruffy beard, rubs his chin. "It'll be bouncing all over the deck."

"I don't care if it bounces off your skull! Just take it out to sea and dump it overboard."

"We'll be late pulling into harbor. Got my official cargo to unload too."

"Tell them you hit a storm."

"I'm just saying…"

"If you don't start loading now, anything official is going to be the least of your problems," Quentin snarls.

"Where's Mr. Amsel?" the captain asks. "He really should be signing off on this stuff."

"He's running late, I assume. He'll be here."

"Well," the captain says stubbornly, "I'll take back our crate, but I'm not loading anything else until he gets here. Could be anything in there."

"Are you sure my associates can't change your mind?" Quentin asks, after taking a deep breath.

The captain looks over to where the truck has, at last, been parked. Jason, Limp, and Shiner have been joined by two more guards, both of whom I recognize from our tussle in the alley. I'm starting to wonder if Quentin has any other people he trusts, or if it's just those five. But they make an impressive lineup. "Well…" the captain allows. "Get things lined up. We'll get the crates ready. When Mr. Amsel gets here, we'll see."

Quentin sputters, but nods. He gestures to Jason, and while the cargo crate is returned to the boat, the goons start to pull boxes out of the truck. Long, narrow boxes.

Adelaide goes pale. "Are those…?" she whispers.

"They do look a lot like coffins," I say grimly. "But there are more than two."

In fact, by the time the process is over, a dozen coffins have been stacked up on the edge of the dock. The captain looks them over dourly, and goes to talk to a few of his crew.

Emil Amsel, the owner of the ship, arrives in a sleek red convertible before Quentin can completely lose his cool. Quentin descends on him like a ton of bricks. "Where the hell were you? We need to get this out of here, and we need to get it out now!"

"Don't snap at me, Quentin. I'm three minutes late. It's not my fault the ship arrived early."

"You should have been here twenty minutes ago!"

"And stand around waiting for trouble? I don't think so. I'm talking to the captain and getting the hell out of here."

He walks over to the captain, while Quentin and Jason step off to one side, lighting cigarettes. "I don't like this guy, boss," Jason says, softly enough that they can't overhear, but not softly enough for us. "Maybe he should follow Higgs, you know?"

"He doesn't know anything," Quentin sneers. "And he's too highly placed. Can't risk it."

"I'm just saying, he knows about the people we've been bringing over. He knows how many of them there are. And now we're trusting his guys to drop twenty-five people in the ocean."

"You'll be there to make sure that it happens," Quentin says. "Problem solved. Stop whining." He looks around. "Where the hell is Liang?"

"I dunno, he thought he heard something and went to look."

Adelaide and I look at each other. Then, together, we turn to look back the way we came, just as Limp comes up the ladder across the way, looks across, and sees us.

"Time to go," I say quickly, springing to my feet. Limp has a pistol, but we've got distance and another ladder, and by the time he fires a shot off we're on the roof.

"Quiet, you idiot!" Quentin shouts at Limp. "Cut them off! Don't let them go!"

"What do we do?" Adelaide asks, looking around.

"Um..." The rooftop only has two exits, both of them ladders. We dash for the one on the other side of the building, and then fall back as Shiner's head pokes over it. He also has a gun. "I have a plan."

"Is it a good one?"

"Absolutely." It is a terrible plan. "Glimmer, come here."

Glimmer flies over, looking cross but staying quiet. Across the way, Limp and Shiner have been joined by Jason and another guy from the alley. This is not a good combination.

"What are we going to do?"

"We're going to jump to the boat, and make our escape from there."

Adelaide looks across the fifty-foot gap between us and the cargo ship. "This is a terrible plan."

"We'll be fine. Glimmer — fairy dust, please."

Glimmer stares at me, and then shrugs. She flies above Adelaide and me, rubbing her bare arms to shake as much dust as possible free.

"Nowhere to run this time, Stark," Jason calls, drawing his gun. "Why don't we go down and have a little chat."

"You're not going to shoot, Jason," I call back. "Too much noise."

"Basil," Adelaide says urgently, "I thought you told me that adults can't hold happy thoughts long enough to fly."

"But we might be able to hold them long enough to jump. Just ... focus on the good things."

"We're about to be killed."

"That is not a good thing."

I turn to look at the ship. It really is a very long jump.

Glimmer drops down to land on my shoulder again. She looks exhausted, and isn't glittering nearly as much as usual. She informs me that she's all dusted out, so if I want to start flying, now's the time.

Jason and his friends are spreading out to surround us. Despite his bravado, and the guns, no one seems to want to be the first one to come into range.

"Well," I say, "here goes nothing."

"Hang on," Adelaide says. "I need to fix some good thoughts in my head."

"Alright, but—"

Which is when she kisses me.

It is not a chaste kiss, and it is not particularly quick. I think that Jason and his boys are caught off guard by it, because none of them try to rush us in the middle of it, but frankly I'm not paying attention to them right now. The whole event probably doesn't actually take more than a second. It feels timeless. It feels right.

Adelaide pulls away first. "Right," she says. "I feel a lot happier. You?"

"Let's do this," I say, with a grin. We turn, holding hands, and leap.

For a moment, the ground falls away. I glance sidelong at Adelaide, feeling like a schoolboy again, and she gives me a smile back. We're rising, soaring into the air, the wind around us, the world at our fingertips. Sadly, the moment doesn't last. We hear Jason shout something behind us. A gun goes off, and a bullet zips past my ear. The world comes crashing in, and that magical moment, just for a fraction of a second, takes a back seat to our fears. And that's all it takes.

Instead of flying, we're falling. A rush of worry replaces the joy, and the entire attempt at flight implodes. It only lasted a couple of seconds, but a couple of seconds got us right over Quentin's head. We hit the deck of the ship hard, rolling across the concrete floor, and I groan as we slam into the side of the cargo crate that the crew has just finished bringing back on board.

Adelaide stands up next to me, and then drops back to the deck as Shiner takes another shot at us, a bullet pinging off the rippled metal of the shipping crate. "Okay. Now what?"

"One moment." I pull her around the side of the crate, so that it's blocking our enemies' views of us. "Oh, dear."

Most of the crew had already disembarked, preparing to load up Quentin's coffins, but two of them are bearing down on us, holding a pair of heavy-looking metal rods. I bring out my pistol, and they stumble to a halt. "Gentlemen. If you wouldn't mind hopping overboard."

The men look at me, look at the water, and jump.

I glance out from the crate to find them being hauled out on the docks by crewmen. "That's a start," I mutter. The crew is gathering around the gangplank, none of them wanting to be the first one up it. "We need a way to keep them from getting onboard."

"Glimmer!" Adelaide says. "Do you see those controls over there?" She points to the crane.

Glimmer nods. They're very nice. So what?

"Think you could drop the crane on the gangplank?"

Glimmer and I both stare at Adelaide for a moment, and then Glimmer laughs. She darts through the air, zigging and zagging in case someone's looking for something to shoot, and lands next to the controls. Putting her back into it, she sends the crane swinging to one side, where it comes within a hair's breadth of knocking the first guy crossing the plank into the water, and then slams both feet on the button to release the winch. The crane smashes through the gangplank, and two goons go back into the drink. Quentin is screaming imprecations at everyone, as Jason and the sailors start pulling people out.

"I might be able to hit him from here," I say, sighting with my pistol.

"You're just going to kill him?" Adelaide asks incredulously.

"If it's them or us?" I try to take a closer look, and then pull back as another bullet ricochets off the crate. "Apparently, no, I am not."

"We just need to hold out for a few minutes, right?" Adelaide asks.

"Assuming that Niall got the message across, yes. We've certainly done a good job of making sure that Quentin won't abscond with the evidence."

"Well, I'd rather he didn't abscond with us."

"I agree. Take the gun." I step over to the crate's padlock, and give it a serious look, drawing out my lockpicks. "I think I can get this open."

"And then what?"

"Swing the door that way, give us some more room to maneuver. Should be wide enough to cover a dash for the bridge."

"I like it. What am I doing with this?" Adelaide waves the gun vaguely.

"Hopefully, nothing. But they're going to start scaling the side of the ship in a minute or two, so you might need to fire wildly to discourage them. Please don't get shot."

"I wasn't planning to, but thank you for the advice." Adelaide risks a very quick peek. "I only see three guards out there."

"Bad sign." I focus on the locks. "Maybe we can lock ourselves inside the crate, if there's room."

"Unless, of course, whatever's in there is a monster."

"Well, in that case, we can take cover and use it as a distraction." I twist the lockpicks one last time, and the padlock pops open. "Only one way to find out."

Taking a deep breath, I swing the crate door wide open, stepping out with it. The extra cover doesn't actually quite reach the crane controls, which are our next spot of cover, but it looks like it's close. Before I can get the gun back, though, I hear a sudden intake of breath from Adelaide. Turning, expecting to see a guard looming over us, I'm instead caught by something infinitely worse.

The shipping crate does not, as it turns out, contain any kind of monster. Inside, on carefully stacked shelves, are fifteen people. For a moment I think that they're corpses, incongruously brought to the island, but then I see the feeding tubes, and the bandages carefully restraining them so that they don't fall off their bunks. All of them are breathing. None of them are moving. Most have extra swathes of bandages around their heads.

Adelaide and I share a horrified look. "They can't be..."

"Cover me." I step into the crate, and check one quickly. Behind me, I hear Adelaide fire a shot, echoing loudly into the space, and the sound of someone on the ship back-pedaling fast. "Head wound," I say. "I think ... I think he's been lobotomized."

"Oh, my God," Adelaide says. "Coma patients."

"What can I say. I'm an entrepreneur." Quentin's voice floats across the ship from the dock. "If you can't find talent, you make it."

"Who are they, Quentin?"

"Nobody. That's the whole point. The world's full of people who won't be missed, and five days on a boat takes away all those nasty urges. Come out of the shipping crate."

"Not likely." I gesture to Adelaide, who hands me back the gun. "But the first person to try coming around is in for a nasty surprise."

"Oh, yeah? Charlie. Get the crane."

"The crane's junked, boss. That damned fairy broke the winch before she vanished."

There is a dangerous pause. "Then get him out of there."

"Uh…"

"Four guys with guns, you can't get one old man out of a shipping crate? Jesus!"

"I resent that, Quentin," I say. "You might as well surrender now."

"Hah. You're a real joker, Basil. I'm going to miss that about you." I hear Quentin moving off. "Jason, I swear to God!"

"Boss! Boss!" I'm not sure which guy this one is. "We gotta scram, now!"

"What?"

"Regulators! Coming around the bay!"

"Damn it!" Quentin doesn't even pause for a menacing threat or quip. A car door slams, and an engine roars.

"Boss?" Jason sounds panicked. "Scatter, boys!" Feet pound the deck, and I hear four splashes in rapid succession as the boys who joined us on the boat hit the water. I emerge carefully from the shipping crate, just in time to almost catch a bullet from Shiner, who's still on the rooftop across the way and seems to have missed what's going on.

I duck back, cursing. "Quentin's getting away!"

"But these people are still here," Adelaide points out. "If we hadn't been here, he would have taken them back into the bay and dumped them."

"I suppose," I grumble. By now, the Regulators have triggered their sirens, and the familiar howl is echoing across the bay. It's probably too late for Shiner, but I can hear a car starting up and expect that Quentin's inside. Sighing, I lean against the crate. "Are you alright?"

"Another near-death experience? I'm starting to get used to them." Adelaide leans next to me and takes my hand. "We're going to have to explain all of this to the Regulators, you realize."

"Actually, you are."

"What?"

"If we let Quentin get to ground, we'll never see him again. We need the Regulators to know everything, and you're a reporter. But I need to cut off his escape."

"You think you can escape a Regulator cordon?"

"Pssh. Easy as pie. I'm a champion swimmer." I shrug off my jacket and shoes. "Keep these safe for me. And make sure no one shoots Glimmer by mistake. Regulators have hair triggers sometimes, and fairies are under their purview. When you finish with them, call Holly and Todd and let them know what's going on. I'll see you in a few hours."

"Basil, where are you going to go?"

I take three steps. "I have to talk to Douglas Schaefer." And before she can point out all of the ways that this is a terrible plan, I dive off of the edge of the boat and into the harbor.

———— 《》 ————

It takes me almost two hours to track Schaefer down. This includes stopping by Silver Donner's to push Donny for information — as well as a temporary coat, shoes, and a towel — a handful of phone calls, and finally leaning on a friend of a friend. By the time I do, it's past six and news is spreading around the city about a massive Regulator raid on the docks. Rumors are flying about what they found — cannibal ghouls, an army of shadow monsters roaring for a fight, three tons of starmetal that someone unearthed, the Crocodile itself. No one seems to know except me, and I'm just as happy keeping it that way. For now. But I eventually learn that Schaefer's just arrived at the London Palace for dinner — a nice little nightclub that he has a large stake in, and where he can trust everyone is on his side.

The bouncer outside the London Palace is a big guy, wearing a heavy leather jacket and with his hair slicked back. He takes one look at me as I approach, starts to raise his hand to wave me to the back of the line, and then catches something in my expression and steps to one side. As I push through the door to the club, I can hear him speaking to someone else in a low murmur. It doesn't matter — I'm moving faster than the news is.

Inside, things are still pretty quiet, but starting to pick up for the evening; a band onstage is playing some old jazz classic, and a dance floor has been cleared near the stage for couples to try out their moves. I glance across the room, spotting Schaefer sitting by the back wall with a good-looking woman across from him and a couple of guards sitting unobtrusively around the corner, and I cut straight across the dance floor to get there. A few people in my way catch my expression and get out of my way.

By the time I reach him, his bodyguards have stood and moved to block my path.

I look at each of them in turn. There are, of course, no weapons allowed in the club. Equally certainly, both of them are packing heat. The thug on the left has his hand in his jacket, ready to draw, but it's the one on the right who steps forwards and raises his hand. "Mister Schaefer is busy," he growls.

I grab him by the outstretched arm, pulling him off-balance, and shove him hard to my left. He stumbles into his friend, whose gun skitters across the floor. I put my foot down on it. "No one asked you," I say grimly. "He'll speak to me."

Schaefer meets my eyes for a moment, and then raises his hand lazily, stopping his guards in their tracks. "There's a protocol to these things, Basil," he says.

"Protocol has flown out the window, Mr. Schaefer," I answer. "We need to talk. Now."

"You want us to send him on his way?" the first thug growls. From the look in his eyes, I know he's anticipating the answer, and as Schaefer stops to consider he takes a step towards me, cracking his knuckles. I tense, ready for a fight.

"No," Schaefer finally says. "Basil's not usually so ... impulsive. I want to hear what he has to say." He turns to his companion. "Katherine, would you be a dear and go fetch a cocktail? This won't take long."

The lady in question looks like she'd rather argue, but nods and stands. She gives me a sour look as she walks past, and Schaefer waves me to her recently-vacated seat. The two goons settle back into their own seats, glaring balefully at me. I pause to scoop up the abandoned gun, dump the clip, and toss it back to the guy who lost it before sliding into the offered seat.

"This behavior is well outside your usual," Schaefer says mildly, meeting my eyes. "For that reason, and because of our earlier arrangements, I am giving you ten seconds to explain why you barged in here like a hooligan and upset my dinner, before I let Frank and Mort do what they do best."

The only way I'm going to get anything is to lay it all out. "You've heard that Quentin and I went to war."

Schaefer nods slowly. "I can see how that might upset you," he says. "But you know the drill. If you have a beef with one of my lieutenants, that's between the two of you. If you want me to mediate, I suppose…"

"We're past mediation."

"Well." Schaefer sits back. "This is a side of you that I haven't seen in a while. What has Quentin been doing?"

"For a start, he killed Victoria Lane."

Schaefer's breath catches in his throat, and his smile vanishes. For a moment I can see a struggle in his expression, and then the shutters come down, and he's back. "Did he?"

"Using a tame shadow."

"What?" Schaefer likes to be seen confused about as much as he likes to be seen vulnerable, but today I'm the rare man who's seen both. "Basil, stitchers are a myth."

"Not anymore. Quentin found a system, with a few of his friends. One of them is already dead. Conrad Higgs."

"I read about that."

"Well, you didn't read about this. The Regulators broke up a shipment Quentin was trying to dump at sea today. A shipment of lobotomy patients that he created. Their shadows are more malleable, you see."

There is a long silence. "Just to be clear," Schaefer finally says, "you are claiming that my lieutenant not only found a secret to the creation of controlled shadows, one he declined to inform me about, but that he has been importing half-dead people to my town in order to create more of them?"

"And then killing them. He's killed at least two dozen. Maybe more."

Douglas hisses slowly. "I didn't know about any of this."

I let out a long breath. It might just be true. "I hope not. Because the lid is coming off it, one way or the other. The Regulators have everything that I know, and right now they're going to be out looking for Quentin. You and I both know that they won't find him."

For a moment, he looks at me, and I look back at him. "Do you want approval, or backup?"

"He's your lieutenant. You have a responsibility."

Schaefer's grimace deepens, but he stands as his cocktail arrives, waving it off. "Frank, call up Hoffman. We're paying Quentin a visit, and I don't expect that it will end with warm wishes."

"Yessir, Mr. Schaefer." One of the goons salutes, and hurries off. Schaefer turns to look at me. "I'll assume you want to join me."

"Just to make sure."

"Fine. He'll be hiding in the safe house that he thinks I don't know about. But we'd best hurry; he must have considered the possibility that you'll go to me."

"What if he runs?"

"Basil," Schaefer says, sweeping past me, "you know as well as I do that there's nowhere on this island that I couldn't find him."

——— «» ———

Say what you will about him, Schaefer moves quickly, and he hits hard. Three minutes after our conversation, two cars are moving through the city, carrying eight armed goons, Schaefer, and myself. Five minutes after that, we're joined by another car with another five people in it, coming from a different direction. We pull up in front of a small, anonymous townhouse on the north side of town, to find a fourth car just arriving. Stephanie Tate steps out of it with a few men of her own. "Mr. Stark," she says calmly. "What a surprise."

"You aren't half as surprised as I am," I say.

"I told you where my loyalties lay." Ms. Tate turns her attention to Schaefer. "Sir. A car pulled into the back garage about half an hour ago. Three people went inside. Quentin, Jason, and Liang. No one else is coming — the others he trusted have been arrested."

"I see," Schaefer says.

"And how do you know about all this?" I ask.

Ms. Tate smiles. "Follow the money, Mr. Stark. Places like this have to be paid for, and diverting some of your personal funds doesn't do the trick. I took the liberty of planting someone to keep an eye on the place. Just in case." She gives me a broad smile. "No one's come out. He's probably glued to the radio, listening to see if anyone's given him up."

"Have they?"

"Not officially."

"Good enough." Schaefer looks around at the fifteen large men and women surrounding the three of us. "It seems a bit much to stop two people," he allows. "Leave four on each door. The rest go inside. Take him alive. And we move fast. There'll be a delay in a police response, but there's no sense making them sweat."

Schaefer's guards move like clockwork. One team takes up position at the front, another at the back, and the third forces the door quick and easy. They vanish into the house, guns at the ready, and I expect to hear a flurry of gunfire when they run in to Quentin and his remaining bodyguard. What I don't expect is for the team leader to emerge from the house almost immediately, walk over, and shake her head.

Schaefer frowns. "He's not there?"

"Well, he's there..." She trails off, looking to her partner, who is following her out, for backup. Getting none, she looks back to Schaefer. "He's just, uh... dead."

I break into a jog, moving sinto the house. "Watch the windows!" I snap. "Turn on every light! Fast!"

The goons look at each other, brows furrowed, and then to Schaefer. I hear him telling them to go ahead and listen to me as I bound up the stairs of the inside. It's a bit garish; crammed with bad paintings and incongruous carpets, poorly offsetting the Victorian wallpaper and wall lamps. It's the sort of home that someone just stuffs things that they don't want in, which for a safe house makes sense.

Quentin is in the upstairs study, slumped on the floor. A last ray from the setting sun is cutting an oddly poetic line across his back, but I turn on every light anyway. Nothing leaps out of the corners of the room, so I move in for a closer look. He's knocked over a chair, and swept most of the things on his desk to the floor, but aside from that there wasn't much of a struggle. It looks like he was attacked just as he was checking the time; his pocketwatch is lying on the floor next to him, the glass face cracked. I kneel beside him, confirming that he's not breathing, and check him for signs of injury. I already know what I'm going to find.

As I do, however, something catches my eye. There's a scrap of paper tucked into the pocketwatch. I pick it up to look at, but then I hear boots on the stairs, and stuff the whole watch into my pocket just as Schaefer and Ms. Tate enter the room, flanked by guards. "No sign of the shadow, Basil," Schaefer says. "It must have slipped away as soon as it killed him."

I stand up. "What does his bodyguard have to say about that?"

"Nothing. He's dead too."

"Damn it." I turn away, looking out the window. "And we have no idea who his partner was."

"On the bright side, the situation is resolved." Schaefer nods to me. "A few of my boys are having a quick look around, just to make sure Quentin wasn't stashing anything that we'd rather not fall into police hands. If you'd like to stick around and keep an eye on them, feel free. I realize that you don't want shadow-stitching to become a weapon in my arsenal."

"I'm not very worried. I don't think you want shadow-stitchers to become a weapon in anyone's arsenal. Too many vulnerabilities."

"True. Still, I thought I would make the offer." Schaefer turns to leave, and then turns back. "And, Basil? That stunt of yours at the Palace had better be a one-time event. Get it?"

"Got it."

"Good. Sorry it worked out like this."

Stephanie Tate walks in after he leaves, looking down at Quentin. She shakes her head. "It's a shame," she says.

"I didn't think you'd be upset."

"For all his faults, Quentin had a certain flair for the business. I'm not upset that he's dead, Mr. Stark. I'm upset that it came to this." Ms. Tate shrugs. "I don't suppose that he committed suicide?"

"I doubt that very much."

"No, you're right. Quentin would go down fighting."

"And you have no idea who killed him."

"Nor do I want to. If I knew, I might have to do something about it. I'm just as happy to accept that the situation is resolved."

I grunt.

Stephanie turns to look at me. "It is resolved, isn't it? Quentin is dead. The scientist is dead. The man bringing bodies to make more shadows has been arrested, and Mr. Schaefer will be keeping an eye on anyone trying something like that again. The only loose end is the money man."

"The money man with his own personal shadow."

"A shadow who'll be dead soon, unless he solved that too. But no, if he did, they would just need corpses, not coma victims. So there you go. Within a few days, there won't be any living shadows. It's a shame you can't catch your broker, whoever they are, but they'll go to ground, and that will be the end of that."

I grunt again.

Stephanie pats me on the shoulder. "You just don't like it when people get away, do you?"

"I just don't like loose ends," I say, walking out the door. "And this one seems like it's going to come back to get us."

— «» —

I call Holly's house from a pay phone, and learn that Adelaide is still with the Regulators; she was able to get a phone call out to assure Holly that we were alive, but is otherwise busy. I tell Holly to meet me at the office, hang up, and start down the street.

Of course, Holly has a car and I don't, so by the time I arrive half an hour later, she's already at her desk, looking over a small stack of envelopes. "Nothing very interesting," she reports. "But I guess we weren't actually gone for very long."

"Where's Todd?"

"I sent him to work when you said the war was over. He skipped last night; did you know that? If he misses two nights in a row they'll kill him. I put the kettle on, by the way, but it hasn't had time to boil. So Quentin's really dead?"

"As they come, I'm afraid."

"Did Schaefer do it?"

"It wasn't Schaefer. He had no reason to do it, and every reason to want to have a word with Quentin — and it doesn't look good for him to have his men die of unaccountable issues. No, it was the money man." I head over to the fridge for some milk, talking over my shoulder. "Quentin kept him in the loop, and he had to have known that we were closing in."

"How many options do you have?"

"Not many," I admit, pausing at the fridge. "I thought it might have been Ms. Tate, but I don't think so. She had every reason to kill Quentin, and to lure him into a mistake, but she spends too much time where Schaefer can see her. If she were our culprit, I think he would know. No, I think it's his contact at the port, the one who introduced him to his shipping contacts, who arranged the security schedule for him. I think that I know who to confront. I'm just missing a few pieces, and I don't want to do this without being totally sure"

"So walk me through it."

"It's not that complicated," I say. I open the fridge door, and a black shadow leaps out from inside and latches itself around my head.

I react almost instantly, but when a shadow is involved, almost isn't nearly enough. My hand is up to my neck by the time that the shadow has plastered itself across my face, and I stumble backwards as it pours itself into my nose and mouth. The creature's substance becomes immaterial almost immediately once inside, but that doesn't really matter, because I can't breathe and I'm already feeling faintness setting in. I grab at the thick, rubbery substance covering my face, trying to force my fingers under the creature's edges, and overbalance, landing on the floor of the small kitchen with a resounding crash. Faintly, I hear Holly's cry of alarm, but the shadow is already oozing over me and I'm very much afraid that I've made a critical mistake.

Desperately, I reach into my pocket, searching for my last packets of salt, and my hands brush something round and engraved. The shadow hesitates, as though feeling the touch, and pulls back for a moment. I grasp the object, pulling it out and swinging wildly. Whatever it is, the shadow seems confused for a moment, but then redoubles its assault, ghostly fingers crushing down on my throat as it attempts to choke the life out of me. I feel my vision going dim, and darkness seeping around the edge. Holly is kneeling over me, and I try to push her aside. No sense both of us dying, and she won't be able to get the shadow off me. She seems to get the idea, and steps away, possibly to try and find some salt of her own. It's probably too late for salt. The darkness is closing in around me, and I try to redouble my efforts to pry the blasted thing off me.

And then, in a frozen moment, my sight fails me completely, and the room falls totally silent. I take a shuddering gasp, trying to force down panic, and only then realize that the shuddering gasp was, in fact, possible. For a few moments, I can only breathe raggedly.

"Uncle Basil?" Holly asks, forcing down a tremor.

"I'm here," I croak, trying to blink. I appear to still be blind. "What happened?"

"I pulled the breaker," she says. "Shadows can't hold corporeal form without light, and the shades are still down."

There is a long, silent moment. "Well," I say, rubbing my sore neck. "Good job."

"Thank you."

"No, and very seriously, thank you."

I hear Holly moving around. "Is it still here?"

"Hard to say," I answer. Moving very slowly and carefully, I inch over to the light switch and flick it off, and then move through the office, repeating the process. "Alright. Open the blinds. We need a bit of light."

"Right," Holly says. There's another moment, and a ray of light slices across the room. In the dim shadows, I see something pool under the door and vanish.

"It's gone," I report. "But stay there. I'm turning on the light, and we may need to move quickly."

"Okay," Holly says. "So … that's what a shadow looks like up close."

"That's what a shadow looks like up close."

"Can we never meet one again?"

"I'll see what I can do." I look down at the object in my hand. "Quentin's pocketwatch," I murmur.

"Why do you have Quentin's pocketwatch?"

"The shadow hesitated when I…." I freeze. "Of course."

"Uncle Basil, you're doing that thing again, where you don't explain things."

"No time," I say, grabbing my coat and rushing for the door. "I need to get to the Port Authority before that shadow does."

"Yep," I hear Holly faintly say as the door slams behind me. "That thing."

———— «» ————

I flag down the first cab I see, and offer him double to get me to the port in under fifteen minutes. He makes it in ten, dropping me off just outside the front gates. It's just past six, and the lot by the port's front offices is empty. I flag down the first guard I see and ask him where I can find Jack Harding.

"Mr. Harding? He was in his office…" The guard trails off, and then smiles. "Wait, no. He was taking that reporter down to the secure holding area."

"Reporter?" I ask, feeling a chill run down my spine.

The guard nods. "Some broad from the mainland. Showed up out of nowhere, wanted to have a look around." He looks me up and down, and I wish I had my cane on me. It makes me look less dangerous, ironically. "Say, aren't you that guy Mr. Harding hired last week?"

"Exactly what this is about," I say. "Where's Mr. Sanderson?"

"Uh … I dunno. Saw him a couple of minutes ago. Said he got a call, and would be right back."

"Did he."

"Yeah. Is everything okay?"

"No." I break into a run.

"Hey! Hey, you can't go back there! Hey!" The guard rushes after me, but I don't have time to run through the entire situation with him, and I don't know who he would trust. Instead, I dash through the nearest door, grab a chair and wedge it under the handle. I hear the guard shouting at me that he's going to call the cops, but I'm already down the corridor and through the back door, sprinting towards the long, large warehouse where the port authority stores suspicious goods until someone can come to inspect them — the perfect place to hide one last comatose patient.

As I approach the building, I see two figures about to go inside. I decide to risk it. "Hey! Wait!" I wave my arms as wide as I can. For a moment, I don't think that it was enough, but the taller of the two spots me, and pauses. And my luck is holding. It's Harding and Adelaide.

"Mr. Stark!" Harding is shocked. "Whatever are you doing here?"

"Yes, Basil, what's going on?" Adelaide asks suspiciously.

"Sanderson is inside," I say, out of breath. I reach out, and Harding supports me for a moment while I recover. "Not as young as I used to be," I wheeze softly. "Barely even ... sprinted..."

"Of course Sanderson is inside," Harding says. "I asked him to meet us down here."

"You what?" Adelaide frowns. "I thought I said we had to be quiet."

"We are being quiet. I told him not to tell anyone."

I groan. "Let me see if I can guess what happened here. Adelaide, the Regulators want to move on the port, but they're caught up in red tape."

Adelaide looks abashed. "I called your office, but there wasn't anyone there. But then I thought, why not just go directly to the source? If there is any evidence here, our mystery man will want to see it. And I still had Harding's number, so I told him I was coming."

"And he told Sanderson." I sigh. "He'll be inside right now, getting ready to kill you both."

"What?" Harding looks at me, wide-eyed. "He wouldn't! I know that we had our differences, but..."

"Sanderson was working with Quentin Lark. He must have used his new position to act as a middleman. He could get money, rearrange the schedules, and hire Quentin's boys to be his new security staff. He even planted Angela to keep an eye on you."

"Angela?" Harding is now staring at me. "That's impossible."

"She got cold feet, so he got rid of her. I think that's why she left. She thought that she could keep you safe that way."

Adelaide reaches for the door. "If all of that's true, we need to get in there right now. By the time the Regulators get here, Sanderson could dispose of the evidence."

"We do." I stop her, and look over to Harding. "Do you have a gun?"

"Well, uh, of course, but I'm not much of a shot..."

"That's fine. Two pistols between us should do. I don't think Sanderson has any backup. Let's go."

I push open the door, with a baffled Harding right behind me. Adelaide is a step behind him, worried but determined.

All of the lights are on inside, and one of the farther doors is open. I run forward, my pistol drawn, and spin around the corner. "Stop right there, Mr. Sanderson."

Sanderson freezes. The room that we're in is a large one, mostly empty aside from a sheet-covered crate near the far corner. He's standing by it, hands in his pockets. I don't see a gun on him. "Stark," he says bitterly, as he turns. "I should have known."

I take a step into the room. From here, it's going to be very, very tricky. "Sanderson. I guess this is it."

"I guess so. Did Harding tell you that I was here?"

"He did. I only have one question for you. Did you love Mercy?"

Behind me, Adelaide and Harding have stepped into the doorway. I hear, without turning, Harding grunt. "What kind of a question is that?"

Sanderson looks at me, and his expression collapses. "Yes, I loved her, you bastard."

I nod. "I think she loved you too."

"What the hell are they talking about?" Harding asks Adelaide.

"Shh!"

Sanderson is staring at me. "What?"

"In this whole, sorry mess, you're the only one she told her real name to. That was the thing that was bothering me. The thing I should have noticed. When I mentioned her, back at the Jane Arlett, you almost shot me on the spot. But you shouldn't have known her name. Schaefer didn't. Harding certainly didn't. Even Todd didn't, and he was her closest friend. But she told you. She trusted you." I lower my pistol. "She was right to, wasn't she?"

Sanderson swallows, and I see tears glittering in his eyes. "No, she wasn't. She died because of me."

"Basil." Adelaide's voice is urgent.

I start to turn, and Harding speaks, his voice suddenly sharp. "Uh-ah. Not so fast, Mr. Stark. Just place your gun on the floor, if you please."

He's standing there, right behind Adelaide. She looks concerned. "I assume he has a gun on you?" I ask.

She nods.

Grimacing, I carefully set my gun down, and kick it toward him. "So, it was you the whole time."

"I must admit, I was hoping you were dead in your office, but this will have to do." Harding nudges Adelaide. "Into the storage room, please."

Adelaide steps forwards, leaving Harding to train his gun on all three of us. Sanderson steps up beside me, but I grab him by the arm before he can try to rush Harding. "I should have realized. The security chief makes recommendations, but it's the head of HR who hires the guards."

"Yes, it is." Harding gives me a little bow, his eyes never leaving mine. "You really made a hash of things, Stark. All I wanted you to do was find the girl and go away. But you had to make this personal, and now my operation is in a shambles."

"Quentin's operation, you mean."

"Quentin? You think *Quentin Lark* could organize something like this? Don't make me laugh!" Harding's hand tightens on the pistol. "I was the one who found Higgs, and recognized the potential of his work. I was the one who approached our funders in the American government, people desperate enough for a new weapon in Korea that they would overlook a few ... irregularities. Do you know how hard it was to find a man with the right blend of ambition and foolishness like Quentin Lark? A man who could find me bodies, and grease the wheels, without ever realizing how thoroughly he was being used?" Harding snorts. "I was always planning to remove Quentin once we'd perfected the operation. Higgs ... that, I regret. But in the end, there are more scientists."

"Do you regret Mercy?"

"She was just a pawn, Mr. Stark. An amusement. When I found out that she'd contacted a Stateside newspaper, well ... she wasn't amusing any more. I don't like people who betray their purpose."

Adelaide is staring at him in horror. "Why?"

"Money, of course. And a splash of patriotism, I suppose, but primarily money. The power of life and death didn't hurt, either." Harding shrugs. "Pedestrian motives, I guess. But I think it's important to know what you want, and work towards it."

"And now what? You lock us in here, run away with the formula for shadows, and sell it to the highest bidder before we break out?"

"Not exactly." Harding's shadow ripples and flickers, and suddenly he has two — one that matches his body, and a taller, slender shadow with a wide-brimmed hat. "I don't relish the life of a fugitive. It's time for the three of you to be tragically slain when Sanderson tries to summon the shadow to kill you." Sanderson growls and starts to lunge, and Harding slams the door shut. He looks at us through the thick glass, and reaches into his pocket, pulling out his pocketwatch. "Goodbye, Mr. Stark," he yells through the glass, his words faintly visible. "I hope you know this isn't personal."

"I hope you know that it is," I say grimly, reaching into my pocket and producing a watch perfectly identical to the one he's waving at me. I open it, and place my hand over the face. "Would you look at the time."

I have the intense satisfaction of watching a series of emotions flicker across Harding's face — a moment of pure confusion, then dawning realization, and then absolute horror. By then, however, the shadow is pooling up his body, coiling around his arms as he tries to run. He falls out of our view, and there is a brief, horrible scream, immediately choked off.

"We have to—" Adelaide starts.

"We're locked in," I say mildly. "Nothing we can do. Shame, really."

Adelaide stares at me. "He's dying out there!"

"Not for long."

Sanderson gives me a long look, while Adelaide goes to try the door. "Whose watch is that?"

"His."

"But then ... whose watch was he holding?"

"Quentin Lark's, I'm afraid." I open the watch I'm holding. "They're rigged; the watch face holds a small piece of shadow. Whenever Harding or Quentin checked their watches, they were actually controlling their shadows. But Harding sabotaged Quentin's watch, so that it couldn't do what it was supposed to. When Quentin called his shadow earlier today, it killed him."

"But ... how did you get Harding's watch?"

"Clumsy me. I must have grabbed the wrong one when I was leaning against him earlier." I glance at the watch again. "One last thing to do. It's high time that shade destroyed itself."

Adelaide turns back to look at me. "You knew Harding was the killer the whole time?"

"I couldn't risk revealing it while he was so close to both of us, and I couldn't think of a way to warn you without warning him. It seemed better to play for time. And Harding helpfully provided us with a locked room to hide in." Through the watch, I can faintly feel the shadow tearing itself apart, powered by my disgust and shame.

"So you killed him."

"He tried to call the shadow."

"You ordered it to kill him."

"He would have opened the door and killed us all if I hadn't."

"We could have…"

"No, we couldn't!" I shout. "This is always how this was going to go down! Harding was never coming out of this alive, not after what he did!"

Into the sudden silence, we hear the sound of sirens. That guard followed through on his threat. Good man.

"Well," Adelaide says grimly, "it looks like everything worked out just how you wanted it, then. Congratulations."

She walks away, and sits in the corner, her arms around her knees and her eyes closed.

Sanderson steps up to me. "Shouldn't you go talk to her?" he asks quietly.

"I don't think there's anything left to say."

The police are remarkably prompt. They're on the scene two minutes later, and have the door open ten seconds after that. We step outside to find a half-dozen officers looking over Harding's body, and Commissioner Darling giving me one of his best glares. "Ah, here you are, Commissioner," I say. "I'm sorry to say that there's been a terrible accident. Mr. Harding has been killed by a nearly-tame shadow that he was attempting to use to murder Mr. Sanderson, Ms. Evans, and me. On the other hand, I have destroyed the shadow, saved my friends here, kept Harding from disposing of the evidence, and incidentally solved the murder of Mercy Nelson." I pause, and smile. "How was your evening?"

I am, of course, arrested immediately.

Chapter Ten

Saturday, March 8th

The next three weeks are more than a little chaotic. I spend four days in jail for Harding's murder before Darling admits that they don't have any evidence to use against me. Sanderson gets arrested too, but sticks to the story that Harding's watch malfunctioned on its own. I have to admit that I'm a little touched; I wouldn't have expected him to have a loyal streak.

By the time I'm let out, the story has hit all of the newspapers, tinged with romance and more than a little outright lying. Sanderson comes out of it a hero, the man that discovered irregularities that led him to suspect his boss of major connections to organized crime, but who knew that he couldn't trust the local police, and so played a long game, finding the evidence that led to the Regulators' now well-publicized arrests at the docks. I'm painted with a more sinister brush; no one seems clear exactly what role I played, but it's generally agreed that I must be responsible for Harding's death, even if the police couldn't prove anything. A few people are convinced that I was involved in the smuggling operation myself, others think that I was Harding's crooked enforcer who spooked. A few guess the truth, but it's buried in all of the lies. The mayor's office has gotten enough spin on the whole thing that Higgs' research is uniformly painted as dangerous and unsuccessful, an attempt to control shadows that resulted in the deaths of everyone who tried to use it.

For a week after I get out, I can't leave Piccadilly Cross without being mobbed, and even there I have to deal with reporters at my door every hour of the day. Panther catches one trying to sneak through a back field in the middle of the night to snap pictures and beats him black and blue, which cuts down the intrusiveness, but not the frequency, of the press.

It doesn't take long for the story to shift. Sanderson is photogenic, happy to take credit, and quick to say that I was just a good detective who helped him out of a jam. More importantly, Darling is taking advantage of the rush of public outrage to try and cut into the west precinct's corruption problems, and soon reports of police officers fighting for their jobs are pushing the first wave of stories out of the papers. The reporters gradually stop bothering me, and my name starts to vanish from the stories — and a good thing too, because 'discretion guaranteed' doesn't work quite so well when there are five cameras stationed at every entrance to my office.

The last reporter to talk to me, to my surprise, is Adelaide.

She arrives at my office a little over three weeks after the night at the warehouse. I'm manning the front desk, while Holly packs up for the night, when Adelaide pushes open the door and waltzes in, wearing the same blue blouse that I met her in. I stand, nodding to her. We haven't spoken since I was taken away. I didn't try. "Good evening, Adelaide. Can I get you anything to drink?"

"Coffee," Adelaide says bluntly. She raises an eyebrow. "I heard that you weren't giving interviews."

"Not to those jackals," I say, crossing to the coffee pot and starting it brewing. "Showing up after everything is over and causing trouble." I pull a chair up to Holly's desk and sit back down. "Were you looking for one too?"

"I'm sending my final report back to the Times," Adelaide says, studying me thoughtfully. "It sticks pretty close to the official story, although I hinted that Higgs might have gotten one shadow under control for a while. It seemed like Mercy deserved that much truth. I'm not sure if I should add anything about Harding."

I don't answer immediately. Instead, I walk over to the coffee pot, let it finish boiling, and come back with a steaming mug for Adelaide. "I would say that you shouldn't," I finally say. "The official report seems to be good enough for everyone here." I smile crookedly. "Unless you want something specific."

She narrows her eyes, leaving the coffee sitting untouched in front of her. "You're going to make me ask?"

"I'm hoping that you won't."

"Were you always planning to kill Harding when you found him?"

I sit down heavily in my chair. "I don't know."

She frowns, looking me up and down. "Who are you, really?" she asks. "I thought that I knew you, but that night … it was like you were a totally different person."

"I'm complicated. We all are. The problem is, you want me to be a good man or a bad one. No one's quite that simple." I sigh. "Why did you really come here, Adelaide? Do you want to find that one piece of evidence that will make me fall into place? To decide whether I'm a good man that you should support, or the evil man Darling thinks I am? It doesn't exist."

She stands up abruptly and walks back to the door, collecting her hat. "I think that this was a mistake."

"Far be it for me to disagree with a lady. I suppose you'll be taking the next boat back to New York?"

"For the time being. The Times is considering opening a branch office here. They think that Everland is a city to watch."

"And after everything that's happened, you still want to come back?" I raise an eyebrow. "I thought you had better sense than that."

"If you dislike it so much here, why don't you leave?"

"I wouldn't last out there," I say after a moment. "This island gets into your blood, if you stay here long enough. It's quieter these days, but don't mistake quiet for tame."

She smiles sadly, shaking her head. "That's an excuse, Basil. It's just an island."

"That kind of thinking kills people, here. That's what killed Harding."

Adelaide's smile vanishes as if I'd struck her. "No, Basil. That was all you. Goodbye."

"Goodbye, Adelaide." I stand, nodding to her. For a moment, my voice fails me, and by the time I can think of anything else to say she is gone.

Fifteen minutes later, as I sit at Holly's desk with a cooling cup of coffee in front of me, I am surprised to hear the sound of the front door again. For a moment, I think that Adelaide has come back, but it's Todd this time. I spare him a tired smile and a brief nod. "Good evening, Mr. Malcolm."

"Come on, Mr. Stark," he says, rubbing the back of his neck. "You can call me Todd."

"Only if you call me Basil."

"Sure, I can do that." He sits down next to me and pulls out a pack of cigarettes. "Smoke?"

"Don't touch the stuff."

After a moment, Todd puts the pack away without lighting up and glances over at me. "How you doing?"

"I should be asking you that. I barely knew Mercy."

"Turns out," Todd says sadly, "neither did I." He shakes his head. "Hard to believe it, you know? I really thought she was this sweet little thing, and she was running a whole con on the side. She had me fooled." He plays with his lighter, and then smiles bashfully. "Or, you know, maybe she didn't. Maybe I just saw what I thought I'd see, and she didn't have the heart to tell me the truth."

"Why, Mr. Malcolm — I'm sorry — Todd. That is absolutely profound."

"Well, ya know, I'm not just a pretty face." Todd grins. "It's hard, not having her around. She was a good friend. But if she saw me moping around, she'd slap me upside the head and tell me to go out and party."

"I wish I'd known her better. At least her death had some kind of meaning. She didn't get out like she wanted, but she did get Harding shut down."

"Why do you think she did it?"

I consider slowly. I've had a lot of time to myself to think, over the last few weeks, and I think I have the last details ironed out. "It started off innocently enough, at least for Mercy. She'd probably been working this scam her whole life, or at least as far back as she could remember, trading on her looks to get ahead and using her smarts to keep out of trouble doing it. She was living the short con, probably enjoying herself immensely and not feeling guilty in the slightest. The men she was with knew the score, after all, so why worry about it? It was a clean transaction. Cleaner than most, in fact.

"I expect things started to go wrong with Schaefer. For the first time, Mercy had tied herself to a man who would, in fact, take it the wrong way if she broke it off. She could wait for him to get bored, but she was nervous about what came next, and not sure about operating in his town. And with good reason — I don't think he would have hurt her, but the man can be frightening when he puts his mind to it, and Mercy had gotten used to having the power in her relationships. She started putting together an exit strategy, which was when she met Sanderson."

"Who was working for Quentin," Todd says with a nod.

"More or less. He wasn't in very deep, but Quentin was pulling him deeper, and he knew that there was something up at the docks that Quentin was keeping quiet. He and Mercy hit it off in a big way, and they started making plans. They didn't want a gang war breaking out, but they figured that if Sanderson could find what was up, they could blackmail Quentin and Harding, and have some real power and independence, use that to get out of town with a nest egg. Quentin was dangerous, but Harding always seemed so nice. A real pushover." I can't fault her for the assumption. I'd made it too. "I don't know if it was his idea, or hers. In the end, I don't think it matters."

"Oh, are we discussing the details?" Holly sticks her head around the corner of the outer door.

"I thought you were gone for the night."

"I was bringing back some food from Glimmer. She's been tetchy lately. I thought *you* were gone for the night."

"Well, I'm not."

"I hid the wine."

"I'm not staying here to drink," I snap.

Holly, undeterred, flops down in a chair. "How far are we at?"

"Mercy's just started dating Harding," Todd tells her.

"Oh, yeah, that. My poor romantic heart. I really thought she was in love."

"She was. With Sanderson." I point out. Holly makes a face, but nods and lets me continue. "It took her a few months, but she wasn't moving too quickly; I don't know if she was being careful, or just enjoying the game. But at some point she put the pieces together, and realized the full scope of what was going on. And then she got scared. If she went to the police, even if she managed to find the ones that weren't in Quentin's pocket, what she'd been doing would come out and Schaefer would come after her. If she went to Schaefer, it would be even worse. Either way, Sanderson was going to go down with her.

"Blackmail wasn't going to work, and she was probably worried that she'd left a trace. She left some kind of vague message for Sanderson, called the New York Times to spill the story, and dropped out of sight. My guess is that she was going to go to Sanderson right before leaving town, tell him everything, and either ask him to come with her or tell him that she'd be back.

"But Harding knew something was wrong. Quentin found out about the Times, and Harding put two and two together. I don't know if it even occurred to him that she might actually have an accomplice. He didn't seem jealous when we first met because he wasn't. He was just worried about his business interests being compromised. He stuck a shadow on my tail so that he could find her quickly, and while he killed her, Quentin organized a fake to throw Adelaide off the trail. And as far as they were concerned, that should have been the end of it. No one would have questioned how she died, I wouldn't suspect Harding, because I wouldn't have told him where she was, and he knew that Mercy wouldn't trust me enough to tell me the whole story."

"But that wasn't the end of it," Todd says. "I mean, it really, really wasn't."

"Well, no. Adelaide didn't buy the cover-up, I didn't buy the cover-up, and Sanderson didn't buy the cover-up.

The hell of it is, if Sanderson and I had compared notes, we could have wrapped the whole thing up in two days, and Higgs would still be alive. But we kept butting heads instead of talking. Damned stupid of me."

"And I think I've got everything else after that," Todd says. "At least they're gone."

"Yeah," Holly says, giving me a slow look. "Has Adelaide been by?"

"She stopped in to say goodbye," I admit.

"And did you two make up?"

"There's nothing to make up, Holly. She isn't going to forgive me for what happened."

"What?" Todd is looking between us, baffled. "What happened?"

"I murdered a man in cold blood."

"What? Who?"

"Harding," Holly hisses.

"Oh. Oh! But … wasn't he trying to kill you?"

"I knew he would. I could have prevented it. Instead, I gave him the tools to hang himself, which he helpfully took." I shake my head. "Adelaide thinks I'm a monster."

"And because you're busy agreeing with her, you didn't do anything to stop her walking away," Holly says. She sighs. "Todd, are all men idiots?"

"Yeah, generally," Todd says easily. "Least, all the men I know."

"What are you two on about?"

"Uncle Basil, look. What happened with Harding? Not good."

"I dunno, I think it was pretty good," Todd says.

"Yes, because, and I really hope you don't take this the wrong way, Todd, you're kind of violent. Like, in a good way, usually, but that's literally how you met Uncle Basil. Punching without thinking." Holly taps me on the chest. "And you, Uncle Basil, are a former pirate."

"Meaning what?"

"Meaning that when you make a horrible mistake, you spend a lot of time pretending it didn't happen, privately blaming yourself, and finding ways to hurt yourself over it.

I can tell you exactly what happened. Adelaide wanted a sign that what happened wasn't you. That it was a lapse, or a horrible thing that you could work through. Instead, you probably gave her one of your dumb 'that's the way things are' speeches."

"That is not a type of thing!"

Holly gives me a serious look. "Todd?"

"Leave me outta this."

"Fine, whatever. The point is, you justified it, told her she'd never understand, or it was your responsibility, or one of your other excuses, and now she's stormed off thinking that you're too dangerous. Right?"

"Well…"

"I knew it!" Holly grabs my arm. "Come on, get in the car."

"What? Where are we going?"

"Where do you think? We're going to the port, you're going to apologize profusely, and then you're going to tell her that you know things are too raw right now, but that you hope she'll look you up when she comes back. God! Do I have to do everything around here?"

"But…" As Holly pulls, Todd lifts me out of the chair and starts effortlessly pushing me towards the door. I try to bat him away. "Holly, she doesn't want to see me."

"If she doesn't want to see you, she won't. Stop assuming that you're the one who gets to decide relationships unilaterally."

"But … I…"

"Basil." Holly lets go of my arm and steps in front of me. "I don't know that this is going to work. I don't know if Adelaide will slap you, or kiss you, or kiss you and then slap you, or even just ignore you. But if you don't at least talk to her, you won't know either."

I look over to my desk, where a bottle of gin is carefully hidden away from Holly's prying eyes. I look over my shoulder at Todd, watching me like a large, mistreated puppy. I look to Holly, who looks more like a volcano about to explode.

And I smile. "I don't know what I did to deserve you as an assistant."

"You didn't give up. Todd, you coming?"

"Sure I will."

"Glimmer?"

Glimmer says that she wants to see me and Adelaide kiss, so yes.

I let them bundle me outside, and into the car, and we drive towards the port to be there before Adelaide's boat leaves, and to the uncertainty of a final conversation. And I don't know if that conversation will end well, or badly, but in the end, how it ends isn't the important part. The important part is that Holly's right. It might be a mess. It might be easier to just let things stay bad, and to sink into apathy with a bottle in my hand. But letting people hurt because you're afraid? That's pirate talk. It's time to take another risk. Time to keep fighting, no matter the odds. Time to do things the Piccadilly way.

I sit in the car, with Holly, and Todd, and Glimmer, listening to their banter and jokes, and for the first time in weeks, life looks good again.

If you enjoyed this read

Please leave a review on Amazon, Facebook, Good Reads or Instagram.

It takes less than five minutes and it really does make a difference.

If you're not sure how to leave a review on Amazon:

1. *Go to amazon.com.*

2. *Type in Shadow Stitcher by Misha Handman and when you see it, click on it.*

3. *Scroll down to Customer Reviews. Nearby you'll see a box labeled Write a Review. Click it.*

4. *Now, if you've never written a review before on Amazon, they might ask you to create a name for yourself.*

5. *Reviews can be as simple as, "Loved the book! Can't wait for the Next!" (Please don't give the story away.)*

And that's it!

Brian Hades, publisher

About the Author

Misha Handman has been involved in writing for most of his life. He started by writing comics for his friends in elementary school and was promptly drawn into the artistic world by their approval, moving on to produce short stories and collaborative works. He has lived in cities across Canada, including Victoria, Ottawa, and Toronto, and refuses to pick a favourite no matter how much his friends bother him about it. For now, Victoria is his home.

Need something new to read?

If you liked Shadow Stitcher, you should also
consider these other EDGE-Lite titles…

Endless Hunger

by Kevin Weir

It's 2133, and Earth has rebuilt after a global catastrophe.

Megacities, wireless tech, and augmented humans are all commonplace. What isn't common, is Kraft. Kraft sees monsters. This tends to get him in trouble, especially when the rest of the world doesn't believe they exist. For Kraft, even an easy job like cleaning a corporation's computer system involves a dark cult, a battle with faeries, and a computer virus that reaches into the real world.

About Kevin Weir

Kevin Weir is an AMPIA Award winning writer of science fiction, fantasy, and comedy. A multidisciplinary storyteller, he has written short films, webseries, stageplays, as well as short stories. These short stories have appeared in places such as Red Sun Magazine, Enigma Front, and In Places Between. He lives in Alberta where he hosts The Third Space Podcast and lives with two dogs that he does not own, but are always around.

Grimenna

by N. K. Blazevic

When Courage Finds Hope...

Evil is roosting in the lord's keep, corrupting the land and feeding off its growing despair. When Paiva Ibbie, a young sheepherder's daughter, joins her aunt to work in the kitchens, she brings with her a flicker of hope from a village in the north that remains untouched by darkness. Her good spirit is a threat to the evil's work and it will stop at nothing to ensure that Paiva's hope is turned into the darkest of despair.

About Natasha K. Blazevic

Natasha K. Blazevic lives in St André D'Argenteuil, Quebec. She studied art in college but, after ayear, fled to the countryside of the Quebec Laurentians where she apprenticed as a stone mason and began to cultivate her love of art and animals in earnest. She is a beekeeper and considers herself a student of life with a keen interest in the natural world. She hopes her book Grimenna can not only entertain and enchant readers, but can help to promote a green renaissance.

Pick Your Teeth with my Bones

by Carrie Newberry

She Has a Tail. Normal Is Relative.

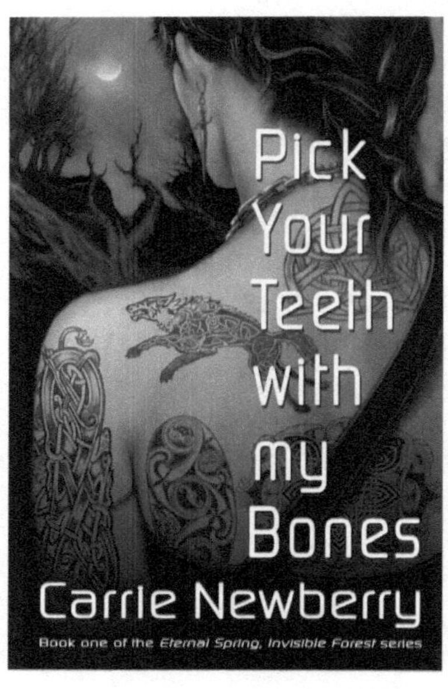

Kellan is a shape-shifter and a member of a secret society, the Sankhain, who protect a fountain of youth hidden in an invisible forest outside Madison, Wisconsin. When a stranger asks Kellan for her help with some documents, documents which shouldn't exist, about the Sankhain, Kellan uses her unique sense of smell to follow the trail, which leads to the very heart of the Sankhain. What Kellan uncovers will shake her world to its core.

About Carrie Newberry

Carrie Newberry is a writer of urban fantasy, horror, and a little bit of everything else. She is a faculty member at All-Writers' Workplace and Workshop and studied Creative Writing at UWMadison. Carrie currently lives in Madison with two rescued mutts and an enormous collection of books.

"Pick Your Teeth With My Bones is an action-packed, emotionpacked rock-your-world tale." — Kathie Giorgio, author

For more EDGE titles and information about upcoming speculative fiction please visit us at:

www.edgewebsite.com

Don't forget to sign-up for our Special Offers